Praise fo:

"In his latest Jack Chastain adventure, Jerry Mitchell captures the landscape and drama of the American Southwest, creating a strong sense of place while keeping the action galloping. His fully-wrought characters, not just steely-eyed men but strong, authentic women, wrestle with contemporary conflicts and issues in an austere and ancient landscape that Mitchell brings fully to life. A great read that doesn't back away from the struggles of the modern West."

—**Mary Taylor Young**, author of *Bluebird Seasons: Witnessing Climate Change in My Piece of the Wild*

"In *Migration of Butterflies and Lies*, J.M. Mitchell has created a suspenseful and complex tale that masterfully interweaves human greed and exploitation with the malicious harm being done to and destruction of our natural world and to native cultural treasures. In the telling, Mitchell explores the root causes and effects of the social pathologies afflicting American culture. *Migration of Butterflies and Lies* not only captivates, it also helps to further educate the reader about the treasures our national parks hold and the never-ending work it takes to maintain their legacy and integrity."

—**Jerry Fabyanic**, author of *Sisyphus Wins*, *The Lion's Den*, and *Food for Thought: Essays on Mind and Spirit*

"Unscrupulous interest groups and nefarious motives rule in this complex, close-to-life Southwestern cross-border thriller of a murderous struggle for gain and control, which is as historic as it is acutely contemporary. Mitchell's book is palpably driven by the author's deep care for our natural environment and cultural heritage, his concern a clarion call to stand up for what so desperately needs protecting."

—**Katayoun Medhat**, author of *The Milagro Mysteries*

"J.M. Mitchell is back with another book featuring his favorite character, Ranger Jack Chastain, who is never far from trouble. The plot is believable, the relationships authentic, and the dialog sounds like real people talking. I urge the readers of *Ranger* to get this book. Mitchell has a big story to tell and he tells it well."

—***Ranger: Journal of the Association of National Park Rangers***

Praise for *Killing Godiva's Horse*

"Rhinos, wild horses, politics—and dead bodies—set a frenetic pace from D.C. to Kenya. Do you like books that hit the ground running and pull you in with multiple plotlines that converge in a heart-thumping climax? Then *Killing Godiva's Horse* is right up your wheelhouse."

—***Colorado Sun***

"Ranger Jack Chastain is an intriguing and welcome series protagonist. Truly refreshing, this novel contains plots that involve western lands rebellion, Kenya, rhino horn poachers and life in New Mexico. Mitchell has taken a big, international, action-packed plot and it works."

—***Roundup Magazine***, Western Writers of America

"That clap-clap-clap sound you heard was me applauding Mitchell's latest work, *Killing Godiva's Horse*. Terrific plotting and writing!"

—**Michael Madigan**, author of *Double Dare*

". . . a pull-no-punches tale of the struggle with outsiders versus residents, urban versus rural, and traditional versus modern. Mitchell gives as balanced a glimpse of the issues, the politics, and the spirit of the West and Kenya in this novel as one will find anywhere . . . He shows how all sides will often find themselves in a different cut of the 'emperor's new clothes.' A good read."

—**Mark Lehnertz,** Tattered Cover Book Store,
Denver, Colorado

Praise for *The Height of Secrecy*

"An engaging mystery with strong characters and a wonderfully authentic setting in the Southwest. Keep your eye on this nascent series."

—**Colorado Authors' League**
2015 Award for Mainstream Fiction

"Loved it! A mystery with strength and realism. Mitchell's background leads to blended masterpieces of plot, setting and characters, complete with insider authenticity. He's got a good series going."

—**Betty Palmer**, op. cit. books, Taos, New Mexico

"This was a fun read. The characters are believable, the rescue and fire scenes ring true, and Mitchell worked in the agency long enough so that he knows how things can go bad. . . ."

—***Ranger: Journal of the Association of National Park Rangers***

"What Grisham does for law and the courtroom drama, Mitchell does for national parks and the politics of land and preservation. His behind-the-scenes knowledge of the subculture creates a believable setting that blends seamlessly with the story."

—**Isaac Mayo**, Developmental Editor

Praise for *Public Trust*

"In *Public Trust,* J. M. Mitchell brings a richness to the wilderness mystery that's not to be missed. Fire starts the novel and it burns fast and furious, but pales to the political firestorm that becomes a battle for nature herself."

—**Nevada Barr,** *New York Times* best-selling author

"[S]o real you think you're reading nonfiction. . . . This is a good read."

—***Ranger: Journal of the Association of National Park Rangers***

Migrations
of Butterflies
and Lies

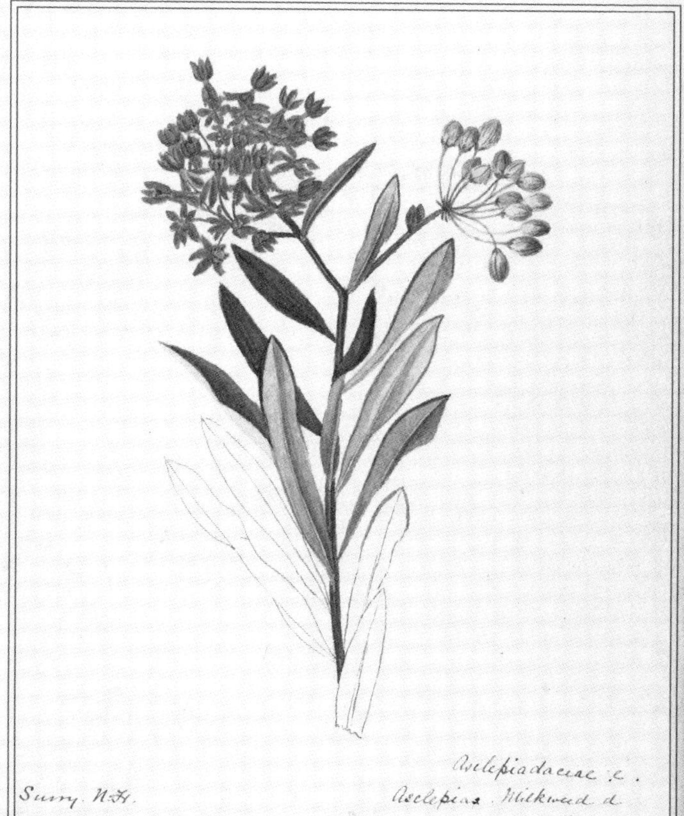
Asclepiadaceae :c.
Asclepias. Milkweed d.
A. Tuberosa. Butterfly-weed. Pleurisy-root.
L.
Surry. N.H.
July 26. 1895.

Migrations of Butterflies and Lies

—

J. M. Mitchell

PRAIRIE PLUM PRESS
DENVER

ALSO BY J.M. MITCHELL

Public Trust

The Height of Secrecy

Killing Godiva's Horse

This is a work of fiction. Names, characters, places and incidents are the product of the author's imagination or are used fictitiously. Any resemblance to actual persons, living or dead, events or locales is entirely coincidental.

Copyright © 2025 J.M. Mitchell

All rights reserved. No part of this publication may be reproduced, distributed, or transmitted in any form or by any means, including photocopying, recording, or other electronic or mechanical methods, without the prior written permission of the publisher, except in the case of brief quotations embodied in critical reviews and certain other noncommercial uses permitted by copyright law. For permission requests, contact the publisher at the address below.

PRAIRIE PLUM PRESS
P.O. Box 271585
Littleton, CO 80127
www.prairieplumpress.com
Email@prairieplumpresss.com

Printed in the United States of America

First Printing, 2025

Print edition ISBN 978-0-9852272-9-6
Digital edition ISBN 979-8-9897792-0-8

Library of Congress Control Number: 2024900040

FRONTISPIECE: Butterfly milkweed (*Asclepias tuberosa* L.) illustration: July 26, 1895, Helen Sharp, *Water-color Sketches of Plants of North America and Europe*, vol 13. plate 39, exhibited by the Boston Society of Natural History, April 1899.

Book design by K.M. Weber, www.ilibribookdesign.com

Dedicated to the memories of
Jan Van Wagtendonk, fire ecologist,
and David Graber, bear biologist.
Great scientists, valued colleagues,
and dear friends.

Prologue

Unseen, a watcher kept track of two hikers, eying them through high powered binoculars.

The hikers, a man and woman, veered off trail, stopping on open rock, turning to gaze over desert lands beyond.

"You've been lucky, Jack Chastain," muttered the watcher. "What you're made of makes things difficult . . . gives you a chance . . . but you've been lucky." Lowering the field glasses, the watcher remembered the political battle Chastain had lost in Montana, years before. A young but experienced ranger—sure of himself, determined to deliver what those who invited him there sought. A national park. Preserving the mountains they loved, by sharing them with others. Or so they had hoped. Dark clouds formed. Division. Then battles. *Poor ol' Jack . . . you left Montana wondering what happened, didn't you?*

You found yourself here . . . in New Mexico, no longer self-assured . . . assigned to a place to which you'd never been . . . Piedras Coloradas National Park. You wanted to hide . . . draw no attention to yourself. The watcher laughed. *Didn't work out that way, did it? The President designated this land a national monument . . . splitting the community . . . those who wanted the monument and those who did not. Warring factions. Again. A powerful man, former state senator Kip Culberson, sought to eliminate the monument and saw you as the enemy.*

But you were lucky. You were beaten, but somehow, while seeking comfort in the wild, a chance encounter gave you strength. Beautiful Kelly. Artist. Troubled, seeing her community torn apart. Little did you know she was Kip Culberson's daughter.

Mysterious provocations pitted neighbor against neighbor. You found yourself trapped between people uncertain about who they could trust . . . but then, a fire changed everything.

You were lucky.

In the aftermath, somehow, they realized that battling their neighbor put at risk the very values they shared. When Kip Culberson and his environmental adversary came together to form a coalition . . . they wanted you involved.

Damn, you were lucky.

What came next wasn't easy. I thought your luck had run out . . . as influential men came on the scene, competing, asserting their power. You refused to suck up to the big shots. Not too savvy, Jack. Their actions opened old wounds from Montana, but you were determined to do the right thing, and not abandon a man from the pueblo—even though he would not share his secret. Somehow you prevailed, and—whether you realized it or not—you got revenge on a man who did you wrong in Montana. You weren't savvy . . . but you were lucky.

And the work of the coalition continued.

Then, you found yourself in the midst of a western land rebellion. You were toast, but the agency director hid you away to let the storm pass . . . sending you to Kenya . . . to finish research of a scientist killed by a rhino poacher. You heard campfire rumblings about connections to New Mexico. How was that not a coincidence? You came home . . . but now, politicians were involved . . . one who had meddled in your work in Montana, and another, a supposed ally. But how did both you and Kelly end up on the river with the aides to those politicos . . . and how did a flash flood pull everyone together? Luck. But it didn't last. The politicians themselves arrived. You were toast. That congressional hearing followed . . . for legislation to negate the work of the coalition. You were warned to stay quiet, but Kelly grew tired of the congressman's political games and took him apart. Somehow, his reaction explained everything, and you went on the attack. Afterward, the coalition's work continued, your ranger friend Johnny Reger—shot during the rebellion—began to heal, and the governor asked Kelly to finish the term of a deceased senator from New Mexico.

Damn, you were all lucky.

The watcher raised the binoculars and spied Jack Chastain and Senator Culberson moving back toward the trail. "Things are about to get harder, buddy boy." The watcher laughed and slipped behind an outcropping of sandstone, then grew serious. "It's hard not to root for a man that lucky . . . but . . . there's a lot to be had on these lands . . . and from here on out . . . you'll need a lot more than luck."

Chapter 1

"Who wouldn't want to protect this?" Hands on her hips, Senator Kelly Culberson eyed a distant mesa and the orange skies beyond it.

Her words settled into the mind of Ranger Jack Chastain, jumbling the thoughts he attempted to organize. He glanced her way. "You know as well as I do. Sometimes it's about who thinks they're more important . . . and what they'll do to prove it."

"But you're past all that. People came together. They see themselves as part of something bigger . . . together . . . even if their needs are different." She slipped an arm around him. "All that's really left is the signing ceremony."

"Hope so."

A gust blew strands of hair into her face. She swept them away. "Are you worried?"

"Can't help but wonder . . . have we done enough?"

"You have. Tonight, schedule the signing, do it, then put it in my court. Legislation based on the coalition's recommendations will give this place even more protection. Be proud."

He locked his eyes on faraway parts of the national monument. "I'll wait."

"Relax." She pointed. "Hey, look."

Downslope, a pronghorn ambled into a grassy clearing mottled by shadows cast by sagebrush and four-winged saltbush. Another pronghorn appeared, then another.

"We should get going." She glanced at her phone. "Meeting starts in forty-five minutes."

He drew in a long, deep breath. "Give me a moment . . . to soak in the reasons this place is special."

—·—

"Why the hell are you listening to him?" came a shout from the back of the cavernous room. A man rose to his feet, pointing at the only uniformed man there, Ranger Jack Chastain, but his eyes locked onto those at the table at the back of the dais.

Chastain cleared his throat. "Sir, who are you asking?"

"I'm not talking to you!" the man shouted back, his voice angry, his eyes fiery.

"I understand. I'm asking you who you . . ."

"Shut up!"

Jack turned to the four sitting at the table.

The old rancher, Kip Culberson—the senator's father—and his environmental counterpart—Karen Hatcher—leaned into their respective microphones, while the other two at the table—a man from the pueblo and a businesswoman—exchanged nervous glances. Hatcher, seeing Kip's move, sat back. Kip nodded, then faced the man. "Sorry, I didn't catch your name."

"I didn't give it," the balding, flat-nosed man shouted.

Culberson, in a brown western-cut sports coat, said, in a calm voice, "Care to?"

"No."

"Okay. Would you repeat your question?"

"I said, why the hell are you listening to a damned fed?"

"Mister, you've got things all wrong. He didn't ask us to listen to him. He asked us to listen to each other."

Jack watched heads turn throughout the room.

"Bullshit!" came another shout from the man. "I know what he's done. He's paid you off. Anyone who doesn't know that isn't paying attention."

"Excuse me?" Culberson leaned closer to the mic. "What the hell are you talking about?"

"Him buying you. All of you there at the table. Making it easy for him and those like him to run the rest of us off our land. The feds, handing out favors, but only to you. The rest of us are gonna be left empty handed. We'll suffer."

Jack watched the man with a feeling of déjà vu as people in the room exchanged questioning looks. Whispers, confusion, rumbles of anger.

Kip Culberson stood. He raised his hands and waited for the room to quiet. "Folks, no one's buying anyone off." He eyed the back of the room. "Mister, where's your land?" He paused, searching among the sea of angry faces. "Where are you, mister? . . . That fella . . . just talking. Where'd he go?"

A woman near the door raised a hand. "He left."

—·—

CENTRAL MEXICO

A man stepped out of the trees. Gray streaks in his hair glistened in the moonlight. He stopped, wiped sweat from his brow, and watched a young woman emerge from the forest. "Careful," he whispered, pointing at the ground at her feet. A crevice in the volcanic rock.

She turned on her flashlight and stepped across.

The man raised his eyes. "Now, look. There."

The black-haired woman spun around, directing the beam at her feet. "¿En el basalto, profesor?"

"No, look up . . . and turn off the light."

The flashlight went dark. "¿Que?"

"Just look. They're right before your eyes. The few that are left."

He watched as her eyes readjusted to the dark. She would soon see fir boughs, and on them a few straggling migrants.

"¿Donde estamos?"

She hasn't seen them. "A place where you can consider your options. For your research." He swept a hand past a bough. "These . . . are wintering grounds."

She gasped. "Mariposa monarca." She let her eye climb to the highest branches. "¿Y habria millones?" she whispered.

"There would be millions, yes, if this were winter. These remaining stragglers will also soon be gone . . . migrating north." He sighed. "Years ago there were so many more, in part because there were so many more oyamel trees."

"¿Profesor Morales, me estas hablando en ingles?"

"To make a point."

"¿Que punto?"

The professor motioned her to follow and stopped at an edge overlooking the valley. "Ramona, monarch conservation could be a good subject for your research. If you choose to accept it, you must be prepared to follow the variables wherever they might take you. They will take you into los Estatos Unidos—the United States—and into Canada. The mariposa—the butterfly—is not simply in decline because of the loss of oyamel forest. They are being impacted throughout their range. You will need to collaborate with others in Los Estados Unidos and in Canada. There, the loss of the milkweed on migratory routes has been devastating. If what we learn from your research is to be used in conservation, I suggest you see it as part of a larger effort, working with colleagues. You know English, yet you reluctantly use it. At some point it must become second nature, because, unfortunately, your English is better than their Spanish."

She laughed. "I understand," she said, forcing the words. "But why bring me here tonight? The drive from university was long. Why not tomorrow, in daylight?"

"One of my contacts in the village heard rumors about a young peasant. Coming to cut trees . . . for timber. I want to intercept him if we can. Try to direct him toward a more promising future. . . . before he does something that sets a course for his life. Maybe he could help on your project. Carry equipment . . . or take readings when you can't."

"Is it dangerous, to . . . intercept him?"

The professor laughed. "No. I never accuse. I understand the difficulties many face, but I can suggest ways to make a living that don't put at risk this very important part of Mexico's heritage." He paused. "Hear that? I was told our would-be logger would be coming to this spot. Remember, we first build trust . . . and hope to intervene before damage is done." The professor turned an ear. "Yes, I hear someone coming."

"A truck? On the road?"

"Sh-h-h." Professor Morales listened. "Not a truck. Footsteps." He turned to the trail.

Two figures emerged from under the trees, moonlight capturing their moves as they slogged their way up the last of the hill, one following the other.

"Buenos noches," the professor shouted.

No reaction.

The men stopped. Moon light glinted off metal. A rifle, carried by the man in the rear.

"Hola," the professor said, forcing the word as he eyed the gun.

"Good evening, professor," the lead man said, his face in the shadow of his hat's brim.

"Do I know you?"

"I do not believe so," the man said, his voice controlled. "If you did, I would be surprised." He chuckled to himself, then removed his hat and wiped the sweat from his brow. A dark mustache appeared in the moonlight. "I know who you are. That is what matters."

The man in the rear, a bigger man, stepped around the first and raised the rifle. Short barrel, minimal stock, curved magazine.

"Why?" The professor gestured toward the rifle. "Why would you . . . ?"

"To stop the lies."

"What lies?"

The mustachioed man laughed. "The lies you are supposedly spreading in the village."

"You're from the village?"

"No."

"What do you mean, lies?" the professor asked, desperation showing. "What did I say? There must be some mistake." Glancing at Ramona, he scooted away.

"We were summoned. A precaution. Our employer likes things working smoothly."

"What do you mean?" Voice cracking, he slid another step from his student.

"What does it matter? Yes, it is true the actual lies are not yours, but what does it matter? It is disruption that matters to my employer."

The professor raised his hands and took a step backwards. "Your boss? Who is he? What can I say to remedy the situation?"

"Stand by the girl," the man said.

The other trained his rifle on the professor.

"Leave her out of this."

"That will not be possible."

The professor waved them toward the edge. "Let me show you something. Over here."

"Stop, professor. I have no interest in belaboring this."

Seeing Ramona moving, the professor broke into a run, darting along the ledge.

A blast came from the rifle.

The professor dropped, pain searing through him. He watched the lead man approach.

The man leaned over him, then turned. "¿La niña, donde esta?"

The other man spun around.

"Encuentrala." (Find her.)

"Run," Morales said. More words ran through his thoughts, but not past his lips. His slowing mind caught the shouts of the men in the chaos of the moment. They could not find her.

As he let go of his last breath, he thought he saw movement. A monarch butterfly, fluttering above him, then away.

—·—

IN THE WILDS OF PIEDRAS COLORADAS NATIONAL MONUMENT, NORTHERN NEW MEXICO

A solo hiker plodded through the night, desert gravel at his feet. In one hand he held a map, in the other a flashlight, both used only sparingly. He did not want light to be seen by anyone who might wonder what another person was doing here at this time of night.

He glanced at the low ridge in the distance. *It's getting closer.* The descending moon set a glimmer upon one spire—what before had been a bump on the horizon. Behind that spire would be a slice in the rock, a drainage, known to exist only by a few.

He tried to imagine what lay within that drainage, besides the man he intended to meet. He'd heard stories. Fascinating stories, but more important than antiquity was the isolation. He preferred his meetings be held in secret. This was beyond the pale. The man he hoped to find was not expecting a visitor. The warning had been, *be careful.*

"All because of a letter," he muttered to himself, slowing to avoid a prickly pear cactus. The envelope's return address had been an illegible scrawl. Contents suggested it came from his most important client. The richest of the bunch. The letter, more dramatic than usual, but hey, rich guys need to entertain themselves, too. It had been simply addressed to Doc, the code name used by a select group of his clients. Doc—consultant to multinational corporations and well-funded politicians—not his real name, Herman Durfey, belittled at university by professors and classmates alike. *If they only knew what I was doing now . . . and what I get paid for it.*

He laughed, then thought again of the letter. With it, a photograph, of a woman—actually a woman and a man, the man being immediately recognizable, the Vice President of the United States. The woman, the obvious subject of the photo. Beautiful, Latina—Hispano, it turns out—with dark hair, dark eyes. Business suit. She held up her right hand for the oath of office.

On the back of the photo, typed words:

Sen. Kelly Culberson, junior senator, New Mexico. Deal with her! Be creative.

Those few words. Cryptic. Dramatic. Nothing to imply this senator was to be drawn into the boss' sphere of influence. Words meaning something different. *Understood. Leave her to me.*

Tonight, phase one.

His performance at the public meeting started things. He chuckled to himself, thinking of the chaos he'd caused.

Doc shot a pulse of light from the flashlight. At his feet, yucca, its spines long, sharp, and threatening. He stepped around it, onto rock etched with lines of erosion, stretching from here to the base of the cliff. *Must be slickrock, the stuff described by the boss' man, Harper Teague. Damned self-important errand boy . . . but let's hope he's right about this guy he has me meeting.*

Ascending, he took long steps up the cross-bedded sandstone, then veered around the base of the spire, around a boulder, and through the brush hiding the entry to the drainage. He proceeded to enter. Inside, a narrows. Rocky floor, hall-like walls. Dark. Starlit sky peering in from above. Turning on his flashlight, he watched for an incline to the left, one he'd been told not to miss. Seeing it, he climbed out of the drainage along rocky steps, feeling uncertain until before him opened a hanging side canyon. Sandy creek bottom. Cottonwood. Willow. Upslope, scattered pinyon pine and juniper.

Through the trees, he saw a flicker of light and marched toward it. Not watching his footing, he stumbled over a rock. Branches snapped under his feet.

From the direction of the light, he heard shuffling, then quiet.

Doc stopped. "Hello."

No response.

He waited, listening, hearing nothing. Absolute quiet.

Then, from behind, "Who are you?" demanded a raspy voice.

Doc jumped. "Hi," he muttered, regaining his composure. "How'd you get behind me?"

"Answer me," the voice growled. "Who are you?"

"Call me Doc." He laughed. "That's how you'll know me." To his left, he noticed a rock. On it, pottery, baskets, ladles, figurines, all lit in the glow of the fire. A metal pot sat on the coals, steam rising above the rim. Doc lurched toward the fire. "Mind if I sit? It's been a hell of a hike, especially at night."

"Stop," the voice commanded, now from a new location. "Don't move."

Doc plodded to a stop and glanced around, trying to locate the source of the voice. "Where are you?" To his right he heard what sounded like a pistol being cocked.

There, a man dropped alongside a boulder, the brim of his hat casting shadow over his eyes and part of his face. In his hand, a pistol.

Doc's spine tightened, watching light glint off silver casing.

"You made a mistake coming here, mister."

"Hold it." Doc raised his hands. "The man you use as a fence told me where to find you."

The man growled, cutting him off. "Damn. I shoulda never brought him here."

"No, it's okay," Doc said. "Let's start over." He stepped forward, offering his hand.

"Stay where you are." The man raised the pistol.

"Whoa . . . I have as much to be careful about as you do, maybe more . . . and my secrets require a good safe spot to talk. That's why I'm here, and, by the way, that's some fine inventory you have there." He nodded at the pottery.

"If you know my fence so well, why come here? Teague can get you this stuff after I pass it off to him."

"That," Doc said, "is not why I'm here."

"The best stuff is packed away." He lowered the pistol. "What'cha lookin' for? This ain't like walking into a department store. You take what I find."

Doc laughed. "You misunderstand me. I'm not seeking artifacts."

"Then why are you here?"

Doc cleared his voice. "Because . . . I avoid being seen with the people I work with. This . . . is the perfect place to meet."

"What exactly do you do?" the man asked, suspicion in his voice. He raised the pistol.

"Consulting." Doc let out a nervous chuckle. "It's hard to explain. Permit me to answer with a focus on you." He cleared his throat. "You come highly recommended. I'm told you have redeeming qualities . . . qualities I can perfect."

The man lowered the pistol. "What the hell are you saying?"

"Your potential."

He raised his gun hand. "That an insult?"

"No, sir." Doc eyed the weapon. "It's a compliment. If you'll permit me to do so, I'll make the world think you're a hero."

"What are you talking about?"

"Turning you into the man the tribe thinks will keep them safe . . . from the monsters endangering those who can't defend themselves."

The man lowered the gun. "Are you sure you know who you're talking to? Maybe you're supposed to be over in the next canyon. Maybe you took the wrong fork in the trail."

Doc shook his head. "What trail? There was no trail." He laughed. "No, sir, I know exactly who you are. I've vetted you thoroughly. I know what I'm getting."

"What *are* you getting?"

"A man I can shape into a lone wolf. A rebel. Someone others see as the rogue who'll make a stand against evil masses. An outsider. Anti-establishment. A gunslinger willing to fight *those other people*." He smiled. "Hell is *those other people*. We all want someone willing to fight *those other people*. You'll be that someone." Doc took a step forward.

"No. No. No," the man said, his words staccato. "Stay. Where. You. Are."

"Of course." Doc stepped back, clearing his throat. "You see, people believe the only way to solve a problem is to find someone willing to give . . . *those other people* . . . a damned good kick in the ass. You'll be that person. Someone I'll transform into the reluctant hero."

"To do what?" the man demanded, confused.

"To seemingly . . . selflessly . . . sacrifice yourself to save the nation . . . or at least the people of New Mexico."

"Me? Sacrifice?" He laughed. "Again, are you sure you've got the right person?"

Doc chuckled to himself. "Yes, your name is . . ."

"Mister," the man shouted, cutting him off. He waved the pistol. "Until you've convinced me of what you're selling, I don't want to hear you even say my name. To anyone. Got it?"

"Got it." Doc nodded. "As I was saying, *you'll* seemingly go after the hidden agenda . . . in Washington . . . but in reality, you'll be there to do a job. It'll be you with an agenda."

"And what will that agenda be?"

"All in due time." Doc rubbed at the flat of his nose, hiding his smile. "All in due time."

A sound. From behind. Doc turned.

Another broken branch. Footsteps. A man came around an outcropping and stopped in the glow of the fire. Salt and pepper beard. Tan, leathery face. Baggy clothes. Floppy hat. Seeing the artifacts, he spun around to Doc. "What did you do?" he shouted.

Doc stared back, not sure what to say.

"Over here!" barked the man in the shadows.

The intruder turned, eyes searching. "Who did this?" he demanded.

"I did," said the man in the shadows, his voice calm.

"How'd you know about this place?"

"You're not as clever as you think, Potts. I followed you."

"Impossible, I cover my tracks, and how do you know who I am?"

"I know. You're Potts Monroe, archeologist. I know your secrets. All of 'em." He laughed. "I might know a little *too much*. I might know more than you do."

"What are you saying?"

"Your secrets. I especially like the one about Spanish treasure. Juan Rivera's treasure."

"Treasure? Rivera?" The archeologist's face lost all expression. "Hold it. I know you."

The man in the shadows laughed, then fired a round into the intruder's chest. The shot echoed up the canyon.

Thrown back, the archeologist steadied himself, eyes wide in disbelief, mouth gaping open. He fell to his knees, then dropped face first into the sand.

The man in the shadows turned the gun on Doc.

"Hold it," Doc said, forcing a smile.

"We got a problem?"

"No. I, uh . . ." He cleared his throat. ". . . would never question your business practices."

Chapter 2

Kelly sat up and stretched, her dark hair tossed by the cool morning breeze. From the foot of her sleeping bag, her brown, groggy eyes moved to the glow on the eastern horizon. The sun would soon peek over. She let out a happy sigh.

"Good morning," Jack whispered.

She dropped her eyes to where Jack's sleeping bag lay empty, then glanced around, finding him on the boulder behind her. "How long have you been awake?"

"Most of the night."

"Why?"

"Thinking."

"About what?"

"Last night."

She sighed. "You've handled worse."

"Yes and no. Somehow . . . last night . . . felt different."

"How?"

He avoided her eyes. "Not sure. Maybe I'm imagining things."

"Remind you of last year with politicians . . . or . . . are you thinking about Montana?"

Jack stood and hunkered over his pack. "Let's not talk about it."

"Okay . . . so that's why we came here . . . middle of the night." She rubbed her eyes. "You were lousy company, by the way." She took a whiff of the breeze. "Smell that. New Mexico high desert.

Restores your optimism, doesn't it? Makes everything feel possible." She stared into his eyes. "No?"

Jack Chastain peeled off his T-shirt and felt the nip in the air. Reaching into his pack, he pulled out a small gray bundle and let it unroll. His uniform shirt, gold badge attached. He slipped it on and began to button. "Gotta go. You've got a flight to catch and I'm on the job."

"Washington, ugh." She let out a tired moan. "I'd rather get lost in those blue eyes of yours."

"On your feet, Senator."

"No coffee?"

"We'll get some in town. Figured you'd need to get moving." He leaned over his pack, stuffed in his sleeping bag, and began to roll up his pad.

"Can you throw me my clothes?"

He picked them off a boulder and tossed them onto her lap.

She crawled out of her bag and stood, wearing only a T-shirt. She slipped it off, dropped it onto her pack, and watched as the sun rose. After a moment, she pulled on khaki shorts and turned, catching his gaze as she tugged on a white linen shirt. She smiled. "Hi, blue eyes."

"Wish I could say '*Take your time.*'"

She made quick work of stuffing her gear in her pack, then pulled on and laced her boots. "I'm ready," she said, hefting her pack onto her shoulders.

Jack did the same and crept past boulders and desert scrub, working his way to the trail, Kelly following. Upon reaching the trace of dirt and desert gravel, he picked up his pace.

Half an hour later, they topped a rise, and a sandstone ridge came into view, beyond which sat the trailhead. Just a few minutes more.

Butterflies fluttered across the trail. Kelly stopped to watch.

"Better keep moving," Jack said, making mental note of the location.

"We're not in that much of a hurry. Smell the roses."

Jack glanced at his watch. "Okay, then give me a minute." He lost sight of the butterflies, then stepped off the trail, into a dry sandy creek bed.

"They didn't go that way." Kelly pointed the opposite direction.

"I know. I saw 'em." He stopped and studied a sandstone outcropping.

Kelly came up behind him. "Did you know, the Aztec believed . . . for those who died in battle, that butterflies took their souls to their final resting place?" She spun around. "What are you looking for?"

He pointed. At the base of the outcropping, in shadow. Dark, moist soil. A seep. Plants with broad, bulbous leaves, and not yet developed seed pods. "Milkweed," he muttered. He inched forward, eyeing a plant. "And, no, I didn't know that about the Aztecs."

She gasped. "A monarch." She followed. "Another tidbit. The Mazahuas people call the monarch the daughter of the sun."

He unbuttoned the pocket below his badge and pulled out a notebook. Between pages he located a sheet of speck-like labels. He removed one. "Where'd you learn all that, Senator?"

"College . . . and quit calling me senator." Kelly rested her hand on his arm. "Cultural studies. What's that?"

"A tag." He stooped. The monarch flew away, then fluttered back, landing on his arm.

"Ah . . . and that means, season of transformation."

In a scissor-like motion, he caught the butterfly between fingers. In gentle taps, he adhered the tag to a wing, then placed the monarch on a milkweed. It flew away. "For research. For a professor . . . coincidently, in Mexico." He opened the notebook and scribbled down the date, location, and tag number. "This isn't likely an important place for monarch, but the professor's not sure if these guys winter in Mexico or California." He put the notebook away. "What do you mean, *season of transformation*?"

"That's what some believe about being touched by a monarch. That they represent transformation . . . kinda depends on what's going on in your life when it happens." She shrugged. "I thought they only wintered in Mexico."

"No, but more winter there. Tagging these guys won't answer

the professor's question. These are migrating north. A different generation will make the trip south in the fall." He turned.

She flashed a confused look. "Why tag it now?"

"Science. If someone sees it, might tell 'em something. Maybe where these guys migrate." He stood. "I'll come back here in the fall." He stared at the outcropping, his mind elsewhere. He brushed a hand across his forehead. "I enjoy this kind of work."

"What's keeping you from it?"

"The coalition report, for one."

"It's almost done. Maybe it's time for transformation."

"Not until the report's finished and we put it in *your* hands."

"But you're nearly there, and . . . change might do you good." She frowned. "I've been so worried about you . . . the mood swings . . . sudden anger."

"Not yet. Transformation . . . transition . . . it can wait."

"I understand . . . but transformation . . . it's a funny thing. It's not always something we have control over. Look at me, and where I am."

"Exactly." He sighed. "Last night, I kept thinking . . . the things that guy said . . . they weren't true, but did he know that? Was it karma . . . bad karma . . . coming around again?"

"Again?"

"Like what happened in Montana . . . the guy last night targeted me, not the report . . . me. But . . . we're beyond the point we were at in Montana."

"Then why worry?"

"Hard to say. The weirdness of it all. His confidence." Jack turned, conjuring memories. "In Montana . . . despite the difficulties, even after the political games . . . we kept it together. But crazy stories started . . . a weird level of certainty about them. I didn't take 'em seriously, expecting truth to prevail. Didn't worry . . . till it was too late." He cleared his throat. "Last night . . . the guy's absolute conviction. Why would he believe those things?"

"You're overreacting. You've handled worse. And you're almost finished."

"Essentially, *it's* done. It doesn't really need to be signed . . .

it's just something they want to do . . . they've worked so hard . . . through so many difficulties." He stared at the milkweed. "But I know this . . . I need to respond to that guy, not wait like I did in Montana."

"You're thinking too hard. You know what? You deserve a distraction . . . doing something you enjoy. Why don't you spend some time on monarchs? Invite that professor up."

"He's been here, but not for this."

"What's that mean?"

"He was here with his wife, an archeologist . . . helping Potts on a project."

"Potts? That loony archeologist . . . retired Park Service guy? Here every spring?"

"Yep, that's Potts. Potts Monroe. He's got a project he wants to show me . . . when the time's right. Being kinda secretive, but he's not loony. *Stereotypical*, maybe, but not loony."

"Whatever." She shook her head. "My point is, you've been so key to the coalition's work, you owe yourself a distraction, a chance to recover."

"Not yet . . . and I haven't been that important."

"You're the only one who feels that way."

Jack shook his head, staring past her. Movement caught his eye. Distant movement. He focused downslope, at a spot amidst sagebrush. A dog. Black, wiry. More movement. A boy. *What the hell?* Jack squinted. The boy, walking a deliberate line through desert scrub. Dark hair. Plaid shirt. The dog staying ahead on a sea of vegetation.

Kelly turned. She gasped. "A child?"

"It is. See anyone with him?"

"No. Is he allowed to have a dog in the monument?"

"No, but I'm more concerned about him being alone."

"Need to go get him?"

Jack studied the boy's gait. Steady. No sign of confusion or uncertainty.

The boy veered, a change in direction. The dog ran and retook the lead.

"He seems to know where he's going." Jack backed toward the trail. "And you need to catch a flight." He gestured for her to take the lead. "Better go."

She headed upslope, glancing back at the boy.

"And hey," Jack shouted. "I want to know the one thing you've avoided talking about . . . whether you're gonna run for your own term as senator."

"Haven't decided." She dropped her eyes. "At this point the governor's probably cursing Senator Baca's death and his decision to appoint me to finish his term."

"I doubt the latter . . . but you need to decide."

She shrugged. "I'm being pressed on it." She sighed. "Someone else might be better."

"Kelly, I've seen your dedication to the work."

A pop came from inside his pack, then a tone, then a voice. Molly, in dispatch, on the radio.

"*Attention, all personnel. We have a report of a lost child. Male, twelve years old. We need all hands available. Stand by for instructions.*"

The boy. Jack spun around. Nowhere in sight. Where'd he go? Jack pulled his cell phone from his pants pocket and gave it a quick check. No signal. He slipped an arm out of a pack strap and swung the pack around. He dug out his radio.

"*The boy's name, David,*" Molly continued. "*Hair color, black. Approximately four and half feet tall. Separated from his parents on a hike. Likely took a different fork in the trail. They believe they were on Saltbush Trail. Some uncertainty about that. Break.*"

The radio went dead.

"We're miles from there," Kelly said.

Jack raised his radio. "Yeah, but we don't know when this happened . . . or where."

The radio popped. Molly continued, "*The boy is diabetic. Does not have his insulin. I repeat, does not have his insulin. We need to mobilize a hasty search, now.*" The radio repeater clicked off.

Damn. Jack keyed his mic. "Dispatch, this is Chastain."

"*Go ahead, Jack.*"

"I saw a boy a few minutes ago. Alone with his dog, off-trail, South Desert."

"*Standby.*" The radio fell quiet, then, "*You're sure about a dog? And the location?*"

"Yes."

"*The report includes nothing about a dog, or taking the trail out of the canyon, but the parents are gone. Freaking out. Disappeared to go look for him, so I can't ask, but . . . can you get to this kid?*"

He looked at Kelly. "Don't see him now. Not sure where he's heading, but . . . I know his direction of travel."

"*Copy. Report back when you pick up his trail. Confirm direction, I'll get someone out in front of him. I'll also put a helicopter on standby, just in case . . . .*"

"Copy. Send someone to the trailhead to pick up Kelly. She's got a flight to make."

"No," Kelly shouted, over his shoulder. "This is more important. Disregard that, Molly."

"*Copy. We're shorthanded so it'll have to be.*"

Kelly took off, jogging downslope toward open desert.

Jack threw on his pack and took off. Working their way off the hillside, jumping rocks, and avoiding pinyon and juniper, they approached open desert. Jack scanned the scene. *No boy. No dog. Where the hell did he go?*

Reaching flat ground, Jack veered in the direction of the spot he'd last seen the boy. Approaching, he saw nothing in the sea of desert scrub. *Maybe we're not there yet. Or, did I miss his tracks?* Eyeing the ground, Jack continued forward.

Should be two sets of tracks. The boy. The dog. Where are they?

"How . . . much . . . farther?" Kelly asked, panting, fighting to keep up.

"Should be here . . . somewhere." Jack dodged a sage, then looked back, up the hill, gauging distance. "We'll slow down when we find his track."

"There," Kelly shouted, pointing. She came to a stop, hands on her hips, fighting for breath.

Good. Jack stopped over the track and traced the boy's likely path across the plain. No obvious destination. "Where's he going?" Jack took off in a slow jog. He glanced back at Kelly.

"Go." She cinched up her pack's hip strap and followed.

They paced themselves, weaving through sagebrush, wasting no time.

How did he cover this much territory? We just saw him . . . what was it? Five minutes ago, maybe ten? Jack glanced down. *The tracks. Gone. Now, where did he go?* Jack stopped.

Kelly came alongside.

"Lost him again." Jack spun around. "Could he've passed out? Did we go past him?"

Backpedaling, eyes on the ground, they retraced, finding the last tracks in the midst of their own. "His tracks just stop."

Scattered rock, a few boulders. Jack circled. No track. Then track. "Over here," he shouted, eying the strange set of clues. Boy's track. Dog's track. Then, no dog track. After a few steps more, no boy.

Kelly stopped over the last set of tracks. "I don't get it." She spun around. "Vanished."

"Yeah." Jack walked a circle around the track, checking in the shade of the largest desert scrub. "Nothing. No dog. Where did he go? If he passed out . . . he'd be . . ."

"He's not here."

"Does he know we're following him? It's like he just . . . evaporated." Jack studied the scene. Outcrops of sandstone. Scrub and rocks. One boulder. Lots of smaller slabs.

Is he hiding? Carrying the dog? He's not behind the boulder. He knelt at a rock near the last of the boy's tracks. Backside, shifting. Soil, pushed up. "Here," Jack muttered. "He's rock hopping. Carrying the dog. But why?" He turned to Kelly. "Maybe the dog's hurt."

More movement of rock, toward an exposed outcropping of sandstone. A ramp, moving a new direction. In the distance, the mouth of an arroyo. Beyond it, sandstone walls. "He's going that way." Jack pointed. "Up that arroyo, into a drainage."

Kelly put her hands on her hips. "Why?"

"Avoiding the sun, maybe? Maybe he knows we're here." Jack slipped into a jog.

In the sandy bed of the arroyo, two sets of tracks. "He was here." Jack bolted up the canyon, taking firmer ground upslope among pinyon and juniper, keeping an eye on the boy's tracks. Then, they disappeared. A rock to the right, other side of the draw. Cross-bedded sandstone. *He's climbing out of the creek bed.*

Around a bend, walls came together. A ledge lay at the base of near-vertical walls. Below the ledge, a drop.

"He's going high," Kelly said. "What if he loses consciousness? What if he falls?"

They picked up their pace.

Around a bend they saw him. Boy, dog, walking toward them, a hundred yards away, fifty feet above the creek bed. *He's backtracking. Must've ledged out.*

The boy turned and ran, disappearing around another bend.

"He's avoiding us," Jack said.

"He must be delirious."

"Go back. Take the creek bed."

She turned.

Jack darted along the ledge. Rounding a bend, he slid on gravel and slipped over the edge, coming to a grinding stop. Glancing over his shoulder, he eyed the drop beyond his feet. Calming himself, he moderated his breathing, crawled back to the ledge, and shook off his jitters. He moved on.

Another bend. Beyond it lay the end of the drainage. An alcove. The boy stood looking out over a precipitous drop, a lip over which water had poured during many a storm. Frantic, the boy looked for options. He had none. The dog stayed close. Seeing Jack, the boy backed to the wall.

Kelly came running up the creek bed, below.

The boy, dark hair, slight frame, eyes wide, glanced between Jack and Kelly.

"We're here to help you," she shouted.

Jack took a step.

The dog barked.

Jack inched toward them.

Darting forward, the dog growled.

Jack raised a hand. "It's okay."

The boy burst into tears. "Don't hurt me."

"We're here to help you." Jack attempted a smile. "Your parents . . . they're worried."

"Go away."

"Are you okay?"

"Leave me alone."

"Wait," Kelly shouted. "Let me try." She ran back down the creek and after a short span of time reappeared on the ledge. Jack let her slip past, holding the dog's attention.

Kelly crept toward the boy. "You okay?"

Eyes scared, he forced a nod.

She slipped an arm around him. "Need your insulin?"

He shot a confused look, then looked back at Jack. "Please don't let him hurt me."

"Jack would never do that. He's a good guy."

"But . . ." He broke into tears. "The spirits . . . their faces . . ."

A hand on each shoulder, she knelt, looking into his eyes. "Spirits?"

The boy stopped talking, his lips clamped shut.

Jack stepped back and studied the little guy. *How strange. Delirious?*

"*Chastain, this is Dispatch.*"

Jack pulled out his radio. "Go ahead, Molly. We've got him."

"*Not possible. He's here with me and his parents. They found him, waiting at their car.*"

Jack scowled. "Standby Molly." He turned and eyed the boy.

The boy pulled out of Kelly's arms and pushed himself against the rock.

Jack drew in a long, deep breath. "So, who the hell are you?"

Chapter
3

Jack signed off the radio and turned to the boy. "Why are you afraid of me?"

The boy pushed back on the wall, as if trying to break through the rock.

"It's okay," Kelly said to the boy. She put up a hand, signaling Jack to step back. "Give him some time. Let him warm up to you. Get us outta here. You lead, I'll walk with him."

Jack pulled off his Park Service cap and ran his fingers through sweat-matted hair. "Make sure he doesn't run. And find out why he's here alone." Jack glanced at the boy's pack. Small but hardly juvenile. "Does he need water?"

"I just checked. He's got plenty, plus overnight gear."

Jack waved her toward him, and whispered, "Molly has no other reports of lost boys. Must be a local kid. Her thinking . . . the Sheriff's in a better position to figure out who his parents are."

"Okay, we drive by there on the way home." She slipped back to the boy.

Jack held out his hand to the dog. Scruff of white on its throat. Otherwise, black. It sniffed his hand, then backed away.

"That's progress." Jack headed back down the ledge.

Staying in Kelly's shadow, the boy kept a slow pace, Kelly holding his hand.

Too far back for Jack to hear conversation, the boy seemed intent on keeping it that way.

Back among desert scrub, Jack pulled out his map and chose a route to the trailhead. It would take a little backtracking, but with a veer to the northeast, up and over a series of gradual rises, they would hit the trail not far from the trailhead.

Cutting across the desert, they climbed onto high ground near the eastern boundary of the national monument. Piedras Coloradas National Park came into view. The plateau and the slice through the rock cut by the river. Then, below the canyon, its path cut toward the hamlet of Las Piedras. Green fields and pastures lay nestled around the village.

Glancing north, he spotted the trail, arcing along the base of an escarpment of red sandstone. In the distance he could just make out the trailhead and a white government pickup with green Park Service markings.

Kelly and the boy still lagged behind. Jack decided to wait for them at the pickup.

Once there, he threw his pack in the back and leaned against the fender to wait.

Kelly and the boy reached the trail, talking, ambling, as if Kelly forgot she had a flight to catch.

A sound. Engine noise. Jack turned.

Pulses of dust hung in the sky beyond a rise in the road. An ATV—a four-wheeler—appeared. Then others, four in all, coming his way. He walked to the other side of the pickup, resumed his lean, and waited.

They accelerated toward him, engine noise growing louder.

The lead ATV slid to a stop, throwing gravel at Jack's feet. The others slowed to a halt and cut their engines. Quiet.

The man in the lead dismounted and folded his arms. Shorter than Jack but of average height, brawny, lips hidden by a bushy mustache, and a pistol holstered on his belt, he glared, and groused, "Why are you here?"

The others—two men, one woman, all dressed for riding—assumed similar poses.

Jack turned back to the man with the pistol. "Working. Chasin' butterflies."

"Very funny."

"No, serious." Jack crossed his own arms and returned their glare. "And, if I wasn't here . . . what would you be doing?"

"We're here to remove you." The mustachioed man turned, improving the view of his pistol. "If you want to stay happy, butterfly man, head down the road and mind your own damned business."

Jack stared at the firearm. "I have a feeling this could turn into what would be . . . very much . . . my business."

"Not in my eyes." The man gave a twisted smile. "Leave."

The boy's dog appeared, inched forward, then jumped back, barking.

"If that damned dog attacks, he's dead," the man muttered, resting his hand on the pistol.

"He's not mine," Jack said, "but he fancies himself as a good judge of character."

Kelly and the boy came around the pickup.

"A boy?" said the woman with the ATVs. "We can't make a scene in front of the boy."

"A scene?" Jack asked.

"We're taking back our road," the leader said, watching the dog. "You feds closed it, now you want our land. That's not gonna happen. We're taking back our road."

"What are you talking about?" Jack asked.

Kelly stopped beside him. "Parts of the trail used to be an old stock road," she said. "Closed years before you got here, mainly to slow the pot hunting. The pueblo wanted it closed."

"Wrong," the man growled. "Had nothing to do with them. Feds were just controlling our lives. Like they want to do now."

Jack shook his head. "Doing now? What are you talking about?"

"You know." The man exchanged glances with the others.

They nodded in agreement.

"I don't," Jack said. He turned to Kelly. "Do you?"

She shook her head.

One of the riders flagged with his hand. "Hide . . ."

The leader cut him off. "Don't use my name . . . or anyone's. We'll be the first ones he sics those land agents on."

"Hey . . . wait . . . it's Senator Culberson?" the woman said.

"Is there something I need to know?" Kelly asked.

The leader took two steps toward her. "Don't play dumb. You know their plans better than we do. Why aren't you stopping them from taking our lands?"

"Private lands? You live on the Enclave, right?"

"Doesn't matter. The feds want to take it."

She turned to Jack and flashed a questioning look. "Do you?"

"I have no idea what he's talking about."

"Lies, lies, lies. You're lyin'. Both of ya."

Jack and Kelly exchanged glances.

Kelly scratched her chin. "Why would they . . . ?"

The leader cut her off. "Because government can't stand seein' people living in freedom, minding our own business. Choosing the life we want. They want our land, probably our guns."

Jack clenched his jaw, then a fist. He stepped forward.

Kelly mouthed, no. She reached for his hand.

"Is that what you *want* to believe?" the boy said.

What? Jack turned to the boy.

The boy stared up at the man with the pistol.

The man sneered. "What did you *say*, little man?"

"Is that what you *want* to believe?"

Red with anger, the man glared, then grew flustered, then turned to Jack, unable to respond. Whipping around to his four-wheeler, he climbed on, started it, and put it in gear. He sped off, throwing gravel at their feet.

"I'll look into it," Kelly said to the woman. "If you learn anything . . . anything about anyone wanting to take your land, contact my field office in Santa Fe."

The woman nodded. She and her companions fired up their four-wheelers and followed.

Jack knelt beside the boy. "Why are you afraid of me, but not him?"

He scooted behind Kelly.

Kelly looked him in the eye and smiled. "You are a funny little guy."

He smiled, then glanced at Jack. The smile melted away.

—'—

They pulled into the modern adobe headquarters of the county sheriff, the boy riding against the door, Kelly between them, the dog in the bed. They parked between patrol vehicles, a pickup and a sedan, both black and white. A deputy climbed out of the pickup and started for the building.

They followed the deputy in, the boy watching him closely.

Inside, they approached the receptionist. Kelly took the boy's hand.

"Buenos días, Kelly," the uniformed receptionist said. "How's life in Washington?"

"Good, Esperanza. Great to see you. We've got a little guy here we found in the backcountry . . . in the national monument . . . South Desert . . . without his parents." She turned to the boy. "He won't tell us his name. Handles himself pretty well, but still, . . ." She leaned against the counter. "We're worried about him. Recognize him? Know his parents?"

Esperanza stood and looked over her counter. "¿Como estas? ¿Como se dice?"

The boy stared.

"Do you not speak Spanish? Or are you from the pueblo? No? What is your name?"

The boy continued to stare.

"Can you tell me who your parents are? Did you run away from home?"

No answer.

Esperanza sat. "Are you wanting us to take him, maybe turn him over to social services?"

"That's probably best," Jack said. "He hasn't done anything

wrong, just seemed odd, a boy his age hiking alone, so far from anything."

"Let's put you in one of the . . ." She paused and tapped her lips. "No, let's don't do that. Take the meeting room." She pointed at a door to the left. Inside sat a table surrounded by chairs. Sunlight streamed in through the windows. "Not as scary as an interrogation room. I'll have a deputy join you."

Kelly sat by the boy. Jack paced the floor, the boy watching him.

"Knock, knock," came a voice at the door. In stepped a solid man in sport coat and bolo tie. Gray hair, a little paunchy.

Kelly got to her feet. "Sheriff Mendoza."

Mendoza nodded at Jack, then gave Kelly a hug. "Senator. A beauty like your mother, but obviously your father's political talents."

She blushed. "I'm not sure that's true. I hear you're retiring."

"Yes, the thought of *not* running for office is appealing. I'll miss the job, but I'm ready to leave the campaigning to you young folks."

She laughed. "It's not appealing to me either. I'm trying to decide if I'll run for my own term."

"You should. We need you there." Mendoza turned to the boy. "Who do we have here?"

The boy watched him. Nothing in his eyes suggested fear.

"What's your name, son?"

He shook his head.

"Did you run away from home?"

"No, sir," he said, his voice at ease.

"Can I call your momma?"

"No sir."

Mendoza appeared confused. "Really? Excuse us, would you?" He signaled Jack and Kelly to follow him into the hall.

He closed the door behind them. "You say you found him on South Desert? Alone?"

"And he avoided us," Jack said. "Covered his track. Pretty good at it, too."

"That could mean trouble at home," Mendoza said. "But I don't see any signs of abuse."

"Strange thing is . . ." Jack said, ". . . he's afraid of me but he's not afraid of anyone else."

"Big, scary Anglo." Mendoza chuckled to himself. "Leave him with me. We have no reports of missing kids, but I'll talk to social services, see if they know who he is." He opened the door and stepped back inside, stopped, and looked back, stunned. "I've never seen that happen. Guess it's time to retire."

Jack peeked inside.

In the corner, a window stood open, a light breeze moving the curtains.

The boy? No sign of him.

—'—

Jack and Kelly climbed into the pickup.

"And he took the dog," Jack said, still marveling at what happened.

"I better go change my flight," Kelly said.

At the sound of a tap on the window, they turned. A uniformed deputy stood outside the door. Gold badge. Gold name plate, Buck Winslow inscribed in black letters. A light-haired man, average size, but appearing slight in his oversized uniform.

Jack lowered the window.

"Where should I start looking for this kid?" Winslow asked. He slipped a toothpick between his teeth and slumped into a lean against the pickup.

"Don't think you'll find him," Jack said.

"That so?"

"He's crafty. Doesn't want to be caught."

"The sheriff said you have no idea what his name is."

"Correct."

"I'll take a spin around. See if I find him. If not, I'll just see if he turns up." Winslow flashed a toothy grin and rubbed at the stubble on his face. "Guess I forgot to shave this morning." He pulled the toothpick from his mouth. "Uh . . . you Park guys have all the fun, don't you? You must love brewin' up trouble."

"What trouble?"

"Out on the Enclave. You got people up in arms over those land agents swarmin' around."

"Land agents?"

"Here to kick them off their land. I saw Hide Mangum this mornin' . . . and again a few minutes ago."

"The guy on the four-wheeler," Kelly said to Jack. "The one with the mustache."

"Yep, that's Mangum," Winslow said. "He's ready to lead an armed rebellion."

"Got a taste of that an hour ago, but I know of no plan to kick anyone off their land."

"Being coy?" Winslow flashed a grin, then a wink. "Everyone seems to know about the land agents. I'd avoid the South Desert if I were you. You'd be provoking ol' Mangum."

"I've got work to do."

"What kind of work?"

Jack shrugged. "Lots of things."

"Why out there? It's pretty remote."

"Everywhere I work is remote. There's lots of work to be done. Today, along the Desert Rose Trail, for example, we found milkweed near the trailhead. Great for monarch butterfly."

"Serious? You'd pick a fight over butterflies?"

"I'm not picking a fight." Jack flashed his own grin and a wink. "I love chasin' butterflies. The thrill of the hunt is in finding their milkweed."

Winslow raised his hands in surrender. "Okay, okay, but if Mangum thinks you're picking a fight, comin' around where he lives, I think you should avoid the place. It's like poking Mangum in the eye. He doesn't seem like a reasonable guy, especially with land agents around."

"There are no land agents."

"Wanna see 'em?" Winslow brushed at his badge with the

back of his hand. “Hop in my rig, we’ll take a spin, look for that kid while we’re at it.”

“Kelly’s got to catch a flight, so . . .”

“No,” she said. “I need to see this.”

They climbed in the deputy’s unmarked patrol vehicle, Kelly in the front, Jack in back.

Stuck to the dashboard, a paper name tag read, ‘*Hello, my name is*’ and scrawled in dark letters, “Deputy Buckity.” Beside it, in a child’s writing, another piece of paper. *Deputy Buckity for Sheriff.*

“Deputy Buckity?” Kelly asked.

“That’s what the school kids call me.” He put on a goofy grin. “Deputy Buckity,” he said, in a cartoonish voice. “Sometimes I even let ’em see my bullet.” He pulled a single 44-magnum round from his shirt pocket.

Not at all scary when presented with a goofy face.

“Gosh, Deputy Buckity,” he cartooned again. “Ever see bad guys? Yuckity, yuck.”

Kelly laughed and tapped on the other piece of paper.

“They’re trying to convince me to run for sheriff. I don’t know. Too much politics.”

Circling the several blocks around the sheriff’s office, they saw no sign of the boy. When satisfied they wouldn’t, Winslow turned onto the main road and drove to the edge of town, pulling into one of the town’s more modest motels, *Desert Sands*.

Winslow pointed at two white sedans parked near rooms at the far end of the motel, no markings, General Services Administration license plates, same as on Jack’s truck.

Jack studied the cars. *Not obviously Park Service but what other agency would be in Las Piedras? It’s not exactly a center of government activity*. “Why does Mangum think they’re land agents?” Jack rubbed his chin. “I mean . . . the actual term would be real estate specialist . . . but why would he think that?”

“Not hard, the way they’re snoopin’ around, asking all sorts of questions. Who owns what, and where? People notice things.”

“But . . .”

“Go ask ’em,” Winslow said. “Knock on the door.”

“Ask the people in the rooms?”

“Yep. Ask ’em.”

Jack got out and started for a door, then stopped. “I’ll ask first at the office. See if there’s something I don’t know about.”

“Let me know what you find out,” Kelly said. “Now, I need to go change my flight.”

Chapter 4

"Goodbye, Senator," Jack said, putting his hands on her waist. "Sorry I made you late."

She kissed him, then removed his hands. "Don't start anything. I've gotta go."

"Get your flight changed?"

"Actually, my flight's running late, but . . . if I miss it, there's a redeye." She kissed him again. "After the signing ceremony, think about coming to Washington, taking some time off."

"Washington hasn't exactly been a fun place for me."

She shrugged. "Don't think about the halls of the Main Interior Building. Think Smithsonian. Think history. Think junior senator from New Mexico."

He patted her on the behind.

She gave him a stern look. "Things have changed. You can't do that. I have a reputation to uphold."

—'—

"Marge . . . still here?" Jack shouted, walking past closed doors before stepping into the office of the superintendent's secretary.

"Not for much longer," she said, her computer off, her handbag on her desk. "Hanging around in case Joe needs something."

"Can I stick my head in, ask him a question?"

"Absolutely not." Marge began watering the potted plants scattered around her office. She glanced at the closed door to her left. "He's on a call. It'll have to be tomorrow."

Jack gave her a slow, accepting nod. "Question. Is there something going on that involves land people? Real estate specialists, here to acquire private land?"

A line formed on her brow.

"There's a couple of government vehicles in town."

"You'll have to ask Joe about that."

Jack scowled. "Seriously?"

Joe's door swung open. He glanced at Marge, then Jack. "Need me?"

"Just for a second. Short one." Jack glanced at Marge, as if he needed approval.

"A second is all you get." Joe waved him in. "Thank you, Marge. Nothing came up that can't wait till tomorrow. Go home." Joe slid behind his big, timber desk. Not sitting, he picked his Stetson off the equally massive credenza and slipped it on, the brim level. Uniform perfect, salt and pepper hair flawlessly groomed. "Get on with it."

Jack stayed at the door. "Two vehicles, government tags, parked at a motel in town."

Joe picked up his briefcase. "What about 'em?"

"Who are they? Realty specialists? Land procurement?"

"That, . . . it turns out, is none of your business. Stay out of it."

"You're kidding?"

"Nope."

"I can't even ask questions?"

"I've been sworn to secrecy." Joe squeezed past him. "Close the door on your way out."

—'—

Jack turned into Elena's Cantina and slowed. *Damn. Packed with customers. Height of the dinner hour.* He circled, searching for a place to park, the tires of his Jeep crunching through gravel.

Squeezing between vehicles, he parked, then ambled over to the steps into the old adobe building. Inside, he noticed Johnny Reger sitting against the back wall, then turned down the hallway to the dining room. As he approached the hostess, he reminded himself he'd be eating alone. He turned back to the bar.

After getting a beer, he worked his way through the tables toward Reger. Not a day in the field, obviously. His blonde hair, usually matted by sweat to his forehead, looked neatly combed.

"What are you pissed about?" Johnny asked.

"I'm not. Where are your groupies?"

"California. Big fire. Wish I coulda gone . . . but . . ." He lifted a hand and twiddled his fingers.

"Sorry it's taking so long to recover."

"Why are you apologizing? You didn't pull the trigger. And yeah, you're pissed. What about?"

"A couple of government cars in town. People out on the Enclave think they're here to force 'em to sell to the government. Joe won't talk about it. Tells me to stay out of it."

"So, you're pissed."

"I'm not pissed."

"You are. And what I happen to know is, Kelly's worried about you."

"How would you know that? And why?"

"She told me . . . at the gas station, heading out of town. You know what it's about."

"Don't you two have anything more important to talk about . . . like . . . your hand? Any closer to arresting the shooter?"

"Haven't heard a thing. We turned it over to the FBI and I suspect they're waitin' to catch the guy when he's not sittin' around with his buddies, cleaning AR-15s." Johnny extended his fingers and watched them move. "But back to Kelly. She wanted to talk about her legislative agenda . . . get my advice . . . right there at the gas station. That lost me right away, but she's right. I may've gotten shot, but you're the one slow to recover."

"I'm fine," Jack growled. "I'm past what happened last year with the politicos."

A chair crashed to the floor. Then another. Across the bar two men faced off. Middle-aged, likely tourists, outdoor garb, poking at each other's chests, voices raised.

The commotion held Johnny's eye. "If you say so. But she's worried, boss."

Jack sighed. "I'm more worried about what happened last night at the meeting."

"Hell with the meeting, it'll blow over." Reger raised his mug. "Where's Potts Monroe?"

"I don't know. He's got a new project he wants to start . . . he may be there. He calls it his little secret. Won't tell me where it's at yet. Wants to take me there."

Johnny flinched, watching a thrown punch. "No one's seen him in a few days. He'd said he wanted to meet today . . . talk about a few things."

The tattooed bartender slipped around the bar and pushed himself between the fighters. A waitress, eyes wide, stood watching, ear to a phone.

Jack tried to ignore the ruckus. "Check his campsite?"

"Yep, checked the whole damned campground. Trailer's there. He's not." Johnny nodded toward the men. "I'm tempted to go see what these guys are fightin' about."

"Not your jurisdiction."

"I'm nosy."

A deputy rushed in the door. Brown uniform, white cowboy hat. He slid between the men and moved one into the hallway, signaling the other—a man in cargo shorts and fishing shirt—to stay put. He spent a moment in the hall with one man, then returned to chat with the other.

"Is that Deputy Winslow?" Jack asked.

"Deputy Buckity?" Johnny said. "Yep. Likely our next sheriff."

"Just met him today."

"He's been here a few years. Kids love him. Don't know about him as sheriff. A sheriff has to be tough when needed. Buckity? Hard to tell. What I know most about him . . . the gags he plays on kids."

"Nothing wrong with that."

"Nope, unless that's all he's got."

They watched Winslow push one rowdy out the door and set the second on a barstool. He turned and sauntered toward their table. "Just gonna sit there and bet on a winner?"

Johnny laughed. "You kinda messed up the odds."

"Didn't want you going broke." Winslow paused. "Learn anything?"

Jack and Johnny exchanged glances.

"Me?" Jack asked.

"I didn't expect Ranger Reger here to know anything. Who do you think I am?"

Johnny chuckled, taking the tease.

"You mean the two cars at the motel?" Jack asked.

Winslow gave a slow nod.

"Couldn't get any answers."

"Figures." Winslow sighed. "You better get some. Folks in the Enclave think they have you guys figured. Especially you."

"Why me?"

"You're the face of the coalition. Mangum figures you're behind the fed's plans."

"Mangum? The guy with the pistol?"

"You're not good with names, are you?" Winslow nodded. "Yep, that would be Hide. Saw him again this afternoon. Quite riled. Not the kinda guy I'd want angry."

"He doesn't need to worry. I have nothing to do with it."

"The effort to take his land?"

"I can't imagine us trying to do that," Jack said. "Why would we? His land's not in the park. It's not in the national monument. We rarely use eminent domain, even when we have a reason to. Why would we use it when we don't?"

"Whether you do or not, be wary about him. Me, I get along with everyone . . . but you? He doesn't like ya. With those government land agents around, I doubt you can trust he won't pull a gun on ya, just to provoke ya. I'd be ready to take him into custody if I were you."

Jack turned to Johnny. "Johnny's the peace officer. I'm just a science guy."

"He thinks you're more than that. I doubt you can change him." One side of Winslow's mouth turned up in a grin. "Mangum suspects you're the architect of why those guys are here."

"He said that?"

"More or less. A grand plan."

"There's no grand plan. Just an effort to find common ground. Bring people together."

"Call it what you want, but Mangum thinks you're going after his home. That the land agents are here because of you."

"Me?"

"You. The government."

"Me, the government? I'm just one guy. A guy who's trying to bring people together, to protect a place they love. Not to run 'em off their land."

"Watch your ass and don't provoke him. Stay away from those damned butterflies." Winslow stood to leave. "Gotta go. Deputy Buckity has Girl Scouts to talk to." He put on a goofy face. "Yuck-ity, yuck, yuck."

Chapter 5

Piedras Coloradas National Park encompassed a region of majestic pine-covered plateaus and deep canyons on the edge of the greater Colorado Plateau. The river that incised great cuts through sandstone strata seemed incapable of the job, but spring runoff could prove it temperamental, and the storms of summer could turn it into a raging torrent. Lighthouse Buttress, towering near the mouth of the canyon, ghostly on moonless nights, could be seen in daylight hours for miles, in directions that included desert environs and the furthest boundaries of Piedras Coloradas National Monument. In many ways the monument and park were different worlds, distinct in their personalities, but the larger monument's high desert—pinyon, juniper, and desert scrub—surrounded and stood sentry over the castle-like plateau, overshadowed, although with its own kind of splendor. While the park had existed for nearly a century, the monument had been set aside only a few years ago. Those acquainted with its quiet demeanor also knew it protected its secrets.

Jack Chastain drove out of the park in darkness, skirted the hamlet of Las Piedras, and turned onto a road toward his favorite part of the national monument, the South Desert.

He parked, watching a hint of the sun's coming arrival. Orange skies in slow eruption through thin, barely present clouds. To the west, over the desert, a pink aura. Desert scrub. No breeze. Early morning quiet.

Grabbing his pack, he slid it across the seat and climbed out of the pickup, taking off down the trail, his gear—tape measures, transect tapes, stakes, and data logger—rattling about in the pack, their sounds fading as they settled in the bottom.

No dew. The crunch of desert gravel at his feet.

He took the bend at the base of the escarpment and caught the view of the expansive scenery beyond the trail. *Good move, getting out here this early.*

In the distance, to the northeast, the jagged peaks of the San Juans, in Colorado. To the west, the Colorado Plateau, continuing beyond the horizon into Arizona and Utah. To the north, the park. To the south, sage brush, four-wing saltbush, rabbitbrush, winterfat, and more, with a scattering of pinyon and juniper.

Four-mile camp. A four-mile hike to the last of the monitoring locations in this part of the monument, put on the back burner as the writing of the coalition report took his full attention. The last camp before turning back to the more heavily used sites in the park.

He headed south on the trail and approached the spot where he'd seen the patch of milkweed. *Won't hurt to check for monarch.*

Eyes down slope, he crossed a sandy creek bed—an arroyo—and stepped off the trail. He stopped. No milkweed. Wrong spot.

Must be behind me. He spun around, stopping to eye the base of the sandstone outcropping. Dark, moist soils. *No, this is it.*

He approached where he expected fifteen to twenty healthy stalks of milkweed. Nothing. Plants eighteen to twenty-four inches tall don't just disappear. Where are they?

Maybe this isn't the spot . . . even if it's similar.

He checked farther down the trail, then backtracked. No other arroyo. That was the place.

He went back and knelt to study the ground. Smooth. Too much so. He caught sight of a stem, broken at ground level, and signs that others had been pulled up from the roots, then the ground patted smooth with gloved hands.

Whoever did this went to a lot of trouble.

He looked for tracks in the soil, and then along the trail. No good boot tracks, but as the sun crept higher, markings appeared. A spot where something had been dragged, possibly a bag. Probably filled with milkweed.

When he saw his own footprints in damp soil, he realized he might be disturbing any evidence Luiz Archuleta or one of the other law enforcement rangers might find.

He returned to the trail, angry, ready to explode.

Four-mile campsite would wait for another day.

Rounding the escarpment, he saw the parked government pickup, and beside it, a four-wheeler. A man stood at a window, peeking inside.

Jack jogged toward him.

The man, hearing him, turned, backed away, and sat on the seat of his four-wheeler. Sturdy build. Pistol in its holster at the small of his back. Hide Mangum.

"What did you do?" Jack demanded.

"Why are you here?" Mangum demanded back.

"Why would you do that? Why would you destroy them?"

"Don't try accusing me of something, government man. Answer my question. Why are you here? I told you, we're taking this road back. Get out of here."

"So, you can do more damage . . . destroying things that need protecting?"

"You won't pin nothin' on me," Mangum said. "Go, don't come back. Leave us alone."

"This is monument land." Jack pointed at the ground. "Belongs to everyone, not just you."

"You're not using that excuse to take our land. We'll fight, and we're retaking this road."

"This road was closed because of pot hunters. Is that what you are? A pot hunter?"

Mangum stepped toward him. "Get out of here. Don't come back. Tell your government land agents they're not gettin' our land." He poked Jack in the chest. "Got that?"

Jack batted his arm way.

Mangum spun, balance gone. He stumbled, falling to one knee.

Jack took a step forward.

Mangum reached for his pistol.

"Do that and you're in even more trouble than you are now."

Mangum snarled. "Not if they don't find your bloody carcass."

Jack dove, landing on top of him, slamming Mangum to the ground, and ripping his hand from the pistol. It slipped out of the holster and Jack hurled it into the brush. He rolled off Mangum, rose to his feet, and backed away.

Mangum sat up on one elbow, dazed, glaring, angry. Equally surprised.

"All I did was keep you from doing something stupid," Jack said, catching his breath.

"This time," Mangum countered. "But never again."

"I for one am not trying to run you off your land." Jack opened the pickup door and tossed his pack inside. "I can't speak for others, but I'm doing nothing that would affect you. Get over it."

"Liar."

"There are consequences for what you've destroyed."

"You're not hangin' anything on me."

Jack climbed in the pickup, started it, and put it in gear.

Mangum lay watching as he drove away.

—'—

Jack blew past Marge's desk, storming into Joe's office.

"We've got to talk, Joe."

Joe looked up from his work. Folding his arms, he sat back. "Okay, talk."

"I need to know what's going on. I was out on the South Desert. Finishing monitoring for that part of the park. There's milkweed I saw yesterday. Today it's gone."

"You sure you just couldn't find 'em?"

"They're gone."

"What do you mean, gone?"

"Gone. No sign of them. Pulled out and gone. Tracks brushed out. Evidence, not much."

Joe leaned forward and picked up a pen, giving it several clicks. "Go on."

"A guy named Hide Mangum and his followers. I'm sure of it. Saw him at the trailhead. Challenged me for being there. Denied messing with milkweed, but threatened to pull his pistol on me."

"Let Barb and her rangers know."

"I will, but . . . Mangum's convinced we want to force them off their land." Jack paused. "He's angry at me for being there . . . just as Deputy Winslow predicted."

"Predicted? What are you talking about?"

"I saw Mangum yesterday. Made a sarcastic comment about milkweed and butterflies. He must've pulled the milkweed to take away my reason for being there."

"How did he know where they were?"

"Not hard to find." Jack scowled. "That's not gonna keep me from working there." He slipped into one of the chairs in front of the desk. "Mangum knows about the guys at the motel." He drew in a deep breath. "What's going on, Joe? Why are they here?"

Joe shook his head. "I can't talk about it. I'm hardly involved myself. This is something much bigger than me, directed from above. I've been sworn to secrecy. That's all I can say."

Jack clenched his jaw. "As close as I am to the people of this community, trying to keep them together, trying to keep 'em from going to war with themselves . . . and you can't tell me?"

"I suppose what you just said is the reason. I was told you—specifically you—could not be in the loop. If you knew what was going on . . . who knows who you might tell, simply because you always want to maintain trust."

"What's wrong with that?"

"Nothing . . . but there are people in higher pay grades than you or I . . . who aren't thinking about trust. They've got another priority." He gave a click to his pen. "That's all I can say. I'm sorry." He leaned forward. "I don't want you talking to anyone about this."

Jack dropped his jaw. He stood, and waited, expecting Joe to redeem himself. When that didn't happen, he stormed out in disgust.

"For your own safety," Joe shouted after him, "stay away from Hide Mangum."

—·—

Jack went to his office and sat, a powder keg about to explode. For a few minutes he flipped through the emails that arrived during the morning, seeing none that required much attention. He continued to fume.

A few minutes more and he left his office, headed for the end of the hall, to Dispatch.

Molly, working at the counter, looked up from her work. "What's up?"

"Nothing. Had to get up and move. I'm grumpy." He reached for the newspaper lying on the counter.

"You don't want to read that."

"Why?"

"You're on the front page. Not much detail but it raises questions."

Jack pulled his hand back, fighting to keep his eyes off the paper.

"Did I tell you not to worry about doing a case incident report on that boy you found out on the desert?"

"I forgot all about the little guy," Jack said. "Thanks for reminding me."

"I'll do the report. I doubt you would've gone after him if not for my call."

"Kind of you." Jack attempted a smile. "That's the only good news I've had all day."

She laughed. "You're easy to please. I only need the kid's name and address."

"I didn't tell you? I don't have it. The kid wouldn't give it. Pulled a grand escape at the sheriff's office. Slipped out a window before we could get his name. Deputy Winslow was assigned to find him, but I doubt he has."

"I'll give Buck a call."

"If anybody needs me, I'm taking a walk. Got to get out of here for a few minutes. If you hear someone screaming, it's nobody dying, I promise. It's just me, chasing off demons."

She nodded.

Outside headquarters, he crossed the bridge and followed the river upstream, hardly noticing the river still at spring flow, the willow along the bank, or even the deer grazing nearby. The only thing that mattered were those words Joe Morgan had said. Whoever gave the orders to him and the land agents—whatever they are—*has their own priority*.

Frustrating. Just like the bad ones up the food chain in Montana, working against the team assigned to help people who lived there, who wanted to leave a legacy for their grandchildren and future generations.

The trail turned upslope, the beginning of a set of switchbacks that would climb out of the canyon. He started back for the road. When it came into view, he stopped and settled onto a boulder overlooking the river. Snow melt from the north, the plateau and the San Juans beyond it. Even the sounds of water left him unsettled. He sucked in a long, deep breath and let out an angry, "Arrrr," screaming above the sounds of the river. Then again, even louder.

"Damn, can't a guy find a little peace and quiet around here?"

Surprised, Jack turned.

Buck Winslow stood on the road, smiling, biting down on a toothpick.

"What are you doing here?" Jack shouted.

"Looking for you," Winslow shouted back.

"Why?"

"I heard you had another run-in with Mangum."

"Who told you that?"

"He did. Accused you of jumping him. Said you accused him of destroying something."

"Milkweed. How'd you know where to find me?"

"Your dispatcher ratted you out." He laughed. "She called to see if I'd found that kid. I was nearby so I dropped in." He kicked at the ground. "Troubled about that encounter, huh?"

"In a roundabout kinda way."

"I told you to be careful about provokin' him. You got me worried, Jack. I don't wanna see you hurt."

Jack slid off the rock. "Thanks, but I'm okay . . . let's not talk about it."

"Okay." Winslow cracked his half smile. "Then tell me about this treasure everyone's talkin' about."

Jack turned. "What treasure?"

"Oh, don't be coy."

"I'm not."

"You were there in the bar last night . . . when those two guys were fighting."

"They were fighting about treasure?"

"Hell, yeah, as if you didn't know," Winslow grinned, looking skeptical. "You didn't hear 'em argue about a guy who hid his treasure somewhere around here? Captain Juan Rivera?"

Jack scratched his head. "Rivera. I've heard that name, but I can't remember how."

"You're keeping it a secret, huh?"

"No, I can't remember where I've heard that name."

"Yeah, right," Winslow said. "The story I heard from those ol' boys last night was . . ." He rubbed his chin. "Rivera was an early explorer in this area. He didn't make much of a splash . . . at least not enough that we know much about him. Rumor is, he may have found gold. Dropped out of sight, hoping to enjoy his riches, but he died before he could get 'em home. Does that sound familiar?"

"Not exactly . . . but kinda."

"Interesting. The story those ol' boys told . . . Rivera stashed his gold on the run, trying to save his ass from Indians. They got the story from a guy named *Potts Monroe*. Know him?"

"Yeah, he works for me . . . a few months every year. In fact, Potts is probably where I heard the name. Need to talk to him?"

"Nope, none of my business. Mostly yours . . . but it's gonna cause problems . . . for you and me. Treasure hunters are gonna be all over this place, causing mischief, digging up anything that even remotely looks like treasure."

"Why's that a problem for you?"

"Gold fever. They're gonna be hauling ass to get here, and they're gonna be rowdy."

Jack sighed. "I'll talk with Potts. I haven't seen him today. If he's not the backcountry, he could be at his trailer . . . in the campground. Let's walk over there and see."

Winslow bit down on his toothpick. "I gotta go . . . just let me know what you find out . . . and stay away from Mangum."

"I'll try."

Winslow flashed a two-finger salute and started up the road toward headquarters.

Jack followed the trail south to the campground, past tents, trailers, and empty spaces. The campground was mostly quiet this time of day.

Monroe's trailer sat in the shade of a cottonwood tree, one of the prime campsites. Potts had agreed to serve as a part-time campground host and in doing so, maintained a selection of park information and reading material, spread out on the picnic table, along with a few of his own journal articles, written about the archeology of the area. River cobbles kept the downcanyon breezes from blowing the collection away.

But as for Pott's pickup, it was gone. Jack decided to catch him later and headed back to the office.

As he passed through employee parking at the back of the building, he noticed words scrawled in the dust on the windows of his Jeep.

"Meet me at Caveras Creek."

Kelly missed her flight?

The only good thing to have happened all day.

Chapter 6

Driving the Terrace Road at a fast clip, he rounded a bend, eager to spot Kelly's SUV parked off the road. But it wasn't there. She must have taken the trail, or even come on her horse. He parked and headed for Caveras Creek, following the path through a break in the sandstone, winding past acacia and cactus, and finally breaking into a jog.

Her first time here since his assignment in Kenya, and since Senator Baca died and the Governor asked her to finish his term. He chuckled, thinking about her adjustment to this new life, how serious she had become, how things had changed in terms of what concerned her. Skinny dipping now seemed risky, she'd said. Before, she would've said to hell with 'em.

Up ahead, travertine pools came into view. Caveras Creek. As he approached, he looked for her at the largest pool, first on her favorite boulder, then in the water. Not there. He turned to the waterfall and the spot where she liked to sit, letting the water cascade over her. Not there either. He glanced right, at the base of the wall where he'd dangled from a rappelling rope, dazed from slamming into the rock, an accident he would come to see as fate, causing him to meet an amazing woman. At this moment . . . no sign of her.

He stopped at the edge of the pool, figuring that he'd arrived first, even after work.

He stripped down, tossed his clothes on a boulder, and dove in. Surfacing, he paddled toward the waterfall, the frustrations of the day melting away.

Intermingled with the splatting of water, he heard a noise. Like a holler, intentional, something to get his attention. Treading water, he scanned the edge of the pool. Nothing but travertine. No Kelly. Not yet. Not on the trail. Not by the rock where he left his clothes.

Where are my clothes?

In a few quick strokes, he reached the shallows and stood, wading toward the edge. No clothes. *Did the wind get 'em?*

"Hello, Jacky boy." Shouted words, carried by the echoes of the alcove.

He turned.

Downstream, in the shade of the cottonwoods, a blonde woman followed the edge of the creek, walking toward him, taking her time. Tall, slender, hiking shorts and running bra. Her devious smile paired perfectly with gray, predatory eyes.

"You!"

"Yep, me." She plopped down on the rock where his clothes had been and ran her eye down the length of his body. "Tempting . . . the water, I mean. Should I join you?"

"Erika Jones. Damn it, what are you doing here?"

"What I'm doing now . . . is playing with your mind. I'm here on business. We need to talk . . . privately. What could be more private than this? And why shouldn't I have a little fun? Your clothes? Not hard to find. I haven't decided if I'm sticking around to watch you search for them."

"Why do you always do this to me?" Jack said, retreating to deeper water.

"Because . . . you're cute when you're vulnerable. That hot springs in Montana . . . you were comical. Almost afraid of me."

"I was your boss."

"That wouldn't matter to a lot of guys."

"You can be unsettling. Intimidating."

"I know. My superpower."

"I thought I was here to meet Kelly."

"I know."

"What is your business?"

"I'll get to that. Yes, I tricked you. I knew Kelly flew back to D.C. . . . but I also knew she was running late . . . her aide told me. She had to take a red eye . . . so I figured there was a chance you two hadn't talked since she landed."

"I'll have to remind her about what her aides shouldn't share with the public."

She donned a mask of innocence. "Kelly and I are old friends. Chums."

He shook his head. "Why are you here?"

"To tell you to stay out of some things."

"Talking about the cars at the Desert Sands?"

"Maybe. Doesn't matter. You need to turn your head the other way, stay out of everything you hear, and anything you see."

"Why? And why me?"

"You get too close to things. Too involved. You could mess things up. There's an operation you don't need to know about. Until afterwards."

"Like, forcing people off of their land, making them sell to the government?"

She smiled, rubbing her chin as her eye followed the canyon wall, chuckling as if to herself. "Can't talk about it."

"Why do you know about it, but I don't?"

She laughed. "I've got better connections."

"Sitting there in the regional office?"

"I'm only in Denver part of the year. The other part . . . well, never mind." She turned, as if checking the trail. "I think I'll strip off and join you."

"Please don't."

She stood and worked the button on her shorts. "It was so hot sitting there by the road, waiting for you to arrive." Watching his eyes, she gave a shake to her hips, then laughed. "You know what,

Jack Chastain?" She sat. "You need a vacation. Get away, so you don't screw things up. Go somewhere you always wanted to go."

"You sound like Kelly," he muttered, fighting a scowl.

"She thinks you need a vacation?"

"In Washington."

"Ooh, you could get in lots of trouble there. Why Washington?"

"She's worried about me."

"Really? If I tell you I'm worried about you, too, would you leave for a while?" Her look turned serious. "Why is dear Kelly worried about you?"

"The occasional short fuse . . . that appears when she least expects it. Thinks I need time to get over what happened with Congressman Hoff and Moony Manson. And with Johnny getting shot."

She let a moment pass, studying him. She gave a slow nod. "But you don't, do you? You don't need to get over that?"

"No," he groused. "I don't." He paused. "Why do you say that?"

"Because . . . you're over what happened here."

"I am?"

"Yes. Congressman Hoff, his political shenanigans. He lost, you didn't. Johnny Reger getting shot? That bothers you, but he's healing. He'll be okay."

Jack waited, treading water, eyeing her.

"You're not angry about what happened here. Not anymore. You're not even angry at Senator Tisdale. He and Hoff, their pandering to corporate interests . . . the kind of pandering that hurt us in Montana, but they got theirs in the end. They lost. You didn't. You won."

"Didn't feel like I won."

"It wouldn't to you . . . but you did. And you know it."

"Then why am I angry?"

"Because . . . even after all that, you know something else could happen. Something could be going on, like what happened in Montana . . . something you didn't understand, that changed the rules. Hoff, Tisdale, even our dear boss Mick Sanders. They were there, too, but you knew they were more symptom than cause.

They responded to something. Something you were naïve about in Montana." Her look softened. "I wasn't naïve, but I didn't see it coming." She smiled. "If I had, I might've used my superpowers to . . . maybe, tweak 'em a little."

"You're full of it."

"Yes, I am." She smiled.

He swam to the shallows and stood. He crossed his arms. "How do you know what I'm thinking?"

"I was there."

"I know, but . . . you . . . you were . . ."

"Unpredictable?"

"Not exactly what I was thinking. In the end, I wasn't sure which team you were on."

"Ooh," she said, batting her eyelashes. "That makes me want to get naked."

"You know what I mean."

"I *do* know what you mean." She eyed the travertine edge of the pool and seemed to flip through the pages of her own memories. "It was so unexpected. The current of misunderstanding . . . that started well before we knew it was happening. You wanted to give people the benefit of the doubt. When they were saying something that wasn't correct, you assumed innocence. That they simply misunderstood, that they picked up part of a story. You stuck to your plan, assuming everything would take care of itself."

"So?"

She glared. "Jack, you're not so naïve now. Don't pretend you are."

"Maybe I am. Maybe I still believe in innocence."

"Innocence?" She laughed. "Innocence is something to take advantage of. You don't know how to."

"What?"

"Such a Boy Scout." She shook her head and continued. "Jack, some of that misunderstanding you avoided so naïvely . . . wasn't misunderstanding. It was a campaign. Lies. Someone planting those lies. Someone, for whom the end justified the means.

Lies, justified by what they were trying to achieve, everyone else be damned."

He stewed, not agreeing, not disagreeing. Remembering. The rumors, some almost laughable. Seemingly not worth rebutting. The wedges they drove between people. The misunderstanding, fear, and uncertainty they caused. He cringed. "You're cynical. Whether you're right or wrong, there's nothing you or I can do about it now."

"You're right," Erika said. "So why are you angry?"

He splatted a hand on the water and screamed, his voice echoing downcanyon. "I don't know." He glared. "Something similar happened here . . . recently."

"But," she shouted, and listened to the word take flight, echoing off canyon walls. She laughed. "It runs against every instinct you have to respond. You can't believe someone would do that, and yet . . . they do . . . and they could do it again." She shook her head. "Such a Boy Scout. You're probably wrestling with how you could've fixed things. But what you won't think about is the stupidity of others."

"What do you mean?"

"Jack, the people in Montana, they split, forming skirmish lines, fighting each other, doing things they were all convinced were the absolute smartest thing to do, while the other side felt just as convinced." She laughed. "Isn't it interesting that people buy into different explanations, and for the same reason?"

"It's sad." He shook his head. "Both sides seemed . . . in the end . . . to fight what they originally wanted. Contrary to their own best interests. Why did they? They hurt themselves. What did we do to cause that? To cause people to go to battle with themselves? Friends and neighbors fighting."

"You're still doing it."

"Doing what?" he screamed.

"Figure it out."

"The people who brought us there to protect those lands, wanting the park. The data that were changed. The grad student and his research. The senator. The congressman. What am I missing? What did we do? What did we not do?" he asked.

"Still doing it."

"What?" he shouted.

"You're ignoring the fact that there were other forces at play. Forces that had their own reasons for doing things. What I said a minute ago. People who see the end as justifying their means. Just because you play by the rules doesn't mean you can ignore those who don't."

"That's rather cynical."

"I call it observant. You and that silly, idealistic grad student. The people in town were his friends. Your reaction—being so understanding, optimistic that things would work out—encouraging patience. He thought you were wonderful, and while what he saw happening in town confused him, he was out there echoing your words, assuring them, lulled into being oblivious to what was really happening." She smiled. "Remember those people ready to sign away property rights to that shady, unknown entity?"

"Yeah, why did they think .. . . ?" Jack said, remembering the confusion.

"That didn't happen by accident. The confusion was the product. Someone planned it."

"And they blamed us."

"They did. That was the last crack, the breakdown. Someone knew how we would respond . . . even counted on it. We played right into their hands. Or, at least, you did."

"How? How did I?" Jack asked, bewildered.

Erika laughed. "Could it be that night at the hot springs, driving back from Missoula? Me, getting naked, insisting you join me? My special powers, blowing a circuit in your wee little brain?" She laughed. "Sorry, I had to find a way to remind you of that." Her face turned serious. "No, I don't think so. I'm afraid my powers don't work that well on you. What did work . . . and not in the way one would think . . . was all that disbelief in who we were. What we were. It never registered that someone might be helping that notion along. That someone might be creating a reputation for us that served their interests."

"We're not perfect," Jack said. "We don't always get it right."

"No, we don't," Erika said. "What if they were correct? What if the government was out to get 'em and you were just oblivious to that fact? Oblivious to what was really going on. A secret government operation, more interested in itself than in them."

"So why are you here now, Erika? Is that what this is about? This operation you're keeping secret. Were you a part of something then, . . . and part of something now?"

"Kinda warm." She kicked off her shoes and slipped out of her clothes. Naked, she stepped into the pool. In water deep enough to do so, she slithered under the surface toward him. Resurfacing, she flashed a predatory eye, then stood—the water waist deep.

Jack raised a hand and stepped back. "Answer me."

She laughed. "Jack, they call it a secret for a reason. Is it questionable? Can't tell you. Is it Big Brother doing all those things people accused us of in Montana?" She slipped down into the water. "Did I figure it out and decide to become part of it, working against you?" She laughed even louder. "Interesting. But let's talk about *here. Now.*" Eyes wide, whites showing, she muttered, "Special mission? . . . Only those willing to do what needs to be done can be trusted to know about it? Maybe. Maybe only those who have that special kind of impaired moral compass are allowed to carry out the mission." She winked.

"Why would you be involved? From Denver?"

"Maybe I'm that kind of person." She flashed a quizzical look. "Could it be that I'm a special kind of devious?" She turned serious. "My involvement is undefined. Who knows how I might be helpful? At present, all you need to know is this . . . I'm here to keep you from thinking twice about doing something you shouldn't."

"Did the guys in the motel call you?"

Her jaw dropped. "Don't tell me you brought attention to them."

"Too late. They did that themselves."

"Stay away from them, Jack."

"So they can force people off their lands? Make 'em sell to the government?"

She floated back toward shallow water, stood, and forced a smile, holding her tongue.

He wondered if he'd just seen her squirm. "Is Erika Jones speechless? Not knowing what to say? That's rare. Tell me. Why would the government need to take their land?"

"Could it be, that it's not what you think?" She dropped all expression from her face.

"Then, what is it?"

She glared. "I've been ordered not to say anything, Jack. I can't even confirm or deny. Orders." She stood. "I'm leaving . . . and I don't have time to watch you prance around, searching for clothes . . . because . . . I have someplace to be."

She walked to the edge. "Stay out of it. Don't mess things up." She stepped over the travertine and picked up her clothes. Likely not wanting to mess up a grand exit, she did not bother to dress before heading up the sandy trail. Water trickled off her backside. "If you can't find your clothes, don't worry," she shouted, without looking back. "I'll leave a clue with Senator Culberson's aides."

Chapter 7

He found his clothes draped over a willow, his shoes nearby. After hiking back to his Jeep, he checked for other pranks, and not finding any, climbed in. He pulled his phone from the glove box. Two missed calls. One from Kelly's father, the other from Karen Hatcher, Kip's partner in collaboration from opposite ends of the political and ideological spectrum. Kip, the former state senator. Karen, the director of a regional environmental organization.

Deciding to wait for a better signal, he started the engine and pulled a U-turn. The phone rang.

He picked it up, eyes on the road. "Hello."

"Sorry to pester you. Wanted to catch you before you made plans for dinner."

"Kip?"

"Yep. You free?" Kip asked, his words cracking amid the road noise.

"I guess. Haven't thought about it."

"Then don't. Meet us at Elena's. Karen, me, maybe others. We'll wait to order."

"Everything okay?"

"Perfect. Just doing a little coordinating." He rung off.

Jack followed the curvilinear road to the edge of Las Piedras, then took the turn toward the plaza, driving past buildings old and older. Hearing music, he slowed and rolled down his window, catching the amplified sounds of acoustic guitar. A cluster of listeners stood around a park bench, where a young woman strummed her guitar and sang her musica, her audience swaying to the song.

At the corner just beyond the centuries-old adobe church, he turned and followed Calle Vicente to Elena's.

He found a place to park and made his way up the steps, into the cantina. Inside, he turned toward the dining room, stopping at the hostess. "I'm meeting . . ."

She turned before he finished his sentence. "They're expecting you." She led him down the hall of whitewashed walls.

The room opened under ornate, massive wooden vigas and branch-like latillas, bathed in the reflected light from the windows overlooking the courtyard. Jack glanced out into the garden—rows of tomatoes and peppers, and beds of herbs, all coming along nicely. He scanned the room, looking for Kip, and spotted Karen Hatcher at the table near the kiva fireplace. The hostess turned to go back to her station.

Karen, as usual, looked fresh off a hike. Gray shorts, hiking shoes, blonde strands of hair matted by sweat to her forehead.

"Where's Kip?"

She gave Jack a hug. "Ambushed. You didn't you see him in the bar?"

"Didn't look."

"Someone grabbed him. Wanted to talk." Karen pointed. "There he is."

Kip wove through the tables, in jeans and a western-cut sport coat. He offered Jack a sun-weathered hand. "Sorry. Didn't intend to keep you waiting." He chuckled to himself. "Used Jack as my excuse to get the hell out of there." Kip sat, shaking his head. "Damndest thing."

"What?" Karen asked.

"Talk of government land agents. Supposedly here to force people off their land."

"You're kidding," she said.

"Nope. Told him I didn't believe it."

"Did he?"

"Took a while to calm him down . . . to listen to reason. Heard it from Hide Mangum."

"Where'd Mangum hear it?" Hatcher asked.

"No idea." Kip eyed Jack. "I kept saying . . . why would the government do something that stupid . . . now, when there's opportunity to lock down the peace?" He gave a slow nod. "Right?"

"Right, . . . uh, you'd think that," Jack said, struggling to find words. He felt a hand on his shoulder. He turned. Thomas, his friend from the pueblo, stood behind him, his long black hair tied back. Thomas, who avoided using his full name with Anglos, having grown tired of hearing it mangled.

"Hello, my friend." He gave another pat to Jack's shoulder, then Kip's, then Karen's. "Sorry I'm late. Sheep on the road . . . on the way to the mountain."

"You're not late. Glad you're here," Hatcher said. "You may be the only one who could make it on short notice. Hold it . . . nope, there's Ginger Perrette." She waved. ". . . and Dave Van Buren behind her."

They navigated their way through the tables. Kip stood, shook hands with both, and pointed them to empty chairs.

"Let's talk legislation," Hatcher said. "But first, let's order."

They picked up their menus and the waitress came.

Jack defaulted—ordering a carne asada burrito.

After the waitress departed, Kip scooted up to the table. "How are we looking, Karen?"

"Coalition members have reached out to stockmen's organizations, enviros, business groups, county and state agencies, others. Gotten feedback on language for legislation. All positive. Support's good. A few suggestions for tweaks to the coalition report, but minor. I've heard no reason to hold off on announcing a date for the signing ceremony."

"Hold it," Van Buren said. "Any comments from ranchers?"

"Why are you worried about them?" Perrette asked, sounding thin-skinned.

He scowled. "We don't need surprises."

Perrette turned red, her fists clenched.

"Hold it, Ginger." Jack turned to Dave. "Got a concern you haven't shared with her?"

"Uh . . ." Dave turned sheepish. "Guess not. Sorry."

"Good. Ginger, anything you need to say?" Jack asked. "Comments from stockmen?"

"No." She worked up a smile. "Sometimes it's a damned good thing you're here, Jack."

"Agreed," Dave said.

Kip laughed. "Yep, it is." He turned to Jack. "But . . . you surprised me night before last. That clown disrupting our meeting . . . you've handled worse, many times. Why'd he get to you?"

Jack nodded. "It was all very strange. His absolute certainty . . . it threw me."

"How so?"

"Maybe I'm imagining things, but . . . I keep wondering, did he believe what he said?"

"Hell, no." Kip shook his head. "He was lyin' his ass off, stirring up trouble, probably for the fun of it. No one's seen him before, and they haven't seen him since . . . and we won't."

"If we do, I can't wait too long to respond. That'd be a mistake." Jack sighed. "What worries me is . . . did people believe him?"

"Don't worry, they didn't." He laid a hand on Jack's arm. "We need you at the top of your game. Kelly thinks a little diversion—some science-time—might clear your head."

"Not 'til we're finished."

"We're essentially done." Kip gave a quick nod and turned to Hatcher. "Where were we?" He paused. "I've coached Kelly on legislative process, and how to get the package moving. She managed to keep a couple of Senator Baca's aides . . . those not delaying other plans. Alex Trasker and Claire Prescott offered to help, both suggesting their involvement be kept under wraps."

Hatcher chuckled to herself. "So, they don't want their old bosses to know?"

"Protecting Kelly, actually." Kip smiled. "Their insights will be helpful. Kelly has statewide priorities to attend to, but thinks she can put someone on this. But . . ." Kip paused.

Karen sat up. "But what?"

"It'd be best if I not look like I'm trying to influence my own daughter."

"No one would hold this against you, Kip."

"They might, and it's not me I'm worried about. It's Kelly. I'll be here . . . but . . . I need to not be the face of the effort. Karen, if you and Jack will be that face, I'll help where I can."

"Hold up, Kip." Jack leaned over his hands. "I can't lobby . . . or even appear like it."

"But you can be yourself," Thomas said.

"Agreed." Karen drummed her fingers on the table. "You always know the line to be careful of." Changing the subject, she said, "We have a few refinements to make to the report, otherwise it's done. I think we ought to set the date to sign the document." Nods around the table. Checking calendars, they tentatively set the signing for two weeks out. After putting calendars away, she said, "I'll confirm that with the others, then call the *Gazette*, let them know."

The food arrived.

"If I may," Thomas said, as others began to eat. "I have been wanting to ask . . . about having a second representative from the pueblo as part of the coalition. Would one of my people—someone looked to for traditional indigenous knowledge—be helpful?"

"What are you suggesting?" Kip asked.

"If Jack has science work to do, that person could help him."

"Jack sat up. "I'm not sure I need additional help."

Thomas set down his fork. "What do you hope to study?"

"Well, for example, the local distribution of milkweed. And with that, butterflies."

"If you hope to learn, wouldn't someone with knowledge of such things be helpful? Traditional knowledge of my people?"

"I think we're talking two different things . . . traditional knowledge and scientific study." Jack paused, stopping himself from saying something insulting. "But yes, more people from the pueblo would be great." He glanced around the table. "And by the way, I refuse to get distracted before we've signed the report."

—'—

They walked out of the dining room and said their goodbyes at the door. Jack lingered, then wandered back inside, finding Johnny Reger against the back wall of the bar.

"Drinking alone?" Jack asked, approaching his table.

"Not anymore." Johnny gave a sweep with his good hand, signaling toward a chair. "Once again, I'm sitting here thinking about not being in California."

"The fire, huh? Next time."

"Maybe." Johnny raised his recovering hand and stretched his fingers. "Sometimes I wonder. Seen Potts Monroe?"

"No." Jack signaled the bartender for a beer. "And he wasn't at his trailer today."

"I didn't see him either. Strangest thing . . . all afternoon, people kept stopping me, asking where everyone was searching for gold. Kind of a dumb question, I thought. Then someone asked where they'd find Potts Monroe. Seemed to think Potts knew exactly where to look. Heard anything about this?"

"Only just today . . . but I don't know much."

"How did all these people know this . . . before we did?" Johnny ran a finger along the handle of his mug. "It's like a dam broke. Quiet, then suddenly it's not. Could it be a joke? We do trust, Potts, right? He wouldn't be a pot hunter, would he?"

"No," Jack said. "Why do you say that?"

"The fact that this would-be treasure hunter asked for Potts by name." Johnny leaned forward. "And he mentioned a Capitan Juan Rivera. I went to the office and googled him. Found some stuff, but not much." Johnny leaned closer, his expression serious. "What I saw was a recent post . . . new even . . . about treasure . . . stashed during an Indian attack on this Rivera guy. Ever heard of him?"

Jack rubbed his chin. "I have."

"So, he's real?"

"I'm trying to remember the circumstances, but yes, he was real." He ran a hand through his hair. "Bear with me, it's coming back . . . I think I heard his name from Potts." He let the memory gel. "Potts was here, on a project he wanted to do last winter. A friend came, she jokingly mentioned Rivera. A real person, lost to history, yet he was the first European explorer to come through this part of the world. Even before Escalante and Dominguez. In fact, those two used Rivera's journals to begin their explorations."

"What was the joke?"

"Seem to remember it mentioning gold, but . . . as a *what if.* I remember them both laughing."

"You won't believe how many I told they couldn't treasure hunt in the park. They argued, cried, begged." Johnny noticed someone across the room. "Deputy Buckity," he shouted.

"Gents," Winslow shouted back as he crossed the floor. Reaching the table, he turned to Jack. "Any more wrestling matches?"

"Of course not."

"Good. Ol' Mangum's talkin'. He's not plannin' on you winning the next one."

"What's this about?" Johnny asked.

"A scuffle."

"Jack Chastain?"

"Fists and everything."

Jack shook his head. "It was nothing."

"That's not how Mangum tells it. He says ol' Jack here jumped him. Rollin' in the dirt and everything."

"Afraid he might do something stupid," Jack said to Johnny. "He was acting tough. I over-reacted . . . thinking I'd keep him from doing something he'd regret."

Johnny's eyes grew wide. "Mangum? Regret?"

"My sentiment exactly," Winslow said. "My advice . . . stay away from that part of the monument." The Deputy took a seat. "You've got more important things to worry about than butterflies. Mangum's telling everyone about those land agents."

"Land agents?" Johnny asked.

"Guys in town . . ." Jack muttered.

Winslow scooted forward. "Learn anything?"

"No. I'm more focused on Mangum."

"I think I'd have a little better reason than milkweed next time I wandered into that part of the world."

"We can't let him get away with that."

Winslow stood. "I'm worried about you." He flashed a salute and headed for the door.

"Get away with what?" Johnny asked.

"Ripped out a whole patch of milkweed. A spot I was hoping to monitor."

"Milkweed? Why?" Johnny whispered. "Who knows about that? Anyone investigating?"

"Why? Hard to know. Told the superintendent. He said pass it on to Barb, but I forgot."

Johnny dropped a five on the table. "Let's go. It's not quite dark." He gave a twisted smile. "You can tell me about kicking this guy's ass."

—'—

They drove through town, turned south, and followed the asphalt road to its end at the entry road to the Enclave, a cluster of homes Jack knew about but had never needed to see. They continued past, along the graveled road to the east boundary of the national monument. Approaching a curve, they slowed, seeing something up ahead. An obstruction nestled between rock walls. Cars. Junkers—bodies dented, paint faded—stacked in the road, only a narrow passage on one side, too small for a highway vehicle. They stopped and exited the vehicle.

A gunshot rang out.

Johnny ducked. "Let's hope that's a warning shot. Let's get outta here."

—'—

Dust trailed behind as they sped away. Asphalt came into view and Jack slowed. On the edge of town, he turned off the highway, cutting along the fastest route back to the park.

Rounding a turn, Jack saw a flagman. Road construction. *This time of night?* He slowed, watching the flagman spin his sign toward them. Stop. Beyond him, a repaving crew. Equipment, men with shovels. Jack took the Jeep out of gear. Anxious, he drummed his fingers on the steering wheel. Detecting movement, he turned. The boy. And his dog. On a side street, walking.

"That's the kid." Jack took hold of the gear shift, then noticed a vehicle behind him. A brown pickup. The driver sat blocking the evening sun from his eyes. A momentary drop of the hand revealed someone who looked familiar. Pudgy face. Dark, serious eyes.

"Remember that guy from more than a year ago? The one Luiz was investigating? Connections to the vehicle fire on the desert? Excess property? Old government truck someone set fire to?"

"Yeah. The guy who gave you so much trouble in public meetings. Luiz never found him. Seemed to've dropped out of sight. Left the state."

"That's the guy. Harper Teague. He's right behind us."

Johnny held his gaze forward. "Whatcha gonna do?"

"Say 'Hi.'" He put the vehicle in reverse and tapped on the gas. The Jeep slammed into the pickup. He killed the engine and climbed out, raising his arms in apology.

Teague backed up, surged into a U-turn, and sped away.

"See ya." Jack watched the pickup disappear into the village.

"What would you call that?" Johnny asked. "*Got hit and ran*?"

"Something like that. He knew it was us."

"Yes, he did. Might have been following. Couldn't see his plates. Too much mud."

Jack turned to look for the boy.

Gone.

—·—

"I'll let Luiz know that Harper Teague is back in town. *And*, I'll talk to the chief about the milkweed." Johnny slipped out of the Jeep, hovering at the car door. "Mark up a map with the location and leave it on my desk. I'll call if I need more information. I'll go out tomorrow and look for clues. Something we can use to hang this guy for resource impacts."

"Be careful. There's another way in. An old BLM road that ends half a mile or so from the monument boundary. From there, go cross-country, hit the trail, come back that way," Jack said.

"Gotcha. I'll be armed."

Chapter 8

Standing at the copy machine, Jack pored over a topo map, found the road, flipped the map over, and pushed the button, making a photocopy. On it, he circled the ranch road and marked the likely spot of the destroyed patch of milkweed—just this side of the Desert Rose Trailhead. "Thanks," Jack said to Molly, as he started out of her office.

"See this?" she said, flipping through the newspaper.

"What is it?" Jack asked, turning back.

She lay it on the counter and tapped on a letter to the editor. "Wants to know about the accusations made against you at the public meeting."

"Do I want to read it?"

"I'm sure you don't, but maybe you should." She flipped the paper around for him to see.

> *Is it true that Jack Chastain has been buying off the people on the Piedras Coloradas National Monument Coalition? Hide Mangum told me it's true, and he told me about land agents, here to buy us out . . .*

Jack sighed and shook his head. He slid the paper across the counter and walked out the door. He left the map on Johnny's desk.

—·—

At the edge of town, Jack turned off the highway and drove to the Desert Sands Motel. He parked near the unmarked GSA vehicle at the room farthest from the lobby.

He banged on the door and heard shuffling inside, then the chain being removed from the door. It swung open. A man peered out. African American, closely trimmed beard. Jeans and a T-shirt. He gave Jack a once over, his eye stopping at the name plate on his uniform.

"Now, you know who I am. Who are you?" Jack asked. "And why are you here?"

The man stuck his head out the door, checking right, then left. "That's not for you to know. I'm sorry, but yours is not a name I've been cleared to speak to."

Jack glanced beyond the man, to a table, covered with papers and a laptop computer. "Meaning?"

"I can't talk to you."

"Who wants to force people off their land, if that's why you're here?"

A smile appeared on the man's face. "I'm not saying anything. I'm not cleared to talk."

"Who does the clearing? Who approves?"

"Can't tell you that, but you sure as hell can't tell anyone we're here. That could make things difficult."

"Too late, it's in the paper . . . and . . . your being here is making things difficult for me."

A perplexed look came over the man. "I got your name. I'll share it with my boss, but . . . for now, we're done talking." He closed the door.

—·—

Holding the topo in his bad hand, Johnny Reger drove a slightly graveled road he'd probably never been on, watching for a stock road that he most assuredly hadn't. The map said it was here, but its whereabouts were not obvious because of the spring growth of grasses amid widely scattered sage and rabbitbrush. Eyeing a rise that would tell him he had gone too far, he slowed. He scanned the lowest ground, mostly flat terrain. The hint of a two-track. Shallow, obviously never graded, rarely used, and camouflaged by windblown sand. He made the turn and followed the road, veering south, to a low area between slopes. A drainage, but not much of one, and an old cow camp. Box canyon, ramshackle corral, and not much else, except one thing of interest. At the end of the road sat a pickup. A grey Ford, F-250, 4×4.

Potts Monroe's.

How did that get here? Nobody's been on this road. There was no sign of recent use.

Johnny pulled alongside and killed his engine. He climbed out, circled the dust-covered pickup, and knelt near the driver-side door, checking for footprints. Nothing. Too much windblown sand.

He checked the door. Locked. He looked inside. Nothing. Nothing on the seat, on the dashboard, or on the floor.

He checked the bed. Not empty. Two similar devices lay in the back. Constructs of woven wire, fashioned to connect to the bumper behind the rear wheels.

He's raking out his tracks.

A little wind and even the drag marks are gone.

What is Potts doing?

Johnny took one last look for clues, pulled out his pack and climbed the hill, going west, topo in hand.

It wasn't long before he came to the boundary fence, just as Jack had said. He climbed through, into the national monument, then, after a half a mile or so he came to the trail. Turning north, he headed for the *X* marked on the topo.

When he arrived at what seemed the approximate place, he kicked around for a moment, not seeing anything that would confirm this to be it. He noticed an outcropping off the trail and headed downslope toward it, eye to the ground. No milkweed. No sign of disturbance. *Maybe this isn't far enough, or maybe too far.* He started to turn back, but noticed a boot track in the moist soil beside the outcropping. *Chastain's boot.* He spotted a broken stem, then more, and a divot where a plant had likely been pulled out by the roots, soil not quite smoothed over.

He spun around, looking for other tracks. Tracks from someone else. He saw none. And no other clues.

He pulled out a camera, snapped a few shots, then put it away.

"This guy is good," Johnny muttered to himself. "But why milkweed?"

—'—

"Knock, knock." At the door stood the Superintendent's secretary, no expression on her face. "Joe wants to see you."

Jack looked up from his work. "Now?"

"Now."

He followed her up the hall and slipped past her desk into the Superintendent's office.

Joe locked eyes on Jack. "I told you . . . mind your own business. The men in town . . . I told you to stay away from them."

"Just trying to learn enough to counter the rumors and innuendo. See the paper today?"

"You disobeyed me. I told you to stay out of it and you went directly to that motel and confronted the people I told you to avoid."

"Are we just gonna let them do what they're doing?"

"Jack, I hate doing this. You're valuable and I consider you trustworthy . . . but you're the one person with whom I was expressly told not to share details. You're too close to people here."

"What's wrong with that?"

Joe gave a click to his pen. "This conversation ends now. I can't say anything more. Stay away from that motel. Mind your own business or I'll ship you off on some detail assignment, like . . . picking up trash in Chicago."

"Make it Washington, D.C."

"No."

—'—

Jack scowled as he stepped back to his office.

Sitting against the wall, Johnny Reger cracked a smile. "Happy to see me, huh?" He threw his arm over the back of the chair beside him. "Margie told me you wouldn't be long."

Jack tried clearing his mind. "Thought you were going to South Desert."

"I did. You won't believe what I found."

Jack turned to face him. "More damage?"

"No, not at the milkweed. That site's sure been worked over. He sure as hell knows what he's doing. Not even a leaf still there. Spooky."

"I thought so, too. What'd you find?"

"A pickup. At the end of the road."

Jack's eyes grew wide. "At the old corral?"

"Exactly. It's Potts Monroe's. No sign of him coming or going, but in the bed of the truck are devices he uses to rake out his tracks."

"What?"

"You heard me right. Strange. They weren't affixed, but they'd been used. There's no sign of him driving in. Inside his truck, nothing. Clean as a whistle. Outside, no track, no sign of where he's gone, just the pickup, looking like it's been plopped down, middle of nowhere."

Jack scooted closer.

"Are you sure Potts is on the up and up?" Johnny asked. "That he's not some pot hunter working against us?"

"He's an old naturalist, turned archeologist. Worked here for years before taking a research position in Tucson, doing archeology all over the country. Loved it here. Been coming back every year since he retired."

"Could he be searching for that treasure? Or could he have found it?"

Jack tried to laugh, then became serious. "Can't imagine any of that being real. If it was, people here would've known about it. When Potts said Rivera's name, it was an obvious joke."

"You're sure?"

Jack nodded. "I think so . . . I trust him to be straight with me."

Reger picked up a sheaf of papers laying on the chair beside him. "I want to show you something." He took the top page and handed it over. "Read this . . . comes from a visitor I ran into this morning. A guy who cornered me, asking questions. I took a few pictures before sending him on his way."

Jack scanned the page. A printed image, of an online article. The title read, *Lost treasure of Capitan Rivera.*

"It says some of the things you told me, but more. This Captain Rivera . . . there's debate as to whether he really was military . . . but he led two expeditions from Santa Fe into present day Colorado. Most historians think he's just a guy who found a little silver, didn't generate much interest, and that was the end of it. Then he was lost to history . . . according to *those historians*."

"*Those historians*? Are there others?"

"Another story. According to this version, Rivera had his reasons for dropping out of sight. Playing down what he found. Acting like he saw no reason to try again, so that no other expeditions would be sent north. And there weren't, until Escalante and Dominguez."

"The Spanish priests . . . that went into Colorado, then along the Colorado River, returned to New Mexico without a route to California, supposedly their original purpose."

"Right. But that's not important to this other story. Except, it should be noted that journals from Rivera's known expeditions turned up in Madrid several years ago. In military archives. How had they been missed? Who knows?" Johnny pulled off another sheet and handed it forward. "But back to the other story. There's this."

Jack scanned it. "In Spanish."

"From an old journal, supposedly found in a chest with a bunch of old letters. Someone from an old New Mexican family. Been here for centuries."

"What family?"

"That seems to be a closely guarded secret."

"How did you get a copy?"

"A website. The story is, the current owner of the journal—quite elderly—let down their guard, let someone see it, who secretly photocopied the journal. They tried finding the place described in the journal but got nowhere . . . even with this." He handed Jack another page.

He eyed it a moment, then gasped, realizing what it was. "A map."

"Not much of one. Detailed just enough to stir up the crazies. The person who copied the journal shared it with a few buddies, hoping for some help. One of 'em told the world and the word's out. That's why we're seeing the crazies here looking for treasure."

Jack tried reading the letter. "Some of those words . . . don't look familiar to me. Maybe a bit more archaic than I'm used to seeing. Maybe the way they talked back then?"

Johnny smiled. "Want me to tell you what it says?"

"You know?"

"It talks about being with Rivera on a third trip into Colorado, then a fourth. Coming back on that fourth trip . . . with a pack train full of plunder . . . somewhere around here . . . Rivera was attacked by Comanches. He and his men stashed the plunder, planning to come back when safe. Rivera made each of his men swear an oath to tell no one, and to only return when they could do so together. Only thing is, farther down the trail the Comanche attacked again and most of the men were lost. Everything we know comes from the survivor connected to that journal."

"What about Rivera?"

"Doesn't say for sure . . . kinda hints that he was one of the people killed, and as I said, Rivera seems to have disappeared from history." Johnny's eyes widened. "But . . . the journal—at least up to this point—doesn't say what they found. It's as if he's writing to himself, not intending the journal to be for anyone else's eyes. He also seems almost fearful someone else might read it, as if he's bound by the oath he swore to Rivera, even when he knows full well there's no reason to honor it. But he's afraid if he goes back, he'll suffer the same consequence at the hands of the Comanche."

"Wow!" Jack sucked in a breath and shook his head. "Didn't know you spoke Spanish."

Johnny laughed. "I don't." He handed Jack another page. "Here's the translation."

Jack turned to the window. "If this is true, then why wouldn't we know this story?"

"Simple," Johnny said. "It was a secret. According to the journal, Rivera was not conducting those later trips with the approval of the Governor in Santa Fe. And he wasn't taking the riches back to Santa Fe . . . or even Mexico City. He had bigger plans. He was taking them to Vera Cruz. There, someone was arranging for boats to get Rivera across the Atlantic to Madrid."

"Madrid?" Jack said, skeptical. "Why Madrid? And why would the guy who wrote the journal need to keep that a secret after Rivera was dead?"

"Because . . . he was afraid of being hung by the governor in Santa Fe."

"Why?"

"He was a co-conspirator, hoping to benefit. Rivera wanted to be governor of everything to the north. He thought the riches he intended to deliver to Madrid would assure that. Titles and riches, cutting Mexico City and the governor in Santa Fe out of the loop."

Jack reached for the map. He studied it a moment. Lines, canyons, the suggestion of a cave. "I don't know why anyone would think this is here in the park. Even if it is, I understand why no treasure's been found. This wouldn't help much. Hardly convincing that it's even real."

"Real or not, I've got a question for you."

"Shoot."

"Would Potts Monroe know about this? You said he had a friend in Mexico, married to that butterfly biologist you work with."

Jack scowled. "Yes. Angelica Morales, an authority on Spanish Colonial history. With that specialization, it did seem odd that she'd be here doing archeology."

"You know where I'm going with this," Johnny said, wearing

a serious look that sat uneasily on the face of a man who was not often serious.

Jack dropped his head into his hands. “Can we believe this?”

“What do we really know about Potts?”

“Plenty. Great reputation. Colleagues in Tucson rave about him. Began his career here, loves the place.”

“Could he have gone bad?”

“No, not Potts.”

“Take another look at the map.”

“Why?” Jack stared at the page. “What am I looking for?”

“What do those clues tell you?”

He scanned the marks on the page. Canyons. Deep ones. High walls. A cave. Pine trees. Pinos piñonero below and pinos altos above. “Pinos altos. Tall pines.” He squinted at the page. “Ponderosas?”

“That’s what I’m thinking.”

“That means the plateau. The park, not the monument.”

“Pott’s pickup is parked on South Desert.”

“So, he’s not looking for treasure.”

“Jack, I saw no tracks, no trailing. Maybe he parked the truck and left.”

“Why?”

“Boss, what do you really know about this guy?”

“What do you want me to do?”

“Good question, because I’m here to get you.”

“Why?”

“A search. The Chief Ranger wants your help in looking around South Desert.”

“I thought you said he wasn’t there.”

“I said I didn’t see any track . . . but the pickup’s been sittin’ awhile. Wind. Sand. You know how that goes. The Chief Ranger thinks we at least need to check it out, see if we can find him. See if he’s in trouble.”

Jack stood and made a quick move to the door. “I’ll grab my gear.”

"Whoa. No rush. Make sure you have everything you need."
"No rush? Why?"
"Because no one's seen Potts in several days . . . maybe a week."

Chapter 9

Jack eyed the contraption in the bed of the pickup. Well used. Heavy gauge wire. "Doesn't want to be followed, does he?"

"Looks like it." Head down, Reger circled the pickup.

"Footprints?"

"None other than ours."

Jack hefted his pack onto his shoulders. "Maybe take separate routes? Go wide to the boundary, then come back together, looking along the fence?"

Johnny pulled his gear from the back of the patrol SUV and slipped an arm through a pack strap. "Got a preference?"

"I'll go farther south." Jack took off.

Walking a line perpendicular to Monroe's pickup, he skirted past the dilapidated ruins of the cow camp. Hitching racks, a rusted-out water trough, and what had been a two-pen corral. He moved upslope, looking down on the box canyon the rancher likely used to trap his cattle. No sign of anything having wandered through the scattered desert grasses. No tracks, other than their own on the two-track road. Reaching the hilltop, Jack turned south.

After what felt like a mile, he veered west, toward the boundary of the national monument. Reaching the fence, he stopped and took in the expansive view of the desert, then turned north, following the fence, eye to the ground.

After twenty minutes or so, Reger came into view, doing the same.

They met up and, without words, climbed over the fence, heading west.

—·—

When they reached the trail, Reger took the lead and turned south. "If there's nothing in obvious places . . . trail junctions, et cetera, . . . ?" He slipped into a quick stride. "Any ideas?"

"This time of year, since it's so damned hot and dry . . . people are preferring the high country . . . the park." Jack gave a rub to his chin. "Potts might be the only person out here. If he is . . . for nearly a week . . . he'll be needing water. There's only a couple of springs I know of, and only one easy route to the river. I say we try those."

"Good." Johnny glanced back. "We have a plan."

"Does Barb know about this Capitan Juan Rivera? Does she know about the map?"

"Some of it. Told her before I talked to you."

"Good. Her thinking?"

"Cover this base first, . . . see if we find him, see if he's in trouble. If he's somewhere else . . . if he's someone other than what we know him to be . . . not a researcher, but a treasure hunter . . . then we're behind the eight ball already. We'll need to find him."

"I'm still skeptical. If any of this stuff about Rivera was true, I think Potts would have told me . . . but he didn't."

"What about that journal?" Johnny glanced back.

"Maybe it isn't real."

"What if it is?" Johnny stopped and pulled off his cap, running fingers through sweat soaked hair. "People have secret sides. Look at me . . . I doubt you'd ever guess I was a singer."

"You sing?"

Johnny let out a long, unmelodious wail, then, "Yeah, yeah, yeah."

"That's awful."

"My Bob Dylan impersonation. Or the Beetles, I forget which."

"I get the feeling you're not expecting to find him. Not here anyways."

"It'll take all day to confirm. What I'm thinking now is . . . where are we gonna camp?"

Jack eyed the sun creeping west. The remaining hours of the day would be hot ones. "By the river?"

They approached a junction, a trail coming in from the west. Johnny stopped. No track. "No point following either trail," he said, as Jack came alongside. "Unless one's the fastest way to those springs you know about." They stared into the distance.

Before them lay an expanse of desert scrub, extending west, bound on the south by the rim of the gorge, and to the north by slickrock, backed by rising walls of stone, forming the plateau—the park. Here—in the monument—lay scores of arroyos, from this vantage disappearing among the desert scrub. Some cuts would be deep. Some more easily crossed near the slickrock.

Johnny sighed. "We better get moving."

"First spring I know of is that way." He pointed toward a break in the slickrock.

—·—

They reached the break and found the spring, seeping into a pool at the base of a wall. Jack knelt, looking the tracks. Rodents. Other critters. No humans. No Potts Monroe.

Farther west, the same proved true at the next spring.

They followed a major arroyo across the plain, then through the cut in the rim of the gorge, scrambling down-slope to the river.

There Jack stopped, hands on his hips, and caught his breath, scanning for tracks in the sand. Nothing. Here, the sand had been worked by up- and down-canyon breezes. There were other cuts through the rim of the gorge, but riskier ones. Potts would know that. This is where he would have come.

Reger walked to the river's edge, eyes to the ground, moving right.

Jack went left.

"Got something," Johnny shouted, working his way across a deposit of wind and water deposited sand. He turned back to the river and knelt. "Never mind. River runners. Must've camped here last night."

Finding nothing where he was looking, Jack turned to join him.

"I know you were hoping for a dry camp," Johnny said. ". . . just because you like the challenge . . . but I think we should camp here."

Jack agreed.

—·—

They threw sleeping bags and bivy sacks out on the sand.

Jack dug into his pack and pulled out his stove and an old, battered pot, and set them on a rock beside the river. He started water to boil, then tossed his pack onto his sleeping bag to keep gusts from carrying it away. The sun dropped below the horizon.

Johnny called in on the radio to dispatch. Getting no after-hours acknowledgement, he broadcasted a report. "No success in finding Potts or any sign of him. Not in this part of the monument. We plan to be back at headquarters after noon, unless we find something or get a better offer."

"*Care to share your idea of a better offer?*" came a response from an unidentified ranger.

"Did I say that out loud?" Johnny signed off and plopped down in the sand.

Jack prepared a well-cayenned pasta, tossing in a few veggies from Reger and pouring half into Johnny's own well-beaten pot.

As they ate, stars began to emerge.

"That Juan Rivera . . ." Johnny picked at his food. "He could've camped in this very spot."

"I still have a hard time believing that story," Jack said.

"He could have been killed here," Johnny forced a swallow. "One thing I learned today . . . while you were getting your gear . . . there's a recent book about Rivera and the two documented trips he made into Colorado. Supposedly a copy at the library in town. Saw an excerpt online. Rivera or one of his men scrawled something on a canyon wall south of Delta, Colorado. They met with the Utes, planning to go to the Colorado River, but didn't make it."

"It's amazing we haven't heard more about this guy."

Johnny broke into a laugh. "Well, me, yeah, but you? You've always got your nose buried in that report you're writing for the coalition."

"Not much longer." Jack sighed. "Soon, there'll be time for other things."

Johnny shoveled in a mouth full of pasta. "Like what?"

"Monitoring I need to catch up on . . . maybe even a study of monarch butterflies. Reminds me why I got into this profession."

"Butterflies got you into this profession?" Johnny garbled.

"No, that's not what I'm saying."

"I just heard you. And it makes no sense to me whatsoever."

"That's not what I meant. I meant critters. Whole ecosystems."

"Too late. I'm gonna start telling people about this image I have of you floating across the meadow . . . swinging a butterfly net, chasing butterflies . . . like my niece . . . my sister's daughter. Plays soccer. Ball keeps whizzing by . . . while she's watching butterflies."

"You saying I'm easily distracted?"

Johnny chuckled. "Nope. You're not. You're pretty damned focused. So much so it's hard to get a joke in." Johnny sat down his pot. "But what you said makes no sense. You're not one to look past what's happening in the here and now."

"I know, and I'm not. First, we'll finish the report and hand it off to Kelly."

"That guy the other night at the meeting. Been thinking about him?"

"Not so much now." Jack sighed. "Why do you ask?"

"I was there that night. I saw the look on your face . . . and the way you disengaged."

"Guess I did. Reminded me of how things ended in Montana."

Johnny laid back. "Boss, how did things end in Montana? You've never told me."

"A stupid rumor. It's not important."

"Then why were you thinking about it?"

The comment caught him by surprise. "Because it destroyed everything we'd worked on, and I didn't take it seriously. Not when it started."

"Why not? And what was the rumor?"

"That some who invited me there didn't really want the park, that they'd brought me in to drive away those who did. I thought it was silly . . . didn't think anyone would believe it."

"But they did?"

"Not all of them, not at first, but it caused suspicions. There were factions that began to wonder if I was going after them. I didn't take it well."

"Going after?"

"To drive them away . . . so that those who remained could do what they wanted . . . and I never understood why they thought I'd do that or what the others would really want."

"You wouldn't. Sounds like they didn't know you. What's happened there since then?"

"Some left, some stayed. Their world changed. But the concept of a park, gone. There's a mine there now . . . changing everything." Jack picked at his food. "Let's change the subject."

"Okay." Johnny sat up and took a bite. "We have one missing archeologist and a rumor mill that says he's up to something."

"I don't believe it."

"Know what I think?"

Jack looked up from his pan, not sure he wanted to hear it.

"I'll tell you anyway. . . . I'd like to think he's out here, but there's no evidence of that. Just a pickup parked out on that BLM road. He coulda hightailed it out of there, going somewhere else. A misdirection, throwing us off his trail. '*Hey, there's his truck. He's doing his research.*' " He laughed. "All the while he could be cartin' off Juan Rivera's gold."

"You really think that?"

Johnny sat quietly a moment. "No, I don't. But with all those rumors, it's fun lettin' my imagination run wild. It does seem odd. Like he's dropped off the face of the earth."

"A few months back, when I visited one of his project locations, I shared a camp with him and his friends. His colleague from that university in Mexico, and her husband, the entomologist studying the monarch. Great people. I sat there all night . . . listening to 'em talk about their research. Scholars, all of them. Angelica, the woman helping Potts . . . they've known each other for years. The husband was just along for the ride. First time in New Mexico."

"The woman? You mentioned she's a historian . . ."

"Yeah." Jack paused, nodding. "Expert in Spanish colonial history."

"As in 'Juan Rivera' era colonial history?"

Hadn't thought about that. "That's a possibility." Jack sighed. "That was the night Potts made the joke about Juan Rivera. His friend mentioned Rivera first. First time I'd heard the name. She talked about early exploration of this area, mentioned Rivera and how he'd been largely forgotten by history." Jack swatted an ear. Mosquito. "Potts, in what seemed a joke, said something like, "*What if there's more to this guy's story*? *What if he chose to disappear*?"

"Was that part of their research?" Johnny asked.

"Hell, no. He was doing archeology."

"Was that the end of the joke?"

"I can't remember much more."

"How about hypnosis, would that help?"

"Get real." Jack scowled. "I remember . . . it was a really dark night. Eerie even. A couple times we thought we'd heard something . . . like someone was out there, listening. That put us all in a silly mood. Potts said something like, '*Rivera probably had some secret he wanted to keep, like treasure*.' Everyone laughed. That's all I remember."

"Wow. Let's give hypnosis a whirl. Maybe you'll remember where he hid it." Johnny swung his hand, moving back and forth. "Relax . . . Jack Chastain. When I snap my fingers . . . you'll remember every secret of Juan Rivera. When done, dance like a chicken."

"Dishes need to be washed." Jack got to his feet and dipped a pot of water from the river.

"You cooked, I'll wash," Johnny said. "I'll figure out what I did wrong . . . we can work on the hypnosis thing later."

"I'm going to bed."

—'—

On the trail in the still cool, early morning light, they climbed out of the gorge and set a course toward undulating sandstone in the distance. Slickrock. Before reaching it, they veered northeast, Jack catching sight of the side canyon where he and Kelly had caught up with the boy, and the route they'd taken back to the trailhead.

They were back at their vehicle at a little after one, followed the dusty road back into town, hit the blacktop, and were at headquarters before two.

Inside, they passed the dispatch office and continued down the hall to the office of the Chief Ranger. Reger knocked.

Barb Sharp looked up from her desk. Her streak of grey, amidst otherwise black hair, lay tucked behind one ear. She waved them in. "So?" she asked, knowing the answer.

"I wonder if he's even been there," Reger said. "His vehicle's parked in a strange location, some distance from any trailhead. I don't know what that means, unless . . . like these rumors we're hearing . . . he's up to something . . . trying to throw us off his trail."

She turned to Jack. "Think that's what's happening?"

"I don't think so, but I don't know. The rumors about treasure . . . I don't think I believe 'em. It's not an insignificant thing and I feel like Potts woulda told me."

"Is he on the clock?"

Jack rubbed his chin. "He's not a contractor. He's retired, volunteering on projects of interest to us . . . and him."

"Does he ever take a few days off, go someplace like Taos or Santa Fe?"

"He does, but . . . what about the vehicle?"

"All I know is," Sharp said, "we've got someone missing. He

may be hurt, he may be dead, he may be up to no good, he may not even be here. For most of those possibilities, we need to find him. I'd rather be wrong about him being up to no good, than to miss a chance to find him if he's hurt somewhere in the backcountry."

"Me, too," Jack said.

"We have no clues," Johnny said, "other than his vehicle in an odd location. No sign he actually went into the monument. No missing person's report, other than from us."

"He could be anywhere. He could've dropped off his vehicle, had someone shuttle him to the beginning of a longer hike," Sharp said.

"Possible," Jack said.

"Is Johnny still working for me?" Barb looked at Jack. "He hasn't been released by the doctor yet, right?"

"Right."

"Most of my seasonals haven't started yet, so I don't have manpower to cover both the park and the monument plus a big search, without having to back-burner something. Yet, we don't really know we've got a problem. Unless we see a reason to need a helicopter, I'd rather not spend that kind of money . . . when we have no clue where to start looking." She sighed. "Johnny, let's put you up in a fixed wing for an hour. That'll cost us less. See if there's anything that catches your attention. You've been up in a fixed wing before, right? Cessna 182? Contract operator out of Farmington?"

"He knows the drill," Jack said. "He does fire flights on occasion, and I might join him. Another set of eyes."

Chapter 10

The Cessna 182 reached altitude of over a thousand feet before turning out of the wind, banking north toward the monument. The pilot, a slender, gray-haired woman they had both flown with before, wore jeans and a burgundy polo, not her usual *Air Service* uniform, likely because the flight had not been on the books until an hour before. She adjusted the trim on the nose, then pulled her headset off one ear. "Okay, where do we want to start?"

Reger, in the seat beside the pilot, glanced back in deference to Jack.

"Start at the pickup?" Jack said.

Johnny nodded and turned to the pilot. "Burn, let's go . . ." He paused. "Why do we call you Burn, by the way? Kinda scary name for a pilot, don't you think?"

She smiled without looking. "It's not b-u-r-n. It's b-e-r-n. Short for Bernadette."

Reger sighed. "That's a relief. I was wondering if there was something you needed to tell us . . . or, if you needed my help in finding a better name."

"Better name? I like Bern."

"Okay . . . if you don't want a name like Ace, or Mad Dog, or Viper, then . . . stick with Bern." Johnny looked out the side window. "Anyways, . . . there's a pickup on BLM land just east of the monument, a little bit north of the gorge."

"I'll get to the gorge. You show us where to go from there. What are we looking for?"

"One man," Johnny said. "Always in baggy khaki pants and a floppy hat . . . but we're more likely to see his camp. His tent."

". . . if he's using one," Jack added.

"Yeah, if he's using one. His tent is kind of a dirty white. Dome tent. We could be looking for an SOS, some sign of him needing help. Sound good, Ace?"

"Sure. Can I call you Mad Dog?"

"Sure." Johnny turned in his seat. "That leaves Viper for you, boss. Good name for a biologist, don't you think? Unless, of course, you'd rather be Butterfly."

Ignoring him, Jack turned his attention to the park's shoebox-sized radio in the seat beside him. He slipped on the headset and called into dispatch, letting Molly know they were in the air. He signed off and peered out the front windshield.

Within minutes, the gorge lay straight ahead. A span of open desert to the north, ending at a broken run of sandstone, slickrock ascending in undulating masses. Potts could be anywhere out there. In the monument, in the park, in Italy, for all they knew.

From the gorge, Johnny pointed the pilot to the approximate location of the monument's boundary, then to where Potts' pickup sat. Seeing it, the pilot pushed the yoke forward, easing off the throttle, letting the Cessna descend. Jack searched out the left side. Johnny took the right. No sign of anyone. Johnny signaled with his hand to set a flight path midway between the gorge and the slick rock.

Below lay sagebrush, four-wing saltbush, and winterfat. An almost uniform pattern. Agreements and compromises made in the battle for water. Sameness, and nothing. No sign of a person. No sign of anything, other than sage, saltbush and winterfat.

"Any reason to check the west desert?" Johnny asked.

"Potts once told me there wasn't much reason for him to ever work there," Jack said.

"Aw-w-w . . . sure sign of evasion . . . misdirection." Johnny gave a wink to the pilot. "That must be where the treasure's at."

The smile faded. "Except . . . there, the treasure would be hiding in plain sight."

"Tell me about this treasure, Mad Dog," Bern said. "I just heard about that." She laughed. "In fact, I had a call this morning from a guy wanting to book a flight to look around. Is this Potts guy the same one who knows where everything is?"

"Well, Ace, Jack doesn't believe there is a treasure. Me? . . . I'm starting to wonder. Yeah, same guy." Johnny turned back to the window. "Next pass, let's try a little north."

She banked the plane right, into a tight turn, settling onto a line over slickrock. Stone with much of the red bleached out of it. Swells and cuts, some with depths impossible to discern at this height. Downslope, arroyos began across the plain.

Jack caught a flash of white below. "Can we circle this spot?"

"What'd you see?" Johnny asked.

"Don't know." Jack stared down as the aircraft banked, wingtip pointed at the ground, terrain in a slow spin, his stomach lurching. He caught sight of the white. Flat ground. Sun must've hit it just right. "Never mind. Nothing there."

The pilot leveled the aircraft back onto its course. They reached the end of the run and started another, farther north.

And so it went, crossing the monument. No Potts, no camp, no SOS or signs of distress.

"Now the park?" the pilot asked.

"Yeah," Johnny said. "Follow the path we use for fire flights over the high country. That'll do it, then we can head back to base."

She turned toward the edge of the plateau, putting the airplane into a gradual climb. On approach, a great void seemed to form below, as always. The massive wall, a barrier, a denial, transforming as they flew over the rim, the wall now gone. Now, only the plateau. A different world. Hospitable. A realm of ponderosa and pinyon pine, of grass waving in the breeze.

Jack gave a quick scan. People, one or two or groups of three, scattered but not in solitude, young to middle-aged. None in khaki. A few in floppy hats, but not the kind Potts wore.

"Seems busy, doesn't it?" Jack said.

"Look, there," Johnny said, pointing. "Lone hiker. Off trail."

Jack let his eye follow his point. Bearded man. Hiking shorts. Blue T-shirt. Lean. Feet planted, reading a map. "That's not Potts."

"No, but betcha dollars to donuts he's a treasure hunter."

The man took his eyes off the map and watched them fly past, following, as if his feet pulled him along so as not to miss a clue someone else might have seen.

Jack noticed a ponderosa, its trunk huge for this part of the world. At least forty-inch diameter. Beside it, a dark spot, maybe a cave. No second ponderosa, but a lot could have changed in two hundred and fifty years.

The pilot spoke, shattering his thoughts.

"What?" Jack asked.

"*Gold fever*. More people will come." Bern looked out her side-window. "The guy I mentioned who called. He offered a percentage of the booty if I'd fly him for free."

Johnny laughed. "What'd you say?"

"I said, first, I'm not supposed to fly over the park at low altitude. Second, cash on the barrelhead, or no flight."

"Ace, you're the best," Johnny said.

They made passes over the plateau, never seeing Potts, an SOS, or a dirty white tent.

"Let's head back to base," Johnny said.

The pilot turned the plane toward Farmington.

At the airstrip, the Cessna taxied to the hanger, stopping outside the open doors. As Bern finished securing the plane, affixing tie downs to the wings, the rangers made their way to the fixed-base operations office to sign for the flight.

The office door opened. Buck Winslow held it open, a manila-colored parcel tucked under his arm. "Looking for treasure, or plotting which land you're gonna buy?"

They stepped inside. The pilot, following, paused to take the parcel from Winslow. "Santa Fe?"

"Yep." Winslow turned back to the rangers. "I think you better get back to the park. Hide Mangum's putting up smoke signals, planning something. Says he has proof of conspiracy. From what I'm hearing, I'm glad I'm not a Fed."

"You're serious?" Jack asked.

"Can't be good." Winslow turned to leave. "He's talking armed rebellion. Hit squads."

Bernadette handed Jack a clipboard, a form attached. "Hobbs meter has it at 1.3 hours."

Jack signed. "Thanks, Bern."

"Next time, Ace." Johnny turned to Jack. "Need to head to the Enclave?"

"Let's stay focused on Potts."

Johnny cleared his throat. "I saw a place or two I'd like to check out for treasure."

"Not allowed. Any treasure in the park would be protected."

"Sometimes you're a pain, boss."

"Change the law," Jack said, thinking about a big ponderosa.

—·—

Reger stopped at the door to the Chief Ranger's office. "We saw nothing."

Barb Sharp waved them in. "That leaves me not sure what to do. He's as good as our employee but other than worries and suspicions, we don't have much to act on. He could be taking a hike. He could be somewhere else, except that with all these rumors . . . I don't know whether to worry about his welfare or worry that he might be up to something shady."

Jack nodded, taking the seat across from her desk. Johnny took one near the wall.

"Before I forget, Jack . . . the superintendent's looking for you."

"About?"

"Potts. These rumors."

Jack stood. "I'll leave the two of you to talk about it. Make a plan for tomorrow."

"Meet ya at Elena's. Your turn to buy," Johnny said. "We'll work out the details."

Jack turned down the hall, passing his own office, stopping at the door to the Superintendent's secretary. "Looking for me?"

Marge attempted a smile and gave a pat to one side of her perfectly groomed head of hair. “Let me think. Hmm. Who hasn’t been looking for you?”

“Serious?”

“Joe,” she said, voice raised. “Jack’s here to see you.”

“Send him in,” came a dour voice.

Jack rounded the corner. “What’s wrong?”

A glare. Cold. “What’s not wrong?”

“I don’t know.” Jack took the nearest seat.

“First, the RD called. Word got to her about you harassing those guys in town.”

“Wasn’t harassing them. Just trying to get answers.”

“For something that’s none of your business. If you approach them again, you can expect disciplinary action.”

“I haven’t talked to him again, but how could what I did be seen as wrong? I wanted to understand what’s happening. If they’re doing something contrary to what we’re trying to achieve with the coalition, why wouldn’t I want to know? People are asking me questions. I don’t know how to answer. Silence is seen as tantamount to a lie.”

“You’ve been told to stay away. Just do it.”

“What’s the regional director hiding?”

“As I’ve said, it’s none of your business.

“Joe, an hour ago I was told Mangum is getting his tribe together to do something, because of those guys. And he thinks I’m involved. I’d have half a mind to join ’em if he wasn’t such an ass.”

Morgan sighed, regaining his composure. “I understand the difficulties this causes you. Be patient . . . and hope it’s over soon. I’ve been ordered to put you in a place where you can’t cause any damage. So . . . use some annual leave! Get a hobby.”

“You and I have played that hobby game before. It didn’t keep me out of trouble.”

“You’re not a troublemaker, usually, but this time you seem determined to be one.”

“Maybe I am . . . more than you know.”

“I’m not buying that . . . keep your nose clean. Take a vacation.”

Joe picked up a pen and gave it several clicks. "Now, change the subject. Potts Monroe . . . these rumors going around."

"What about 'em?"

"The RD heard 'em, too. Wants to know if we did our due diligence hiring this guy."

"He's a retired agency archeologist. Everyone knows him. His reputation is impeccable."

"Does he have a record of any kind? Did you check?"

"He . . . uh . . . didn't need a background check. He's not an employee, per se. He's not a contractor. He's a volunteer."

Joe gave the pen another click. "Think his previous office did a background check?"

"I . . . uh . . . I don't know."

"Ask," Joe said. "This talk of treasure . . . has people swarming the park . . . doing things they shouldn't. Where do you think Potts is?"

"Been trying to find out for the last two days. No sign of him, but his trailer's still here."

"These rumors make his disappearance seem suspicious . . . especially in the eyes of the RD. And Washington."

"The only time I've heard Potts talk about this Juan Rivera character, and the possibility of treasure, it was a joke." Jack paused. "Hold it." A memory began to form. "That night he said, '*There's plenty of treasure in Piedras Coloradas, but it has nothing to do with Juan Rivera.*' "

"What's that mean?"

"Simple statement of appreciation. He loves this place."

Joe gave his pen a click.

"I'm worried about him."

"You can worry on lockdown. Barb and her people will look for Monroe . . . using Reger while his hand is healing. You . . . you're on lockdown. No going out in the park, or the monument. Make yourself scarce. Don't you have writing to do? Coalition business?"

"Yeah . . . it's nearly finished. The signing is scheduled, but . . ."

"But what?" Joe put a hand on his phone.

Jack noticed. An impending end to the conversation. "Those

guys at the motel. They make things difficult. It's not a good time to be doing what they're doing."

"Don't change the subject." Joe picked up the phone and started to dial. "We're talking about Monroe. If you hear from him, let me know. If he should be arrested, don't sit on it."

Jack stood. "He's not a crook." Seeing no response from Joe, he slipped into the hall and into his office, dropping into a chair. *Potts is no criminal. Gotta protect him, somehow.*

One person can confirm the likelihood of the Rivera story . . . and any connection to Potts.

Jack pulled out a stack of business cards and flipped through them one by one. Hers was not among them. Only her husband's. On it the professor had scratched out his home address—given as the best place to mail any butterfly information. But the card had only one phone number, the professor's office. Jack dialed the number. It went to voicemail. The recording, in Spanish—and not the professor's voice—said not accepting messages. Jack stared at the card.

There is another option.

The address.

—·—

Jack trudged up the steps to Elena's, spotting Johnny in the crowded bar.

Johnny waved him over. "I started without you. Had to buy my own beer." He tilted his chair back on two legs and rested against the wall. "We decided the best thing to do is look at your files, see where Potts worked in the past, check some of his old research locations."

"Makes sense." Jack leaned forward, lowering his voice. "You know where the files are but . . . you've got to be careful. Arch site info is protected. Not to be made public. Pot hunters."

"Then I'll let you worry about the files, just tell me where to go. I'll act like I have no idea where I'm at when we get there . . . which might not be far from the truth." Johnny looked up. "Deputy Buckity's here. Must be checking for rowdies." He waved him over.

"It'll have to be you looking at files," Jack whispered, watching Winslow turn their direction. "I'm taking a vacation."

"You're kidding," Johnny muttered, "I had no idea."

"I didn't either, till today."

Deputy Winslow, in uniform, stopped at their table. He remained standing. "Gents."

"Kinda loose with your language, aren't you Buck?" Johnny said. "Still working?"

"Treasure hunting hooligans . . . I'm sure I'll be here several times tonight."

"Smart. You and me, workin' but . . . Jack here, he's going on vacation." He turned to Jack. "What do you mean, you didn't know till today? Something Kelly wants you to do?"

"She suggested it, and so did the superintendent, but the destination wasn't either's idea."

Reger raised a hand to Jack. "Hold it. I need to say something." He stood. "I've got an announcement. Jack Chastain, workaholic, is going on vacation." He dropped into his seat.

Heads turned. Heads at tables. Heads at the bar. Most flashed looks of confusion, then returned to their drinks.

Jack scowled.

"Where you goin'?" Winslow asked.

"Play tourist. Relax. Short trip."

"Where?" Johnny raised an eyebrow.

"Don't know." Jack felt the bore of disbelieving stares. "Mexico. Mexico City."

Johnny stood. "He's going to Mexico City. To relax, he says. I for one don't believe it."

Jack slumped down, avoiding eyes beginning to look strangely interested.

"You can't go on vacation," Winslow said. "Your buddy Mangum will start causing mischief."

"Might be good if I'm not here. Might calm him down a little."

"You can hope." Winslow looked out into the room and gave his chin a rub. "Then again, . . . you won't be here to defend yourself."

Chapter 11

Using a website he had heard about from Kelly, Jack found a flight that cost less than expected. A last-minute opportunity to snap up an unsold seat on a near empty flight, requiring only that he be in Los Angeles before noon tomorrow, achieved easily with a six o'clock flight from Albuquerque, that flight costing the most of the two.

He arrived in Mexico City in late afternoon, departing the jet and making a hasty departure through customs and immigration, slowing only to find a currency exchange, trading a few bucks for pesos. He then ambled out on the street to find a cab.

He stopped at the curb. A cab—a green Volkswagen Beetle—pulled forward. "University City," Jack said, as the cabbie took his backpack and tossed it onto the back seat.

"¿Donde?" The young male cabbie looked confused.

Jack climbed in the front. "Cuidad Universitaria."

The beetle darted into traffic. Before even getting out of the airport, Jack began to deduce the rules of the road. Only a bumper length's advantage over the car in the next lane gave one the right to move over, even if the next guy had to slam on the brakes. Who needs a stinkin' rear view mirror?

Outside the bounds of the airport, the ride remained unsettling. Maintaining a death grip on the door handle, Jack took in the cityscape of Mexico City. Grand classical buildings, modern skyscrapers, business parks, and compressed neighborhoods served by simple, single story, poured-concrete shops.

They crossed a major portion of the city heading west, then southwest, then onto a freeway headed south. The city seemed to take on several different iterations, from different times, serving different approaches to living. Mexico City, population, nine million. The greater metro area, over twenty-one million. A monster of a city.

After forty-five minutes, signs appeared for the old Olympic Stadium, a central library, a cultural center, an ecological reserve, various museums, and, of course, the main exit to the Universidad Nacional Autónoma de Mexico, the nation's largest university.

The twists and turns through the city made Jack begin to wonder if the cabbie had understood the name he'd given for the hotel, or if maybe he didn't know where he was going. Overwhelmed with both the ride and the city, Jack held his tongue. When the cabbie came to an abrupt stop at the curb, outside a glass-faced building, Jack checked the name on the sign.

"Yep, this is it," Jack mumbled to himself. He paid the cabbie and climbed out of the Beetle. Standing at the curb he stared, realizing he was staying at a hotel like any he might find in the states. *Damn, where's your sense of adventure, man*? He sauntered into the building.

Approaching the desk, he caught the eye of an attractive, dark-haired young lady with an eager smile. She checked him in and gave him his key, pointing him to the elevators.

"¿Tienes un mapa?" he said, asking for a map.

She reached under the counter and produced a folded version, and a page on University City's major attractions. "¿Puedo ayudarte a encontrar tu destino?" She handed them over.

"Yes, please. Uh, . . . sí." Jack unzipped a pocket on his pack and pulled out the professor's business card, pointing at handwritten words. "This address. La direction, esta casa."

She glanced at the card, then studied the map. "Muy cerca. Cerca de la Universidad." She pointed. "Aqui." Tapping the location of the hotel, then an intersection, then—walking her finger down a street—she showed him the vicinity of the residence.

"That close?" Jack said, eying the map. "Lucky. And close to the university? Gracias."

She handed him back the card. "De nada."

Making his way to the elevator, he made note of the lobby and the locations of a restaurant and gift shop, then rode to the fifth floor. He surveyed the room—nothing unusual—and dropped his pack on the desk. Sprawling out on the bed, he lay a moment, then grew restless, having no desire to hang out in a hotel room. There was ample time left in the day, enough to get to know the surroundings, and even confirm the location of the professor's home. Then he could find a place to eat. Sticking the map and business card in his shirt pocket, he headed downstairs and struck out. Turning left on the sidewalk outside the hotel, he followed the busy street.

After somewhat less than a mile, he turned at the intersection pointed out by the desk clerk. A mix of shops and homes. He eyed the business card. The correct street. He passed several side streets before seeing the address written on the card. A stately home, not large, not modern, but refined. Columnar wooden posts. A carved wooden door at the end of a terra cotta walkway lined with subtropical plants. He noticed a light shining through one of the windows.

What the hell? He approached the door and knocked three times.

After a long moment, the door inched open.

The professor's wife stood in the door, in a robe, her hair mussed, dark lines under her eyes. She shook her head, seeming to struggle with focusing her eyes. "Señor Chastain?"

"Yes. Sorry I didn't call in advance, I didn't have your number. Could I set up a meeting with you, maybe tomorrow, to talk. Some things have happened at home, and . . ."

"Something that would bring you here?" She appeared close to tears—and confused.

"Sorry . . . it's hard to explain."

"Señor Chastain, I . . ." She paused. "What is this about?"

"Potts Monroe."

"How do you mean?"

"Could Potts be a treasure hunter these days . . . more than an archeologist?"

She wiped at her nose with a Kleenex. "I'm sorry, but I'm in no mood for such talk. Not now. Not when it's something so silly."

"Silly? I promise, it's become quite serious."

"It may be, but today is not the day." She wrapped her arms around herself. "Today, I have buried mí amor . . . my husband. I cannot talk about this now."

"No!" Jack stepped back, his mouth gaping open. "I'm so sorry, I didn't know. What happened? Was he sick? Was it an accident?"

"Neither. He was murdered. I cannot talk about it now. I had just gotten people to leave. I need time alone. Maybe tomorrow, mid-morning." She wiped away a tear.

"No, I'm sorry, never mind. Forget I came. This is not important."

"Please Jack, come back tomorrow. It might do me good to think about something else. But let's do that tomorrow. Until then . . . I can assure you . . . Dr. Monroe is no treasure hunter. Okay?" She awaited his response.

"Okay."

She closed the door.

Jack stumbled onto the street, turning back the way he came. *What a jerk! Why didn't I find a way to call first? Poor woman. How tragic. Such a wonderful guy, her husband was. And how could I be so insensitive about Potts? Didn't even try to whitewash it. This was a bad idea. Shoulda stayed in New Mexico but . . . to do what?* He sighed.

Tomorrow, come back and give condolences, then leave. This Potts issue doesn't have to involve her. Maybe the university library . . . check there. He stopped and shook his head.

It would be difficult to even know where to start. But what if the rumors are true? What if she's involved? What if she said that about her husband to get rid of me?

He trudged forward. *Ridiculous. Don't be stupid. But be*

prepared to do this alone. Go to the university library and see what you can learn. You know enough Spanish to do this yourself.

If only you knew where to start.

At a corner, the name on the street sign hardly registered. *Did I go too far?* He pulled out the map and took a glance. *No, this is it.* He looked up the road, then across the street, hoping to see a familiar landmark. At the back corner of a modern, glass-fronted building stood a man—in a mustard-colored ballcap—studying him, or so it seemed. Jack held the man's eye for a moment, then the man turned away and stepped behind the building. White guy. Pudgy face, dark serious eyes. Familiar, even in the evening shadows. Can't be Harper Teague. How would Teague even know he was here? How could he find him?

Would he come all the way to Mexico just to play his political games?

Probably some random white guy . . . and his mind playing tricks on him, he thought. He was so screwed up after hearing about Professor Morales.

But Teague had been following in that pickup in Las Piedras.

Someone must have heard Johnny's silly stunt in the bar. *Damn his big mouth.*

But why Mexico? Why would Teague be following me here? Rivera's gold?

Jack glanced at traffic, then jogged across the road, stopping at the alley behind the building. No sign of the man—if it was Teague.

Jack sighed. *You're imagining things.*

Chapter 12

Sitting in the hotel restaurant, Jack finished breakfast and planned his day. Too early to drop in again on La Profesora—the name Potts called her that night in camp—he drank a little more coffee, then ambled back to his room to kill some time. He turned on his cell phone and pulled up the number for Kelly's desk.

"I've been worried about you," she said, answering. "I tried calling . . . all day yesterday, and the day before that. You never answered."

"Sorry. Day before I was in the backcountry, then flying the park. Got busy planning what I'm doing now, then yesterday, I never turned on my phone. Guess where I am."

"Taos?"

"Nope. Not *New* Mexico, *old* Mexico."

"Say that again."

"I'm in Mexico City."

"Work?"

"Kinda, but not exactly. I guess you'd call it a vacation."

"You're taking a vacation without me?" she said, feigning sounding hurt.

He laughed. "Sorry. Superintendent's idea. It was this or locking me in the office."

"Why, and why did he think you should go to Mexico?"

At the window, he stared down at the busy street below. "Mexico was my idea. Joe reacted to me cornering those guys Hide Mangum calls land agents. I demanded to know what they're doing. I was told to mind my own business. No going into the park, or the monument, and maybe even into town."

"I can't talk long . . . I've gotta a committee meeting to get to, but . . . today I'm letting the committee chair know I'll be working on a bill to adopt the coalition's recommendations . . . after the signing ceremony. Why Mexico City?"

"Research. Potts Monroe is off somewhere, and I've been trying to defend him. Quick trip to find anything that can put the rumors to rest. It's complicated."

"Father told me . . . something about treasure, but why Mexico City?"

"An expert who lives here . . . but I'm not sure I want to bother her now."

"Gotta go," Kelly said, abruptly. "We need to talk."

"Announcing your candidacy?"

"No. Controversy in Las Piedras."

—'—

Jack left the hotel and followed the route he'd taken the evening before. The traffic, now heavier, felt unsettling. Hugging the outside edge of the sidewalk, away from the road, he eyed the passing cars, prepared to make an evasive jump. He checked the occasional passersby on the other side of the street, trying to convince himself that Harper Teague would not be there, that it hadn't been him the day before.

He took the turn into the residential area and strolled past several side streets. The farther he got from the noisy boulevard, the more his attention fell on the jardins—the gardens. In the stillness and light of the morning, colors and fragrances pulled at his attention. Flowers. Cacti. Agave. Trees with blue and lilac-colored flowers. The botanic scents of central Mexico.

Ahead he could see the house. Their casa . . . rather, her casa. No cars. Maybe she was alone.

He slipped past the timber columns, slowing as he approached the door, his eyes adjusting to the shadows cast across the walkway. He knocked.

The door swung open. Light settled on La Profesora as she stepped into the doorway. This time, not in a robe, but dark slacks and a white, cotton blouse, her brown, almost black, hair pulled back, her eyes still sad—or suspicious—the lines beneath them gone, probably hidden by makeup. This was the beautiful academic he remembered from before—now somewhat restored—but without the sparkle he remembered in her eyes. *Would it ever be reignited*?

"Come in," she said, stepping back.

Jack attempted a smile. "Not necessary. I'm only back to pay my respects and tie up loose ends. I'm sorry for your loss. Your husband was such an impressive man. A pleasure to get to know. With that, I'll leave . . . I won't bother you. I'll check the university library, see if I can find a few answers. Then I'll consider myself done."

"Thank you, but please, come in. If our conversation becomes difficult, I will let you know, but come in, let me see if I can help."

"You've got more important things to think about."

She bowed her head, acknowledging the comment, then swung her arm, gesturing him in.

He followed her through a sitting room, into an office or library. Both, he realized. The room held two desks. Two facing walls with distinctively different bookshelves and contents. One shelf extended to the ceiling. Mostly modern books and cases for reprints and separates. Titles, in Spanish and English, some the same as the books on his own shelves. On the opposite but longer, door-less wall, shorter shelves, more knickknacks, books almost all with Spanish or Latin titles, an occasional one in English, or French, or Portuguese, and with a noticeable difference in the variability of age. Some incredibly old. Some in collections. Above the shelves, framed pictures of archeological digs, people with trowels in hand, others of workers in old buildings or in town squares, with calipers, planes, draw knives, and mallets. Tools for studying or restoring historic fabric of one kind or another.

La Profesora moved a few items from the chairs at a table near the window, as Jack glanced between the two desks. One, classical—dark wood, leather writing surface. A stack of papers and periodicals sat neatly assigned to one corner of the desktop. The other desk, fanciful, turquoise blue, books laying open over strata of papers. A picture in one book—a portrait from another century—suggested historical content. La Profesora's desk.

"You are welcome to sit." She waved him to the chair facing her side of the office and settled into the other. Tapping her lips with a finger, she squinted, eyeing him. "Tell me what it is you want to ask. And why you would think Dr. Monroe is anything other than what he purports himself to be?"

"Are you sure you want to do this?"

"If we need to stop our conversation, I'll tell you, . . . but Dr. Monroe is my friend. I'm willing to help if I can." An uncertain look came over her. "Why did you think of me? Why come all this way?"

"I came to you . . . because of a name I'd never heard . . . before the *two of you* mentioned it that night in camp. First you. If you remember, I'd hiked in to join the three of you at Pott's research location. The name you mentioned is now part of a rumor. That rumor includes Potts."

She leaned over her elbows, setting her head on steepled fingers. "What is the name?"

Locked onto her eyes, he watched for a reaction. "Juan Rivera."

An amused look came over her. "Rivera? ¿Que in el mundo? What in the world did I say?"

"You said he'd explored nearby lands . . . on his way to what is now Colorado."

"Which he did." She shook her head, confused. "Remembering that brought you here? I'm sure I didn't have much to say . . . Rivera was a man largely lost to history. His explorations were overshadowed by that of Escalante and Dominguez. Only in the last few decades has more become known of the significance of his explorations, and only because his journal was found in a military archive in Spain. A journal that helped Escalante and Dominguez on *their* travels."

"That night in camp . . . you said all that. It wasn't those things that brought me here. It was something that started as . . . or felt like . . . a joke. An inside joke . . . by Potts . . . to you. Not your husband, not me. It so much felt like an inside joke that I'm not sure I really listened. But I heard enough . . . and the other day, when I first heard the rumors, they triggered that memory of Potts, you, and that seemingly inside joke."

"Okay," she said, now very interested. "What did Potts say? What was this joke?"

"It went something like this . . . What if Juan Rivera wasn't lost to history? What if he chose to disappear? What if he actually found what he was looking for but reported otherwise to the governor in Santa Fe, then quietly slipped back into Colorado to get what he found?"

She threw back her head and laughed. "And . . . what had he found? Are we assuming riches? Gold? Silver? *Treasure*?"

"Yes, treasure. That's what this is about."

She let out a sad little chuckle. "He was joking."

"Then you said something like . . . to enjoy the good life."

"I was joking."

"That's what it felt like, but now we have these rumors . . . Capitan Juan Rivera . . . treasure . . . the details are uncanny. I couldn't help but think, *I thought that was a joke.*" He leaned forward. "The rumors have treasure hunters swarming the park. People suspect Potts knows where this treasure is."

"You asked him . . . right? What did he say?"

"Potts is nowhere to be found."

"What do you mean?"

"He's disappeared. He's not at his camp trailer. We found his vehicle, in the most unlikely of places, . . . so he could be on a hike. We've looked for him. Found nothing. Even people in the agency are growing suspicious. Questioning his integrity. His reputation. Then I remembered that night in camp . . . I figured you were the best person to ask. The best place to start. The only person who might help me preserve his reputation."

"Because I'm the person who first mentioned Juan Rivera . . . to your ears at least?"

"Correct."

She let out a sigh. "I remember that night quite well. I suppose it will become an enduring and haunting memory now that I no longer have my husband. I was there helping my old friend and colleague, Dr. Monroe. My husband agreed to go but I could tell, he felt like a third wheel . . . until your arrival. The work you do absolutely thrilled him. The hike you took him on . . . requiring ropes . . . what did you call it?"

"Canyoneering."

"Yes, he so enjoyed the rappels, the dry waterfalls, and when the two of you saw la mariposa monarcha he was ecstatic. He is . . . was . . . encouraging me to help Potts again next year, so he could tag along, do more work of his own."

Jack let out a sad little chuckle. "I planned to contact your husband. I found a few monarchs and a nice patch of milkweed not far off a trail."

She smiled, appreciatively.

"Unfortunately, those milkweeds are gone. Destroyed."

Her smile dissolved. Her eyes went blank. "What does that mean? That sort of thing happens?"

"Milkweed destroyed? Not in a park . . . usually. It was odd. Never seen anything like it."

"By a person?"

"Yes."

She mumbled something to herself, her eyes now wide. "Are you safe?"

"I'm fairly certain who did it. We've had our little scrapes, but . . . I can handle myself."

Tears formed in her eyes. "Are you being naïve?"

"Those things . . . go with the job."

Anger flared in her eyes, flashing amidst the tears. "Just as it does with being a researcher de la mariposa? You can handle yourself?" She dropped her face into her hands. "My husband thought he could handle himself. And now I am a widow. He worried about me. He should have worried about himself." She sobbed into her hands.

Jack felt himself pushing back in the chair. "I'm so sorry."

"My husband was killed taking a graduate student into the butterfly reserve. Authorities have yet to find the body of the young girl." She glared. "He couldn't just do his research. He had to let himself get pulled into also protecting the butterfly, and that got them killed. Now I am alone, in his city, not mine . . . and without him."

Jack searched for words. None came.

Tears kept flowing. "I ask you again . . . are you safe?" Then, she whispered. "Is it possible my husband's death and your destroyed milkweed are connected in some way?"

Tears held his eye. His first impulse, a dismissive no. He stopped himself. "Connected? I can't see how. Am I safe? I think so. The risks I face are the ones I normally face."

Again, she dropped her face into her hands and sobbed.

"I'm sorry," Jack said. "This is too painful. I should leave."

"No," she said, an abrupt reaction. The sobbing stopped. "No, I haven't yet answered your question." Chin up, brave face, she drew in a breath. "Let us return to that."

He smiled. "How about this? A little small talk. Your specialty is Spanish colonial history. Potts is an archeologist. How did you know each other?"

She forced a smile and wiped the tears away with her sleeve. "We were grad students in Arizona, working on archeological projects together. We became fast and dear friends."

"But you're an historian."

"Yes, it was I who changed course, but there are historical archeologists."

"I guess I didn't think about that."

"Yes . . . there's looking for answers in the dirt, or among the musty pages of old letters and ledgers. I am drawn to both." She lay back in her chair. "Juan Rivera . . . his story . . . his mission included looking for silver and gold, but also finding a route to the north and establishing trade relations with the Utes. He made two trips. On the second he got as far as present-day Delta, Colorado. He found silver . . . not enough to stir much interest. He was—for the most part—lost to history. Even his journals, found in Spain, don't share much about the man. Rivera may have simply returned to Mexico when the governor finished his term."

"Considered a failure?"

"No. I wouldn't think so. He made friendly contacts with the Utes, found routes used by Escalante and Dominguez."

"So . . . there's no chance Rivera kept his head down, sneaked back into Colorado, picked over the mother lode, and retired to a life of wealth and sangria on the coast of Spain?"

"Interesting." Her eyes suggested a mind tugging on the strings of the last point. "Tell me more . . . the details. And how is Potts supposedly involved?"

Jack leaned over his hands. "The rumor goes like this. The writings of one of the men who traveled with Rivera were found among old family possessions somewhere in New Mexico. The person who found them was uncertain what they had, and what to do with them. Shared them, hoping to understand what they represented. Supposedly . . . getting the journal entries interpreted. These suggest a third and fourth trip, that Rivera returned to what's now Colorado to get treasures he found earlier but didn't report. The journal suggests Rivera didn't intend to go back to Santa Fe. He didn't even intend to go to Mexico City. His plan, according to the journal, was to avoid both capitols, to go directly to Vera Cruz."

"Stop." She sat up. "The journal says Vera Cruz?"

"Supposedly."

"Go on."

"He wanted to sail to Madrid. He'd already booked passage."

She gasped. "That's why you came to me. Because of what I said that night in camp." Her eyes narrowed. "So, if you wonder if Dr. Monroe is a pot hunter—or rather, a treasure hunter—then you have the same question about me. You wonder if I'm in cahoots with him."

"Why would I think that?"

"Because I'm from Vera Cruz."

"I'm not sure I knew that."

"Then . . . go on."

Jack rubbed his forehead. "Well . . . the story . . . it doesn't play out the way Potts said that night. This journal says Rivera had hopes of becoming governor of all lands to the north. He was taking the riches to Spain . . . to impress . . . not to seek the good life in Madrid."

"Interesting." The look in her eye softened. "Go on."

"Why did Vera Cruz trigger that response?"

"It's an unusual detail but one that would be historically accurate . . . or likely. The port city of Vera Cruz was the primary connection between New Spain—Mexico—and Spain."

"Why your reaction?"

Red flushed over her. "I know that city well. I taught at the university in Vera Cruz before coming here to be with my husband. I loved Vera Cruz. The old city. The ocean." Her nostalgia dissolved. "Continue, please."

"There's not much more. Simply that Rivera returned to Colorado, loaded up the treasure and was attacked by Comanche . . . the enemy of the Utes and about everyone else in that part of the world. Rivera may not have survived. Unable to move quickly, burdened with treasure, they stashed the loot in a cave and tried to sneak away . . . to return when it was safe, but they were caught. The cave is thought to be in what is now Piedras Coloradas National Park."

She tapped her lip. "Interesting."

"Oh . . . and there's a map."

"Of course." Her expression suggested skepticism.

"Or so it's called. More a description of the lay of the land and a drawing of a cave. Put together from memory, supposedly."

"Okay," she said, trying not to smile. "You have seen this map?"

"Yes. A ranger I work with found a photo . . . online . . . and printed it off. Scrawls mainly . . . looks to be on old, browned paper."

Mirth gone, La Profesora stared at the wall.

"That's not the expression I expected to see," Jack said.

"It is not the expression I expected to give."

Chapter 13

"Enfrair los ánimos," La Profesora said, her eyes boring into him.

"What?"

"Clear the air," she said, eyes unchanged. "You think I'm involved, don't you?"

"I didn't say that."

"But you do."

"No."

"Logic . . . your reason for being here . . . all suggest that is a lie."

"Not true. I'm here for Potts. Rumors suggest he knows where the treasure is, that he's going after it himself." Jack stood and began to pace the room. "He knows the park like the back of his hand. People know that. Doesn't help. The night before I left, I went online and read through the discussion threads. There were claims that Potts was the first person consulted by the owner of the journal. That he had possession for months, then returned it, acting as if it was no big deal. Then, the owner mentioned the journal to a historian. After that person translated the first few entries, they told the owner a different story, that the contents could be important."

"And you haven't discussed this with Potts?"

"Haven't seen him in over a week."

"Is that common?"

"No, but . . . he works alone . . . as a volunteer. Any time he wants to do things of personal interest, he can . . . he's not an employee. He likes to hike, visit old research locations, that sort of thing. In fact, he may've shown up by now, but we've looked and . . . haven't found him."

"Is there *evidence* Potts had possession of the journal?"

"None that I've seen."

"Do you believe the rumors?"

"I didn't . . . don't . . . but it's been falling to me to defend him . . . and that's become difficult. It's getting to the point where I don't know what to think."

She picked up a pencil and squeezed. She turned to the window. "Now you have me feeling the same way. At first I was amused. Now I don't know what to think."

She went to her desk, moved a stack of papers, and uncovered a laptop computer. Going online, she ran a quick search and found the stories Reger had seen, and the threads about the journal supposedly written by a member of the Rivera party. She stared, studying the words on the screen. "I don't know if I can believe this or not." She frowned. "There's a new clue, dated today. A name connected to the port in Vera Cruz." She sighed. "Seems too much coincidence."

"Why?"

"For me? Because of my own connection to Vera Cruz."

"Why is that a coincidence?"

"Because, somehow, it makes me feel as if I'm part of this. Potts is my friend. And despite what you say, I can't dismiss the possibility that you are here because you think I am part of something, too."

"Promise, I don't." Jack slipped into a chair with a view of the screen. "I'm here because of your expertise, and because you know Potts and the Rivera story. And I'm sure you want to protect him as much as I do. Can we disprove the rumors?"

She stood. "Before I answer that . . . let's go to my office at university. Maybe the library. It's easier to look at digital collections from there." She looked around the room and picked up a ring of keys. "We'll take my car."

—·—

She drove a gray BMW 335. She understood the traffic and how to take charge. Weaving through streets and crossing one major road, she had them on campus in minutes.

A couple of minutes more and she pulled into a parking space outside a building marked, *Facultad de Filosofia y Letras*. Faculty of Philosophy and Letters.

She climbed out of the car and, without slowing, dashed into the building, leading him upstairs, then down a mostly empty corridor. "I don't need anyone to see me. I'm in no mood to be showered in sympathy," she whispered, ducking her head as she passed two young men—students. She turned down a quiet hallway, produced her keys and unlocked a door. Pushing Jack inside, she followed him in, then closed the door.

In the moment before he'd felt her push, he'd read the placard posted in the hall.

Dr. Angelica Vargas, PhD
PROFESORA DE HISTORIA

"Dr. Vargas . . ." he muttered, mostly to himself as he looked around the ten-by-ten-foot office. Her desk, in a similar condition to the one at her home, sat layered with papers and open books. "I'm not sure I really knew your name. Without thinking, I thought of you as Profesora Morales . . . but . . ."

She plopped down at her desk. "Common mistake for norte-americanos." She tapped the computer keyboard. The monitor came to life. Pounding out a string of familiar keystrokes, she glanced up. "My name is Angelica . . . Lucia . . . Medina . . . Vargas. Doctor Vargas if you wish, but Angelica is perfectly fine." She turned back to the monitor, typing in a few keystrokes. "Maybe you never heard my name. My husband only used his terms of endearment . . . like, mi criatura encantadora." A hint of a smile appeared. "Such a biologist." She shook her head, as if teasing him. "And Potts . . . Dr. Monroe . . . only calls me La Profesora, his own term of endearment, I suppose, even though he's known me since well before I finished my doctorate. Maybe La Profesora is less personal. We were never lovers, but there were times I wished we were. Other times he did." She laughed. "Never the same time. He was older, but I had a huge crush. Now, I'm always La Profesora and he's Dr. Monroe." She gave two quick key taps, then spun the monitor around for Jack to see. "Speaking of names. The dates check out."

Jack leaned in to see the words.

Secretario Colonial Julián de Arriaga

"Who's that," Jack asked, "and what do you mean, the dates check out?"

"Colonial Secretary in Vera Cruz, Julian De Arriaga. He was there in 1765." Angelica turned back to the screen. "That's the name I saw today on the web page . . . the latest entry related to the Juan Rivera rumors."

"What's the significance?"

"Arrianga was supposedly Rivera's contact in Vera Cruz, arranging passage to Madrid."

"And he's real?" Jack leaned in, studying the name.

"Yes. A man with connections to Madrid. And, he had his own little battles. If I remember right, that was a period of turmoil . . . and infighting . . . between bureaucrats and merchants in Vera Cruz." She smiled. "In many ways the Spanish in Vera Cruz were more influential than those here in Cuidad Mexico. Many merchants were quite wealthy, and with wealth comes the expectation of influence. Entitlement." She turned back to the screen.

"Could this mean the rumors are true?"

"I wouldn't say that. Something about this troubles me." She scowled. "If Rivera was working with Arrianga, it would have been dangerous for both. They would have been keeping it secret. Neither Rivera nor Arrianga could afford to anger the powers in Cuidad Mexico. And for Rivera, Santa Fe. Would Rivera's men know about a connection to Arrianga? Maybe a trusted lieutenant, or someone he hoped to include in his plans?" She squinted at the screen. "But."

"But, what?"

"Scholars have never thought of Rivera as a man with connections or influence. The Governor in Santa Fe chose him to lead an exploration. Nothing suggested it was for any other reason than he could get the job done. Maybe they were close, but connections? Influence?"

"Does it matter?"

She sighed and gave a rub to her chin. "Maybe not, but . . . if he had connections to Arrianga, he likely had influence. If he had influence, why has he been forgotten by history?"

She closed the result block and typed in a new search term. "Thinking ahead . . . If Rivera didn't survive an attack by the Comanche, and we only know of his secret because of this journal by a survivor . . . it just seems odd that Rivera didn't keep his mouth shut. Seems out of character for a man whose journals are so spare . . . a man who, from all evidence, seemed unassuming, unaffected." She chuckled to herself. "But how would I know that? I'm speculating. We have to follow the evidence, and often history denies us insights into the very drivers for the events that occurred." She turned to him. "If true, it seems more likely his secret would have died with him, considering the risks."

"So, you're discounting the possibility?"

"You would think, wouldn't you? Except . . . this Julián Arrianga . . . had his political battles. He was ambitious. If currying favor with Madrid would be a chess move to outflank his political opponents, then . . . from what I know of Arrianga . . . he might have done it."

"Did he leave journals . . . anything we could check?"

"Yes, reports, and they would be in the digital collection at the university in Vera Cruz. Still, that will take a lot of work, and I'm not sure he would report on giving support to someone such as Rivera . . . because of the risks." She gave her chin a rub. "But . . ."

He watched as the cogs seemed to turn.

"Let's do this. The central library next door has a copy of the old records for the port of Vera Cruz . . . ships coming in and out, records of who and what were on those ships. Who booked passage, etc." She stood. "The Spanish were tremendously good bureaucrats. Their records might have something that tells us if it's worth doing a deeper dive."

She grabbed her keys and circled the desk. Peeking into the hall, she waved him to follow, then closed the door behind her, leading Jack back along the route they came in on.

They crossed the parking lot to the adjacent building, a tall, blocky edifice, covered in shapes and what looked to be Aztec and Spanish forms.

"How did I not see that?" Jack asked.

"You were terrorized by my driving." She raised her arms and presented the wall before them. "That," she said, "is the largest mural in the world." Moving on, she entered the expansive first floor, leading him past a crowded entryway, the central desk, and a line of other patrons. As if she owned the place, she advanced to a staircase.

Jack followed as she bounded up the steps, taking entire flights in short order, then exiting the stairwell in a way that suggested a well beaten path.

A quieter floor, with rack upon rack of books.

Passing several, she made her choice and ducked into a canyon that continued all the way to a far wall. Jack watched as she scanned, appearing to know for what she was looking. Starting at a top shelf, she made her way to the bottom, scooted past a break in the racks, then started over, making a sudden stop and pulling half a dozen books off the shelf, all with the same blue cover. She handed the books to Jack, did a quick scan for other titles, picked a few, then led him out of the canyon.

"Here," she said, turning to a table.

Flipping through the books with blue covers, she stopped occasionally to study a page. After half an hour she looked up from her reading. "No mention of a Juan Rivera booking passage for Spain in 1765, 1766, or 1767." She reached for another volume and flipped it open.

He began to wonder if she would ever need his help. She glanced up, as if hearing his thoughts, then returned to scanning, running a finger down the page. As she flipped to another, Jack caught a movement, in the next aisle over, behind the next rack of books.

He turned his attention back to her reading but noticed the figure in the shadows changing their position, as if trying for a better view.

"I had thought we might be finished, but . . ." She flipped one of the books around toward him and tapped at a line on the page.

He glanced at the words. "My Spanish . . . those words might be a bit more archaic than I'm used to reading."

She leaned forward. "It indicates passage being held for two passengers, to go from Vera Cruz to Spain. It gives no names." She shot a curious twist of a smile. "There's no indication whether they made the trip."

Over her right shoulder, the dark outline made another shift in position. Jack glimpsed the brim of a ballcap. Jumping to his feet, he said, "Is there a bathroom nearby?"

Taken aback, she pointed.

He ambled a few feet, then darted to the head of the aisle, rounding the corner. He saw no one. Gone. He followed the rack to the end, into the aisle along the far wall. Still, no one, but there had been.

What the hell?

He strolled back to where Angelica Vargas sat reading.

Don't scare her. Keep it to yourself. For now. "Sorry, now I can concentrate." He smiled and retook his seat. "Where were we? Passage held for two. What year?"

"1766. The year following Rivera's last recorded expedition."

Chapter 14

"1766." Jack repeated, before stealing a glance into the shadows of the next aisle. With no one there, he dropped his eyes to read the passage.

"That would be a strange time for what is suggested in this rumor." Angelica's eyes narrowed. "Or . . . would it?" She ran a hand along her chin. "I need to think about this."

"Why? What?"

Staring at the table, she gave successive slow nods, as if checking off the details running through her mind. "Earlier that century, the Bourbons ascended to the throne. By 1766 the king was Charles III, a highly successful king, determined to reform and modernize Spain. He put limits on the influence of the church."

"What bearing would that have on Rivera?"

"That, I need to think about." She paused. "If I remember my dates correctly, reforms had not yet come to New Spain . . . in fact, I believe the new Viceroy of New Spain arrived in Mexico City that very year, mid-year 1766. Reform came quickly, but not that quickly. He expelled the Jesuits, doing so before the end of 1767 . . . throwing them all on a boat, deporting them to Italy. But reform . . . I need to think about." She stood and paced along the rack. "Charles wanted administrators who were *peninsulares.*

Disinterested professionals. Usually meaning military men. Men with long records of service."

"Online, he was referred to as Capitan Juan Rivera."

"Yes, I'm aware. Historians assume it's in reference to his leading the exploration. No actual evidence has been produced confirming Rivera was military. Likewise, I'm not aware of evidence that he wasn't . . . but finding *no* evidence that something *didn't* happen is hardly evidence at all. In fact, it isn't. So, let's assume there's a chance Rivera was indeed a military man. If so, that could have been part of their intended pitch. That *here* is a man capable of being an administrator, one of the king's peninsulares."

"And what of this?" Jack inserted. "They were to come bearing gifts. Gold, silver."

She sighed. "Yes, and there is that. The persuasive power of gold."

"So, the rumor's possible?"

"We're talking about a king whose focus was reform. And a new Viceroy whose sole principle was absolute obedience to the king. Administrators represented the king." She made an abrupt stop. "That would have been well established by 1766, at least in Madrid, with rumblings—within the bureaucracy Arrianga was in—that reform was coming to Mexico, which it did. If this is true, what risks would Rivera and Arrianga be willing to take? Something as bold as going to Madrid, bearing riches they were honor bound to disclose to their higher-ups?"

"Would that sort of thing have been done?"

"Seems unlikely."

Jack leaned forward, elbows on the table. "So, a reason not to believe the journal."

"It's speculation . . . unless we find something of evidentiary value." She picked up her bag. "Let's go back to mi casa . . . give this more thought and make a plan."

Jack picked up a stack of books.

"Leave them for library staff." She led him back to the stairs. Before reaching the landing above the main floor, she paused—checking for anyone she might know—then continued down.

Outside, Angelica started toward her car.

Now, Jack took over the job of looking. His eyes, behind sunglasses, searched the lot for anyone who might be watching—among the cars, under the trees surrounding the parking lot, at the corners of buildings—but without saying so, for fear of causing her worry.

At her casa, they settled into her office. She sat quietly at her table, tapping her lips, staring at a blank pad of paper.

"Are you sure you want to do this?" Jack asked, breaking the silence. "I'm intruding. I can take it from here."

"I want to do this. It . . . occupies my mind. Let me think tonight and we can start again in the morning. Would you like me to drive you to your hotel?"

"I'll walk."

—·—

Evening seemed to have come quickly. The angle of the sun, the cooler temperatures. As he walked, he made subtle checks to see if anyone might be following, time and again seeing no one. Admit it, you're paranoid. He's not here. The prospect of Harper Teague being in Mexico City seemed crazy. But someone was there in the library, whatever they were doing.

As he walked on, the perfume of vegetation—so different than in New Mexico—claimed his attention, even as thoughts of possibly being following stayed lodged in his mind. *Think about the evening*, he told himself. *Think about being in Mexico. These flowers. A café on a plaza somewhere.*

He made the turn toward the hotel. After a couple of blocks, he thought he saw movement to the right. On impulse, he started to look, but caught himself.

Businesses lined the avenue. From professional buildings to small shops. Behind them—obvious at the next intersection—an alleyway. He paused at a placard and pretended to read, head down, facing it, but checking for movement along the alley. After killing enough time, he continued to the hotel.

"Buenos días," the doorman said, grasping the door handle and swinging it open.

Jack nodded and strolled into the lobby, past the desk and the concierge, past the bar, and into the alcove housing the elevator. He pressed the up button and waited, watching the lighted floor numbers descend. His mind went back to the movement he thought he'd seen. *Silly.* It's ludicrous to think Harper Teague would be here.

The elevator door slid open. Jack glanced back at the lobby. No familiar faces. He checked the bar. People enjoying after-work cocktails. No Harper Teague. *What the hell, go have a drink. Wash away the paranoia.*

Before reaching the bar, he noticed the gift shop. A stack of newspapers lay on the counter. He slipped in, picked up a *New York Times*, and got in line to pay. A dark-haired woman in a bikini, likely returning to the pool with newly purchased reading material, picked through her coin purse for pesos, then slipped into the hall. Next in line, a pudgy boy buying candy bars. As Jack watched the boy leave, he noticed someone at the registration desk, a man in a mustard-colored hat. His back to the room, he leaned over the counter in protected conversation with the same young woman Jack had checked in with the day before.

Jack slipped behind a potted palm to watch.

The desk clerk stood stiff, wary, her eyes turning to co-workers, then to the hands of the man. She stepped back, politely, otherwise looking tight-lipped.

The exchange ended.

The man made an abrupt, stiff move for the door, head down, barging past the doorman, and once outside, turning right onto the sidewalk.

Jack put down the newspaper and headed for the desk.

She saw him approach. Her eyes grew wide.

"¿Era eso sobre mí?"

With a slow nod, she said, "Sí."

"¿Puedes . . ." He struggled for the word. " uh . . . decirme qué . . . quería?"

"He wanted to know how long you would be staying."

"Did you tell him?"

"I told him we are not allowed to share information about our guests. He offered a bribe. I did not take it."

"Thank you.

"He also . . ." She glanced at the other clerk. "He wanted a key to your room. He said it was a matter of national security. He said he needed to install a listening device. He claimed to be federales."

"And?"

"I asked to see his badge. He left."

"He's following me. I don't know why . . . but thank you."

"De nada."

Jack slipped over to the window and caught a glimpse of the man, waiting at the busy intersection. Stocky, taller than the others crossing the road, he wore a pale green guayabera and that mustard-colored ball cap. He never turned to show his face. Must be Harper Teague.

The man crossed the intersection, disappearing into the steady flow of pedestrians.

Jack turned to go to his room, then stopped.

Two can play this game.

Jack dashed outside and, forgoing the intersection, crossed the road, dodging cars. At the crossroads, Jack turned to follow. Pedestrian traffic seemed to be increasing. End of the workday. The sidewalk climbed a hill. Teague would have a hundred yards or more on him, so he jogged, passing others on their trudge upslope, seeing no one ahead wearing a ball cap. College students. Businesspeople. Humanity. Then he saw it, the mustard-colored cap. He slowed, keeping his distance.

The crowd thinned. Students at an apartment complex, businesspeople heading into their neighborhoods. Jack let himself slip farther behind as the man began to slow.

The reality sank in. It really could be Teague. If it is, why? Why would he be following me? How did he know I was here?

Could this be about Rivera? Digging for clues? Trying to find where to look for treasure?

Another block and Jack could see a bend in the road. Instead of following it around, Teague crossed the road and marched up to a two-story building on the outside curve, never looking back as he entered. A sign over the door read, *El Palacio*.

Jack crossed before reaching the building, trying to stay out of sight. Close to the wall, he crept to a window and peeked inside, a subtle move, avoiding the glare of the inside lights now that the sun had slipped below the rooftops.

Against the far wall, a registration desk. *It's a hotel.*

A young man in tan, probably a teenager, stood at attention, waiting for the lone guest in the lobby. The man, putzing about, turned. Teague. His serious eyes settled onto a newspaper laying open on the counter. Without looking up, Teague spoke to the desk clerk, who turned to the back wall and retrieved a brass key from the key cabinet, handing it to Teague, who departed.

Jack submitted the key's cubby location to memory, then watched as Teague ambled down the steps into a covered courtyard, past tables and a jardin, disappearing through a far door.

Jack stepped into the entryway. Spanish tiles. *Nice. Now what*? He ambled in. On the walls at both ends of the desk, paintings, depictions of scenes from centuries back. A Spanish gentleman, the central focus of one, a stunning, remarkably dressed Spanish lady on the other.

Potted flowers and tropical plants seemed to invade the room from the courtyard below.

The young man behind the counter, said, "¿Puedo ayudarlo?" When Jack didn't answer, he followed with, "May I help you?" He ran a finger across the thin beginnings of a mustache.

Jack glanced around. "I'm . . . not sure."

"Do you have a reservation with us?"

"Uh, . . . no. I have a room at the bottom of the hill."

"Are you meeting someone?"

Jack didn't answer.

"You are welcome to look around. We are not as big as your hotel, . . . but . . . it has been in our family for generations. My father is proprietor." Getting no response, he rattled on. "Someday the responsibility for meeting the needs of our guests will fall to me."

"Nice place. That man that just came through here . . . I would swear I knew him."

The boy smiled.

"Could that have been my old friend Harper Teague?"

His eyes grew wide. "You know Señor Teague?"

"So, it *was*?" Jack said. "Amazing. I'm here for just a few days and who else is here . . . enjoying the beauties of Mexico . . . but Harper?" He shook his head, feigning amazement.

"Maybe a coincidence for *you*, but not so for Señor Teague."

"How so?" Jack asked, playing along.

"Señor Teague stays with us quite often."

"What?" Jack stepped closer. "¿Perdon? What do you mean, often?"

"I would estimate that Señor Teague spends three days to a week with us every month."

"Are you serious?"

"Very serious. We're his home in Cuidad Mexico. His office when here." A suspicious look came over the boy. "Are you sure Señor Teague is your friend?"

Trapped, he attempted a smile. "Should I say yes or no?"

He laughed. "Say yes."

"Okay . . . yes. We know each other. Not well. I know him from up north, the states. Caught him following me today, so I turned the tables on him . . . to see what he's up to."

The boy nodded. "Do not worry. Señor Teague is not a very nice man. He complains to mí padre when I've done something not to his expectations. Papá knows his kind of man, but . . . he is steady business."

"What does he do here?"

The young clerk reached into the cubby for room 24. He pulled out a business card. "I should not share, but . . ." He handed it over.

Jack stared.

Harper Teague

Avocado Broker

"Avocado broker? What is an avocado broker? And . . . why no contact information?"

The young man laughed, unable to conceal his amusement. "An avocado broker is what it is. Contact information? People he wants to find him, they know."

"Everyone else?"

"Everyone else, I believe he prefers they *not* know. But . . . if you know, you come here." He nodded toward the courtyard. "Breakfast, 9 a.m., every morning, meeting someone or not."

"That's it? That's how he connects to the world?"

"That or a fax . . . received in our office." He nodded to the back room. "We get it to him."

"Interesting." Jack flipped the card over. No other information. "Strange."

"This one, Papá keeps, as he does for all regular guests. He places them in the key boxes as reminders that these patrons deserve individual attention."

"I see." Jack turned his eye to the painting of the Spanish lady and rubbed his chin. *Maybe Teague's more surprised than I am. Maybe he's wondering, what the hell is Jack Chastain doing here? But he initiated the cat and mouse.* Jack studied the room. More character and culture than the monstrosity at the bottom of the hill. "Have any rooms?"

"No señor, not for tonight."

"Just as well. How about tomorrow?"

The boy pored over the register, then his computer. "Sí. We do."

"Then please reserve one room for a Mr. Smith. Uh, . . . Mr. Juan Smith."

The boy smiled. "Pleased to meet you, Señor Smith." He offered his hand. "And I assume you wish to surprise your friend Señor Teague on your own terms?"

"Yes, please," Jack said, shaking the boy's hand. "Let this be our little secret."

Chapter 15

The next morning, Jack prepared to check out of the hotel. To keep from telegraphing a departure, he would need to avoid taking his bag to Angelica's. Everything needed to appear as it had the day before in case Teague had someone waiting and watching.

After paying his bill, he asked to leave his pack in the hotel's bell closet.

The desk clerk waved the doorman over.

The doorman attached a red numbered tag to a pack strap and handed Jack the stub, then walked the pack to a closet behind the concierge's desk. Jack slipped him a few pesos and headed off to see La Profesora.

—·—

Another beautiful morning for a walk. He strolled the same route, no sign of being followed, but this time of day might not be Teague's hours for trailing. But how did Teague manage to do what he did? Without waiting around all day.

Jack knocked on Angelica's door.

She answered, in jeans and a blue silken blouse, her hair pulled back. She appeared shaken, uncertain. "Come in."

"Something wrong?"

"I have a visitor coming. Later."

"I can come back, just tell me when."

"No, come in. We will work until then. I have a few things we can look at. When my visitor arrives, you can continue working." She stepped back from the door, ushering him in.

"Are you sure? You look . . . uh, . . . forgive me, you look rattled."

She sighed. "Yes, but . . . it will be good, unexpected but good, and yes, I'm rattled." She continued into the office where a marked-up pad of paper lay on the table. Her thoughts, possible sources, circles, and arrows.

Not wanting to be seen as prying, he kept his eyes on a page in an open book. Nervous, she seemed all over the board, unable to focus, finally settling on the book before him.

"This is from my personal collection," she said, laying a hand on the page. "Does Juan Rivera live within these words?" She gave a nod to her computer. "Or . . . in the records we can search online?" Wringing her hands, she looked away. "I am confident he does not. If you happen to think I am part of an effort to find treasure, I can assure you my uncertainty is real."

"Understood. I wasn't thinking that."

A frown on her face, she nodded, avoiding his eyes. "Anything that would suggest an intention on the part of Colonial Secretary Julian de Arrianga might be our only clue. An explicit mention of Rivera, yes, but I'm not confident that would happen, even if this rumor is true. Reports of a connection between Arrianga and Rivera in official records or in a journal entry seems unlikely. A planned trip to Madrid by Arrianga during the subject time frame might be a clue. Maybe some pattern of his life changed temporarily . . . something we could use to fashion a hypothesis or a framework for further investigation. But . . ."

"What?"

"If this journal in New Mexico is real, and there is gold to be found, nothing here will help you find it."

"I know." He sighed. "I'm more concerned about Potts' reputation. That's why I came. Put me to work."

She handed him a book. "Start by looking for any mention of Arrianga or his office, Colonial Secretary in Veracruz. And, of course, any mention of Juan Rivera."

He opened the pages. Handwritten documents, alternating between official records and bookkeeping. Mind-numbing work, scanning page at a time. Jack finished one book after half an hour and slammed it shut. "Nothing in that one." He reached for another. "I don't know what to think. It just seems so unlikely we'll find anything. I see bureaucracy that's worse than anything I see today. No mention of a Rivera. If truth is hiding on these pages, how will we know it? One book and I'm already wondering if we're done. Should we call it quits?"

Angelica gazed over the frames of her reading glasses. "You expect an answer tied up in a nice little package? To find *truth*?" She let out a chuckle. "Truth, our constant tormentor."

"I want to defend Potts . . . but I'm afraid of what we'll find . . . but I'm also afraid of missing the truth."

"If you do not find the facts that prove these stories to be true, that does not mean that they're not . . . although I rather doubt they are. And, finding something that suggests the possibility of it being true, . . . also does not prove they are. You are wrestling with a very common dilemma in my profession. Trying to make inferences . . . using what you have, to make interpretations hundreds, sometimes thousands of years afterwards. Most clues are gone. Those that remain may be irrelevant."

"Was I silly coming here? Speculation has reached people who demand answers. Important people. Wanting details . . . asking questions. And Potts hasn't been there."

"I understand, Jack. For now . . . sometimes, in the effort to gather facts . . . it's more fruitful to focus on what might *not* be true."

"Why?"

"Falsifiable hypotheses. Errors . . . and lies . . . are sometimes less elusive. More easily disproved, and yet, easily believed. And that's the irony."

"Irony?"

"They are often more easily accepted . . . believed . . . or wanted

. . . thus they have longer shelf life than fact . . . or truth. Yet, often, they are easily taken apart and disproved. Truth? It is what it is."

It is what it is? He flashed a confused look.

She shrugged. "No importa. Doesn't matter. Keep looking."

Echoing through the house came a knock. Angelica got to her feet, took a deep breath, put on a strong face, and left to answer the door.

Jack listened as she welcomed her visitor. A girl's voice, unintelligible words, then a man's, more easily understood.

Angelica invited them to sit.

The girl's voice, barely audible. Fragile. Tears. Hushed exclamations. Only when she began speaking louder could Jack make out her words. Some words and phrases went right past him, but he began to understand the gist of what she was saying.

This was Profesor Morales' graduate student. The missing girl presumed dead.

Profesor Morales had taken her to the butterfly reserve to discuss research for her doctoral dissertation. She had been excited about the topic and he had encouraged her, and told her to consider the larger, international implications of the project. She had thought it odd he had chosen to take her at night, but Professor Morales had learned of a young man planning to cut timber. Morales hoped to divert him to work that wouldn't harm the butterfly reserve, maybe even pay him for logistical support to her research . . . to help him find a better future. She thought Morales had wanted her to see the compassion he had for the people who lived there.

Only it wasn't a boy who showed up. It was the cartel. Two men. Morales was killed, but diverted their attention long enough for her to slip away, into the darkness, hiding in the forest, avoiding being found. When her fear subsided, she found a church, and stayed hidden, telling no one what happened for fear of the cartel. Days later she caught a ride to Cuidad Mexico.

She was here to tell La Profesora that her husband had saved her life.

Angelica sobbed.

The man—Jack guessed him to be her husband's department

head or a university administrator—tried to console her, but soon fell quiet.

At last, Angelica stopped crying. "¿Que vas a hacer?" (What will you do?")

After a pause, the girl said, "Plaeo terminar mis estudios." ("I plan to end my studies.")

"Mi marido vio esa promesa en ti." ("My husband saw such promise in you.")

The girl did not respond.

After they left, Angelica stayed in the sitting room by herself.

Jack waited the better part of an hour, remaining quiet, giving her space. Finally, he stepped over to the door.

Curled up in a chair, knees tucked beneath her chin, tears streaking her face, La Profesora rubbed her eyes and looked up.

"What can I do for you?" he asked.

"Nothing . . . I'm a mess. I'm sorry."

"I couldn't help but hear. Don't apologize. I should leave . . . unless you need anything."

She nodded. "Can we continue tomorrow?"

Jack nodded. "Yes. You must remember the good he did."

She nodded, attempting to smile.

At the door, he paused, the gears in his mind jammed. "Tomorrow." He closed the door.

He strolled up the street and onto a sidewalk.

Damn. What a loss. Poor Angelica.

At the road to the hotel, he turned left instead of right, to wander, to think.

She'll be haunted by the way he died. Her husband, such a great guy. So dedicated to his work. For her, life, but never the same.

He stopped at a cafe, ordered a beer, nursed it until he felt ready to eat, then asked for tacos and another beer. He sat killing time and decided to give Kelly a call.

Her phone went to voicemail. No talking with the one person who could pull him out of a fog. "La cuenta, por favor," he said to the waiter, who produced the check. Jack left him a handful of pesos.

He started for the hotel to get his bag. A few blocks down

the road, a feeling of being followed settled over him. He stopped at a storefront. A travel agency. He turned as if to read the posts on the window. In the reflection, he noticed a man on the other side of the road, slow pace, looking his way. A Mexican man, wiry, dark clothes.

He let the man go past, then continued down the sidewalk.

Before reaching the hotel, he stopped again, this time at a store. Somewhere after the travel agency a switch had occurred. In the window reflection he saw Teague peering from behind a building.

Continuing to the hotel, Jack nodded to the doorman, the same as the day before.

Inside, he walked past the bell closet. *Need a plan. But what*? He passed through the lobby, stopping in the elevator alcove. He turned to watch. No Teague. Would he try, after what happened the day before?

Jack slipped across the hall, into the gift shop, taking his position behind the potted palm.

No Teague.

Then he showed, walking in with the ease and unfocused attention of someone returning to their hotel. He paused, as if remembering something he forgot. He approached the registration desk. A desk clerk slid down the counter to greet him. A different woman. Teague produced a stack of pesos, covering them with his hand, then leaned in, proceeding to make his request.

She glanced at his hand, typed on the keyboard of the nearest computer. She shook her head, then leaned into the screen, checked more closely. She shook her head again.

Teague glanced around, as if suspecting a trap, a look of confusion on his face. He turned back to the clerk. She typed in another query, and again shook her head.

Teague headed for the exit, pausing for the doorman to swing the door open.

The clerk watched him go, then glanced down, frowning as she picked up the single bill he'd left on the counter.

What could Teague be thinking now? He followed me in. He

has to know something's up. But what? Maybe he thinks he got what he needed. Maybe he thinks I'm leaving. But where did I go? Where will he go? Will he stake out the entrance, to see if I catch a cab to the airport? Will he think I'm traveling incognito?

Incognito.

Jack headed for the pool to kill some time and figure out what to do.

He stopped. That's it. He turned and crossed the lobby. He approached the blue-suited bell man with the receipt for his bag. As the man handed over the backpack, Jack slipped him a tip. "Gracias. Una cosa más."

"¿Sí?"

"¿A . . . un barbero?"

"¿Barbero?"

"¿Sí, y hay un otra puerta?"

The doorman smiled and broke out his English. "There is another door at the back of the building." He motioned Jack to follow, leading him through the lobby, past the pool, to a service door. "Un barber, dos calles abajo. Pepe's."

Barber, two streets down. Pepe's. Jack passed him more pesos, gave him an appreciative slap on the shoulder, then slipped out. The door closed behind him.

He crossed the parking lot, staying in the shadows of vans and larger vehicles, watching for Teague or his accomplice. Seeing neither, he slipped behind a departing bus, walking alongside it, then darting into an alley. The alley put him on the next street over. One more to go. The next alley ended at a road lined with small shops and cafes. Pepe's overlooked a small plaza.

Jack walked past Pepe's and plopped down on a bench, checking for anyone who might be following. After several minutes, seeing no sign of Teague, he approached the shop.

Inside, he took a seat.

The barber attended to an older man having his pompadour spruced up a bit. When finished, he spun the man around to the mirror and watched with pride as an approving smile hit the customer's face.

The customer left, the barber cleaned up, sweeping a path to his barber's chair, then turned to Jack. "Próximo."

Jack stood. "¿Pepe?"

He smiled, raising his arms, as if for an embrace. "A su servicio."

"Pepe, I want a shave. Un afeitado. Everything. My face, my head. Mi cara, mi cabeza."

The barber's smile melted. Confusion. "Tan bueno cabello."

"I know. It'll grow back." Jack looked in the mirror one last time before seeing it gone. *What the hell am I doing . . . to such a good head of hair*? He sat.

Pepe popped the cape, let it settle over Jack, then proceeded to buzz cut his hair down to stubble. Leaning him back, Pepe covered his head with a hot, steamy towel, then applied shaving cream. He pulled out his straight razor, shaved off the remaining stubble, and spun Jack around to see the result.

Pepe attempted a smile.

Jack stared. "Wow. Look how white my head is."

"¿Que?"

"Blanco. I'm gonna stand out like a sore thumb."

Pepe laughed. "Sí. La farmacia tiene bronceado en aerosol."

"Huh? ¿Que?"

"Aerosol." Pepe patted his head, then made the motion of spraying an aerosol can.

"Oh. Spray tan?"

"Sí, o ir a la tienda para estudientes de teatro." Pepe pointed out the window. "Al otro."

"Theater students?" Jack repeated. "What?" He looked across the plaza, at other shops. "¿Un tienda?"

"Sí." Pepe pointed. "Para estudiantes de la universidad."

Jack paid up and made his way across the tile-lined plaza. The storefront posted no name, only ornamentation. Sock and Buskin, the ancient masks of Greek Theater, or more accurately, Melpomene and Thalia, the muses of tragedy and comedy, were painted in gold on a window. A door stood open. A spry, older Mexico woman in a long, flowing dress, went about her work. Something about her suggested a very worldly woman.

He stepped in. "Speak English?"

"Yes."

"Makeup. Got my head shaved but didn't think about how white I'd be. Don't want to stand out like a sore thumb."

Covering her mouth, she let out a chuckle. "I see." She led him to a display of grease paint, studied his face a moment, then chose a hue. She handed him a plastic tube with a black screw top. "Do you need help with the first application?"

"Sure, if you don't mind."

"Come this way." She motioned toward a mirrored makeup table at the end of the aisle.

As Jack followed her back, his eyes were pulled to other theatrical wares. He stopped at a rack. Hair pieces. Beards of all kinds. Mustaches. A Fu Manchu.

She patiently watched, a smile forming.

Jack took down a pencil mustache, then the Fu Manchu, both wrapped in cellophane.

"Are you an actor?"

"No." He eyed the beard.

"What are you trying to do?"

He turned to face her. "Frankly? . . . I want to hide in plain sight."

"Then you don't want those." She took the mustaches and placed them back on the rack. "As an Anglo . . . you want something like this." She reached for a bushy brown mustache.

"Not very exotic."

"No. It's not. That and a pair of sunglasses . . . because your blue eyes stand out . . . and a change in posture, maybe a . . . ¿Cómo se dice? . . . a slouch . . . you'll blend into any crowd. You'll look like a tourist ready to get on the bus."

"The bus? I want to watch a guy without being seen." He caught the surprise in her eyes. "Nothing illegal . . . just . . . you know, like in a restaurant." The answer didn't seem to satisfy her.

"Don't worry."
"Hamberguesa."
Squinting, he asked, "What?"
"Order the hamburger."

Chapter

16

He walked out of the shop and into the sun, feeling overwhelmingly self-conscious. *Don't leave yet. Got to get used to this.*

He ducked into the café next door, feeling like a clown in vivid colors needing to go unnoticed. Taking a seat, he watched the eyes of a waitress as she approached. She exchanged pleasantries and hovered to take his order, a cup of coffee. No reaction that he could see to his grease-painted pate and newly acquired bushy mustache. Not that she cared.

The waitress turned to the kitchen.

A person plopped down at the seat across the table. It took a moment to realize who joined him. The theater shop owner, wearing a smile. "I thought I'd add to your cover by having a strange woman drawn to your now average animal magnetism. I assume this is not the restaurant you plan to case."

He laughed. "It's not. Gotta build up my confidence . . . see how people react."

"With a little time in the sun, you won't need the grease paint." She stood and shook a finger. "Remember, you promised I will not become a . . . ¿cómo se dice? . . . accomplice."

He arched a brow. "You won't, I promise . . . but what if there's treasure at stake? Are you waving off your cut of the booty?" He laughed.

She let out a slow, uncertain chuckle.

—'—

He approached the Palacio Hotel by way of the backstreets. Waiting until nearly sunset, he peeked in the window to assure the coast was clear. No Harper Teague. Only the desk clerk. The same young man. White shirt, black tie appearance.

Jack opened the door and stepped into the entry. Spanish tiles, freshly waxed. He paused, adopting his slouch. The muscles in his back tightened. *Can't do this for long.*

He sucked in a breath and stepped around the corner.

The young man looked up. "Buenos días."

"Buenos días." Jack said, glancing into the courtyard and seeing no one. He dropped his pack and leaned against the counter. "Un quarto, para Señor Smith. Juan Smith."

The boy moved to his computer before realization hit. He looked up and eyed the face before him. Confusion morphed into concern.

Jack laughed. "I thought I'd have a little fun with it." For the first time, he noticed the boy's name tag. Carlos. No last name.

Carlos forced a smile. "How did you . . . ?"

"Nice, huh?" Jack tested his fake mustache's adhesion. "Got a room for me?"

"Sí, but do I need to be worried? I am wondering what you are up to."

"I understand, but don't worry, I don't plan to do anything but watch. If he recognizes me . . . no big deal. Maybe he'll have a good laugh. But . . . he was the one following me . . . and I'm not sure why. I'm turning the tables . . . to see what I learn."

"You promise you won't do anything inappropriate . . . or illegal?"

"I promise. Is he still here?"

"Sí."

"Do I need to worry about him walking in on us now?"

Carlos glanced at the key cabinet. "No, he's in his room."

Jack eyed the cubby for room 24. No key. A paper, rolled up, held with a rubber band, jutting a few inches past the cabinet frame. "Can I use cash? Cash kinda goes with the disguise."

"Sí, you can pay with cash . . . upon departure . . . but we hold the room with a credit card."

"Sure, no big deal." He pulled a card from his wallet and slid it across the counter.

Carlos turned to the computer before picking up the card. "I assume it's not in your name, Señor Smith?"

"Correct. Consider it a loaner." He laughed. "From a guy I know."

Carlos picked it up and eyed the name. "Jack Chastain. Sounds fake."

Jack gulped. "It does?"

The young man laughed and slid the credit card into the card reader.

—·—

His room sat two doors down and across the hall from Harper Teague's. He slowed passing room 24, hearing voices—maybe the television, maybe Teague on the phone. He unlocked his own room, number 27, and peered inside. Homey. Not as modern as the rooms in the chain hotel monstrosity at the bottom of the hill, but more in keeping with the culture of Cuidad Mexico. He dropped his pack on the table, turned on his cell phone, and brought up Kelly's number.

She answered on the first ring. "I'll have to call you tomorrow. I'm in the middle of something. Getting Alex Trasker's take on what happened today."

"What happened?"

"A wild ass claim that money is flowing into campaign coffers for me from California and New York."

"You made your announcement?"

"No."

"Whose claim?"

"Hard to know. It's all over the airwaves. Television ads in Albuquerque and Santa Fe. Radio, all over New Mexico. Call me tomorrow."

—·—

The next morning, Jack left his room early to be in the courtyard before Teague's 9 a.m. arrival, picking a table in the opposite corner from his.

A dozen tables, half of them occupied. Mostly couples. Teague's preferred table sat empty, not reserved, but not in the most inviting of locations. Bright sun, no trees or greenery, set off to the side by itself. Clear lines of sight in all directions. He must have an arrangement with the hostess.

A young waitress, her black hair in a bun, brought coffee and took Jack's order of huevos rancheros. Waiting, he read the paper and watched for Teague over the top of his sunglasses.

Right on time, Teague arrived. Tucked under his arm, a newspaper. The one by his door.

Teague appeared just as Jack remembered him from a year or more ago. A little over average height, stout, dark serious eyes. Anxious. And wearing that mustard-colored ball cap.

The waitress brought him coffee. A few minutes later, she brought his breakfast. Not once did he make eye contact with her. His eyes remained locked on the newspaper, even as he ate. When he finished, almost on cue, another man arrived and took a seat. The same skinny man Jack caught following him the day before. Teague and the man exchanged words, Teague appearing to give him an assignment, but with uncertainty and irritated gestures. The man left, walking past Jack's table without so much as a glance his way.

Teague finished a cup of coffee and stood to leave. He looked around the courtyard, but seemed to see nothing, his mind elsewhere. Leaving his newspaper, he strolled toward the lobby.

Jack stroked the hair on his lip. *It worked. It really worked.*

He waited a few minutes before asking for his check. He paid the waitress and left the hotel through the lobby, nodding to the gentleman at the desk—an older, more filled-out version of Carlos, gray at his temples, clean shaven face.

Taking the same backstreets he'd used the night before, he crossed the main road, then found backstreets to Angelica's casa. Hovering beside bushes across from her house, he checked for onlookers. No skinny fellow. Jack approached her front walkway and pulled off the mustache. He knocked on the door.

It swung open. In slacks and a black silk blouse, she waved him in. "Buenas días," she said, before being jolted by the sight of him. Her eyes grew wide. "What did you do?"

He laughed. "I thought it might be cooler."

"You were hot? What will your Kelly think?"

"It'll grow back."

"What is on your head? It looks like . . . grease paint."

"You know grease paint?"

She led him into the office, eyeing his noggin. "I uh . . . have some, uh . . . thoughts on what we can research today."

She had checked out a couple of volumes from the university's special collections and brought them home, preferring to work here.

The volumes had communications between the Colonial Secretary in Vera Cruz and officials in Cuidad Mexico.

Angelica waded confidently through reports while Jack felt of little value in understanding the text. Archaic terms and expressions. Yet, he could look for names.

"Mí amor's department head called me yesterday afternoon with details he did not wish to dwell upon while with the grad student."

"Are you okay?"

"Sí. I didn't sleep well last night, but . . . I am okay."

He could see pain in her eyes, details tugging at her emotions.

"The main purpose of the trip was to educate the grad student about lowland forests, pine and oak, and their importance to preserving oyamel forest y la mariposa monarcha. They visited a café in Ocampo, mí amor's mas favorito, having decided not to visit Angangueo, their original destination. A waitress told them of a young man who would be logging that night. The student paid little attention, not realizing its importance until mí amor took her to the trail . . . at night."

"Oyamel, that's where the monarch winter?" Jack asked, acting oblivious, trying to distract her from going into painful details.

"Sí. They absolutely cover the trees of the preserve in orange wings."

"So, he was also trying to protect the lowlands outside the oyamel forests? Why the lowlands?"

"The pine and oak forests cool the air from Michoacan's warm western plains . . . rising upslope toward the oyamel forest. Deforestation threatens oyamel and the ground water table. It is a complicated issue."

"I'm sure."

She sighed and looked longingly out the window. "I remember the first time I heard mí amor talk about the work of so many to preserve la mariposa monarca and the oyamel. He was so impressed." She let out a sad little laugh.

"Why are you laughing?"

"Because, I listened, hearing every word, but I didn't like him . . . then. I saw him as an arrogant ass, someone who undoubtedly thought his work was more important than mine."

"So, this was before you two were together?"

"Yes. At the conference where we met. We were a panel, just the two of us."

"You, the Spanish colonial historian, and him, the ecologist?"

"Yes, and that was the point. Cultural versus natural. Or at least that is how I took it when I was asked to share the stage with the great Profesor Morales."

"A debate?"

"That's how I approached it. I went first, making every argument I could about priority being given to the preservation of Mexico's cultural heritage. Very protective. Dogmatic. I'm sure I looked ready to spit in his face, daring him to better my arguments."

"And him?"

Tears formed in the corners of her eyes. "He proceeded to make his point. Beautifully, about the tremendously diverse natural heritage of Mexico. Plants, animals, ecosystems. Then, abruptly, he changed course, and agreed with everything I had said, agreeing with the importance of our cultural identity, and going so far as to . . ." She wiped tears from her cheeks. ". . . apologize for even being so bold as to share the stage, . . . for attempting to offer arguments to put alongside mine. He apologized . . . for failing so miserably."

"What did you do?"

"I grew angry. I glared. I thought he was patronizing. Making fun of me." She sobbed and wiped again at her eyes. "Then, he said, something like, "May I make it up to you? May I offer retribution for my deficiencies? Take you to dinner to compensate your excellence and having to endure my failures?"

"In front of everyone?"

"Yes."

"What did you do?"

"I grew madder. Damned Mexican machismo. A wolf in lamb's clothing." She sniffled, wiping away another tear. "He was so charming, making me look like a jerk, before these people important to my future. I sat thinking I've ruined my reputation. People see me as a bitch."

"What happened?"

"Women in the audience started chanting. *Di que sí. Say yes.* Men joined in. I was embarrassed."

"And you said *yes*."

"What could I do? I had to get off that stage. We ate dinner in the hotel restaurant. People saw us. We were the talk of the conference. Everyone seemed so happy for us. No one seemed to remember what a bitch I had been. I accused him of doing what he did . . . to restore my reputation." She began to cry. "He denied it. Always did. He said he was under my spell." She laughed. "My spell. From that day forward, I was under his. I moved here from my beloved Vera Cruz to be with him, to live my fairy-tale life." She wiped her eyes. "Now it's over." She looked up, into Jack's eyes. "I'm sorry. You didn't want to hear that."

"I did." Jack nodded. "I love that story. A memory to find strength in."

She nodded, then scooted a book across the table. "Look." She tapped on an entry. "The Colonial Secretary reported an envoy . . . wanting to book passage on the Crown's ship to Spain."

"When?"

"1765."

Jack sighed. "That doesn't help."

"Not if you're wanting to disprove the possibility of treasure."

At the end of the day, Jack prepared to leave. "May I go out the back way? I want to lust for your BMW. After you scared the hell out of me on the streets, I may have to get one."

She laughed. "Want me to drive you to your hotel?"

"No, my heart couldn't handle it." He flashed a smile and slipped out the back door, onto a road that crossed his usual route. After two blocks, he took the first road north and followed the backstreets to El Palacio.

—·—

Mustache in place, Jack peeked in the window of El Palacio. No Harper Teague. Good. He slipped inside.

Carlos looked up. "Buenos días," he said, his expression morphing to wary.

"¿Como estas?" Jack asked, then whispered, "Is our friend still here?"

"He is." Carlos sighed. "Unfortunately, encuentro malo. Bad encounter today with him."

"Sorry to hear that. He might not be a fan, but I am. I also love this hotel."

"Gracias. Mi padre would be pleased."

"I saw your father this morning, after breakfast. You're a spitting image of the old man."

Carlos looked confused. "Old man?"

"Never mind. Your run-in with Teague . . . what happened?"

"I should not say." He shrugged. "A fax, he didn't get as soon as he would have liked."

"Who uses faxes these days?"

"Señor Teague. He doesn't use email when he's in Mexico. Doesn't trust it. He thinks someone might hack into his communications. I believe the word is paranoid."

"But faxes . . . that's interesting."

"According to my father . . . faxes are harder to intercept than emails. More secure."

"What about encryption?"

"I don't know. I don't ask questions. If Señor Teague wants to communicate by fax, it is not for me to question. I simply need to get him his faxes in a timely manner." He sighed. "But some of his faxes are silly. Like one word. *Go*, or *start*, or *now*. Others tell him to go places. When those arrive, he checks out and leaves, anytime day or night."

"Go where?" Jack caught himself. "Never mind. I shouldn't ask that."

"Most often the faxes send him to Michoacán. Recently, he had two faxes, sending him to Zitacauro and Angangueo . . . in the same week."

"Angangueo? I've heard of it," Jack said, more to himself. "Is that the butterfly reserve?"

"Sí, I believe so."

"Wow, what I would do to see *those*."

Carlos reached under the counter, produced a clipboard, and plopped it on the counter.

Faxes. A whole stack of them. "No, I meant . . . the reserve . . . to see the butterflies."

Carlos reached for the clipboard.

"Hold it," Jack said, placing a hand over the top page. "Why do you have these?"

"They're reports produced by our machine when we send or receive a fax."

"What for?"

"For billings. And for when someone challenges a room charge." He eyed the top page. "Señor Teague and whoever it is that communicates with him . . . they likely assume Señor Teague's is the only copy." He chuckled to himself, flipping back several pages. "This one sends him to Michoacán." He flipped another page and squinted at the miniaturized version of the transmission. "This one reads, 'Doc says to start the those other people treatment.'" Interest piqued, Carlos leaned in to take a closer look. "That's what it says, *the those. The those other people treatment.*"

"Typo."

"It's handwritten, but yes, an extra word." He laughed.

Tempted to flip the clipboard around to read it himself, Jack resisted, not wanting to violate Carlos' trust or get him in trouble. "Michoacán. Butterfly country," he muttered, just to say something.

"I cannot see Señor Teague being interested in mariposa monarca, but what do I know?"

—·—

In his room, Jack pulled up a map on his phone. Angangueo in Michoacán.

He checked the distance from Cuidad Mexico. Not exactly close. But not far either.

Chapter 17

Jack checked the time, then called Angelica, asking if she minded if he changed their plans for tomorrow. "I'd like to see the butterfly reserve."

"The peak of mariposa migration is past."

"I know, but still . . . I'd love to see the place, give you a break from all this silliness."

Heavy quiet settled over the moment. "Would you like me to drive you?"

"No, that would be difficult for you, I'm sure . . . after all you've learned. I'll take a bus. They leave once an hour from the central station. A cab to there, then . . . by bus to the reserve . . . there I can think about the importance of your husband's work."

"Very well, but I will not take a break. I thought of a new angle. I'll work on that. But . . . be careful, please."

"I'm a tourist. What trouble could I get into? I'll be back before sunset. Hey, where was that little cafe Profesor Morales loved so much?"

"Ocampo. A village between Zitácuaro and Angangueo. I don't remember the name, but it's on the road from Ocampo to El Rosario Reserve. You will need a guide in the reserve."

"Are guides hard to find?"

"At this time of year, maybe. Ask at the café."

—·—

He snuck out of the hotel before sunrise. The cab he called sat waiting at the curb. It got him to Terminal Poniente while still dark. There he bought a ticket for the next bus for Angangueo. Too dark to watch the landscape, he fell asleep, waking after crossing into Michoacán. The road lay in a wide valley between volcanic peaks, their range extending north to south. Through the windshield, he saw a town in the distance, maybe a small city. He checked the map app on his phone. Zitácuaro.

Out the side window, from the highway to the foothills, stood groves of evenly spaced trees interspersed with other farmland, though the groves were the most prominent feature.

The bus passed the industrial edge of the city, then entered Zitácuaro. At the station it off-loaded most of the riders, added a few, then departed for Angangueo on a twisting and turning road that connected several towns along the foot of the mountain.

He noticed a sign for the village of Ocampo, but chose to wait, wanting to check out Angangueo first, wondering what deserved Teague's attention.

Angangueo lay in a valley, along an ascending road that felt like an entry to the mountains. An old silver mining town, it bore its identity as both a center for past wealth and a mecca for those now seeking la mariposa monarca. Getting off the bus, he studied the town and got his bearings. The tower and dome of the Temple of the Immaculate Conception stood tall over Angangueo, the roads in this part of the little city narrow and cobbled. Evidence of past and future festivals hung on plastered walls and light posts. Houses on terraces sat above the main road, overlooking it all.

Why would Teague come here? What would he be doing? Carlos doesn't see him as a butterfly kinda guy. Agreed. Doesn't seem like a festival kinda guy either. So, why here?

Jack walked the cobblestone streets for half an hour, seeing nothing helpful. No clue as to what business would bring Teague this way. Twice in a week. '*Why did I think it might be obvious*?'

he asked himself. *With such sketchy information to start with. No way it's connected to Rivera. Or is it?*

His stomach growled. Okay, first breakfast. Then make plans for the day. But where?

He remembered Professor Morales' chosen café and caught the bus to Ocampo.

Smaller, not confined to a narrow strip of valley, Ocampo lay in a grid. He walked several blocks, finding a few cafes, but none he had confidence in concluding to be on the road to the butterfly reserve. He would have to guess the most likely, so he did, a cafe that looked fairly busy. Good sign.

He reached for the door handle, catching a shocking image in the glass, a bald man reaching his way. He glanced back, then laughed. A reflection.

Slipping in, he took a small table near the window. Throughout the cafe, chatter, most in Spanish but a few pockets of English, the tables around him taken by people at various stages of their meals. Several sat talking over cups of coffee. A few solo guests ate in silence.

A waitress in a blue apron brought him a menu. "¿Agua?"

He caught himself before risking Montezuma's revenge. "No, gracias. Solo café, y huevos rancheros, por favor."

"Buena opción." She picked up the menu and scurried away, returning with coffee.

"Speak English?" he asked her, and awaited a response, ready to attempt his Spanish.

"Yes. Some."

He took a sip of his coffee, holding the cup in both hands. "Is it true someone was killed here in recent days? Someone connected to la mariposa monarca?"

Her head bobbed, not a yes, not a no. "A man was killed, yes, but he was . . . how do you say, un forastero?" Struggling to find the word, it suddenly came to her. "Outsider . . . he was an outsider, here to cause trouble. You need not worry."

"It's safe to go to the reserve?" He took another sip.

"Yes, but you missed the migration."

"Really." Jack feigned disappointment. "Too bad. Wanted to see it. This man who died?"

"Do not worry."

"You said he was here to cause trouble. What kind of trouble?" Jack set down his cup.

"Esas otras personas. Telling us how to live our lives. Rich men in Cuidad Mexico paid him to cause trouble. Why? Only the rich know why they do such things. But, the man who died, he hoped to bring ill to our village."

"He was no troublemaker," Jack said, emotion taking charge. "He was a scientist. A researcher."

The waitress made no attempt to respond. Without checking his cup, she said, "I will bring more coffee." She departed.

In a few minutes, she returned with his food.

After she left, a voice, in a whisper, muttered, "He was set up."

Jack looked around. No eyes met his.

At the closest table, a man—dark hair, maybe Mexican, maybe not, in jeans and a plaid flannel shirt—head down, sat picking at food. He switched to his coffee, took a swig, and stared out the window. Then, he set the cup down and turned his eye back to his plate.

Jack glanced at the other tables. No eyes were on him.

"Don't look," the voice said, "Keep your voice and your head down."

Jack couldn't help it. He looked.

"Don't look at me," the man whispered, eyeing the window, holding his cup at his mouth.

Jack picked up a fork and glared at his huevos rancheros. "What happened?"

"Cartel."

"Cartel set him up?"

"No. They reacted to rumors."

"What rumors?"

"You heard the essence of it. That the professor isn't one of us. He's a troublemaker. Sent to control us, stop the farmers, that sort of thing."

"Who started the rumors?"

"No idea. Someone with an agenda."

"Why would the cartel kill him?"

"Control. Farmers pay protection money. A rumor like that gets started . . . farmers feel threatened . . . especially the new ones . . ." The man fell quiet, watching the waitress. He picked at his food and waited as she poured him coffee, then Jack, then moved to the other side of the room. He raised his cup to his mouth. "Cartel must have thought they needed to make good on protection . . . scare anyone threatening their control." He took a sip. "Obviously, not a tourist."

"I am. Just wandering through."

"But?"

"I knew the professor."

"Then be careful."

"How do I get to where he died?"

"Sure you want to do that?"

"I'm just a tourist. I want to see the butterfly reserve."

"You're kinda late."

"Depends on what you're looking for."

The man set down his fork and picked up his napkin. He wiped his mouth, holding it there. "Don't go to the end of the road . . . where tourists go. Go south at the big intersection. You'll know it when you see it. Go to the end of that road, take the trail. Stop at the overlook on open basalt." The man stood, eye on the window.

"How do I get there? I came on the bus," Jack said, head down, cup to his mouth.

The man stretched and gave his mouth another wipe with the napkin. "Use your thumb."

"Do I need a guide?"

"At this time of year?" He left pesos on the table and headed for the door.

—·—

Jack asked for his check and paid the waitress. "Is that the road to the reserve?" He pointed out the window.

"¿El Rosario? Sí."

He stood. "Gracias."

Out on the street he turned toward the mountains. After walking several blocks, he stopped at a sign that read, *Santuario El Rosario*. There he waited. In a few minutes, a green, banged up old pickup approached. He stuck out his thumb. The pickup slowed to a stop. The driver, his window down, gave his head a half turn.

Jack repeated the words on the sign, "Santuario El Rosario?"

The man—unshaven, gray, thin, the dark tan of a worker—nodded. "La mayor parte del camino." With his thumb, he pointed to the bed of the pickup.

Jack climbed in. *Most of the way, good.* He sat against the cab and watched Ocampo grow small in the distance as the pickup ascended the mountain. They passed farms, dwellings, forests of pine and oak, and openings with the same kinds of groves, in grids, he'd seen outside Zitácuaro. Big trees. Small trees. He squinted, not recognizing it. Citrus? Probably not.

He noticed a cardboard box, a few inches tall, near the tailgate, holding tools. On its side, one word most prominent. Avocados.

He looked back at the trees. *So that's why Teague came here. Avocados.*

The pickup wove through curves in the shadow of pine and oak, then emerged into full sun. Eyes on the road behind him, Jack noticed an intersection. It took a moment to register. Is it major? More than any another other he'd seen. He gave the roof of the cab two good slaps.

The man pulled to the side of the road and stopped, flashing a curious look.

"Gracias," Jack shouted, hopping the gunnel. He waved and watched the old man go, then hiked back to the intersection, taking the south road.

A few hundred yards in, past a scattering of houses and barns, he reached the road's end and the beginnings of a trail into the forest.

A mile or so farther, the trail merged with a two-track road from the west, climbing to higher country. Alongside the road, evidence of tree cutting. Stumps. Slash. The pine and oak gave way to fir, likely the oyamel. The road ended, leaving only the trail. After a trudge uphill, he stopped on open ground, and took in the scene. To the south, a volcanic peak and a trail appearing in an opening in the trees. To the north, a basalt rim, overlooking the slope down to the road. To the northeast, a band of oyamel forest. Farther, on the next mountain, El Rosario.

Professor Morales and his student were somewhere near here. Why? Because of a rumor about a young man coming to cut timber. Oyamel? Or Pine? Or Oak? Could be any of them.

He heard engine noise and the rumbling of tires on rocky ground. He turned toward the sound, seeing nothing because of the trees. Then it emerged. A pickup, newer than the one he'd ridden up the mountain. It stopped at the end of the two-track.

Two men climbed out, one wearing a hat, both stocky. The driver went to the front of the pickup, head down, eyes on the ground. He stopped, stood upright, and turned back to the other man, pointing. Both went back to the vehicle, pulled out their gear, and hit the trail. Jack lost sight of them in the trees.

Glancing at the ground, he noticed tracks, in addition to his own, in the dirt laying over the basalt. None seemed fresh, but still . . . must be a popular hike.

He pulled a bag of nuts and dried fruit from his pack, and nibbled as he studied the landscape, remembering Angelica's description of the ecology. The loss of downslope pine and oak increases the temperatures affecting the upslope oyamel forest, and even the ground water dynamics. Thus, Mexico intended to protect the area. To preserve what's left. Good for Mexico.

After a few minutes, he heard the sounds of the men on the trail. Boots on rock, lungs fighting for air. He kept his eyes turned away—a matter of habit, not intruding on the men's solitude.

He heard a few words between fights for breath.

A shot rang out.

Jack slammed himself to the ground. He looked back, over his shoulder.

The men stood at the edge of the clearing, one standing, one—the bigger man—stooping over his knees, gasping, holding a rifle. An automatic weapon.

The other man wore a brown fedora that cast a shadow over dark, angry eyes. "That shot . . . " he said, and paused to get a breath of his own. "That shot . . . was to get your attention." He stepped forward. "Before you die, tell us . . . do we have the right man?"

Jack's heart pumped. "Obviously not . . . I'm not him."

"I haven't told you who we're looking for."

Jack got to his feet. "I'm not him."

"Were you in the café in Ocampo?"

Jack held his tongue.

"Asking questions?" The man sucked in a breath. "About things of no concern to you?"

"I'm a tourist."

"Who came to see the mariposa . . . after the migration." He took another deep breath. "You are either not well informed, or here for some other purpose. Which is it?" He waited a moment, then smiled. "I believe you are here because of another man . . . a man who came to this very spot . . . a man who died . . . for reasons that don't concern you."

"I came to see butterflies. There are still a few, aren't there?"

The man gave a dismissive wave of his hand. "No."

"But I love butterflies." Jack froze, noticing for the first time—dried blood, dark, almost black, on the basalt on the rim. Holding still, eyes darting, he checked his options. To the right, open ground. Then up the mountain. *Never get there. They'll shoot.* Behind him, a run for the forest, a slog through downed limbs. *Wouldn't even make it to the trees before being cut down.* The only other option, over the rim. Jump. Hope for an incline and the chance to hit the ground running. If no incline, maybe break a leg, but if not, a chance to get to the trees before he takes a shot. Jack eyed him.

The big man managed to stand upright, still fighting to catch his breath.

"Why are you here?" asked the man in the fedora.

Do it now, before the one with the gun catches his breath. Jack took two steps and jumped, dropping below the rim. He could see where he would land. Sloping ground, covered with duff. Fir trees and rock all around.

He hit ground, left leg absorbing the shock, right leg ready to move. His feet slipped on duff, momentum carrying him downslope. He slid a past an oyamel and stumbled over a rock, sending him flailing. Dropping to his rear, he slid to a stop, then rolled into the shade of an oyamel.

He took a deep breath, regulated his breathing, and listened.

Above, shouting.

Run? No. To run is what they expect. Never make it to the trail. Never survive if you do. Not in the open. They'd cut you down. What would be a good weapon? A rock? He noticed a broken branch, three inches in diameter. A Louisville Slugger. He picked it up and gave it a swing. *It'll have to do.*

Above, confusion. Orders shouted. *They'll probably go down the trail, try to cut me off.*

Through foliage, he saw the man with the gun appear at the rim, staring over gun sights.

The other man stopped alongside him. "Vamos. Cazarlo."

Hunt him down? Jack moved farther under the tree.

"Vamos," the man in the fedora ordered, then did something unexpected. He pushed the other man over the edge.

The big man hit ground and tumbled head over heels, coming to a stop in brush at the base of a tree. Fighting obvious pain, he forced himself to his feet, rifle at his side.

The man above hollered, unable to see where his compadre landed.

Moving fast, Jack stepped out from behind the tree, heart pounding. He swung the branch, catching the big man on the back of the head. He dropped. Out like a light. The rifle lay beside him, its strap still slung over the big man's neck.

Get the rifle.

Before he could, he heard the other man's voice. A different location.

"¿Cosiguele?" the man shouted.

Did he get me? No, he didn't. Jack slipped behind the tree and listened for where the other man would appear. Within moments, rustling came from across the slope.

The fedoraed man appeared. "¿Cosiguele?" he repeated.

Jack slipped behind the bole of the tree, in shadow.

The man saw his compadre. "Tonto torpe," he grumbled, angry words. He lurched across, slipping on duff. Reaching the other man, he knelt to pick up the weapon, and tugged at the strap, trying to free it.

Jack stepped out from the tree and drew back on his bat. He sent it helicoptering toward the man in the fedora, ready to rush him if it missed. It didn't. It slammed his head and ricocheted into the brush. The hat went flying. The man dropped, sliding headfirst downslope. He crashed into a rock.

Both men lay motionless.

Hope they're not dead. Jack crept toward them, ready to pounce. Both men, face down, would be out cold for who knows how long. He pulled the rifle strap out from under the big man's shoulder. He saw no weapon on the other guy, but noticed the back pocket of his jeans. The faded outline of a wallet. He slipped it out and thumbed through the contents. Among them a driver's license. Jack chuckled. "Hola, Umberto. Who would have thought killers like you would carry a driver's license? Maybe it's fake." He slipped it into his own pocket, returned the man's wallet to his, then checked the other man. He too had a wallet. And a driver's license.

With the men still out cold, Jack headed across the slope, carrying the rifle. Finding the trail, he went back to the overlook to get his pack.

One last thing before leaving. He disassembled the rifle and smashed its components with a rock, limiting his handling of the stock, trigger and trigger guard, preserving any remnants of the big man's fingerprints. Then, using the tail of his shirt and a splash of water from his canteen, he washed away his own. At the edge of the clearing, opposite the trail, he hid most of the rifle under a log. The gun barrel, now bent, he sent flying, downslope, into the trees.

Try finding that.

He took one last look out over the oyamel, pausing in reverence at the dark stain of blood.

Then, he picked up his pack.

Time to get out of here and onto the next bus to Cuidad Mexico before these guys wake up and talk to their friends.

Chapter 18

Jack waited in the shadows not far from the bus stop, not wanting to be seen by anyone even remotely resembling the waitress or the old man in the pickup, or a member of the cartel. He doubted the old man had anything to do with it and who could say what cartel members even looked like, but at this point he felt he could say about as well as anyone. He doubted it was the man in the restaurant. It was likely the waitress. If not her, someone she knows, someone she talked to.

Don't think about that. Just get the hell back to Cuidad Mexico.

The bus to Angangueo appeared. He started to ignore it, but a realization settled over him. First things first. Cover your tracks. Get out of here. Don't wait for the bus to Zitácuaro. Stepping out of the shadows, he waved it down, then settled in for the short ride to Angangueo. There, he took a quick walk, circling several blocks, glancing back on occasion, checking for a tail. As one last precaution, he strolled into a hotel, as if to get a room, passing through the lobby, into a breezeway, staying several minutes to see if anyone followed. Seeing no one, he headed for the bus stop, taking a backstreet.

The bus sat at the curb, no line yet forming. He saw a gap between buildings and slipped in, waiting, eye on the bus. He pulled out his cap, slipping it over his now sunburned head. Then, his jacket. One last measure, his pack—he would not wear it. Instead, he would carry it like a bag. Anything to look different. *Damned mustache . . . shoulda brought it.*

The driver strolled out of a café and stepped up into the bus. A line formed. Jack crossed the roadway, head down, and joined the line pulsing onto the transport.

He picked a seat near a gray, grandmotherly-looking woman who huddled against the window to herself. He threw his pack in the overhead and plopped down. The bus began to roll. It would be difficult to relax until it crossed the state line out of Michoacán.

Countryside flew past the window.

What am I doing in Mexico? Here because of some crazy rumor about gold. Then, I come to Michoacán, because of something even crazier, and unrelated. Almost gets me killed. All because of Teague, who may be simply wondering what the hell I'm doing here.

The murder of Professor Morales, how would Teague be involved? Not likely, unless he's wrapped up with the cartel, which wouldn't be smart. But . . . could he?

Bottom line, it's all a distraction. Nothing to do with disproving—or proving—the rumors of Juan Rivera and treasure, or Potts Monroe's involvement.

I should be in Piedras Coloradas, helping to put finishing touches on the coalition report.

The bus came to a stop in Ocampo. Jack kept his head down. Then on to Zitácuaro, and the state line into the Estado de Mexico. They reached Cuidad Mexico before sunset.

Jack took a cab to the hotel, having it drop him off on a backstreet. He trudged up to the front window and peeked inside. No Teague. Opening the door, he slipped inside.

Sitting in the back room, Carlos turned to the sound of footsteps. "Buenos días."

"Buenos días." Jack paused at the counter. "Our friend still here?"

Carlos nodded.

—'—

In the morning, Jack went to the courtyard, mustache in place, a thin layer of grease paint now hiding red, not white skin. Choosing a different table, a little closer to Teague's, he waited and read his newspaper, finishing breakfast before Teague made his appearance. Hiding behind the paper, he watched as two men came in from the lobby. The skinny, middle-aged man, and a more sophisticated-looking younger man, in well-fitted clothes and a fedora.

Hope that fedora's not a sign of something.

He could not hear many words as they conducted their business, but he recognized uncertainty, anxiety, and Teague's verbal chest thumping. Teague scribbled on a napkin, straight lines one direction, then straight lines for another. A grid. Circles and taps on the napkin. Teague giving assignments. *They haven't given up looking.*

Yesterday must have thrown them. Why don't they assume I've gone home?

They concluded their planning and departed. Jack sipped at his coffee, then left by the same exit, the lobby. Carlo's father, at the hotel desk, offered a *buenos días*. Jack replied likewise and slipped out the door, making sure no one waited outside. He made a wider loop on the backstreets, checking for followers. Before reaching the main road, he made a call.

"Angelica," he said, when she answered. "Are we on for today?"

"Yes. How were your travels?"

"Tell you when I get there. I'm coming in the back way . . . don't be frightened."

Slow to respond, she muttered, "This has nothing to do with my car, does it?"

"I love your car. I'll see you in a few minutes."

He made a wide loop along backstreets, then found an alley, staying close to walls, out of sight of windows. He saw no one. No Teague. No skinny, older guy. No man in a fedora. Must be staying close to the main road.

He rounded a corner and saw the back of Angelica's casa. Ducking into vegetation, then crouching behind her car, he approached the back door.

He gave it three knocks. She opened the door immediately. He slipped in. She closed the door and locked it, her hands shaking.

She turned, putting her back to the door. "What is going on?"

Jack sighed. "I don't really know. I'm confused by it myself," Jack said, giving his best performance of calm. "I've been followed the whole time I've been here."

"You didn't tell me?"

"Didn't know at first, and still don't know why. Could be, they're just as surprised to see me here as I am to see them."

"You know them?"

"One. Turns out, he spends quite a bit of time here."

"So you went to the mariposa reserve to see if they followed you?"

"No, but to see if I could find clues as to what they're up to."

"Something to do with the mariposa?"

He shrugged. "I don't know. I came here because of the Juan Rivera rumors and Potts, so I wondered if their following me was about that . . . but what I've learned is . . . the main guy has a reason for being here, and surely has no connection to Juan Rivera."

"So why are they following you?"

"Don't know."

"Are they following you now?"

"I think they tried."

She broke into tears. "So, why go to the reserve?"

"One of the men . . . the one calling the shots . . . he was called to Angangueo and Zitácuaro twice in the same week, two weeks ago."

"How did you learn that?"

"Desk clerk at the hotel. Don't worry, he's a good source. But . . . at the monarch sanctuary . . . I learned a little." He pulled the cards from his back pocket and offered them to her.

"What are these?"

"Take them."

She glanced the cards. "¿Licencia de conducer?"

"Yes, driver's licenses. What I learned, I learned from those guys."

"Who are they?"

"They're the men who killed your husband."

She gasped, eyes wide. She studied the cards. "How do you know that?"

"They told me . . . as they were telling me their plans to kill me. Whatever you do with those cards, be careful. Those guys are cartel."

A card in each hand, her eyes went from one to the next. "How did you get these?"

"Borrowed them."

"But they wanted to kill you. How . . . did you . . . ?"

"Let's say . . ." He attempted a smile. ". . . in the wild, I have home field advantage."

"You're not from Mexico." Confused, she did not get the joke. "What did you do?"

"In so many words, . . . I left 'em in the forest, out cold. Hid their rifle. Unless I killed 'em, they're gone by now. If the police search the scene, they'll find a rifle . . . an automatic weapon . . . in parts . . . hidden. Got carried away disposing of the barrel, but if the police look, they'll find it." He noticed her hands shaking. "Let's change the subject."

"How did you find them?"

"They found me. I must've asked a few too many questions at the café in Ocampo."

She stood shaking. He guided her into her office, where books sat stacked on the table and on the desk. She took her seat, her mind elsewhere.

Jack picked up a book, a scrap of paper jutting from between pages. "What are we looking for?"

"No," she said. "No yet. These people following you . . . are they cartel?"

"I don't think so."

"Then, why are they following you?"

"I don't know. I wondered if it was the Rivera treasure rumor, but I really don't know."

She turned, staring into a back corner.

Minutes passed.

Jack broke the silence. "Now . . . you can tell me something."

"What?"

"What's with avocados?"

"What do you mean?"

"A man I talked to in Ocampo . . . said the Cartel was reacting to rumors . . . somehow related to farmers . . . not drugs, not drug running, but farmers . . . especially young farmers. Said the cartel requires them to pay protection money. The only thing I could see being farmed in any abundance was avocado . . . at least I think it was avocado."

"It was, yes."

"Why would the cartel be there if it's not drugs? Why farmers? Why would they be concerned about a butterfly biologist?"

"Cartel are into more than just drugs. Avocados are called *green gold*. Markets keep growing, especially in los Estados Unidos, the U.S.A. There is pressure to put more land into production, to keep growing the market. Avocado farms and timber cutting are the two great threats to the mariposa reserve. Protections are in place, but other forces are at play, . . . people who know how to game the system, get others to take the risks."

"Risks?"

"The risks and the effort involved in starting a farm. The risk of government attention."

"Attention?"

"There are protections, but things work differently here than in the U.S. It is not uncommon for young men to feel encouraged to clear land for avocado production . . . to do the work, to take the risks, then, when they are out of money . . . broke, before the plantation can earn any real profit . . . someone else comes in, maybe a wealthy, established landowner, or an international corporation, maybe even the cartel . . . but . . . they come in, give the poor farmer an offer he cannot refuse, and he sells. Then, the cycle starts over, somewhere else."

"And the avocados end up on a truck to the U.S.?"

"Yes, except not there. Not yet."

Jack shot a look of confusion. "Why?"

"The plantations around Zitácuaro are not yet able to ship to U.S. markets. They want to, but haven't yet satisfied USDA requirements."

"Then why the demand?"

"There are many markets, but avocado value increases when shipped to the U.S.A. The demand there is unquenchable. Seven percent of annual production goes to satisfying desire for guacamole at your Super Bowl parties. Then there's the growing demand for avocado toast. Healthy food for you. Environmental costs—to forests, the diversity of wildlife—for Mexico."

"Then why not stop it?"

"Because it brings economic benefit to many. And many more wish to share in those benefits. But . . ." She glanced at the window, almost involuntarily.

He leaned closer.

"Where there is money, cartels find opportunity."

"But the butterfly . . . that is opportunity, too, right?"

"Yes. Sustainable opportunity. Tourism. But that pales compared to green gold. Much land is burned, intentionally, to bypass Mexican protection laws, using another law that allows producers to change land use to commercial agriculture if lost to fire."

"So, suddenly, out of nowhere, spontaneous combustion. A forest fire."

"Yes, and with the opening of the forest, higher temperatures, and dryer. Erratic rain."

"And that's a trend the cartel intends to protect."

"Many wish to protect that trend, including multinational corporations, some based in the U.S.A. It is not a simple thing to fix."

Jack sighed. "The man following me has a business card, says he's an avocado broker, though I know him in New Mexico not for that. In fact, I've never understood what he does."

Her eyes grew wide.

"And since the reason I'm here has nothing to do with avocado, there's a chance he's even more surprised at seeing me. I saw him in New Mexico recently, so this may have something to do with the Rivera rumors, but . . . now I'm not sure." He let his eyes fall on the stack of books on the table. "What've you found?"

"Nothing."

"What about all these scraps of paper?"

"In that stack, things I saw that might yield information in another book." She turned to her desk, and two smaller stacks. "In that one . . ." She pointed at the stack on the right. "Books from the university's special collections. In the other, my books. Neither yielded anything. Other than the reference I found to passengers booked for one of the Crown's ships to Spain."

"What can I do to help?"

"Nothing. Maybe tomorrow, we can go online and take another look at the digital collections in Vera Cruz but . . . after everything you've told me, I'm feeling fragile. I'm not sure of my powers of concentration. I'm sorry."

"Don't be. My fault. Maybe I shouldn't have told you."

Shaking her head, she muttered, "I needed to know." She glanced at the driver's licenses lying on the table. "I'll be careful with these. I know someone who can give me advice."

Jack stood. "Rest. I'll come back tomorrow. I'll see myself out."

"No, you will not. I need to lock the door behind you."

—'—

Jack ducked behind the BMW, then behind a hedge running the length of the driveway. From there, he headed the opposite direction from El Palacio Hotel, finding a mercado where he could kill a little time. Catching Kelly at lunch, he made small talk over the phone but shared few details from his last forty-eight hours. She would only worry. She didn't need that. Not now anyway.

Someone was still putting out misleading radio and television political ads and she had no idea who, or why, but they continued. She ended the call to run to the floor for a vote.

After a beer at a cafe, Jack put on the last of his disguise, the mustache, and followed the backstreets to El Palacio.

He peeked in the window. Guests stood registering at the

desk, a middle-aged couple, their bags on the floor behind them. Carlos kept a smile on his face as he transacted business. Maybe old friends, or regular customers, or Carlos being Carlos. After he reached back and pulled a key from the cubby, the new guests headed toward the courtyard.

Jack slipped in.

Carlos looked over. "Buenos días."

"Buenos días." Jack approached the desk. In nearly a whisper, he said, "I know I shouldn't ask . . . but . . . the faxes our friend receives. Do they ever mention avocados? Or cartel? Or anything like that?"

"No, I do not remember seeing such things. But it is no business of mine." He gave a sheepish grin. "It is rare for them to have much detail at all."

"Really?"

"I can show you." He glanced toward the door, then the courtyard, then reached under the counter, retrieving the clipboard. "He is such an ass," Carlos said, as if to himself. "Insists that faxes be delivered right away, but he had nothing but profanities when I delivered this one, minutes after its arrival." He scanned the top page on the clipboard. "As if blaming me for what it says. This one . . ." He eyed the message. "Interesante." Spinning around, he checked Teague's cubby. A white envelope jutted out. "Must have arrived with Padre here . . . me running errands."

"What is it?" Jack asked.

"Tickets. He's being sent to Madrid. Tomorrow."

Jack glanced at the fax. "Madrid?"

Carlos gave him an uneasy stare. "If you'll excuse me, I have work I need to complete." He handed Jack his room key, then pulled the envelope from Harper Teague's cubby. "If you'd like me to leave a message for your friend, address it as this person has done. I will deliver them both tonight." He disappeared into the back room.

Jack picked up the envelope. Unsealed. He pulled out the contents. Two tickets. The first to Madrid, Spain. Before checking the second, he realized that contents included a passport. From Saint Lucia. Jack stared. *Why would Teague's passport be from*

Saint Lucia? He flipped open the cover. Teague's picture. Jack felt a tremor in his hands. He glanced at the courtyard. No prying eyes. His were the only ones doing any prying. He returned the contents to the envelope.

The clipboard. Carlos had also left *it* on the counter. Jack slid to the end of the registration desk, pulling the clipboard with him. Behind the cover of potted plants, he turned it toward him. A record, not the fax itself. A miniaturized version of the contents. Jack quickly read it. Teague was to go to Madrid to make an exchange. But the second ticket was not the return trip as he expected. Instead, it was to Paris. The fax had airlines and flight numbers.

He wanted to ask Carlos for paper and pen to make a few notes, but that would be inappropriate. Carlos was taking a risk as it was. And Jack could not stand here all night. He pulled out his phone and snapped a shot of the fax. He turned to leave but stopped. Flipping through the faxes, one by one, he made quick work of photographing each fax to and from Harper Teague, Room 24.

The oldest, four months old. Simple message. *Don't use email.*

That explains a lot.

Jack turned the clipboard around and pushed it back to where Carlos had left it. "Gracias," he said, in a shouted whisper. Then, he slipped away to his room.

Chapter 19

Jack stared at the picture, the latest fax, sending Teague to Madrid. An exchange. Strange. Maybe a connection to treasure in New Mexico.

If Juan Rivera's journal was found in Spain, maybe Teague has someone there doing research. Maybe they found something. But Paris? Why Paris? And who is pulling his strings?

Or maybe it has nothing to do with any of that. Maybe it's about butterflies or avocados.

He slid a finger across the screen, pulling up another picture. Another fax. Vague words.

Put it in play.

What does that mean? He checked the date. Probably the fax Teague had gotten mad at Carlos over . . . he wanted this sooner. *Why?* He flipped to the next photo, expecting the one Carlos had read him a few days before. Different fax, not the one with '*the those*.' Instead,

Not your doing. Move on.

Two faxes earlier, he found it, the hurried message with the extra word.

Initiate the those other people treatment.

He flipped to the next fax in chronological order. One sent from Teague.

Unintended consequence from Doc's plan. Problem fixed too permanently.

To which the response had been the message he'd just read,

Not your doing. Move on.

Jack checked the dates. Three faxes, all in the last two weeks. Is it a coincidence that they come before and after the death of Professor Morales?

Jack flipped through the faxes. No way to tell. *Why are the messages so damned cryptic? Why can't they say what they mean?*

Because, then you'd know what they're doing.

What are they doing? He reread Teague's fax.

Unintended consequence from Doc's plan. Problem fixed too permanently.

Who's Doc? And who sends these faxes? He checked the tiny little capture of the phone number on the edge of one of the faxes. Toll free . . . but, why does the number look so strange. He counted. One too many digits. *How can that be? Not a Mexico thing. Angelica's number is ten digits, same as mine. Maybe some sort of strange country number, registered to who knows where?*

Too weird.

He scrolled back to today's fax. *Could be nothing. Could just be an avocado broker going somewhere to expand his market.*

But with a passport from Saint Lucia? To do that why would he need a passport from Saint Lucia? Teague is American if I've ever seen one.

Jack opened the phone's browser and googled *Saint Lucia passport.* Buried in the details, an interesting fact. For $100,000 a passport and citizenship can be bought.

Why?

Why would they do that and why would he need it?

While he had the browser open, he checked last minute fares for empty airline seats. Departing city, Mexico City, destination, Madrid. A list of flights popped up. He cross-checked the list with the airline and flight number in the photo of Teague's ticket. *Bingo.* Iberia, departing early afternoon, arriving mid-morning the next day. No way he wouldn't see Jack. On an airplane? Tailing him . . . in an airport? Jack checked the fare. Three hundred bucks, one way. Better than expected.

Gonna do it or not? He pulled out his credit card and made the purchase.

Then, for the short flight to Paris on Air France.

He closed the browser and plugged in the phone to charge. It would need a good one.

Craziest thing you've ever done, he couldn't help thinking.

Better get some sleep.

—·—

Sitting at breakfast, Jack watched Teague hold court over his minions, the pressure seemingly gone, orders cursory at most. He dismissed them and turned his attention to eating.

He thinks I'm back in the States.

Jack scratched an itch under the mustache, causing one side to come loose. He raised his newspaper and pressed it back into place, then checked his sunglasses.

Watching Teague, he remembered being plagued by him in New Mexico. Maybe more than he knew. A ghost hiding in plain sight, and possibly before that in Montana. The games Teague played so openly, politics to drive the coalition apart, a convincing act as a right-wing activist fighting for freedom. Then, in the oddest of coincidences, an unlikely courier in Kenya carrying a rhino horn to a powerful Congressman beholden to someone. Someone seeking favors from a Saudi prince.

Teague sure gets around.

And he's a ghost to the park's investigative ranger, Luiz Archuleta.

A trail that starts and ends in New Mexico, with crumbs popping up in Montana, otherwise nothing but fairy dust. Connections to events, seemingly coincidences. Now, Mexico, the strangest of all. Some kind of game, but what? Does his time here have more to do with butterflies or Juan Rivera and gold? He knew I was here. There's no way Teague would've stumbled onto me by accident.

How does a guy who looks like a bump on a log get in so much trouble around the world? Without leaving a trail?

A passport from Saint Lucia might help.

Teague finished his meal, folded his paper and stood. He pulled on his cap and stretched. Glancing around the courtyard, his eyes fell on Jack.

Jack froze, heart thumping, head locked, as if reading the newspaper.

Teague's eyes moved to the next table. Two Mexican cuties.

His eyes lingered, a smile forming, then he walked through the jardin to his room.

Jack sipped the last of his coffee, then dragged his backpack out from under the table. He headed to the lobby to check out, sauntering up to the registration desk.

Carlo's father stood at attention, the ever-disciplined innkeeper.

"Checking out," Jack said, handing him the key. "Love your hotel. Hate having to leave."

"Gracias," he said, staring into the computer monitor. "We anxiously await your return." He squinted. "Okay, Señor . . . Smith."

Jack felt a shot of adrenalin. *Damn, forgot about the alias.*

"I see . . ." His eyes moved across the screen. "Uh . . . that you've been with us three nights. Is that correct?"

"Yes," Jack said, not exactly certain, after the blur of the last few days.

"And will we be using the credit card we have on file?"

Has he seen the name? "Yes, please."

The printer pulsed out two copies and Carlo's father presented one for signature. Not a word. Either he didn't notice, or one doesn't question such things. Jack signed.

"Your copy," he said with an obligatory smile. "We look forward to your next visit."

"Count on it." Jack picked up his day pack and slipped the copy into the top pocket.

"You are traveling light, señor."

"Always do." He pulled out an envelope. "Almost forgot. Your son . . . extremely helpful."

"Is he now? I'm so pleased." His father's smile changed. A different smile. Authentic.

"You should be." Jack slid him the envelope, addressed to *Carlos.* Inside, two U.S. twenty-dollar bills and a vague but appreciative note, signed, Señor Juan Smith. "Buenos días."

Outside, he made his way to the backstreets, following the same route he took the day before. The same precautions.

Angelica answered the door as quickly, her eyes tired. "Adelante . . . come in."

"Have you been digging through books?"

"Yes."

"Find anything?"

"No."

"Then stop." He slipped in, letting her close the door. "I've put you through too much." Keeping his pack on, he hovered at the door. "I can fly home today. I can quit putting this burden on you. I've prolonged your pain, especially yesterday."

"No, dear Jack, I'm not asking you to go. There are angles we can check in the digital collections in Vera Cruz."

"I'm sure we won't find anything."

"Why so pessimistic?"

"You don't have the look of someone who's optimistic. It's just . . . look at the toll this is taking on you. My revelation yesterday didn't help. And Potts . . . his reputation. I'm not sure of what we could find that would help . . . but I'll continue to defend him. If I hear anything at home, I'll let you know."

"But. . . ."

"It's okay. Thank you."

"Your gratitude is unnecessary. Thank you for getting me

answers . . . about mí amor . . . and for showing such concern for my friend." She paused. "When you see him, tell him I will join him next field season. I will need something to occupy my mind." Tears appeared in the corners of tired, hopeless eyes.

Don't drag this out. "I will. I'll tell him." Jack smiled. "Thank you," he said again, then slipped out the door.

Emerging from the hedge at the end of the driveway, he turned onto the back street.

Now, one last stop.

—'—

Jack glanced down the aisle of hairpieces and fake noses, as the proprietor approached, having heard him come in the door. "Hola, señora." Eyeing the merchandise, he dropped his pack to the floor.

The gray-haired, matronly woman wore a long, multicolored skirt and matching vest over a white blouse. South American look?

"Hola," she said. "Am I an accomplice to serious crime?" She flashed a crooked smile.

"Not yet. Maybe after today."

—'—

Jack approached airport security. Not seeing Teague, he got into the line as it inched forward. Once at the front, a security agent signaled him forward.

"Pasaporte."

Jack handed it to him.

"Boleto o tarjeta de embarque."

He handed him the phone, his boarding pass showing on the screen.

The agent eyed the screen and handed the phone back, turning his attention to the passport, glancing between the passport photo and the top of Jack's head. "Pelo . . . tu cabello."

"Shaved it." Jack forced a laugh.

The agent let out a chuckle and handed back the passport. He waved Jack through.

After screening his bag, Jack headed down the corridor to the gates, head down, still seeing no sign of Teague.

Time to add another part of the disguise. Be a different person, the theater shop owner had said. He pulled out a pair of eyeglasses—dark frames, gray tinted lenses. The same rules as before. Keep it simple. Hide in plain sight. Dark frames will make you a different person. Gray lenses to hide the blue eyes. She had selected a lesser mustache and told him to use it sparingly. And another, should he need to change personas yet again.

Near the gate, he slipped into a bar, ordered a beer, and watched the boarding area.

He spotted Teague near the door to the jetway, wearing a gray sport coat over a baby blue polo shirt. Reading nothing. Talking to no one. Checking his watch every few minutes.

A gate agent made an announcement over the public address system. The only word Jack could make out was Madrid. He watched as Teague and a small group formed a line. Everyone else stayed seated. Must be in first class.

Teague disappeared through the door.

Leaving pesos on the table, Jack sauntered toward the gate. The easy part was over. Now the difficult part. *Hard to miss with him at the front of the plane.*

Jack got in line and began his shuffle forward. Once on the jetway and nearing the cabin door, he dropped his shoulders and assumed his back-hurting stoop. Head down, he stepped on board, turned down the aisle, and—seeing Teague to his left—faced straight ahead. For a moment it seemed Teague looked his way. Would a bald man with glasses trigger a memory? Nearing his seat, he slipped off his pack and put it in the overhead. He gasped. *My pack! He could have recognized my pack from the streets of University City.*

Jack dropped into his seat on the aisle. Hiding behind the man in the next row, he watched first class. Teague seemed intent on looking out the window.

Hold it. I never took my pack to Angelica's. Except this morning.

A flight attendant handed Teague a drink.

You're thinking too hard. Teague's not looking for a backpack.

After takeoff Jack settled in and read the novel he'd gotten at the first hotel. When the lights were turned off, he slept. Cat naps. With a long flight to Madrid, he would get several.

—'—

The jet landed at Madrid-Barajas Adolfo Suarez Airport and taxied to the terminal. When stopped, the flight attendant popped open the door and Teague quickly departed. Jack stood in the aisle, waiting his turn to disembark. The consequence of taking coach. *Now I could lose him.* Tapping his toes as the forward rows emptied, he waited, pack in hand, along with the customs form passed out by the flight attendants. When his turn came, he dashed up the jetway and jogged through the concourse under the rippled roof of the airport, finally seeing a stout man in a gray sport coat. Teague.

Slowing, Jack trailed at a distance, watching Teague amble through the concourse. Please, Teague, make the exchange in the airport. Teague turned toward immigration, pulled out his passport and chose a line.

Damn. Jack watched, then chose a different line. Quickly processed, Teague started down the hall to baggage claim. When finished, Jack hurried into the hallway. No Teague.

Catch him at customs. Jack started to jog, rounding a corner in time to spot Teague slapping a customs form down on a counter, without stopping, then turning toward the sign for the exit. *Salida.*

No bags? Teague's making an exchange but has no bags?

Jack jogged to the exit, following Teague's lead, placing his form on the counter.

"Detente ahi," shouted a uniformed customs agent.

Past the gate, Jack turned. "Nothing to claim. Nada que reclamar."

The agent nodded, waving Jack on.

He dashed to the terminal door.

Teague stood outside, taking in the day it seemed. He strolled to the curb, glanced right, then left, then walked left.

Jack watched. *Please don't make this hard, Teague.*

A hundred yards down, Teague crossed two lanes of road to a center island packed with people.

Jack slipped out and followed, staying on the sidewalk alongside the terminal, parallel to Teague. Teague walked past lines of waiting people.

If someone is picking him up, I'll lose him for sure.

Teague approached a man in a reflective yellow vest.

After an exchange of words, the man turned to a line of taxis. He waved the first one forward, a white cab with a diagonal red stripe on its side. It stopped at the taxi stand. The attendant opened the rear passenger-side door, leaned in, saying something to the driver, then stepped back. Teague slipped in and the taxi bolted into traffic.

Jack watched it round a curve and disappear.

Chapter 20

Now what?

Jack started back to the terminal.

What a stupid idea. Waste of time and money.

Why did you think you could make this work? But . . . you're giving up.

He turned and dashed across the road, across oncoming traffic. Horns blared.

The taxi attendant saw him coming. "¿Necesitas un taxi?"

"Sí. ¿Habla Inglés?"

The attendant shrugged. "Un poco."

"You just put my friend in a taxi. That last man. He forgot his papers. Do you know where he's going?"

"Barrio de Salamanca."

"Some kind of business district?" Jack asked. *A place an avocado broker would go?*

"It is many things."

Jack shifted his weight from foot to foot. "Near here?"

"Cerca del centro de la cuidad." He caught himself. "Near city center."

"Big place?"

The man gave a shrug, maybe, maybe not.

"Can you get me a taxi . . . and ask the driver to take me to the same place?"

The man blew a whistle and waved the next taxi forward.

The taxi sped to the curb. Another white taxi, red stripe. The attendant jerked the door open. "Barrio de Salamanca," he shouted, followed by a run of words Jack couldn't follow.

Jack climbed in and the cab pulled away from the curb.

"Barrio de Salamanca?" the driver confirmed, looking left, into oncoming traffic.

"Yes. Sí."

"¿Y donde?"

"I'm not sure where. Do you speak English?"

He nodded. Stubbled face, a few days' growth.

Jack stared into the rear-view mirror, watching the driver's eyes. "I hope your English is better than my Spanish."

"The attendant said you want to catch your friend. I can call his cab on the radio . . . it's one of ours. I can ask his destination or ask to meet somewhere." He reached for the mic.

Jack jolted forward. "Whoa, whoa." He leaned over the seat.

"What?" the cabbie asked, accelerating into the lane leaving the airport.

Jack sighed. "I uh, . . . he's, uh, . . . he's not exactly my friend. I don't want him to know I'm following him."

The cab began to slow. The cabbie eyed him through the rear-view mirror, a suspicious stare. "Why do you follow him?"

"Turning the tables. He was following me and I'm trying to figure out why."

The cabbie glided the car smoothly down the middle of the lane, eyes still looking back. "None of my business . . . I'm sure I've transported my share of people doing illegal things . . . maybe even un asesino o sicario . . . a hit man, or two, but . . . I prefer not to." He awaited a response.

Jack forced a chuckle. "I promise, I just want to see what he's doing."

The cabbie turned his eyes to the road. "We can wait, get to Barrio de Salamanco, *then* I use the radio. Take our time. If our driver knows where the fare is going, patience on your part won't be a problem. If he doesn't, your friend is a few steps ahead, somewhere in the barrio."

Jack let out a sigh. "Good plan. Any suggestion on what I should do to blend in?"

"Blend in?"

"Look like a local."

"Oh." The cabbie glanced over his shoulder and laughed. "You look like an American."

"I am an American."

"Perceptivo." He laughed, giving his head a good shake. "Perceptive, huh." He glanced left, changing lanes. "Stop at a vendedor. Street vendor. Buy a scarf. Long one. Bohemian look."

Jack gulped. "What if I don't have any cash?"

"What are you telling me?"

"Sorry, I didn't think before jumping in the car . . . do you take credit cards?"

The cabbie laughed. "I can, but if you have dollars, I can give you euros."

Jack pulled out five twenties. "Hundred bucks?"

"One to one?" the cabbie asked.

"I have no idea what the exchange rate is, but that sounds fair to me."

"Mejor para mi, pero no por mucho." With one hand he rifled through his change bag. "Better for me, but not by much." He passed back seventy euros, a mix of tens and twenties. "I kept thirty. Cab to city center is thirty euros."

"Tips customary?"

"Not expected."

Jack dropped a ten over the seat.

"Gracias."

After the cabbie turned off the freeway, he drove the city like he knew it well, arriving in an area of both wide and narrow lanes and densely packed, multi-story buildings. Five, six, seven stories, elaborate architecture. Curves, arches, turrets. The cabbie picked up the mic and hailed Teague's cab, exchanging rapid fire words with the other driver. Setting the mic on the dash, he hung a hard right for a short drive through the barrio, stopping mid block on a street crowded with pedestrians.

"Barrio de Salamanca." He pointed at a five-story building. "That is your destination."

On the ground floor, a shop. A rather high end one at that, bookended by other high-end shops. Gold, gilded letters hovered over the door, partially hidden by the trees lining the street.

"I expected something shady . . . almost dangerous."

"These businesses have very wealthy clientele. Art patrons. Gente who collect the rare and the valuable."

"But the guy who followed me is supposedly an avocado broker."

"Maybe avocado brokers are collectors." He pointed at a cart on the opposite side of the street. "A street vendor. She will have a scarf but don't pay too much."

Jack opened the door. "Thank you. You've been really helpful."

"Be careful, my friend. I am of the impression you do not know what you might be getting into."

"You're right." Jack closed the door.

The cab inched away from the curb, then accelerated into traffic.

Jack approached the street vendor. "Scarf?" he muttered, slipping thirty euros to the youngish, wavy-haired woman, adorned in clothing like her wares. "Básico. Simple."

She studied him a moment and reached up, removing his glasses, studying his eyes. She ran a finger over one brow, then pulled a long, woolen scarf off a rack. Brown with threads of burgundy. She slipped it around his neck and let it drape. "Muy guapo."

He laughed. "You should've seen me with hair. ¿Suficiente euros?"

She smiled. "Sí."

He pulled on his glasses, dropped into his stoop, and crossed the street.

Need a plan, but how do I plan when I don't know what's there?

A bell rang as he opened the door and stepped inside, the

room dim and in shadow. He stepped away from the windows, hoping to let his eyes adjust to the dark.

"¿Puedo ayudarlo?"

Jack turned.

A young, attractive woman came into focus. Light brown hair. Green eyes. Curvaceous but slender. A tight-fitting red suit. Shadows seemed to accent her curves.

Jack forced his eyes away. "May I . . . uh . . . look around for a minute? Quiero mirar."

"American." She sounded almost accusatorial.

"Obvious?"

"No." She put on her best smile. "But you are our second American in the last five minutes. We must be experiencing un estampida americana . . . a stampede of Americans."

Jack laughed, not sure that he should. "Small world." He turned to eye the merchandise. Paintings. Statuary. Collectibles under lock and key.

"The other gentleman . . . we see him with some regularity." Without thinking, she glanced to the rear of the shop. "So, how can we make you a regular customer? Are you a collector?"

"Uh . . . sometimes. I heard this was an interesting place. Just wanted to see for myself. Give me a few minutes."

She nodded and melted into the shadows.

He approached a painting. Trying to appear interested, he shifted his position, as if looking for a different angle, his real interest locked on the well-lit office at the back of the shop.

Glassed in on three sides, the office held two men. Teague, in his gray sport coat, standing, the other man with a salt and pepper goatee and a tweed coat and vest, sitting at a desk. He spun around to face Teague, then turned back, occupied with something on the desk.

Jack slid down the wall, a few steps at a time, checking one painting, then the another, keeping his back to the office.

Light poured through the office door, knifing a cut through the shadows cast over dark wooden floors. Similar slices came through windows, keeping Jack close to the wall. Taking the appearance of eyeing painting details, Jack listened to the mutterings from the office, mutterings that became clearer as he moved down the wall, yet words remained inaudible.

"This was a unique deviation from your usual ," the proprietor said. "As is other request. Unusual at best."

Jack scooted closer.

"If you can't meet our we and you have a problem," Teague said.

"Oh, you'll be satisfied but it is just these are different risks. so much more susceptible to " He paused. " questions from authoritative voices."

"Immediately?"

"Maybe not. I've done the best ."

"If the questions don't come up right away, we'll be fine. You'll be fine."

Jack heard a squeak from the room. He glanced back.

The proprietor had turned in his chair to the desk. He did something, then spun back, causing another squeak. He faced his visitor. "Are you sure, Señor Teague? "He held a book bound in leather. "Many of the people who in such treasures know how the game is played. They can accept certain secrets being hidden the provenances. That will not be an issue and that is I've given you."

"So why do we have a problem?"

"The problem is not with ." He waved the book. "This my specialty."

"What are you saying?"

"I'm saying I'm suspicious of the authenticity. If I am, why wouldn't others be?"

" the stuff is real."

"In such abundance? With no historical record?"

Teague laughed. "Well . . . it is kinda old."

"Maybe to you. To me, it is a sliver in the long history of man. Who could have owned such treasure without the knowing it existed?"

"No one knew. That's the issue. It was just recently found. ."

The last inaudible words caused Jack to drift to the next painting. *Teague found it*!

"You expect me to believe it?" the proprietor said. "Why act as if it has long been held?"

"I do expect you to believe it," Teague said. "And there's more where they came from. Your job is to give them a history. To make the sale possible and prevent others from looking for where they actually came from. It needs to appear like they're in someone's collection."

"Very well. I've done that." The proprietor sighed. "But if there are more, what will you do next? You can't play this game every ."

"Let me worry about that." Teague stood and paced the floor. "Can I trust you?"

"Of course." The proprietor handed Teague the book.

"Impressive." Teague flipped through the pages. "I'm more worried about what happens afterwards."

"Afterwards? How so?"

"You're not in a need-to-know position, but . . ." Teague cleared his throat. "The proceeds . . . they're to fund a very special project."

"Something honorable . . . like a hospital, or the poor?"

Teague shook his head. "Hell no. Nothing that silly."

The proprietor gave a quizzical stare.

"It's more in the *control the world* category." He laughed. "Just joking. Don't worry about it. It needs to appear to be a legitimate transaction by an anonymous collector, with a purchase by an anonymous collector. Where the money goes? Who knows? Who cares? Magically it needs to reappear with no connection to the transaction. It's just money, floating by on a comet, magically landing in its intended bank account."

"Money laundering is not my specialty."

"It's not really money laundering. It's just . . . nobody's business." Teague studied a page. "Think the boys in Paris will honor playing the game . . . the way my guy wants it played?" He cleared his throat. "It is to appear . . . a trustworthy transaction on its way to Freeport."

"Freeport? Again, this is not my area of expertise, but . . . they have a reputation for being protective of clientele, both seller and buyer."

"Good."

Jack shuddered. *His guy? Freeport? Appearance of a trustworthy transaction?*

"If going to Freeport, why the auction? Why not there?"

Jack took a half step, to hear. *Freeport, Texas? New York? Maine? Which?*

"Prospective buyer wants the pieces to have a history. Both on the market, and with this." Teague gave the book a shake, then flipped again through the pages. "And this is perfect. Old, as if it's been in some family for decades and decades."

"I would have preferred to have more time," the proprietor said. "I was limited by the materials I had on hand . . . but yes, I used my usual methods. Giving leather an appearance consistent with the story I hoped to create. Age and wear. Paper and binding present their own unique challenges, but . . . the product should adequately meet your needs." He stood and pointed at a line on the page Teague had open. "The writing. Feel the entry."

Teague slid a finger over a line of words.

The proprietor flipped to another page. "Now here."

Teague repeated the move. "Seems different."

"Exactly. Early entries would have been made with a quill. Later entries with different types of pens."

"I see. No way someone will think this is fake."

"Only if they question the actual pieces. My work? I stake my reputation on it. My services never fail, but I have no control over the work of others. If the pieces are not authentic, if they come under question, I will deny any connection . . . to you . . . to the collection . . . to the provenance I have created."

"But the pieces are real."

"If you say so."

"Stop worrying." Teague approached the door. "Gotta go. Paris waits. Pico is waiting."

A voice came from Jack's right. "I see you've taken a fancy to this particular painting."

Noticing both Teague and the proprietor swing around to the voice, Jack turned to the woman, then the wall. "Uh, yes. The realism . . . I love . . . the . . . uh . . ." The painting. *Damn. Impressionist.* "Seemingly real . . . even in the absence of detail."

"Yes." She staked out a position behind him. "A special addition to any collection."

"Yes," Jack agreed. *Should I run*? Heart pounding, body frozen in place, he listened as two sets of footsteps left the office. One paused. The other footsteps—deliberate, metered—continued past the door, then stopped. The steps started again, continuing to the door. Jack glanced around, catching sight of Teague exiting the shop, the leather-bound book in his hand.

"May I be of assistance?" the proprietor said from behind him.

Jack turned, and noticed the face of the man's assistant, blushing. "I think I'm pretty well taken care of, thank you."

"Are you now?"

"Yes, I may want to come back tomorrow. Look at this one with fresh eyes. See if the love is lasting." He laughed.

"Another American. What a coincidence," he said, voice dry, no sign of wonder.

Jack pointed. "That guy? He was an American?"

"Yes."

Jack mustered his most friendly smile. "Another collector? What does *he* collect?"

"That," the proprietor said, folding his arms, "is strictly confidential."

Jack dropped the smile. "And that is the right answer," he said, his voice deep, resonate.

The proprietor scowled, his eyes narrowing to slit. "Why?"

Now what? Uh . . . "Because . . . I just *may* have a client, who just *may* have pieces that could appeal to the right collector."

The man's arms eased to his side. "Can you share what you know about these pieces?"

"Maybe a Picasso, maybe a Dali, maybe a pair by Miró."

He smiled. "How can we be of help?"

"No offense," Jack glanced at the young woman. "But your lovely assistant is a little easier on the eyes."

The man laughed and gave a stroke to his goatee. "Of course." He returned to his office.

Jack turned to the woman. "I'll be in touch."

The woman smiled and slipped him a business card. "Buenos días."

"Buenos días."

At the curb, he glanced back. *Or, maybe not.* He waved down a cab, and began to ditch the scarf, changed his mind, and instead stuffed it into his bag, along with the business card. "Aeropuerto, por favor," he told the cab driver.

Chapter 21

Jack stared out the window of the cab as Madrid screamed past, his thoughts on the leather-bound book and its contents. *Might not be real, but the treasure apparently is. According to Teague. So, he has it. At least part of it.*

Who is his guy? The sender of the faxes? Could it be Potts Monroe?

The cab began to slow. Ahead on the freeway, cars sat stopped. The cabbie offered no explanation. Minutes passed.

"Got a one o'clock flight. We gonna make it?"

The cabbie shrugged. Man of few words.

Makes two of us. Jack turned to the window, drumming his fingers on the door handle.

The jumbled mess dissolved, and the cabbie accelerated, speeding north, then east, then onto the exit for the airport. He dropped Jack off at the curb.

Half an hour before takeoff. Could make it.

He threw his pack over his shoulder and jogged across the terminal, making it through security with little waste of time, then found his gate. People stood watching the displays, waiting.

Disheveled, he ducked into a bathroom and changed into a button-up shirt of a different color—blue. He smoothed the wrinkles, then left to watch for Teague. Stopping two gates down, he found a spot to view the boarding area, making a quick scan, then searching person by person. *No Teague. He isn't here.*

No gray sport coat. Could he be wearing something different?

He scanned the crowd again. Faces only. *He's gotta be here.*

A male gate attendant made an announcement. Several people stood and made their way to the boarding gate. First class. No Teague.

The attendant admitted the last of his first-class passengers, sorted through boarding passes, then announced general boarding. The mass of remaining passengers got into line.

Wait for Teague. He may yet come.

Almost too late, Jack rushed the attendant as he started to close the jetway.

One seat sat empty in first class.

No Teague. Where is he?

Jack ran his eye along the rows, all the way to the back. Not here.

He took his seat as the flight attendant closed the door to the plane. She made her preflight announcements. French, not a word understandable, even with hand gestures.

Did Teague miss the flight?

—·—

The jet arrived in Paris. Jack disembarked and headed for the terminal exit.

What do I do now? I don't know where I'm going.

Did Teague change his plans? Did the proprietor in Madrid warn him?

He turned on his phone and pulled up the photos of the faxes sent to Teague. The last fax—more detailed than most but still cryptic. Only a few lines. Flight numbers and times. One line at the bottom, a mix of numbers and words. Maybe an address?

Outside, he found the taxi attendant and showed him the line on the photo. He waved a cab forward.

The words had meaning. Jack jumped in and showed the photo to the cabbie.

The cabbie sped into traffic.

After a long ride, Jack found himself in a city not unlike Madrid, a maze of block after block of five to seven story buildings. Roads like tunnels through expanses of often elegant buildings. Wasting no time, the cabbie navigated turns and narrow streets, then, with no warning, he came to an abrupt stop, and pointed at the building on the corner.

Hotel something. Same name as the street. *Must be where Teague's staying. It's a start.*

He paid with the last of his euros and slipped out of the cab.

At the curb, three people approached holding placards. Jack glanced at the words, no idea what they said. Eyes suspicious, the protestors stared, then let him pass.

He spotted a door and ducked inside. People, but no registration desk. No bellman.

Strange.

A woman in black tight-fitting slacks and gray loose-fitting sweater started across the lobby toward him. Auburn hair, not young, not yet middle-aged. Attractive. Confident. She offered a brochure as she approached.

Jack reached to take it.

She said something in French.

"Speak English?" he asked.

"Of course."

"Is this a hotel?"

An almost haughty laugh. "No. This is an auction house."

"But the name . . ."

"You Americans," she said, as if that explained everything. "We are an auction house. One of the oldest in Paris."

Jack flashed a confused look.

"If you need lodging, there are options nearby."

"I don't, but . . . auction house? What do you auction?"

Her eyes lit. "Anything of interest. Objects d'art, fine watches, jewelry, antiquities, stamps, even automobiles, but not at this location."

"Are the auctions over for the day?"

"No, no, no, no," she said, in rapid fire. "Some have not yet started."

"What's being auctioned?"

"You are holding the listing."

He glanced at the brochure. Everything written in French. "Can I go in?"

"Of course. All of our auctions are open to the public. If you would like, you may preview what is available in each auction room."

"Now?"

"Oui. Will you be wishing to bid?"

"Maybe. If I understand what's happening."

She laughed. "Of course." She swung an arm, motioning him down the hall.

Several large rooms opened from the corridor. One, with walls upon which hung paintings, most in gilded frames, the auction ongoing, the auctioneer guiding bidders from one offering to the next. The next room held tapestries. The next, sculptures, modern, blocky. The next, a large, rectangular glass case filled with expensive watches, and a smaller group of bidders. The next room, a full house, the bidding not yet started, the auctioneer visiting with prospective buyers.

Jack glanced at the brochure. The description had one word he recognized. Antiquités.

He peeked inside. Objects on the wall, including kachina masks. Most of the bidders stood clustered around glass cases, waiting. He tried approaching one of the cases. No one moved to allow even a peek, for fear of losing their place.

He walked back down the hall, finding the woman handing out the auction schedule, waiting as she finished with a mustachioed man holding a numbered paddle.

She saw Jack and excused herself from conversation. "May I help you?"

"The room with antiquities . . ."

"Yes?"

"Too many people to get in . . . but . . ."

"Highly anticipated, yes."

"What's on the block?"

"The block? Oh, yes." She glanced at the card. "Roman gemstones, Greek ceramics, Egyptian amulets, Byzantine coins, Chinese jade, and . . ." She looked up and caught his eye. "The big attraction today . . . and this may be of interest to you . . . treasures from the Americas."

"Treasures?"

"Oui. One highly anticipated lot that may or may not . . . *go on the block*. We will see."

Before Jack could ask why, over her shoulder he noticed Harper Teague coming in the door. Harried, in a rush, like a man who missed a flight. Jack moved alongside her, his back to Teague, and whispered, "Thank you." He slipped away, out of Teague's path.

She turned back to her work and saw him. "Monsieur Teague."

As he approached, Jack glided in behind him, seemingly into conversation with a pair of French ladies carrying on about something, maybe their success for the day or their plans for the next sale. They shot Jack a wary look. He smiled, then ignored them, inching closer to listen in on Teague.

"Bonjour, Babette. Sorry I'm late. Has it started?"

"How many times have I told you, Monsieur Teague? My name is not Babette. It is Amélie."

"Sorry." He looked past her, down the hall. "You look like a Babette."

She scowled, staring at the leather-bound book barely larger than his hands. "The provenance?"

"Yeah." Teague said, not taking his eye off the people in the hall. "They found it . . . hidden where they probably had it last."

"I'll take that, please. If everything is in order, we can proceed."

He handed it over. "I might stick around and bid on a few things."

"Very good." She nodded. "You know where to register."

"I do." Teague walked away.

Jack watched him make a turn off the hall, likely to register, and waited for his reappearance on the way to the auction room.

Within minutes, the woman Teague called Babette announced the beginning of the next auction. Jack followed others into the room, slowing at the door, glancing around the corner. *Where is he?* He touched the mustache, making sure it was secure, then continued in.

Teague stood over a glass case, somehow having jostled his way to the front.

Jack slipped behind the back row of bidders, hiding behind a big man of similar height. He watched over the man's shoulder as Teague stared into the case, two men in suits behind him, exchanging glances, sneering, probably plotting to move him out of the way. For a moment the crowd parted, providing a glimpse of the items under glass. A figurine in gold. A circular piece with figures and possibly writing, also in gold. Down the length of the case, other passing moments gave views of other pieces, all in gold or silver.

Juan Rivera's treasure? Antiquities. Taken from the park? They should be protected for the public. He wanted to scream, for law enforcement, or whoever. But who? Interpol? How would that work? And what evidence did he have?

The auctioneer stepped to the front of the room and announced himself, his tiny microphone hardly noticeable, but the sound system effective enough that no one could question what he had said. He stopped at the case nearest Teague, running off a long introduction that included frequent use of the word antiquities, and the long list of countries Amélie had mentioned. An assistant unlocked a second glass case along the back wall.

Paddles came out. Serious bidders crowded forward.

Teague had his number: 86.

The auctioneer started with Byzantine coins, setting the pace, establishing his method for stepping up the bidding. He quickly finished the coins and moved on to Egyptian amulets, then a few Greek ceramics and pieces of Chinese jade.

He turned to the glass case at the front of the room.

Teague jostled for position.

The auctioneer's assistant stepped forward with the first item from the case, a gold figurine, four or five inches tall, fat little arms and legs, glistening under the light of the room. The auctioneer began talking, likely a description. Then bidding began, paddles raised.

Jack leaned in to watch. *How do I stop this? If I try, would I be escorted out to the street by a French policeman? Or arrested?*

Could Potts be involved?

The number of paddles raised began to slow. The bids? Who knew. Jack couldn't follow. Some numbers sounded similar, like numbers in Spanish, but before he could figure out the bid, the auctioneer moved on to the next.

Teague raised his paddle.

Was that ethical? What was he doing, running up the bid?

The auctioneer acknowledged his bid, then turned to the other side of the room, accepting another bid. Before Jack could locate the other bidder, Teague bid again. The other person must have responded in kind, keeping the auctioneer moving from one side to the other, back and forth, until no additional bids came. The auctioneer brought down his gavel. The unseen bidder prevailed.

Jack glanced at Teague. A crooked smile. You win some, you lose some.

The next item, another figurine in gold. The bidding started, running up to something quite pricey before Teague flashed his paddle. The auctioneer looked around the room, finding a bidder, maybe the same one as before. The duel continued for several rounds, then ended with another bang of the gavel, the other bidder prevailing again.

The next item, a shield, in gold.

And so it went. A good half hour, maybe longer. More shields, gold vessels, bracelets, earrings, pendants. Then the lot was gone.

The auctioneer turned to the masks positioned along the wall—kachina, half a dozen, showing deterioration. Those that looked oldest appeared made of plaster, maybe selenite—gypsum—the others made with leather, horns, feathers and faded paints.

Teague became anxious, fidgety. He made a move to the door. A man stepped in his way. Teague turned, looking for another path.

Jack stepped right, ready to follow. The crowd cut him off. No way to the door.

Over the shoulder in front of him, Jack watched Teague grow more anxious.

The gavel came down on the first mask, after a bidding war like the ones for the gold figurines. Same for the second mask, eating more time, as the back and forth ran up the bids.

Teague because jumpy. Animated.

Jack watched for an opening. The man blocking his escape now stood blocked by others.

No path out.

When the last gavel dropped, the crowd stayed put, as if expecting more.

Teague forced his way through the throng. Jack felt his eyes, but Teague didn't see him, his focus more on the gaps he exploited as he clawed his way across the room.

Jack circled the man beside him, staying out of Teague's way, then followed his zigs and zags to the door.

In the hall, Jack stopped and pressed himself against the wall, letting others pass as he kept an eye on Teague.

Forcing himself past a woman, Teague slapped a man's back. An acquaintance. Blond-hair, well-dressed, lawyerly, the man shared a few words before Teague melted into the crowd.

Jack moved forward and caught Teague talking to "Babette" in the lobby. He gave a dismissive wave then slipped out the door, into the Parisian evening.

Amélie stood along the edge of the departing throng, exchanging words with patrons, directing some to where they could settle up on their purchases.

Jack approached her. "Tell me about the lot with the gold figurines."

"The gold figurines? I would have taken you for having interest in the final lot."

"The masks? Sure, but the gold and silver pieces . . . I didn't understand their story."

"Poor American . . ." She let the twinkle in her eyes pass

between them. "Of course. A remarkably interesting story. Anonymous owner, but this we can share. They are from a family originally from Spain. The items were in the personal collection of a Spanish military officer sent to the New World."

Yeah, right. He smiled. "Okay, and how did he end up with that kind of treasure?"

"Cortez promised the crown one fifth of all gold and silver found. But the remainder? He kept a large portion, and the rest was split between his officers and men. The original owner was one of Cortez's senior officers."

"Really?"

"Oui. What is unusual is that the pieces were not melted down," she continued. "Most of those types of treasures were seen as pagan, and of little interest in that form, but they were gold, and the Spanish crown was in need of gold, so most were melted down and sent to Spain."

Good story. Good details. "So why didn't this guy melt his down?"

"There are many mysteries in this line of work, but to your question, I came to the conclusion that he found them fascinating. Kept them as mementos . . . souvenirs. This is a man who returned to Spain with his memories rather than choosing to stay in the New World."

"I see. Seems unlikely we would just learn about such a collection," Jack said, making no effort to hide his skepticism.

"They have sold pieces over the years, a few at a time, to keep from raising suspicions."

"Suspicions of what?"

"I do not know. He may have had more than his fair share. Or maybe he did not want to come to the attention of the Spanish Crown. Of course, that would not be a problem in the present century."

"Why?"

"Because of the Spanish Civil War."

"The Spanish Crown was . . . ?" Jack said, unable to remember details of Spanish history.

"Exiled, but more importantly, the generation that held the collection escaped to the south of France, avoiding slaughter at the hands of Franco."

Wow, that guy in Madrid sure knows how to concoct a history. "Interesting."

"Yes, it is. We've been fortunate to have been chosen to show the collection."

"The pieces. They're very unique."

"Some are. Especially those from a location for which there are so few collections."

"Like New Mexico . . . maybe Colorado?"

The words caught her by surprise. "What did you say?"

"New Mexico, maybe Colorado, in what's now the United States."

The confusion on her face lingered longer than he expected. Then she laughed. "No, no, no, no, no. These are not from those places."

"They're not?" *Yeah, right.* He chuckled to himself. *She believes everything written by the man in Madrid.*

"No, why would they be from there?"

"I just . . ." He caught himself. "Sorry, go ahead with your story. You said, a location from which there are few collections."

"Yes. In today's showing, a few were from the location best known for having its treasures plundered."

"And that is?"

"The Aztec capital, Tenochtitlan. Now known as Mexico City."

Not expecting that, he muttered, "Okay."

"But *most* of the collection was not Aztec, including the little gold men."

"Then, who?" he asked, playing along.

"Tarascans."

"Who are they?"

"Their history is less known to the world, but they too were skilled workers in gold, silver and copper. Fewer examples of their craft remain, making these quite special. Elaborate shields and spearheads. Earrings, bracelets and pendants."

"So, today's collection . . . it was . . . Taras . . . ?"

"Tarascan, yes."

"I've . . . uh . . . never . . ." Uncertainty took away his words.

"I'm not surprised that you've not heard of them. The region they were in is today better known for other things."

"Such as?"

"Or vert," she said, reverting to her native tongue, then, "Avocat."

Jack gulped. "Excuse me?"

"Green gold. Avocado. The Tarascan occupied what is today known as Michoacán."

—'—

Jack slipped out the door, drunk on uncertainty. He turned down the sidewalk, stunned, going nowhere in particular.

A man holding a placard rushed him. Angry, wild-eyed, waving his sign in a threatening manner. Shouts, in words Jack could not understand.

Jack stopped, confused, not wanting to make the man more agitated. He listened, with no idea what the man said.

Once the man blew off enough steam, he blurted out his final threat and turned, calling it quits.

Jack sighed. *Seen worse.*

He took a step, then stopped. Curious, he pulled out his phone and clicked a quick picture of the man's sign, to translate later.

He turned back to his own thoughts.

Michoacán, green gold, and most confusing, real gold.

Chapter 22

Jack plodded down the sidewalk, nowhere to go. Noticing a bench, he plopped down.

So damned confusing.

Teague's provenance is fake. Yet everything Amelie said about the origins of the gold pieces is plausible, even likely. Possibly the reason Teague kept going to Michoacán.

To steal their treasures . . . as a collector . . . and avocado broker.

But it had nothing to do with Juan Rivera. Or Colorado.

The good news. Potts wouldn't have anything to do with it. No way Potts could be complicit in sales of little gold men from Michoacán.

But why was Teague following me? He has no clue I followed him here, so all's fair, but to what end? All it tells me is how he moves around the world, but that's about it.

He is up to no good, but it doesn't appear to have anything to do with New Mexico.

Look at yourself. In Paris, by way of Madrid. How in the hell did you let that happen?

Might as well go home.

A taxi screamed past.

He opened the map app on his phone. The Louvre sat a few miles away. The Eiffel Tower, a little farther. He sighed and checked the time. He called Kelly instead.

It rang twice.

"Senator Culberson," she said, answering, something holding her attention.

"Hello, Senator. Busy?"

"Always." She recognized the voice. "How's Mexico City?"

"No idea."

"You're home?"

He ran his eye along the buildings on the street. "Nope."

"Where *are* you?"

"Paris."

Silence, then, "That was unexpected."

"Following Harper Teague. Thought I'd catch him in some big conspiracy . . . but in the end, got nothing. Nothing that involves us anyway. So, here I sit. Also saw Madrid."

"You're kidding. What'd you think he was doing?"

"He's involved in selling a treasure trove of gold figurines and wares. Antiquities. I thought maybe Juan Rivera's treasure . . . but unless he melted it down and turned it into something in the style of a people in Mexico. . . ." He paused. He hadn't thought of that till now . . . but, no. He dismissed it.

"You're sure it's not related."

"Pretty sure. Wasted time and money . . . but . . . what the hell! What are savings accounts for?" He let out a sad little laugh.

"What'cha gonna do?"

"Go home, I guess. See if I'm needed on any updates to the coalition report."

"Maybe you should stay . . . enjoy Paris."

"Maybe you should come join me."

"Ooh," she cooed. "I'd love to, but I'm busy . . . and you need to be."

"When we get off the phone, I'll check on airline tickets."

"Come here. To Washington. Call it coming to see me." She attempted a sad laugh. "I'm fluttering my eyelashes. If you could see me, your heart would melt."

"You'd be working, Senator."

"Not all the time."

"Okay. The boss would be happy if I'm gone a few more days. I'll do it."

After ending the call, he stayed put, working from the bench, the sounds and smells of traffic a few feet away as Paris got its second wind.

He managed to get a seat on a Swiss Air flight departing the next morning. One stop in Zurich, then D.C., thirteen hours of flight time, and not a bad fare.

He texted Kelly. His arrival at Dulles would be at 3 p.m.

Then, a quick text to Reger, checking to see if Potts had made an appearance. His prompt answer: Nope.

Now, a hotel. *But . . . who knows how long it takes to get around Paris in the morning? Sleep at the gate.* He checked for trains, learning there were regularly scheduled departures to the airport from a nearby station. Throwing his pack over one shoulder, he started for it.

He turned down a narrow street and caught himself walking fast. He slowed. *No need to rush. Get the feel of the place. Experience Paris. It's costing you enough.*

Ahead, a pair of young lovers walked hand in hand. Another couple approached, older lovers on an evening stroll, the woman grasping the upper arm of her male companion. Up the street, a man left a building and descended steps to the sidewalk. *So, this is Paris?*

Realization hit. The man coming down the steps. Stout. Gray sport coat. Harper Teague.

Teague reached the sidewalk and started toward him.

Jack spun on his heels. He noticed a café, crossed the street, and ducked inside. Huddling against a wall, he peeked out the window and watched Teague continue up the sidewalk.

At some point he's gonna wonder why the same bald guy with a mustache and scarf is everywhere he goes.

"Salut," came a woman's voice behind him. "Suivez-moi." A tired look about her, she picked up a menu and motioned for him to follow.

A hostess. Jack followed her to a table, keeping an eye on

Teague through the window. Teague kicked about, in no hurry to get to his destination.

Did he see me?

Leaving a menu and motioning him to sit, the hostess departed. A waiter in an apron that nearly reached the floor delivered meals to a young couple at the next table.

Head down, as if reading the menu, Jack watched Teague bound up the steps of a building, tug open its tall wooden door, and slip inside. Beside the door, a tile embedded in the wall. A sign, one word. Hôtel.

The waiter arrived, using words Jack could not understand.

Jack made a selection and pointed, trying to say the words, "Vin rouge." Then, "Boeuf bourguignon. Soupe á l'oignon."

The waiter fired off a flurry of words.

"I'm sorry, I don't speak French."

"But you tried," the waiter said. "The wine. A glass or the bottle?"

Jack smiled. "Just a glass. Is there one you recommend?"

"Oui, monsieur, one you will love, and I'll bring your soup right away."

"Merci."

The waiter left for the kitchen.

Hôtel. Jack stared out the window. Turning his eye down the street, he noticed the building where Teague had first appeared, a building dripping with elegance. Beside the door where Teague had emerged, a sign, simple but stylish. Banque. He let the word rattle around in his brain. Banque. Ban que. Bank. It's a bank. But too late for banking hours.

At that moment, a man in a suit and tie and long brown overcoat stepped out the door, sat down his briefcase, and turned to lockup.

On impulse, Jack jumped to his feet and dashed to the door, raising a finger to the hostess—one moment please—as he stepped out and jogged across the street.

At the bottom of the steps, the man turned the opposite way down the sidewalk.

Jack ran up behind him. "Monsieur," he shouted. "Monsieur."

The man glanced over his shoulder, uncertain if he or someone else was being hailed.

Here goes nothing. Hope he speaks English. "Mr. Teague sent me to catch you. Did he happen to leave any papers in your office?"

"Papers?" The man—gray, slender, small nose, not a hair out of place—looked confused. "Just his wiring instructions."

"Uh, . . . wiring instructions. Nothing more?"

"Why anything more?" the banker asked, agitated. "All I need is the wiring instructions."

"No papers with the money?

"He brought no money." Disdain. "This is a trust account transaction."

"Did the wires go through?"

"It will be days before the accounts settle. I explained that to Monsieur Teague. He need not worry. Now, what kind of papers did he think he left?"

"Something he was reading when he walked in."

"I saw no papers."

Jack smiled. "Merci."

With an agitated groan, the man turned and departed.

Jack returned to the cafe, noticing as he retook his seat that the door to the hotel opened. Out stepped Harper Teague.

Hope he didn't see all that.

Teague stopped at the bottom of the steps and waited for a break in the traffic. Then he crossed the road, stepped over the curb, and stared in the cafe window, twenty feet away.

Jack covered his face, adrenaline pulsing. Nowhere to hide. *Get ready to say hi . . . old friend . . . not.*

A blue Peugeot stopped at the curb. Teague climbed in. The car pulled into traffic.

Jack watched it all the way down the street. It made a turn at the next corner.

The waiter delivered his soup.

Jack picked up his spoon and let out a sigh. Relief.

Can't believe it. Still haven't been caught. But why did you do that? he asked himself. *You didn't learn anything, and you didn't need to.*

He glanced across the street. Hôtel. Maybe Teague's started a war with the desk clerk.

Don't press your luck, Jack. You've wasted enough time. And money.

The aroma of the soup hit his nose, sending tremors all the way to his stomach. When had he last eaten? *Eat,* he told himself.

Who would've thought this spy stuff could make a guy this hungry?

—'—

Sleeping on airport seating did not work out as planned. After a fitful night, managing sleep in short spurts, he gave up trying and at a little after five went searching for a cup of coffee.

He returned in time for boarding, feeling little better. Still dead tired, only a tiny bit of caffeine-induced recovery.

The gate agent announced boarding for first class.

One of the people in line was the man Teague had slapped on the back at the auction house, the blonde-headed acquaintance with the look of a lawyer. The man had obviously gotten a full night of sleep. He smiled and exchanged pleasantries with a young blonde woman. His suit—if the same one he wore yesterday—looked freshly pressed. Immaculate.

Once on board, Jack fell immediately asleep, even before the jet left the ground.

He was awakened by a flight attendant upon reaching Zurich. "What?" he said, not understanding her words, then noticing they were the only two still on the plane.

She recalibrated her language now that he'd given a clue. "Do you have a connection?"

"Yes, to Washington, D.C."

She glanced at a list. "Two gates down. Hurry."

He stumbled to his feet as the attendant handed him his pack. He rushed up the aisle in a stupor, and staggered to his gate, boarded just in time, and found his seat against the window.

He woke hours later to the slamming of overhead bins at Dulles International Airport.

He stopped for a cup of coffee in the terminal, and while in line he turned on his phone. He had a message with a number to text when he arrived.

He texted the number and a few seconds later, received a phone call.

"Jack, it's Alex Trasker. Here to pick you up."

"You're not Kelly."

"No, but some people say I'm better looking."

"Not this one, and. . . . you'd need documentation to prove anyone else does."

He laughed. "Get your bags. Call when you reach the door . . . give me the door number."

Jack found the exit and called. In a few minutes a German sedan pulled up to the curb, Trasker at the wheel. He wore a dark suit, pressed shirt, and tie, his dark beard with its usual neat trim.

Jack climbed in and shook the offered hand. "Kelly busy?"

"Always." Trasker pulled into traffic. "Calendar filled up. I heard her giving an aide your number, asking to leave you a message to get an Uber or taxi. I offered to come get you."

"Kind of you. And it's also kind of you to help Kelly get her feet on the ground."

"It's only for a few months. I start in the fall at a university in Indiana. Teaching economics. Until then I'll help where I can, laying low, not wanting people to know what I'm doing." He gave a pat to the top of his head. "What's with the . . . ?"

Jack let out a gasp. "I forgot." He swiped at a spot on his head. A hint of stubble. "You don't want to know, really. Silly idea."

"Something to do with the heat . . . or humidity?"

"Neither, but that makes for a better story." He let out a self-deprecating chuckle. "Your old boss, the Congressman . . . is he why you're lying low?"

"He's still licking his wounds, but what's done is done." Trasker got into the lane to exit the airport. "I'm more worried about giving people another reason to go after the Senator."

"Another reason?"

"Don't be naïve." He shot an abrupt look. "In fact, naïvety is why I wanted to talk."

"My being naïve?"

Trasker laughed. "You are, but I meant Kelly. She's naïve as hell. Almost proud of it."

Jack shared a chuckle. "I can see that."

"She's getting hammered. Ads running all over New Mexico by people who know how to create bad reputations."

"Why would they do that? I mean . . . she's hardly had time to show what she's made of."

"It's not unusual. It's politics. What is unusual is Kelly's response. She's determined not to raise money to counter it, even when it's being offered."

"That would be Kelly."

"I respect her for it, but she's getting killed. She's got to come to terms with some aspects of playing the game."

"But the way the game's being played is her point. She feels it shouldn't be money that gets her attention. It should be the needs of her constituents."

"I respect her for that, too, but I want her to survive long enough to fight those battles. That's why I'm here to support her. I'm just sayin'. . . ." He sighed. "And she needs to make her announcement. Is she going to run for the office or not?"

"She hasn't told me either."

"Seriously?"

"Yeah."

Trasker sighed. "I think you should nudge her . . . and if you want to see her succeed, encourage her to fight back." He stroked his beard. "So where have you been?"

"Everywhere, feels like." He shook his head. "Mexico City, Madrid, Paris. Today, Zurich, but just to change planes. I could sure use a shower."

"Sounds like a great trip."

"Shoulda been, but no, it was a waste of time."

Trasker cast a curious eye. "How would Paris be a waste of time?"

Chapter 23

They arrived at the Hart Senate Office Building before Kelly returned from her meeting. The receptionist had no update on her status.

"I'll wait here," Jack said to Alex, taking a seat in the reception area of the office suite.

"Not so fast," Trasker said. "Give me a moment." He walked down the hallway, reappearing with a woman in tow. "This is Vera Martinez."

The woman nodded. Dark suit, Native American. Average height, quick friendly smile.

Jack extended a hand. "Jack Chastain. I've heard about you from Kelly. You worked for Senator Baca, right?"

"Yes."

"Where in New Mexico?"

"Ohkay Owingeh. San Juan Pueblo."

"Been there."

Vera nodded and waved him to follow as she started down the hall. "Come on back."

"I know you're busy," Jack said. "And it's the end of your day."

"Nobody worries about the clock around here."

Trasker gave him a gentle nudge. "Let's put you to work. Tap into your expertise." He laughed. "By the way, Vera looks young, but she's been here over a decade."

Martinez made a left turn into an office. Behind the desk, against the wall, stood a credenza with a computer and two monitors. Chairs sat scattered around the room.

"Sit here," Martinez said, steering him to a black ergonomic chair.

"But I'm . . . ,"

Trasker blocked his retreat. Standing on either side of him, Trasker and Martinez spun him around to the monitors.

She pointed at the closest screen. "This is a draft of a bill. Rough, based on what we see in the coalition report. We won't do anything until after the signing ceremony, but . . . the senator wants us thinking about what will be in the bill."

"You do know I can't do anything that looks like I'm lobbying?"

"We know . . . but you can answer questions," Trasker said. "You know the report better than anyone."

Martinez pointed at a line of text.

He stared at the words. "Makes sense, but this was given to you by someone, and they know the answers as well as I do."

"Nope." Trasker pointed at another line. "Both Kip and Karen Hatcher deferred to you."

Jack's eyes followed Trasker's finger across the screen. "Okay, captures how the monument protects the shared values of the people of the region . . . but . . ."

Trasker cut him off. "Good. Now . . ." He paused, reaching for an already worn copy of the report, pages folded and dog eared. "My thinking . . . where your input would be most helpful . . . ," He waited while Vera used the mouse to scroll down the page. ". . . is here. I'm feeling somewhat uncertain about all we need to capture in the authorities and general language to allow future modification and program refinement without having to rehash old battles. The report speaks to a commitment to monitoring resources, reporting results, assuring accountability by the managing agencies, National Park Service and Bureau of Land Management, answering both to the general public and to an advisory committee made up of equal parts environmental, rancher, tribal, business and local government."

Vera faced him. "Will the bill saying that be enough?"

"Am I the one to say? . . . I mean, with the restrictions of lobbying . . ."

Trasker cut him off. "Jack, you were the principal facilitator of the coalition effort. You took the lead in organizing the report and pulling in contributions from others. You wrote a good portion of it. If it's not in your wheelhouse, whose is it?"

"Writing this kind of bill is your expertise, not mine."

"True, with respect to writing the bill, but you are the expert on the subject."

Kelly breezed into the office. She stopped and put her hands on her hips, her dark eyes piercing against the lighter brown of her suit. Her jaw dropped, catching sight of Jack. "What happened to you?"

He attempted a smile. "Haircut."

She glanced at the other two, then locked her eyes again on Jack. "Go home, you two. It's my turn with this gentleman." A smile formed. "I hadn't counted on spending the evening with a strange man." She feigned a shudder. "Could be exciting. Could be scary."

"I know a little place off DuPont Circle," Trasker said. "Your strange man is probably tired of eating food from Mexico, Spain and France, so maybe try Italian. This place I know has the best chicken piccata. You could go there, get to know each other."

"That's an idea," Kelly said. She turned to Martinez, who seemed to be missing something. "It's alright, Vera, go home. Tomorrow's a new day. Me, I'm gonna enjoy the evening not talking to a bunch of old, white guys."

Jack gave her a face, a signal. Maybe she shouldn't be talking like this. "You know . . . someday, I'll be one of those old, white guys."

"Not yet, you're not. Just bald." She laughed.

Vera giggled.

Trasker had caught Jack's look. "It's my fault. I started that one night after a tough day. I was worried she was blaming herself . . . when it was them being set in their ways. We try to keep her sane."

Kelly flashed a smile. "Go home, both of you." She led Jack to her office. Unpacked boxes sat in a corner. On the wall, under sixteen-foot ceilings, hung two paintings. Her own. A panorama of New Mexico canyonlands and one of the state's Pueblo and Hispano cultures.

She shut down her computer, grabbed her briefcase, and pushed him into the hall.

In the elevator, just the two of them, he let the door close. "My turn to be inappropriate."

She shot a wary look from the corner of her eye.

"Nice ass, Senator. You look great in a suit."

She raised a finger to her lips and shook her head, fighting back a smile.

"You do."

When the elevator opened on the ground floor, she slipped past, leaving him behind.

A capital policeman, walking toward the elevator, slowed. "Everything all right, Senator?"

She glanced at Jack, then back. "Yes. He's with me. Thanks."

Outside, she gave him a thump on the chest. "Look here, mister, *I am* a U.S. Senator."

He laughed. "Your point?"

"I don't have one . . . about that. It's just . . . it's amazing the security they have here . . . and they're very dedicated. I have no idea how many cameras and microphones there are, but Capitol Police protect people like me, and I don't want someone thinking they need to protect me from you. Especially when you look nothing like your driver's license. Got it?"

"Got it." He smiled. "Can I follow you? It's the best view in Washington."

She flashed a bug-eyed glare. "What's with you?"

"Been in Paris alone . . . and what do you mean, I look nothing like my driver's license?"

She gave a dismissive wave, then turned, but stopped. "By the way . . . you're gonna tell me why you did that, but not yet . . . not until after the strange man thing rubs off. Cause . . . I kinda like it." She laughed and pointed at the ground to her left. "Beside me. I don't need you looking like a stalker."

They took the metro to the station at DuPont Circle. After minutes at the fountain, walking through throngs of people enjoying the evening, they headed down a spoke road off the circle. Kelly took his arm and guided him into a restaurant.

"Good evening, Senator," the hostess said, as they entered. She led them into a quiet part of the restaurant, seating them at a booth for two.

Looking around the room, Jack leaned in and whispered, "You've been here before?"

A blonde waitress in a tuxedo shirt and bow tie approached. "The usual, Senator?"

Kelly nodded. "Yes, please."

"And you, sir?"

"Same as the Senator." He waited for the waitress to leave. "I like saying that." He cleared his throat. "Same as the Senator." He glanced around the room, checking for anyone listening, or faces he might recognize. "I really could've used a shower."

"You're fine . . . and the only reason she knows is," Kelly said, "this is the first place I came with Alex and Vera. They made a silly point of calling me Senator every time she came to the table . . . knowing it made me self-conscious. Regarding a shower, I've seen you worse."

"But we're not in the park." He checked for sweat stains. "Come here often?"

"Restaurants here are amazing . . . Italian, Chinese, Thai, you name it . . . really good restaurants. There's only one thing I avoid . . . Mexican food. One place I tried . . . made guacamole with mayonnaise . . . I'm afraid to even try another place."

A shiver shot through him. "That'd be an effective way to reduce avocado consumption . . . which might be good, by the way."

"Why's that?"

"Long story, connected to butterflies and land use change."

"Before you tell me that one . . . tell me about this new look."

"It'll grow back."

"I'm not worried . . . I kinda like it . . . but tell me."

"Impulse. Didn't think about how long I'd have to live with it."

"Why'd you do it?"

"Disguise. Harper Teague was in Mexico, following me. Wanted to turn the tables on him, figure out what he was doing, which I did." He scowled. "But . . . a waste of time."

"Harper Teague followed you to Mexico?"

"Thought so, but no. Turns out, he spends time there, working. Has a hotel he stays at . . . near where I was going."

"Too much of a coincidence. Know how big Mexico City is? Twenty million people."

"I know." He shook his head. "The trip was a waste of time. I wanted to find a way to defend Potts Monroe, but I found nothing. Nothing that helps, nothing that hurts, . . . waste of time. Little tangents I stupidly followed. The butterfly reserve. Following Teague to Madrid, then Paris. Wastes of time."

The waitress returned with two glasses of pinot grigio and took their orders.

"Did Teague ever see you?" Kelly asked after the waitress left.

"Not after my fancy new haircut. Unless of course he was playing along . . . but I don't think so. He's up to something. Something no good, but it doesn't have anything to do with the park or the monument, or Potts Monroe."

"Why did you say we should cut back on guacamole?"

"Increasing demand for avocados simply increases the pressure to clear land needed to protect the monarch butterfly. The Super Bowl alone drives up demand for avocados by a third . . . over eight million pounds of guacamole made on game day. Growth in avocado production has been good for many in Mexico. Except, where there's money, there's the cartel, and where the cartel is—at least in butterfly country—there's one more powerful force making it difficult to protect the butterfly and its habitat. The cartel takes money from farmers and it kills people." He paused, catching himself before mentioning his run-in or Professor Morales' death. "Anyway . . . guacamole . . . we contribute to a growth industry with consequences for the monarch butterfly."

"Is that the real reason you went?" Kelly sipped her wine, her eye moving over his head.

"What do you mean?"

"Butterflies." She stared a moment, then laughed. "It's the kind of work you love."

"You're thinking too hard." He leaned over his hands. "Butterflies were a coincidence. I was there because of Potts." He sighed. "Had a little talk with Alex on the drive from Dulles."

"About me?"

"Yes."

She took another sip. "He thinks my pledge not to make the office about money isn't practical."

"Maybe it's not."

"If it's not, then maybe I'm not the right person for this office."

"He thinks you are. You need to make your announcement. Are you running or not?"

"I don't know yet. I don't know if I'm effective. What if I don't see any signs that I am?"

"You will. What will it take to convince you?"

"Evidence that I am of real service to the people of New Mexico."

"You're serving them every day."

"But doing things anyone could do. Responding to requests and inquiries. Serving the basic needs of constituents. Working on what they bring me. But I don't see evidence that I can do this job better than anyone else who wants it."

"You're hard on yourself. Alex thinks you can do great things, but you need to defend against people spreading misinformation."

"I've heard what he has to say." She forced a smile. "Are you still thinking about that guy spreading lies at the public meeting?"

"Not anymore. I was, but your father and Karen Hatcher claim no one's heard anything more from the guy . . . and they don't think anyone believed a word he said." He chuckled to himself. "I guess truth prevailed. Unlike what happened in Montana."

"Good." She took another sip. "Because I've been worried about you . . . worried you're searching."

"Only for a way to defend Potts Monroe. I was told to make myself scarce, so I did. I went to the one person who might have answers. Turned out she's in mourning . . . her husband died. I only made things worse for her."

She gasped. "What happened?"

"Another time. I'd rather not think about it tonight." He shook it off.

"But what about butterflies . . . as work . . . even if the professor died?"

"Maybe." He gave a long rub to his chin. "Wish it could honor him in some way. Your people have the report and are working on legislation, so maybe it's time."

"I promise, we won't move forward until it's signed." She sighed and took a slow sip of her wine. "After all the things that have happened. All the times things could've gone to hell . . . you didn't let that happen."

"Wasn't me. It was everyone."

She nodded, letting out a knowing chuckle.

Chapter 24

The waitress brought out their meals, two plates of chicken piccata.

"How long can you stay?" Kelly asked, picking up her fork.

"I should get out of your hair, huh?"

"No. Tomorrow's Friday. I'm flying to New Mexico." She smiled, giving a twist to a sprig of hair. "Stay in my apartment, relax a few days. I'll be back on Sunday."

"I'll go with you."

"I'm not going to Las Piedras. I've got a meeting in Santa Fe on Saturday, then a town hall in Las Cruces Saturday night . . . the other end of the state."

"I can find a way home." He took a sip. "Coalition report might need final touches, and I shouldn't risk the appearance of lobbying. Not now." He sighed. "I don't want you dragged into some ludicrous smear campaign."

"I've got plenty of that already." She pointed at his plate, hardly touched. "Eat."

—'—

After dinner, they took the Metro to a station in Arlington, then an uphill walk to Kelly's apartment. She cracked open a bottle of red wine and poured them each a glass.

Jack backed toward the master bath. “I’ll let mine breathe a moment. If you don’t mind, I’d like to take a shower.”

She smiled. “Go ahead . . . I’ll start on what I need to have read before morning.”

After a shower and shave, Jack returned to the living room, wrapped in a green towel. He plopped down on the sofa.

A stack of papers on her lap, her briefcase open, the glass of wine half gone, Kelly tore herself away from her reading. “I should get comfortable, too.” She set the papers aside and disappeared into her bedroom.

He checked the time. Nine-thirty. Seven-thirty Mountain Time. “I’m gonna make a quick call,” he shouted. “Will that bother you?”

“Nope, go ahead,” she yelled back.

He opened the contact list on his phone. The Kid. The graduate student in Montana. He thought a moment about what to say, took a sip of wine, tapped the phone number, and listened for the ring.

“Hello,” came a quick, cold response.

“Toby LeBlanc . . . this is Jack Chastain.”

A pause, then, “Wasn’t expecting *you*.”

“I’m sure you weren’t. How are you?”

“I’m doing,” he said, no emotion. “Can’t talk long. I work nights.”

“Got vacation time you need to use?”

“No. Why?”

Kelly returned, wearing flannel bottoms and a T-shirt. She picked up her papers and settled in beside him.

“I need someone with your expertise. A whiz on GIS, who can do a few analyses looking at geology and ground water flow, maybe surface geography, and tell me where to look for water.”

“You mean, like, springs and creeks?”

“No, that’d be too easy. I want damp soils, and that’s a relative description. Damp in New Mexico would be considered dry where you live.”

“What’s this for?”

"Monarch butterflies."

"Monarch butterflies like damp soil?"

"No, monarch like milkweed. Milkweed likes damp soil."

"Uh, . . ."

Jack let it sink in, hoping to piqué Kid's interest. Pushing wouldn't work.

"Uh, . . . how much work is there?"

"I've got some data layers. I just need someone who can use 'em to make inferences about where to look. It'd be great if that person could spend a little time on the ground to test or truth their results."

"I work ten-hour days. The way my schedule works, I've got six days off coming up. The end of one pay period, the beginning of another, but I don't think that's enough time."

"Maybe not, but . . . it'd help."

"Can you pay for my travel?"

"Yeah. What else do you need?"

He seemed to think about it. "A place to throw a sleeping bag."

"For that, the options are limitless. Think about it," Jack said, ready to end the call. "I'll call you Monday. If you're game, we'll nail down some plans." He ended the call, sat back, and let his thoughts bounce around in his head.

Kelly put down her papers and slid into his lap, facing him. She picked up her wine and offered a sip from her glass. "I love it when you talk dirty."

"That, Senator, wasn't talking dirty." He took a sip. "Thought you had work to do?"

"Why Mr. Chastain, it sounded like a brazen attempt to grab my attention."

"Senator, I need to teach you the meaning of brazen."

"Good." She kissed him, then glanced at the stack of papers. "Those'll wait."

—·—

They woke to the sounds of morning activity on the streets of Arlington.

Jack climbed out of bed and stood at the window. Several stories below, a steady stream of pedestrians made their way to the Metro Station, most for a short trip to whatever hall of government employed them. A sudden pulse of traffic exited the station, a pack of others going the opposite direction—to organizations based outside the city. In the distance, he saw buildings. Landmarks of a nation lay spread across the landscape. Arlington National Cemetery. The Pentagon. Beyond them, the spire of the Washington Monument and the Capitol dome.

Kelly headed for the shower. When done, she returned to the bedroom, naked, drying her hair with a towel. "Stay . . . rest. I'll call, meet you for lunch . . . unless the day goes to hell."

He took her by the waist and pulled her onto the bed.

"Are you trying to make me late?"

"Something like that."

She kissed him, then forced her way out of his arms.

He watched her get ready, choosing a burgundy suit and slipping a pair of heels into her briefcase. After putting on makeup and a comfortable pair of walking shoes, she tossed a few things into an overnighter and rolled it toward the door. She turned back to Jack. "You could come into the office, help a little on legislation."

He buried his head under a pillow.

"I'll call." Before closing the door to the apartment, she shouted, "Lock up. I won't be back here till Sunday."

He dozed, then made coffee, then enjoyed the luxury of another shower. Using his freshly recharged phone he made airline reservations, getting on the standby for the same flight Kelly would be on, departing on an afternoon American flight from Reagan National.

While getting another cup of coffee his phone rang.

"Coming to the office?" asked a male voice. Alex Trasker.

"Maybe."

"I'd like to take up where we left off yesterday. Vera would like a better understanding of how far authorities for action should go."

"Kip and Hatcher would have opinions on that."

"We asked."

"What'd they say?"

"Each was open to expansive authorities, but . . . for their own group's interests, and a bit more *qualified* when it came to supporting other needs. Cautious would be a better term."

"Doesn't the coalition report already answer the question?" He took a sip of his coffee.

"Kinda. Kinda not. Your interpretation would be helpful."

"Is that your only issue?" Jack asked.

"Here, let me put Vera on." The background noise changed as Trasker switched to speaker phone. "Vera, Jack asked if that's your only issue."

"Depends on how pretty he wants it to be," she said. "Maybe it doesn't matter. Who knows if it'll even make it to committee, much less to the floor?"

"She's joking," Alex said, an aside. "She's got a dry sense of humor." He seemed to turn away from the phone. "It'd be good if we knew what Mr. Expert here thinks, right?"

"Agreed."

"Jack?"

He sat a moment, sipping his coffee, imagining Alex giving a stroke to his beard. "Yes?"

"Just give us a few minutes of your time. This *one* topic. Us asking questions."

"Okay. Tell no one I was here. You've only worked with Kip and Karen Hatcher."

"Agreed."

Jack stuffed his gear in his pack, turned off the coffee, and locked up. Within minutes he was on the metro, standing in a crowded train car. At the Capitol South station, he departed and headed north, skirting past the capitol to the Hart Senate Office Building.

In the Junior Senator's suite, Vera took Jack to her office and sat him at the computer. Working from notes Vera made from talking to both Kip Culberson and Karen Hatcher, Jack leveled the playing field—working through the lunch hour—crafting authorities to give the federal agencies what they needed to manage the monument without giving away the farm or causing itself excessive headaches any time something needed to be acted upon or changed. Both preservation and utilization had authorities for action in the monument, within defined limits.

"There. My thoughts," Jack said, pulling back from the computer. "I'm done."

"Should I give it a quick read?" Vera asked. "In case I have any questions?"

"Too late if you do," a voice said from behind them.

Senator Culberson stood thumbing through a handful of notes. "I've got to get to the airport. Jack, are you coming?"

He stood. "Yeah."

"Got calls you need to return?" Trasker asked, eyeing the notes.

"These can wait."

"Any from important people? Prospective contributors? Should someone call back, tell them you've been called out of town. Suck up a bit."

"It can wait . . . and . . . on the sucking up part, no."

Trasker sighed. "I respect your position on that . . . but, as I've said before, I'm worried. You're letting others define you."

—·—

The standby list came through, giving Jack a seat on the flight.

They arrived in Albuquerque and met the aide who staffed Kelly's office in New Mexico's largest city, a man with salt and pepper hair who had been with Senator Baca for over a decade and would be leaving at the end of the term. On the drive to the office, to pick up Kelly's personal vehicle, they discussed a constituent's complaint about the Small Business Administration.

Jack sat in the back, his mind wandering.

After getting her vehicle, Kelly and Jack took off for Santa Fe.

At the hotel, she studied a package of briefings in preparation for meeting the staff of the governor.

The next morning, after she left, Jack wandered Old Town, circling familiar landmarks, killing time. He made his way past the Palace of the Governors to a restaurant called The Shed.

Kelly's meeting lasted well past noon, at which time she called and asked to meet him on the square.

"Good, that's where I'm at."

He left the restaurant. In a few minutes he spotted her across the way. She approached, stopped, and sighed. "Father would be better at this."

"In his words, it's time for the next generation." Jack looked into her eyes.

"I hope so." She attempted a less than confident smile. "Mind if we grab a bite to eat? I was thinking, The Shed." She pointed. "It's that way."

He allowed himself a chuckle. "Sounds great. Been a long time."

—'—

As they talked over lunch, uncertainty melted away. Something about being back in New Mexico. The person who was Senator Culberson was not a great deal different than the woman he met at Caveras Creek years before, but the layer of formality she wore in Washington, D.C. took a bit to get used to. Mostly for her.

Here, formality dissolved away. The hour was theirs. Then, she would need to depart for Las Cruces, on the way dropping him off at the bus station.

"Do you realize, on most of our trips to Santa Fe . . . or Taos . . . or wherever . . ." Jack paused, not sure what to say. He took a sip of his margarita. "You were the artist, sharing yourself. Maybe at a gallery, maybe with someone wanting to commission a piece."

"Feels different, doesn't it?"

"Yes, but you wouldn't think so."

"Why?"

"Because most politicians seem to do just that, focus on

sharing something of themselves. Know what I mean? It's about them. You? You don't seem to be that way."

"I'm not sure I know what I'm doing."

"You know what you're doing. You just need to get to know yourself in this role."

"The people of New Mexico need someone who knows how politics work."

"Like your father?"

"Yes, like my father. All those years I tried not knowing what he did. Throwing up my arms and treating politics as a dirty word. But he did his work . . . and I don't know how he survived it."

"How?"

"I don't understand it yet. There are people in Washington trying to do good things. Important work . . . trying not to get caught up in contrived battles . . . trying to bring people together . . . to find solutions. But the politics, . . . it's amazing."

"How so?"

"You haven't heard the ads?"

"I've been out of the country, remember?"

She sighed. "The ads say I've sold out to Washington special interests, accusing me of the very things I've taken a stand against. The ads call on constituents to demand my position on issues, even though I feel strongly that my positions need to come from the people I represent."

"You've made that known. It may take a while to sink in." He took a sip of his drink. "People will come to know what you're about. The governor did. He watched you take on Congressman Hoff and saw something there."

"Yeah." She rubbed at her brow. "I've given myself a week to decide if I'm running for my own term. I've reserved the big meeting room at the Inn of the Canyons for next Saturday. Same day as the coalition's signing ceremony. A town hall to talk about issues that matter. I'll either announce I'm running, or that I'm not.

"Which way are you leaning?"

"I don't know yet. Maybe I should come back to New Mexico, let someone else have a run at the office."

He smiled. "Or maybe you'll realize they need you."

—·—

Kelly dropped Jack off at the bus station.

With his pack slung over one shoulder, he waved as she turned toward Interstate 25 on her way to Las Cruces.

Chapter 25

Complete waste of time. And money.

Jack stared out the bus window, oblivious to the landscape flying past, thinking about the places he'd been in the past week. *A waste of time. What was I thinking? Distracted, by talk of treasure, or looking to defend Potts Monroe? Wild goose chases that turned out to be irrelevant.*

Defend Potts as best you can until he returns . . . and ignore the distractions.

The bus turned off the highway and crept into the hamlet of Las Piedras. Beyond the edge of town, the plateau rose—the natural boundary for Piedras Coloradas National Park, more meaningful than the legal description he knew by heart. His eye moved to the slice through the plateau, the canyon—a sliver from this angle—and down to where the river lay, a quiet, unassuming force, even in these late days of spring flow.

Somehow, everything felt different. Maybe just from being gone.

Felt like months.

The bus came to a stop at a gas station in the middle of town. Jack slipped on a baseball cap, in no mood to explain his new look, and followed the few others departing the bus.

He pulled out his phone. *Who do I call? No one. There will be someone on the square or coming out of Elena's.*

He stretched, loosened the knots in his back, then his arms and legs. Walking, he eyed the distant bell tower of the centuries old church that stood over the square. He passed other buildings, added in more recent times, some in architectural styles that hadn't aged nearly as well to the eye as the old adobe church.

Rounding a corner, he caught sight of people on benches, on sidewalks, and sitting on the ground in the shade of cottonwoods. He recognized no one.

A dark sedan passed, then slowed. The driver put it in reverse and stopped beside him. The driver's side window slid down. Sheriff Montoya, wearing dark sunglasses. "That boy you brought into the office," he said, as if a question. "Couple weeks back."

Jack eyed his vehicle. Unmarked. "Slippery little guy?"

"Yeah, that one. I just saw him."

Another vehicle rolled past, an unmarked SUV. Montoya reached for his radio microphone. "Deputy, you just drove past my location. Got a second?" He watched the vehicle pull into a parking space. "He might as well hear this. Keep me from repeating myself."

Buck Winslow got out and sauntered over to Montoya's sedan. "You're back," he said to Jack, as he pulled a toothpick from his shirt pocket. "Where you been?"

"Mexico."

"Oh, yeah, I remember Reger saying something about that."

"You need to hear this," Montoya said to Winslow. "That boy Jack and Senator Culberson tried handing off to us a couple of weeks ago. Just saw the boy . . . and managed to slip up on him, trap him in an alley. Got him to talk, but not much. Asked him who his parents are. Asked him if it was common for him to be hiking by himself that far from home, like that day out on South Desert."

"South Desert," Winslow said, stepping closer. "I hadn't heard that part."

"He was, yes."

"By himself?" Winslow looked to Jack to confirm.

Jack nodded and turned back to the sheriff. "What'd he say?"

"Nothing. Not about that." The sheriff rubbed his chin. "I'm wondering . . . now that I've talked to him . . . if we need to bring him to the attention of social services."

"Why?" Winslow asked.

"I assured him he wasn't in trouble, but he still wouldn't say much. The one thing he did say, and he seemed to regret it, was . . . he worries what might happen to his mom. I asked him if his father was hurting her. He said he didn't have a father. He wouldn't tell me who his mother is, but it's all about something that happened that day. I got the impression he hadn't told her. Afraid it'd put her in danger . . . so he's not talkin'. What I couldn't get out of him . . . is this. What happened that day? Why's he afraid?"

Winslow squinted, processing the information, his eyes moving in their sockets.

Another distraction. "Doesn't sound like you need me involved," Jack said.

"Maybe not," Montoya replied. "Only if you can think of why he woulda been afraid of something out there." He locked eyes on Jack. "What did you see that day?"

"Nothing, really. He was crossing the desert. Seemed strange, being there all alone. Got a call on the radio about a lost boy, thought it was him, so we went after him. Seemed to be hiding his tracks . . . pretty well, too . . . and he was afraid of me. I gave him no reason to be. He said something about spirits . . . or maybe it was faces."

"Spirits," Winslow's eyes moved between the sheriff and Jack. "Ah, the boogeyman."

"Maybe," the sheriff muttered. "But . . . I lost him. Still don't know who the boy is."

"Lost him?" Winslow said, aghast.

"Yeah." Montoya sighed. "I tried making him comfortable. Sat him down. Sat beside him in the dirt. I figured I'd take him home after we talked. Talk to his mom. Get some answers. He musta figured that out. I tried getting up. My old bones didn't work too fast and he saw his opening. Darted right past me. By the time I was on my feet, he was gone, no sign of him. No clue where he went."

Winslow laughed.

"Deputy, if you think I'm old, you're right but don't be laughin'. Someday you'll be slow, pickin' your own ass up out of the dirt."

Winslow let out a chuckle. "You're not old. You're as nimble as a jackrabbit."

"Don't suck up to me, deputy. By the way . . . it's the voter you need to suck up to . . . without it lookin' like you're doing it." He rubbed his forehead with the back of his hand. "You spend a lot of time at school. Ask around, see if you can figure out who this kid is."

"But I haven't seen him . . . so I don't know what he looks like."

"You might see if we still have the recordings of the office video feed from the day Jack brought him in. That might help."

"I take it you don't need anything from me," Jack said.

"Just to think about what coulda scared that boy."

"Probably happened before we saw him, but I'll think about it." Jack turned to Winslow. "Heading anywhere near the park?"

"I can."

"Can I get a ride?"

Montoya drove off.

Jack followed Winslow to his SUV and climbed in the passenger side, setting his pack at his feet. He noticed a new, *my name is Deputy Buckity*, sticker on the dashboard.

"Still got your bullet?" Jack asked.

Winslow shot him a look, then laughed and guffawed, "Yuckity, yuck, yuck." He backed the vehicle onto the street, circled the square, and took the road toward the park.

Jack watched out the side window as Las Piedras slipped past.

"Your old buddy, Hide Mangum . . . he's been looking for you."

"Glad he missed me." Jack pointed at the sticker on the dashboard. "It's great that you do that sort of thing in the schools."

"It's rewarding." He shot Jack a glance. "Changin' the subject? Mangum's tellin' everyone in the Enclave that you and those land agents of yours are about to go after their land. They're gearing up for war."

"Never been part of anything that goes after people's land."

"You need to tell him that." Winslow braked at a stop sign,

then turned toward the park, hitting highway speed for the short drive to the entrance. “Did you really go to Mexico?”

“Yeah. Waste of time.”

“Really. I guess you shoulda stayed here . . . for the excitement.” Eyes locked on the road, Winslow dug into the vehicle’s console. He found a toothpick. “You didn’t miss it. Just late.”

“For what?”

“Excitement. For what, I’m not sure. Something about Juan Rivera’s treasure.”

“Decided I don’t believe all that talk.”

“Well, don’t, but everyone else seems to. Apparently, the story’s gotten interesting.”

“How so?”

“Not sure. Too busy dealing with treasure hunters to figure out what’s got ’em goin’.”

“Any sign of Potts Monroe?”

“Nope.” Buck took his eyes off the road. “Think he’s involved?”

“I don’t want to think so.”

They passed the park’s sandstone and timber entrance sign. Ahead, cars sat at a standstill on approach to the station, a line of a dozen or more cars. Winslow slowed to a stop.

“Kinda busy for this time of day,” Jack said.

“No worse than yesterday. All this because of treasure.”

“And you really don’t know what the breaking news is?”

“Heard a thing or two but I didn’t know what it meant. Sounded like . . . something about arrows.” Winslow wagged a finger at the cars metering one at a time through the entrance station. “Last night this line went all the way back into town.”

“Arrows? Like . . . a direction marker? . . . or what?”

“I don’t know. Ask around. Next fight you see, ask the guy who’s left standing.”

“That wouldn’t be wise, would it?” Jack sighed. “They’re wasting their time.”

Winslow laughed. “*You* are a cynical man.”

The car in front of them pulled up to the entrance station, the driver flashed a permit, and the ranger waved them through.

Winslow followed, stopping at the kiosk.

The ranger, a young blonde woman Jack had never seen, stood in the open window. Full uniform. Big smile. “Deputy Buckity.” She let out a giggle. “What brings you to brave the line?”

“Just giving a ride to one of your own.”

Jack leaned into view. “We haven’t met. You must be new. I’m Jack Chastain.”

She smiled. “I’ve heard about you. Senator Culberson’s beau.”

He laughed. “I guess that’s who I am.”

“I’m Jen.”

“Jen, who?”

“Last names are for wanted posters. Just Jen. I don’t want Deputy Buckity hauling me in for some crazy thing I did in the seasonal dorm at my last park.”

“Don’t worry about Buck. If you play your cards right, he’ll show you his bullet.”

“Oh, I’ve seen it. Surprised he hasn’t lost it.”

Jack laughed. “So, it’s been like this all weekend?”

“People pouring in, headed for the backcountry looking for treasure.”

“And they know they can’t treasure hunt in the park?”

“We’re handing out this.” She held up a flier. The word *Warning,* in red letters, crossed the top. Below it, *No Treasure Hunting.* More words below that. “I’m not sure it’s doing any good. People are wild eyed and crazy.”

Winslow gave her a two-finger salute and accelerated away.

“Take the first left,” Jack said.

They followed the main park road for half a mile before the junction came into view.

“Turn here and go to the end of the road. I’m the last cabin. Base of the wall.”

Winslow slowed at the circle drive, stopping at the farthest cabin.

Jack climbed out, dragging his pack, then turned to wave.

The deputy’s vehicle pulled away, disappearing down the road.

Vertical cliffs tugged at Jack’s eyes as he unlocked the door.

Inside, everything looked as it did when he left. He dropped his pack on the kitchen counter. A blank pad of paper lay by the phone. *Hold it. Isn't that where I wrote down my flight to Mexico?* He stared a moment, trying to remember, then shook it off. *Must've taken it with me. Enough with the paranoia.*

In the cupboard sat a single can of chili. *It'll have to do.* He dumped the can in a pot and turned on the stove. His phone rang, vibrating in his pocket. "Hello," he said, without looking.

"Boss, heard you're home." Reger.

"Yep, I'll see you in the office tomorrow. Talk to you then."

"Hold it, boss. You should know . . . this place is crazy with treasure hunters."

"Saw that coming in. Deputy Winslow said there's a new wrinkle on the Rivera story."

"What wrinkle?"

"Something about arrows. Who knows? He wasn't sure."

"Arrows? What else did he say?"

"Not much . . . but I've wasted enough time on Juan Rivera. No more. I'm gonna eat and go to bed. I'll talk to you tomorrow." He ended the call.

He dished up his chili and sat. So, what is the latest on the Juan Rivera story? He reached for his laptop, then stopped. *No. Quit wasting time.*

And stop worrying about Potts. He'll turn up.

The boy came to mind, and the sheriff.

What could the boy be afraid of? Why make such an effort to avoid talking about it?

The boy's a distraction. Another waste of time. There are more important things to do.

Like polishing up the report and getting it signed. Then . . . maybe getting into the field. Doing some science.

He thought about Mexico. Then, Paris. The lunacy. *Why did you do that? The money it cost. And Madrid. Listening to Teague and his accomplice make the treasure seem so real.*

And it was real. It just isn't relevant. To here.

Not to Potts, not to Juan Rivera, not to Piedras Coloradas.

Just a waste of time.

But Teague was up to something. What?

Words crept into his mind. Words that flowed out from the windowed office. . . . *send to Freeport.*

Which Freeport? Texas? New York? Maine? Or where? And who's in Freeport? Some rich collector or museum that wants little gold Mexican men in their collection? And shields and spearheads and bracelets?

If it's a museum, enough time has passed that they might be bragging about new acquisitions. Might not be hard to find. *Local museum makes haul at Paris arts auction.*

He reached for his laptop. Flipping it open, he toggled the switch and pulled up the browser. He typed in Freeport, Texas, and scrolled through the latest news. Nothing remotely related. He typed in Freeport, New York. Nothing there either. Freeport, Maine. Same result. Freeport, Illinois. Nothing. No mentions of museums. Collectors? That would be unlikely. Those people wouldn't be putting their acquisitions in the news. But . . . just in case . . . he typed in *artifact acquisition by collector in Freeport.*

He scrolled down the screen. Nothing remotely relevant.

The way Teague said it, definitely Freeport, not a word in some other language. What about England? He entered *Freeport, England.* No such place. As he scrolled down the screen, he spotted a news brief. The English prime minister wanted to set up a special economic zone where the usual customs laws didn't apply. freeports. Little *f*, freeport, not big *F*, Freeport.

Buried among the details, a description. The purpose of freeports, and mention of the world's largest, a huge facility in Switzerland. Zurich.

Zurich.

Where the man in the fancy suit got off the plane.

Jack pounded out a new query, *Zurich freeport*, and scrolled down through the results. The Zurich freeport, a building larger than thirteen soccer pitches. More space being built. He opened an article. ". . . *where arts and antiquity are stored to avoid taxes and hide future transactions.*" He closed the article and opened another.

"... filled with art" "No one, except the very secretive administrators of the facility and the individual owners of the items in each locker, really knows what is there." "... where sale transactions take place hidden from the eyes of the tax collector."

Jack stared at the words. ... *hide future transactions ... largest in the world. Zurich.*

The well-dressed man at the auction. And on the plane. *Could he have had ... ?*

Maybe a buyer. Maybe escorting another buyer's purchases from Paris to Zurich.

Stop. What does it matter? Jack sighed and closed the browser.

You've wasted enough time. And money. This has nothing to do with Potts Monroe or that silly rumor about Juan Rivera.

He slammed the laptop shut.

Enough distraction.

Chapter 26

The desk for the superintendent's secretary sat empty. Jack checked his watch. Still early for Marge. He stepped past her desk, pulled down his ball cap, and knocked on the door to the right.

"It's open," came a voice from inside.

Jack slipped in.

Joe Morgan glanced up. "You're home." He turned back to scribbling on a yellow, legal note pad. As always, the superintendent appeared neatly pressed. He finished a thought and set down his pen.

"Anything changed?" Jack asked.

For a moment, a look of curiosity formed, but Joe made no mention of what he did or didn't see in terms of hair. "For you?" he asked.

Jack leaned against the doorframe, then nodded.

"Nope. The regional director still has no interest in hearing your name."

"I'm tired of being on the road, but . . . what if I take leave and work on a personal project? Milkweed and monarch butterfly?"

"Where?"

"Backcountry. Both in the park and the monument. I'll stay out of people's hair."

"Why would you take leave? Those things fall under your purview."

"I just thought . . . if I took leave . . . you could tell the RD I wasn't working."

"Her concern is you sticking your nose into something that's not your business."

"Joe, what happens here is my business. I, and you, we've put in a hell of a lot of work getting people to tolerate each other, listen to each other. Us listening to them."

"That's why they don't want you here. Everything somehow connects back to you, and if anyone asks, you feel you need to answer. The powers that be don't want that happening."

Jack stepped inside and plopped down in a chair. "What are they doing, Joe?"

"I can't tell you. Every time I talk to the RD or Washington I swear again that I haven't told you a thing. It's that simple. This is driven by someone else, not us. It's way above me, and I'm not controlling it." He sighed and shook his head. "Jack, if anyone gets hurt . . . I want it to be me, not you." He picked up his pen and gave it a click. "Sorry, but that's the way it's gotta be. Now, change the subject. Milkweed. If you keep your nose clean and focus on the project, I'll take the heat if someone asks."

Jack gave a grudging nod. "I'm not a rabble-rouser."

"I know that, but you've got your moments. Promise me you'll be in the backcountry."

"Promise. Thought I'd bring in a guy I know to do some analysis, then go into the field. Have a little project money to get him here. We can do the analysis using the geographic information system here in the office, then go into the backcountry, ground truth the effectiveness of his work. After he leaves, I'll stay focused on the backcountry."

"Good. Where's this guy from?"

"Are you sure you want to know?"

"I was mostly making conversation, figuring a university, but if you put it that way, yes."

"Montana."

Joe sighed and gave his pen several clicks. "Keep your nose clean."

Jack stood and slipped out the door.

In the hall, he made his way to his office.

First things first.

He called the number for the Kid. No answer.

Turning on his computer, he checked email and waded through a backlog of messages.

In twenty minutes, he tried the Kid's number again. No answer.

Twenty minutes later, still no answer.

Maybe he changed his mind. Maybe he had more important things to do. Can't blame him. Jack waited a few minutes and called again, leaving a message, ending with, "If you've changed your mind, I understand. Take care of yourself."

At the sound of a knock, he looked up.

Reger stood in the door wearing Stetson, service belt, and weapon. "Gotta talk, boss."

"About?"

"Juan Rivera."

"I've wasted too much time on that already."

"Hold it boss, hear me out." He stepped in the office. "The latest is not about arrows . . . though I see how someone could think it's about quivers, thus arrows."

Jack stood. "It's about quivers? For arrows?"

"No, boss. The word is not quivers. The word is Quivira. You know the word, right?"

"Remind me."

"Coronado."

"Coronado was south of here, looking for Cibola, seven cities of gold. Turned out they were pueblos."

"Boss, there's more to the story. Quivira. The motherlode. Coronado went all the way to Kansas looking for it." Reger braced himself against the desk. "He looked in the wrong place, boss. The Turk misled him. Took him onto the plains, hoping Coronado would get lost and die."

Jack's head began to pound. "Now, how would that involve Rivera? Wrong century."

"This might make me look dumb, but . . . I read the latest from the journal." He swallowed, then sucked in a breath. "Quivira is in Colorado."

"What?" Jack spun in his seat. "Impossible." He pulled out his cell phone and found the international number for Angelica Vargas. La Profesora. It rang twice.

"Buenos días, Jack," she answered. "Are you home?"

"Yes. Got a minute?"

"Sí."

"Quivira? How likely is it that Juan Rivera found Quivira?"

"Quivira?" She laughed. "Virtually none. Quivira is in Kansas."

"What if Coronado was misled? What if Quivira was not in Kansas?"

Silence. After a long moment, she muttered, "I will need to reacquaint myself with something. I will call you back." The phone went dead.

Jack pointed Reger to a chair. "Have a seat."

Two minutes later, his cell phone rang.

"Hola, Angelica. Learn anything?"

"Nothing. Everything is as I remember."

"Enlighten us."

"The place Coronado traveled to in search of Quivira is present day Kansas. At one time, some believed it might have been Texas. One site is in what is now Hutchinson County, others to the east and south. But the consensus now, supported by artifacts—Spanish items—is, he was in Eastern Kansas. He encountered indigenous communities but found no gold. You know the story, yes?"

"He went from New Mexico to Kansas. That does seem odd."

"Let me explain the context." She cleared her throat. "The factors at play. The desperation. The deceit." She paused. "The Viceroy of Mexico shared with Coronado the stories from a friar named Marcos de Niza. De Niza had supposedly seen the Seven Cities of Cibola. Golden cities, supposedly filled with riches in what is now

New Mexico. Gold, precious stones, fine clothes. Coronado, the governor of New Galencia—what is now largely Sinaloa—offered to fund an expedition from his own wealth, actually his wife's family money. Mendoza, the Viceroy, contributed to assure he would have a stake in the riches.

"Coronado's expedition," she continued, ". . . was huge. Over three hundred soldiers, a thousand natives, supplies, beef cattle, horses, all headed north with de Niza as their guide. This was February 1540. When they reached the first city, it was not of gold or grandeur. It was a crowded little village, not much in appearance. Coronado demanded surrender. The people refused and he attacked. It was a difficult battle and Coronado was wounded, but the Spanish prevailed. Expecting piles of gold, he found nothing of the sort, only to learn de Niza had never actually been in the city, he had only seen it from afar. Disappointed and bleeding money, he sent a report back to Medoza that no gold had been found, and he sent de Niza back to Mexico."

"But it didn't end there, right?"

"Coronado met a native of the Mississippi River region, a man kept as a slave by the Cibolans. Coronado's men referred to him as *the Turk*. The Turk told Coronado about a land of fabulous riches, known as Quivira. He offered to lead him there. Coronado set out with the Turk as their guide. Along the way they raided villages, killing natives, raping women, stealing supplies. All manner of cruelty. The Turk kept assuring Coronado it was only a little farther. Finally, when in Kansas, the Turk was tortured for answers. He admitted he wanted to be free, to go home, that others had encouraged him to mislead Coronado, to take him deep into the plains where they hoped he would become lost and die in the wilderness."

"So, the whole thing was made up?"

"So, it would seem. Except . . ."

"Except?"

"Hold it. I just noticed . . . ," Angelica said. "I . . . never noticed this before." She paused. Momentary silence. "Maybe it's nothing."

"What?"

"First, tell me more about this rumor."

Jack turned to Johnny, against the wall, his foot tapping. "Gonna put you on speaker."

"Who's this?" Johnny asked.

"An expert in Spanish colonial history." Jack turned to the phone. "Angelica, this is Johnny Reger. He's followed the rumors more than I have. He's the one who showed me the website. Johnny, tell us the latest. Quivira."

"Does she know about the journal?"

"Yes, part of the story."

"Then I'll start at the end." Johnny scooted up to the desk. "Things had gone quiet . . . you know . . . the effort to understand the journal. The writing is difficult to read, some language is unfamiliar to these guys. Leaks to the public stopped . . . maybe they found something big . . . or they didn't know what to do with what they learned. There was uncertainty about words, some disbelief, that sorta thing. So, yes, it turns out the latest is about Quivira."

"Go on."

"There's lots of talk about the guy named the Turk."

"It wasn't his name, but yes, he was a historical figure."

"Really?" Johnny said, his eyes lighting up. "Good."

"What else?"

"Well, this Turk guy misled ol' Coronado, taking him far away from the actual Quivira, to somewhere in Kansas."

"Jack and I were discussing that. The reference to Kansas . . . was that in the journal?"

"Nope. There were discussions between these people, trying to understand it. Why?"

"As you know, there was no Kansas when either Coronado or Rivera made their expeditions, and the likelihood of any mention of the Turk, in any journal from the late 1700s . . . seems unlikely."

"Right, gotcha." Johnny looked a little deflated. "But . . . these guys got excited about where they think this is leading. Want me to go on?"

"Yes, please."

"Word has it . . . on his second trip into what is now Colorado, Rivera encountered a Ute who wanted to trade for some of his gear.

The only thing he had of interest to Rivera was an item he was slow to show . . . made of gold. They followed this guy into the mountains, lost track of him, got lost themselves. They decided not to mention the gold when they reported to the governor in Santa Fe, and they planned another trip north. On the third trip they made camp near the settlement of one of the friendly chiefs on the Uncompahgre River, waiting for others to come trade with the chief and his people. They followed a trading party back into the mountains, getting lost several times, having to backtrack, then they found tracks. Then they found people, high in the mountains, in a place they likely wouldn't be in winter. But this wasn't winter, and the travel routes were open, and there it was, in the high country. Gold, silver, precious stones."

"The things the Turk had promised Coronado," Angelica said.

"I suppose, yes."

"Where?" she asked, sounding wary.

"San Juans, and you won't believe where they think it is?"

"I don't know the area."

"Just as well, because these guys interpreting the journal have ideas but nothing solid to go on."

"Got it, so . . . ," Jack said, interrupting. "Where do they think it is?"

"Near Telluride."

Angelica went quiet. No immediate response.

"Do you know Telluride?" Johnny asked.

"I've heard of it. Mining town. Where is it relative to your location?"

"North."

Jack leaned into the phone. "A minute ago, you said you noticed something."

"Yes, give me a moment," she said. "I want to check Castañeda's account. Coronado's chronicler." Papers rustled through the phone line. "It's something I've paid no attention to before." She paused. "One of my source materials claims the Turk said Quivira was to the north and that he offered to take them there."

"What's strange about that?"

"He didn't take them north. He took them east, first into what is now Texas, then into what is now Oklahoma, then Kansas. He didn't take them north, and, of course, I know the reason for that."

"Which is?" Jack asked.

"Not only did the Turk want to return to his own people, he admitted after being tortured, but he'd been told to lead Coronado into the wild, hoping he'd get lost and die. But . . ."

"We're listening."

"What if in the Turk's first mention of Quivira, he really did mean north? What if . . . when he agreed to lead Coronado the wrong direction—the reward being his freedom and returning to his own people—he changed his plans? The Cibolans could see the desperation in Coronado. So far, he'd found no riches. Coronado was desperate, and in that desperation, maybe they saw opportunity. Opportunity for a lie, and one that the Turk could make even bigger. Ever growing illusions of riches. Could Coronado have forgotten the Turk's earlier words, let himself be lured east, not north? Is that possible?"

"Hell, yeah," Johnny said. "Just look in the eyes of people here . . . looking for Rivera's cave. Gold fever. It's contagious. People are delirious."

"So, the journal could be real?" Jack muttered.

She waited before answering. "I have a deep feeling of skepticism, but . . . I'll admit, my heart is racing." She sighed. "There have been too many years without finding a golden city. In Kansas . . . or Colorado." She paused. "And I'm sorry, I must get off the phone. I have a call I must be on."

"We'll let you go," Jack said. "Thank you. We'll keep you in the loop."

Johnny sat looking uncertain. Caught between excitement and deflation. Finally, he left.

Jack stared at the ceiling. *Quivira? Could it be? Or just another waste of time.*

A knock sounded against the door.

Fighting the adrenaline coursing through his system, Jack took a deep breath and forced his eyes onto a bearded man in the hallway. Somewhat tall. Thin. Long, dark hair, tucked behind his ears. Worn jeans and T-shirt. It took a moment to register. The last time Jack had seen him he looked different. Very different. No longer did Toby LeBlanc have the look of an All-American boy. "Toby?"

He nodded. No emotion.

"I just tried calling you . . . but . . ."

"Still need someone to work on your project?"

"Uh, yeah. Sorry, my mind's on something else . . . but just a distraction . . . come in."

Chapter 27

"I didn't think you could be here till . . ."

"I have to be back on Sunday. Boss changed my schedule . . . needs me to cover someone's shifts, so I traded days. I'm here."

"That's great." Jack jumped up and extended a hand. "Great to see ya."

LeBlanc shook his hand. Almost grudging. No confidence.

"How did you get here? I mean, I was going to pay for your travel."

"It'd be good if you could. Cost an arm and a leg."

"I'm sure. Hard after the fact but I'll find a way." He pointed to a chair. "Have a seat."

LeBlanc sat and looked around the office.

"Get a room?"

"I bought a sleeping bag."

"Perfect. You can camp on my lawn, or my sofa."

"That'll do."

"We'll get into the backcountry as soon as we can."

He nodded. "Put me to work."

Jack glanced around the office. "I could find a workstation in another office, but . . . I think I'll let you use my desk . . . my computer. It has GIS and the data layers."

"What'll you do?"

"If you need quiet, I'll find someplace to work."

"I don't."

"Then, I'll just read, be here to help where I can."

He nodded.

"So, how have you been?"

His eyes moved away. "Gonna tell me more about why I'm here?"

"Oh, yeah. Sorry, I'm distracted."

"That's okay. I'll just get to work. Give me something to read." He stood.

Jack pulled a natural history volume off a shelf, setting it on the corner of the desk. "Intro to the area." He reached back and grabbed a book for himself on the history of New Mexico.

LeBlanc ignored the books and pulled up a directory on the computer. He took a few minutes to scan the files, then opened the application he wanted to use first. He leaned forward, studying a list. "The Park and monument are on separate maps?"

"Yes," Jack said, standing over him as the cursor floated over the directory, Quivira still occupying his mind.

"Which do you want to do?"

"Oh . . . uh . . . both if we can."

"Which has better data?"

"The Park." Jack noticed two mentions of Quivira in his book's index. He flipped through the pages to each. Nothing substantial.

LeBlanc clicked on a file—correct in his interpretation of names. Shapes began to form, lines, then labels. Piedras Coloradas National Park. "Okay, base layer for the Park. If we get this figured out, and if there's time, we'll do the monument." He closed the file and clicked on another. "I want to study the orthophoto, then tell me what you want from the analysis." An image came up on the screen. Aerial photos, highly detailed. Landforms, uniform scale and geometry. Deep canyons. Pine covered highlands. "Is the Park mostly plateau?"

Jack set his book aside. "Mostly. The place I found milkweed isn't in the park. It's on the monument."

Eyes still locked on the orthophoto, Toby muttered, "Then

maybe we should start there . . . where you know what you're looking for. Where is the monument, relative to this?"

Jack ran a finger down the screen, along the west, south and east boundaries. "Surrounding the Park. Everything downslope of those boundaries. Everything north is Colorado."

LeBlanc closed the file and reopened the file listing, clicking on another set of orthophotos. The image popped onto the screen. Slopes, open desert, rivers, creeks, arroyos, slickrock swells. Without words, he studied the terrain.

"Very different," Jack said.

He nodded. Without closing the orthophoto, he opened the data layer for hydrology, studying for a minute before closing it and opening another for geology. He continued through several more data layers, then stopped and turned away from the computer. "Is it easy to get to this place you have milkweed?"

"*Had* milkweed. Yeah, it's not too far in."

"What do you mean, *had*?"

"Let's not worry about that."

"Can we go there? I want to see it. We can talk about what you want done."

Jack opened a desk drawer and pulled out a set of keys. "Let's go."

He led him down the hall and out the back entrance, into the parking lot for government vehicles, all of them white with arrowheads and green stripes down their lengths.

They pulled out of the parking lot, onto a service road. At the highway, they waited for a break in traffic.

"Is this normal?" Toby asked, watching the line of cars streaming by.

"No, it's not actually. There's this rumor going around about treasure. It's got people wild eyed and crazy, coming to search, even though they can't, supposedly."

"Can't?"

"Can't treasure hunt in the Park."

He nodded.

A break in traffic, a slow-moving RV. Punching the gas, Jack turned onto the road toward the Park exit. "We'll skirt the edge of town and go out to what's called the South Desert."

LeBlanc nodded.

"Kid, maybe we'll . . ."

"Don't call me that," he said, cutting Jack off. "I don't go by that. Not anymore."

Jack glanced at LeBlanc, forgetting what he intended to say.

—·—

Leaving the blacktop, they dropped onto gravel. The tires began to rumble.

Ahead lay a bend in the road.

Jack slowed, feeling a knot in his gut. Those cars. Stacked in the road. *Forgot about that.*

He rounded the bend. *No cars. Gone.*

County road department must not have taken kindly to Mangum's game.

He sped up, passing the turn into the Enclave, then the boundary sign for Las Piedras National Monument. At the end of the road, the trailhead sat empty.

"I didn't bring water," LeBlanc muttered.

"Won't need it. Won't be gone long. We're close."

Jack led him up the trail, thinking about the earlier conversation. *Can't call him Kid. Who knows what other hot buttons he has now, poor guy?* "Ever been to New Mexico?" Jack asked, tossing the words back over his shoulder.

"Never."

"What do you think?"

"Different."

"Give it time. You'll love it." When LeBlanc didn't respond, he glanced back.

LeBlanc forced a nod.

Ahead lay the escarpment. Once past it, Jack watched for the dry arroyo. It came into view. Jack pointed off trail to the right, then at the sandstone outcropping.

Leaving the trail, they headed toward it, downslope, through rocks, sage and snakeweed. After a hundred yards, Jack veered toward the rock.

"Did you lose all your hair?"

"What?" Jack said, barely catching the words.

"Sorry, that's being an ass, isn't it?"

Jack laughed, the words having sunk in. "Temporary. Trying a new look."

"As a bald guy?"

"Yep."

"If you've got all your hair, why?" He caught himself. "Never mind. Not my business."

Jack laughed. "Kid, don't worry." He paused. "Sorry I said that." He started over. "It's okay, Toby. I'm okay with anything you have to say. It's a funny story. I'll tell you all about it later." He turned back to the outcropping "This is why we're here."

In the shadows of the rock—soil. Dark, red, moist.

LeBlanc watched as Jack walked the perimeter, a curvilinear line of thirty or more feet, an area five to ten feet wide, emanating out from the stone.

LeBlanc studied the setting. "How did you find this place?"

"Monarch butterflies. Saw 'em, came to see why they were here."

"There was milkweed here?"

"Yes."

"Where'd it go?"

"Long story."

"Give me the short version."

"Someone ripped 'em out."

°Toby pulled out his phone and snapped a few photos—the outcropping and a scattering of shots across the landscape. "Surface features," he said as he put the phone back in his pocket.

They ambled upslope toward the trail.

"So, why'd you shave your head?"

Jack laughed, turning in time to catch the first hint of a smile since Toby's arrival. Where to start. "I was in Mexico."

"When?"

"A few days ago. I got home yesterday. When I called you, I was in Washington, D.C."

"Why were you in Washington, D.C.?"

"Not relevant to the story. Anyway, I was in Mexico. I suppose I could say the barber didn't understand my Spanish?" He started for the trailhead.

LeBlanc stayed close. "He didn't speak Spanish?"

"No, he did." Jack laughed. "But I didn't. I do, just not very well."

LeBlanc let out a chuckle. "So, that's what happened?"

"No."

Another chuckle. "Then what?"

Jack sighed. "I needed a disguise."

"Why?"

"Someone was following me."

"Why?"

"I'm not exactly sure, but I thought . . . with a good enough disguise I could figure it out."

"Did you?"

"Nope. Big goose chase. I did learn something about the guy but . . ." He caught himself.

"What?"

Jack sighed. *Don't go there.* "A guy from Mexico I met last year started me on this project. A butterfly researcher."

"Are you changing the subject or are these stories related? You learned something from the butterfly researcher?"

"No, . . . he died."

Behind him, the sound of footsteps on gravel stopped.

Jack turned.

LeBlanc stared through him. "What are you not telling me?"

"It had nothing to do with this."

Cold moment. "Really?"

"Promise. Totally unrelated." Jack turned and started walking.

Toby waited a moment before following.

In a few minutes the trailhead came into view.

Nearing the vehicle, Jack could see they were not alone. On the backside of the pickup a person stood, fidgeting, working at something.

As he got closer, Jack noticed words scrawled on the windshield, in white. A man stepped out from behind the vehicle.

Hide Mangum slid his holster from the small of his back, the pistol in easy reach.

Jack trudged forward, jaw and fists clenched.

"Why are you here?" Mangum growled. "I warned you."

"Working. Get away from the truck!" Jack stopped at the fender and read the words.

YOU WILL NOT RUN US OFF OUR LAND

Jack banged his fist on the hood.

Toby stopped behind him.

Mangum scowled, eyes moving between men, either not expecting to be outnumbered, or uncertain about the young man with an appearance even rougher than his own.

"I am not running you off your land, Mangum. Don't be starting a revolution."

"I'm not starting it! You are. I'm calling you out."

"I'm not playing that game." Jack unlocked the door and turned to LeBlanc. "We're leaving."

LeBlanc walked past Mangum's ATV and climbed in the pickup, wasting no time.

Jack fired up the engine and threw it in gear, throwing gravel as he accelerated away.

Over the first rise, Jack hit the windshield washer—fluid and swipes by the wiper had no effect. "Damn, it's paint." He slammed on the brakes and dug a razor blade from the glove box. He scraped away the words and climbed back in. "There. No harm done."

LeBlanc said nothing until they reached the blacktop. Then, he muttered, "That the guy that ripped out the milkweed?"

"I think so, yes."

"Totally unrelated, huh?" He sighed. "So, what have you gotten me into?"

Chapter

28

"Don't worry about him," Jack said, after minutes passed. "If you want, I'll promise not to use that road again. We'll work in the Park."

"The road's not the issue." Toby sighed. "Oh . . . never mind." He glanced out the side window. "Isn't the Park different geology?"

"Sits on top of what we saw today?"

LeBlanc pushed a strand of hair from his eyes, then tapped a finger against the armrest. "If you want similar places, seems best to start with what we already know."

"Yeah, but we can try the Park. If it doesn't work out, I know another way in to where we were today. Or thereabouts."

That seemed to calm him. "Get me geology reports. I'll think about both places. It's all sedimentary. Things in common . . . but other factors to figure out."

"I'm sorry that happened back there."

"Not your doing." He turned to the side window. "But you're still attracting hotheads."

As they approached the entrance station, Jack slowed. Another line of cars.

They waited, pulling forward one car length at a time. When they reached the kiosk, the window stood open, the new ranger on duty.

"Just Jen," Jack shouted.

She lit up a toothy grin. "Morning, Senator Culberson's beau."

"This is Toby LeBlanc. Worked with him in Montana. He's here on a project."

"Hi Toby." She leaned out the window, squinting as she looked him over. "Kinda cute."

"A little shaggy, if you ask me." Jack glanced over, catching Toby looking self-conscious. "Be careful with this woman, Toby. She's on wanted posters, supposedly." He turned back to the kiosk. "He'll be here a few days. Hey, the line of cars . . . treasure hunters?"

"Looks like it. The Chief has the law enforcement guys talking to people at trailheads."

Jack gave her a wave, then pulled away.

"What'd she mean, Senator Culberson's beau?"

Jack gave a nod. "The way it sounded. Speaking of women, you've got a fan."

"I'm not good around women these days. Your girlfriend's a senator?"

Jack nodded, pointing back with his thumb. "That one might be a take charge kinda gal."

"She'd end up being like all the others."

"How's that?"

"She'd call me moody." He turned to the side window. "She'd end it."

Jack let it go. He turned onto the service road and parked behind headquarters, then led Toby up the backstairs into the building.

In his office, Jack pulled a few research reports off the shelf and sat Toby down to read. He used his own time to play catch up, returning phone calls and emails, writing a couple of memos. Then, he slipped down the hall, sticking his head into the Chief Ranger's office.

"Knock, knock."

Barb Sharp spun around from her computer. Her eyes grew, an unsettling, whites-of-her-eyes response. She raised both hands, grasping hair, her gray streak caught between fingers. "What happened?"

"Mangum. I ran into . . ." He stopped, realizing the reason for her response. "Oh, you mean this?" He ran a hand over his head. "New look."

"What are you trying to look like?"

"Can we talk about Potts Monroe?"

"No sign of him. I've got more I can say about your new look, but. . . . we searched for days before calling it quits. I wonder if he stashed his vehicle and took off on an extended backcountry trip. I woulda thought he'd get a permit, let us know where he was going. Maybe he's on BLM land."

Jack took a seat. "Got home yesterday. I'm amazed at the traffic."

"It's killing us. No time to deal with anything else."

"Learned about the latest rumors this morning."

"Quivira?"

"Yes. Think someone's just playing games with us?"

"Hell of a game. We've got treasure hunters coming from everywhere, Florida to Alaska. Talked to a guy yesterday, . . . cocksure he knows the mind of Spanish explorers better than anyone, . . . sure he knows where to find the booty. And—he says—when he finds it . . . we'll never know. He won't stop looking. None of them will. Tell 'em they can't treasure hunt in the Park, doesn't matter."

"None of 'em?"

"We've cited some . . . for digging. Some try to act like typical visitors, out hiking. But, where we usually have a few hard-core types going off trail . . . canyoneering to some little-known waterfall or isolated canyon, it seems everyone wants to go off trail. Three medicals yesterday, all needing a helicopter. Broken bones, concussions, people getting in over their heads."

"Johnny told me about a secret chat-room group . . . he's following."

"Yeah, old friends, sounds like. Hoping to get in, get the treasure, and get out."

"Think they've been here yet?"

"Maybe they have, maybe they haven't." Barb leaned over her desk. "Johnny seems to think their leaks in the past happened during periods of frustration . . . trouble translating the journal. Otherwise, we might not have ever heard about them."

Jack sighed. "I'm not sure I buy it. Feels like a waste of time."

"Well, it's wasting ours." Barb sat back in her chair. "Johnny was here a few minutes ago. He's studying chatter from the last couple of days. He thinks the sudden revelation about Quivira came about because of difficulty reading the word. The styling on one letter . . . made the word seem nonsensical. When they realized they'd been misinterpreting the letter, the word hit like a bomb."

Jack rubbed his forehead. "Makes my head hurt."

"If they've just figured this out, like Johnny thinks . . . then it's about to get worse." She sighed. "Gold fever is highly contagious."

Jack stood to go.

"You need to know this," Barb said. "A rumor about Potts. That he found it already."

Shaking his head, Jack lurched into the hall and returned to his office.

Toby LeBlanc sat reading.

After an hour, Jack stood and approached the door. "Want some lunch?"

"Not hungry. You go ahead." Toby continued his reading.

Jack went home, ate a sandwich, and brought an apple back for Toby.

He crunched at the apple as he thumbed through pages. After an hour, he bumped Jack off the computer and revisited the data layers for the monument, scribbling a few notes. Then he reopened a geology paper on recent work on the Jurassic stratigraphy of northern New Mexico, flipping between it and the data layer for surface geology—the exposed geologic features.

Staying out of his way, Jack watched from a chair by the window.

Toby pulled up an orthophoto, found the site where milkweed

had been, then started putting data layers over it, hoping to understand the implications of what each layer represented.

Still work to do, he keyed on other variables. After an hour more, he felt ready to print a preliminary map. “Where’s the plotter?” he asked.

“Two doors down.” Jack handed over his keys. “Locked this time of night. Use the key marked MX.”

Toby slipped down the hall and returned minutes later with a large sheet of paper, twenty-four inches wide, a few inches longer. He laid it out on the desk.

Jack peeked over Toby’s shoulder as he evaluated the plot. Transparent yellow blobs lay scattered across satellite imagery.

“Want contours?” Toby asked.

Jack gave a rub to his chin. “This is cleaner and I always carry a topo.” He eyed the plot’s extent. “Both the Park and monument?”

“I have more confidence in what it picked up for the monument. Made a few inferences about the geology in the Park, where things might be found. Probably garbage.”

“It’s something to work with . . . tomorrow.” Jack slapped him on the back. “Like Mexican food?”

—'—

Jack treated him to dinner at Elena’s, sitting at a favorite table near the kiva fireplace. Already dark, it was too late to see much of the courtyard. He would save the stories about Elena’s garden for another night. Toby asked about ’the senator.’

Leaving after dinner, Jack paused at the bar. Full room, busting at the seams, not a single table empty or bar seat unoccupied. Johnny Reger held court alone at his usual table. He’d managed to keep a few chairs from walking off.

“Need a beer?”

LeBlanc shrugged.

Jack pointed him to the back wall.

Johnny glanced their way. His jaw dropped.

"Don't say it," Jack muttered as they approached.

"How did I not notice that this morning?"

"I was wearing a hat."

"Not that big a hat. Were you in Mexico for some kinda cancer treatment or something?"

"Hell no." Jack scowled. "If you repeat that to anyone I'm gonna kick your ass."

"Well, you sound healthy."

"This is Toby LeBlanc."

Reger stood and shook his hand. "Did you give him the shave?"

A smile tried to break through on the stoic face.

A woman slipped into one of the chairs, having come from the direction of the bar, a fresh margarita in hand. Auburn hair pulled back, her shoulder muscles rippled under the straps of her tank top. Her eyes met Jack's, then migrated to the top of his head.

"Don't ask if he's sick," Reger said. "If you do, he'll kick my ass."

"I like it," she said, sounding sincere. "Tough guy look. Wouldn't have expected that on you, boss, but . . . what the hell? What's Kelly think?" Without waiting for an answer, she flashed a smile at LeBlanc. "You new here?"

Toby swallowed. "Here on a mapping project."

"Christy Manion, fire staff," Jack said to Toby, then turned to Manion. "When did you get back?"

"A few days ago. Burns went well. Lots of acres, landscape scale. Everyone needs to do that."

"Sit," Johnny ordered. "Does this mapping project have anything to do with Juan Rivera's gold?"

"I don't know what you're talking about," Toby said, pulling out the last chair.

Johnny pointed into the room. "Those people, they'll tell ya. That's why they're here, most of 'em." His eyes shot to the door and he let out a holler. "Deputy Buckity."

Winslow wove through the tables toward them. "Everything under control here?"

"You mean the rowdies?"

Winslow nodded.

"No fights so far."

"Good." He turned to Jack. "Saw your buddy Hide Mangum today."

"So did I."

"I've got a solution for you."

"I'm all ears."

"Don't provoke him. Don't go out there."

"I'm working." Jack scowled. "Working the next few days, but maybe in the Park."

"That'd be better. If it's true about forcing him and his neighbors off their land, you might as well make it as painless as possible." He turned his eye on Toby. "You're new."

He nodded.

"Working with these guys or looking for gold?"

"Can't he do both?" Johnny flashed a crooked smile.

Winslow waited for an answer.

"Working," Toby said.

"Good." Winslow offered a hand. "Buck Winslow. When I know you better, I'll let you see my bullet." He smiled and gave a pat to his breast pocket. "Yuckity, yuck, yuck."

LeBlanc glanced around the table, uncertain how he should react.

"We call him Deputy Buckity," Johnny said. "Hey Buck, I saw an election poster today. *Deputy Buckity for Sheriff.* Looked like it was written by a six-year-old."

"Probably was. Kid from school." He gave another yuck, yuck. "I might have to let 'em run my campaign." He glanced around the bar, a return to duty. "Any of you find treasure yet?"

"Nope," Reger said. "Maybe tomorrow. Christy and I have the day off . . . taking a hike."

"You mean, you're going treasure hunting?"

Johnny shook his head in faux denial. "Can't. Just going hiking, like everyone else."

"Have fun." To Jack, Buck said, "Keep things peaceful. Stay in the Park." He left.

"Good guy," Reger said, watching him all the way to the door.

"Johnny, you're not really going treasure hunting, are you?" Jack asked.

"Boss, it doesn't hurt to look does it?" He turned serious. "What's this about Mangum?"

He glanced at LeBlanc. "Nothing serious."

—·—

THE NEXT MORNING

Jack outfitted Toby with an old backpack and divvied up a few days' worth of meals.

Considering how the regional office viewed him at present, Jack avoided the uniform and chose cargo shorts and a T-shirt.

They drove up-canyon early, but not early enough, finding the parking lot nearly full. People hunkered over packs making final preparations. Circling the trailhead, Jack noticed a change. Instead of friendly, casual conversation between groups—the usual—people avoided contact, as if fearful someone might learn something and get a jump on the treasure.

An unusual assortment, both people and gear. Families, few. People ranging from underprepared to overprepared. Bad shoes. Overstuffed backpacks. Down jackets in late spring. Too much weight in the belly and/or backpack. Little evidence of having all the water they'd need. Underrepresented by the young, adventurous. Overrepresented by the older, wild eyed.

"Let's get ahead of the crowd." Jack dragged his pack out from the back of the Jeep.

They crossed the bridge over the river—the late spring flow starting to drop—then up the switchbacks leaving the canyon. Near the rim, Jack stopped and let Toby take in the view.

Thousands of feet of sheer rock, the river flowing past at its base, mostly straight with a few meanders as it made its way to the canyon mouth, then across open lands to the south.

The canyon stood in shadow. No sun yet, except to the south, beyond the canyon, where the plain lay illuminated by morning's glow.

Toby stared without expression, sucking in air. When he'd caught his breath, he turned and started his final trudge onto the heights of the plateau.

Approaching the top, a slow-moving pair of hikers came into view. Jack held back. "Let's look at your map."

Toby pulled off his pack and dug it out, carefully unfolding it.

His own pack still on, Jack unzipped a pocket and pulled out a well-worn topo. He unfolded the map and held it alongside Toby's plot, then tapped on the nearest splotch of yellow.

Another hiker, an unshaven man in green camo, approached and slowed.

They stepped aside but the man lingered, staring at the splotches of yellow. "That's where you think it is?"

"We're looking for milkweed," Jack said.

"Yeah, right," the man said, with a skeptical chuckle. He pulled out his phone, snapped a picture, and moved on.

"Strange," Jack said, watching him.

After more encounters, Jack veered off trail to where the first yellow splotch would be.

Pinyon and juniper gave way to ponderosa pine and scattered oak.

"Might be too high for milkweed," Jack said. "Thought we'd be lower than this."

Comparing maps, they crept to the likely spot on the plot. No spring or damp soil.

Jack tapped on the next yellow spot, this one—from the looks of the satellite image—at the base of an escarpment.

In route, they encountered a man and woman, middle-aged, white, wearing what looked to be street clothes, standing between ponderosas, turning, searching, looking confused.

"Lose something?" Jack asked.

"No," the woman muttered. "It's not what we lost. It's what should be here. My husband saw it on the Earth app. A cave. It should be . . . right in this area."

"Sh-h-h. Don't be talking," her husband growled, staring into an electronic device. "Could this be a shadow?" he said to himself. "Instead of . . . ?"

"Could it?" Her disappointment flared his way. "You said it would be here."

"It looked like a cave." He hunkered over the device, turning his back on the intruders.

"You know you can't treasure hunt the Park," Jack said, just as the radio stashed in his pack blared the beginning of the dispatcher's morning report.

The man gave him a suspicious look. "You a ranger?"

Jack and Toby slipped away without answering. Listening to the weather forecast for the day, Jack headed downslope, keeping an eye out for an escarpment among the pinyon pine and juniper.

The approach led through scattered rock and grass, an occasional oak. They reached the rock. A face of red sandstone, thirty feet high, an erosional remnant.

Toby dropped to one knee and ran his fingers through the soil at its base.

A man dashed up to the rock. The man in camo, carrying a folding shovel, a decades old military type, set for use as a pick. "I was here first," he shouted, dropping to all fours, jostling Toby out of the way. Swinging the shovel into exposed ground, he made several stabs and pushed away the dirt. He muttered again, "I found it first."

Toby stared. Jack signaled him to step back.

The hole grew as uncertainty came over the man. He looked over, as if expecting affirmation, or encouragement. After minutes, disappointed, he stood and trudged up the hill.

Toby watched until the man could no longer be seen. "Can we go back down?"

"Sure. Let's get away from the crazies."

"I think we need to start in the monument. Start with what we know."

—'—

At the bottom of the last switchback, they headed for the river.

Approaching the bridge, they spotted a pair of familiar faces, Johnny Reger and Christy Manion, carrying day packs.

Johnny stopped mid bridge. “Where are you guys going? Gold’s that way.”

“That’s why we’re leaving,” Jack said. “Too many crazies.” Reaching him mid-river, Jack looked out over the current flowing under the bridge. “We’re going back to South Desert.”

Christy slipped past Jack and shouldered up to Toby, exchanging a few quiet words.

An easy smile grew on Johnny’s face as he watched, then turned his attention to Jack. “Didn’t Deputy Buckity say you should stay away from that part of the world?” The smile melted away. “That’s not a question, boss.”

Chapter 29

Potts Monroe's pickup sat at the end of the road, a layer of wind-blow dust over its green metallic paint.

"We're not the only ones out here, huh?" Toby said, as Jack parked beside it.

"It's been here awhile." Jack left it at that, not wanting to trouble him with the details of what was known and what was not. "May see people on the trail, but not many. Starting to get hot. Winter's a better time to be out here."

They threw on their packs and headed west. Strapped now on Jack's pack, a climbing rope, just in case. After climbing over the boundary fence, they made a direct line to the trail, Jack in the lead.

The expanse of the desert opened to the west. Slickrock and foothills lay to the north, in the direction of the plateau.

At the first trail junction, Jack stopped. "Let's look at your plot. See what's closest."

Toby pulled it out of his pack. They commiserated over it and the topo, eyeing the landscape. They could likely hit everything in the monument in this plus two days, maybe three.

The plan would be to start at a cluster of yellow splotches off this very trail, which would eventually reach the edge of the slickrock, but first—before committing to the slickrock—they would check locations close to the original patch of milkweed.

That might be the best odds of finding similar conditions. If they found nothing, Toby feared he would need to go back to the office to tweak a few variables.

They followed the trail north toward the main trailhead. Topo in hand, folded to show only this part of the monument, Jack gave occasional glances at the nearest geologic remnant highlighted, a yellow spot on Toby's plot. Triangulating off a pair of major landforms—a sandstone spire along a ridge below the plateau, and a break in the rim over the river—Jack determined they were close. He veered off the trail.

A sound came in on the breeze. An engine.

Jack turned to the noise.

A single all-terrain vehicle appeared, top of a rise.

He made out the rider. Hide Mangum. *How did he know we were here?*

The ATV accelerated toward them.

Jack checked Toby, standing off trail. Uncertainty.

"My fault," Toby said. "We should've stayed in the Park."

"There's no reason we shouldn't be here. There *is* a reason he shouldn't . . . the ATV."

Mangum slid to a stop. "Get your ass gone," he said, through his bramble of a mustache.

"How'd you know we were here?" Jack asked.

"My little secret."

Jack looked past him. To the west, rolling slickrock. Beyond the trailhead, a pair of buttes, a saddle between them. Mangum must watch from up there somewhere.

"We're not bothering you, Mangum," Jack said, trying to sound relaxed. "We came in another way just to give you space."

"The space I need comes from you bastards leaving, taking your land agents with you."

"I'm not involved with them."

"Lies." He slid off his ATV and took a step toward them. A bluff charge. He smiled and scratched at his beard. "I know what you're up to. You're finalizing your plans . . . to bulldoze everything we got."

"Bulldoze? Colorful. Where'd you come up with that?"

Mangum smiled, his eyes narrowing to a squint. "It'll do, till I figure out what you're up to. And I'm close to figuring out where this is going."

"I don't think so."

"If I tell people I know your plan and let them picture you with a bunch of bulldozers . . . they'll be willing to fight. Besides . . . what else could it be?"

"Not that."

"People are scared. They need to get past being scared and get ready to fight."

"A little dramatic, aren't you?"

"Hell no."

Jack crossed his arms. "Why pick on me? I have nothing to do with those guys in town."

Mangum glanced at LeBlanc, then turned a stare on Jack. "Catch you here again and no one will ever know what happened to you. I'll bury your ass so deep no one will ever find you."

"Hell, you will." Jack took a step, then stopped, watching Mangum's gun hand.

Mangum let it hover at the small of his back.

Jack stepped back.

"Hands where I can see 'em," came a shout on the wind. "Now."

Mangum looked past Jack, in the direction of the voice. "There's four of you?"

Jack turned.

Johnny Reger, jogging toward them, slowed and raised his service weapon.

Christy Manion, behind him, stopped.

Mangum scowled and dropped his hand.

"Why are you here, Reger?" Jack shouted, angry. "Are you following us?"

Johnny stopped, eyes locked. "So you must be Hide Mangum."

"It's none of your damned business who I am." Mangum threw a leg over the ATV, settling onto the seat.

"Gimme your key," Johnny ordered. "You're leaving it here."

Mangum started the engine and kicked it into gear, throwing dirt and desert gravel.

"I'm writing you up," Reger shouted, watching him speed away. "This area is closed to vehicles." He turned to Jack. "I can fire one over his head if you promise to do the paperwork."

"Why are you here?"

Mangum cleared the rise.

Johnny smiled. "He called my bluff. Can you believe it?" He holstered the Sig Sauer semi-automatic pistol, unbuckled his belt, and pulled off the holster. "Now I can stash this." He dropped it into his pack. "The positive side . . . I don't have to lug his body back to the trailhead."

"Why are you here?" Jack demanded.

Reger pointed at Christy and whispered, "I figured she'd like to get to know your friend."

"Bull."

"We're keeping you safe, Boss."

"I can take care of myself."

"Odds weren't exactly even . . . even with two of you."

"Mangum was bluffing." Jack caught Toby still eyeing the trail, it hardly registering that a buff, attractive woman was trying to engage him in conversation.

"I didn't read him as bluffing," Reger said.

"How did you know we were here?"

"Tracked you, Boss. Better question is, how did he know?"

"I wondered about that, too." Jack pointed at distant bluffs, and the saddle between them. "Must have some kind of lookout . . . maybe up in that saddle? Might be able to see for miles."

Toby remained silent. Distracted, and not by Christy Manion.

"You guys leave. We've got work to do." Jack faced Reger. "Go. We'll be fine."

"This is as good a hike as any, and no crazies, unless we count *you*."

"Thought you wanted to go treasure hunting."

"Me? Treasure hunt?" He laughed. "I wouldn't do that. Plus, there's always tomorrow."

"I don't need your protection."

"You might not think so, Boss . . . but you're kinda naïve when it comes to the dark side. In fact, you can be kinda stupid . . . so . . . we're not leaving. Not yet."

Jack growled. "When?" He glanced at his topo. "Toby, where's our next spot?"

He shuddered, then pulled out his plot.

"You lead." Jack said, then turned to Reger. "After our next location, you leave."

Toby headed for a dry wash. On the other side, he sidestepped cactus and sagebrush, climbing upslope to an outcropping at the base of a swell. Ignoring the map, he studied the lay of the land, pointing at elements he expected to find, then zeroing in on the backside. There, in the shade, damp soil, deep red. Among the grass, milkweed. Tall, with developing seed pods.

"You did it!" Jack said, slapping Toby on the back. "That's why we're here. Good job."

A hint of a smile began to form.

Jack turned to the others. "You can leave."

"Late for lunch, you say?" Johnny dropped his pack and settled in beside it.

Manion did the same.

Toby studied the extent of the moisture, then plopped down to join them.

Jack dug out a bag of veggies, pulled out a handful, and bit down on a stick of celery.

A monarch butterfly flew past, fluttering among them before perching on milkweed.

"We should check for eggs and caterpillars," Christy said.

"You know about butterflies?" Toby asked.

"I didn't just study fire science." She flashed a smile. "I'll show you what to look for." On hands and knees, she approached the nearest plant. She held back a leaf. "Here. Eggs."

Small, round, off-white eggs, attached to the underside of the foliage.

She pointed to a rough edge. "Here's where a caterpillar's been getting her lunch." She checked more leaves. After one, she giggled. "There you are little guy." She watched as the black, white, and yellow striped critter nibbled away, Toby peering over her shoulder. "Eat your milkweed," she said. "So you taste yucky and predators won't want you for supper."

"That's why they eat milkweed?" Toby asked.

"I don't know if it's why, but it works. Predators leave 'em alone . . . as well as their mimics—viceroys, which look a lot like monarchs." She let out a chuckle. "Damn imposters."

"I knew you'd need us," Johnny said to Jack, as if he had something to do with it. He pointed at the distant saddle. "We're not leaving yet. Not till he can no longer track your moves."

—'—

The next cluster on Toby's plot, three yellow blobs, south of the trail. It took a bit of hike. Without trails marked on his map, he felt uncertain about exact locations in the open desert. Using a compass, Jack triangulated off a pair of mesas, transferring the azimuths to Toby's map. The intersecting lines indicated their location. Toby continued across the desert.

Thinking they found it, they stopped and confirmed the location. Toby examined the site.

Reger stepped over to Jack and whispered, "You know I carry a GPS, right?"

The location yielded results, a small scattering of milkweed, but no monarch butterflies.

The next two sites were dry. No wet soils, no milkweed, no butterflies.

"It's not a perfect science," Toby said, following Jack back to the trail.

"Didn't expect it to be . . . it's a tool . . . and you've done pretty well so far." Jack glanced around. Flat ground. A few scattered boulders. An opening between desert scrub. A view to the west, streaks of high, thin clouds, and the makings for a pretty good sunset. "This will work." He turned to Johnny and Christy, trailing behind them—Johnny still quizzing Christy about her recent fire assignment.

"Time to go," Jack said, interrupting. "We're camping here. You can leave. Go, before it gets dark."

Johnny turned and pointed at the still obvious saddle between buttes. "Not yet, Boss. If he's there, he knows you're here. We're stayin'."

Jack studied the saddle. "It's miles from here."

"Remember what Deputy Buck said. If Mangum's provoked, who knows what he'll do."

"That's silly. He wouldn't . . ." Jack threw up his hands. "And you're not prepared for an overnight."

"I'm fine." Johnny turned to Christy.

"Me, too. I carry a space blanket."

He turned to Jack. "We're staying."

"Do you have a space blanket?"

"Yep. Always. Right there with my GPS."

"You don't have food."

"We have enough. If we get desperate, we'll look for berries."

"There are no berries out here."

"Then tuna . . . off prickly pear." He gave a sad, puppy dog look. "But they're not ripe, and . . . there's the glochids. I hate glochids . . . they get on my tongue . . . spiny little bastards."

"Shut up," Jack said. "We packed enough food for two and a half days plus a little more. Not a lot, but enough." He frowned. "May have to cut our trip short, but you won't go hungry."

"Aw, Boss, you know how I hate your cooking." He shared a wink with LeBlanc.

Jack dropped his pack. "Then maybe you should cook." He dug out his stove, started water to boil, then turned to set up camp. The distant buttes kept tugging at his eyes, as he laid out his sleeping bag and bivy sack.

When the water reached boiling, he stirred in the makings for pasta, combining two of the meals planned for the trip, creating something of a Cajun fettuccine alfredo with vegetables.

Christy Manion crept up alongside him as he cooked. "Boss,"

she said, hovering, watching Johnny try to make conversation with Toby.

"Glad you're home, Christy." Jack tasted the pasta. "You don't have to do this. We can take care of ourselves."

"Maybe, but we're here." She nodded in the direction of Toby. "Know who he reminds me of?"

Jack stopped stirring. "Who?"

She slipped closer. "He'll talk, but not much. Seems smart when he does, but questions himself. Unwilling to take risks involving other people. Like he's hiding. Sound familiar?"

"No."

"Think about it. A couple of years ago."

"No idea."

She cocked her head and gave him a bug-eyed stare.

"Who?" he said, giving up.

"You!" she whispered.

"You're kidding." He scowled. "Johnny thinks you want to get to know him."

"You're changing the subject." She laughed. "I'm curious. But I saw something . . . in his eyes. Something I'd seen before. Made me wonder . . . what it was, what made him tick, then I realized . . ." She moved to the other side of the stove, watching Toby, not worried about being noticed. "It's you. At first, I thought you were aloof, a bit of a jerk, but I gave you the benefit of the doubt because you knew what you were doing . . . that fire, remember?"

"Yeah."

"I realized you were . . . you know."

"Damaged?" He nodded toward LeBlanc. "Toby was there, going through what I was. He may still be dealing with it."

"You think?"

"Maybe."

"I'm teasing, of course he is." She stepped away to join the other two.

Jack watched them as he turned off the stove. Faced with not enough dishes and utensils, he announced having to divvy out the food on what he had available.

"Don't consider me forward," Christy said, scooting toward Toby. "But, . . . wanna share a plate . . . or a pan?"

Jack put two helpings onto a battered metal plate and set them up with utensils. He filled a cup for himself and passed the pan to Reger.

When finished, they settled back and watched the sun. It slipped behind a thin veil of clouds and made a modest exit. They waited. Then came a glow, and a slow eruption of red, orange, and yellow, unleashed by a furtive sun. It held them in quiet long after it faded.

Well after dusk, Johnny announced, "I'll take east."

Christy got to her feet. "West it is."

"What are you two doing?" Jack asked, rolling onto an elbow.

"Guard duty." Johnny smiled. "We're posting up the trail, both directions, making sure no one sneaks in. If Mangum makes a showing, it'll more likely be from the east, so I'll take that direction, seeing I'm the one with a weapon."

Jack glanced at Toby. He didn't look unconcerned. "Johnny, can you just relax?"

Johnny grabbed his pack and headed for the trail. "See you in the morning."

Christy shot a salute as she headed the opposite direction.

Jack sighed. "They don't need to do that."

Toby sat for a moment, then said, "Why are you so sure?"

Chapter 30

Jack cleaned up after dinner, careful not to waste any water, then ambled over to where LeBlanc sat leaning against a rock. "Just as well. This will be quieter. Johnny's stories can get a bit loud." Getting no response, he plopped down. "A bit different than Montana, isn't it?"

"Yeah."

"Gonna go back to grad school?"

"No."

"I hope you do . . . sometime." Lead balloon. Jack waited for words, his eyes trying to cut through the dark to see Toby's face. "I wish those guys would calm down, quit worrying."

"Are they cops?"

"No, fire staff, both of them."

"Reger's fire staff? Why's he carrying a gun?"

"He has a law enforcement commission. Got it years ago, decided he'd rather do fire work. He's pulled in when extra hands are needed. He's doing that now because of light duty."

"Being a cop is light duty?"

"Not exactly. And he's not a cop, he's a ranger. But. . . . you need both hands to use fire shovels, pulaskis, and all that. It's not the right kind of work for healing."

"What happened to him?"

"Shot. In the hand. Months ago. Not his gun hand but he's on physical therapy. Johnny's the kind of guy that needs to keep busy."

"What's Christy do?"

"Fire. That one can work your ass into the ground."

"She's in good shape. Speaking of ass, she's got a nice one. Cute as hell."

Jack laughed. "You noticed?"

"Hard not to. She wants to visit, but I don't have much to say."

"She's a good person. Don't fret. Just enjoy getting to know her." Jack pointed into the southwestern sky. "Venus and Saturn."

"Who does she work for?"

"Johnny, ordinarily."

"Who does *he* work for?"

"Me. Except now. He's on loan to the Chief Ranger." Raising his hand, Jack traced the arc of the Milky Way. "A bit before the moon comes up. I've come to love the stars here."

"What's your job?"

"What it looks like. Natural and cultural resources. I'm their chief."

"You don't do planning?"

"Get pulled into it. In fact, I'm wrapping up a project with the community now . . . regarding this national monument. Then I'll get back to the kind of work I was hired for."

"How do you keep finding these powder kegs? This is reminding me of Montana."

Jack laughed. "It's not bad here. Pretty nice, actually." He pointed. "Orion's Belt."

"That Mangum guy . . . what are you thinking? It's very much like Montana."

Jack sighed. "He's harmless. Similarities? All coincidence."

"Don't tell me that. It makes me want to run."

"Why?"

"You said I'm here for a *little project*, but I can feel it, something's about to explode. And it feels like I'm being pulled in, and I can't do that sort of thing again."

"It's totally different here."

"Don't say that. Weren't you listening to him? Didn't you hear what he was saying? He was telling you what he's gonna do . . . how he's gonna do it . . . same as in Montana."

"There's guys in town he's misreading. Reacting. Getting angry. As soon as he sees the truth—at least what I hope is the truth—he'll calm down, everything will be okay." Jack paused. "You're not much into stars, are you?"

"That sounds like everything you said in Montana, and yes I'm into stars . . . but not when I'm worried I'm about to be collateral damage."

Jack sat up, the words catching him off guard. "It was different there."

"Don't you understand . . . what those people can do? The lies."

"What are you talking about?"

"The people who start the lies. Who manipulate us, make us do things totally opposite of what's best for us. Opposite of what's in our best interest."

"People lock onto things. Rumors. Details. Half stories. That's life, Toby."

"That's not life. That's someone's plan. Someone smarter than the rest of us. They find people to carry their lies, and those people do it, sometimes unwittingly. They're *groomed* to think they're passing along something important, oblivious to the damage it causes."

"Kid, you're thinking too hard."

"I'm not, and don't call me that!" Toby barked. "That name came from a time when people depended on me, looked to me to help them do great things. They don't do that anymore. Now they see me as a traitor, and . . . they don't do great things. They hurt themselves, and they blame me for it. Their own actions, their own misfortunes."

"It's hard getting past what happened in Montana, but . . ."

"I can't get past it. And I'm not thinking too hard. Those things happened."

Jack let out a chuckle. "You used the word, *groomed*. People, letting themselves be groomed? Really? C'mon, that *is* thinking too hard."

"It's not," LeBlanc growled. "They do."

Even in the dark, Jack felt the eyes penetrating him.

Toby fell silent. Jack held his tongue. No point in continuing this conversation.

Out of the quiet, a sudden shout. "They do." Toby gasped, as if he'd shocked himself, then muttered, "They find people. Naïve people, maybe a little too full of themselves. People with a little too much ego. They tell 'em they're smart, tell them they can be a hero, tell 'em everyone needs 'em."

"We don't need to talk about this. We can change the subject."

"They stroke that ego, teach them to do things. They mold you to their way of thinking. Lessons? They wouldn't call it that, but they plant the seed and they watch it grow. They turn people into tools. Tools to serve their interests. To carry out their agenda."

"Kid, this is getting really hard for me to fathom."

"Quit calling me that." He seethed, then sighed. "Why is it hard?"

"I'm sorry, but listen to yourself. Sounds outlandish."

"You don't know what those people are capable of. In Montana, they . . ."

Jack cut him off. "I was there."

"You didn't control the game. You brought something to the game, but in the end, they turned your strength . . . your value . . . into weakness. They didn't care what you or anyone else thought, or what you or anyone else considered important. They had their plan, their goals, and to them the end justified the means. They created a story that made everyone ignore their own interests. To do their bidding. People didn't even know they were working against themselves."

"I give you that. I saw it."

"You're damned straight you saw it."

"But I don't buy that people were enlisted. That they were part of a plan."

"Then how do you explain what occurred?"

"It happens. Bad actors, yes. Politicians playing fast and loose with the truth. Someone buying them off. Bureaucrats thinking about their own careers more than serving the public."

"But there were worse things happening."

"Kid . . . Toby, I'm sorry, but you're still young. The things you've seen in life are . . ."

Toby laughed, cutting him off. "Are you really going to tell me I'm too young and dumb to know what happened?"

"Not the way I would've put it, but . . ."

"Don't. There are things I saw. Things you didn't."

"I was there, at the tip of the spear."

"Not as much as you may think. There were people there to create lies. Conspiracy theories, the crazier the better. Others were there to repeat them. They did, feeling justified in doing so. They were taught that even when someone calls it a lie, they were to ignore and repeat. Ignore and repeat. If people hear something often enough, they believe it. It's accepted as truth."

"Do you realize how paranoid you sound?"

"Shut up!" he barked. "Listen to me."

"If that were true, then . . ."

Toby cut him off. "It's true. I know it's true." His eyes glared across the darkness. "They picked me. They groomed me. I was one of them."

—·—

Time seemed to have passed, as if the words had knocked Jack unconscious. Coming to, the Kid's words continued bouncing through his mind, his legs in seizure, his fists clenched, his body preparing for the next gut shot. Each echo of words producing stabs at an old wound, an old pain, a numbness he'd mostly forgotten. "What . . . did you say?"

"You heard me."

Jack stared into the darkness at the outlines of the young man. *You thought you knew him. Did you really?* He swallowed at the dry grit in his throat. "When was this?"

"Before I worked for you."

"What'd you get out of it? What was in it for you?"

"Nothing, but I didn't know that at the time. Smoke up my ass, nothing more."

"Couldn't have been."

"It was. They said the right things. A compliment. A favor, turned into grooming. To . . . supposedly . . . make me a leader in the community. Tapping my . . ." He paused, and the next words flowed out full of spite. ". . . natural leadership abilities." He spat out, "Yeah, right."

"Why you?"

"Felt like happenstance, but it wasn't. Started on a weekend home from school. An introduction . . . to a guy named Teague. He wanted to meet me."

Jack shot forward but quelled his own reaction. *Let him talk.*

". . . felt like a chance meeting. It wasn't. The guy played on my ego . . . called me a local hero . . . the quarterback who took the town to state and won. He made sure we met again. He pulled me in. That first meeting . . . looking back, the worst day of my life."

Jack held his tongue. *Don't tell him. Not yet.* "What'd he want?"

Toby exploded. "Damn it, Jack, I told you already. Change the subject."

"Okay."

Toby sat in silence, no sound but the rustling of feet against rock and dirt. Then, he muttered, "All that leadership bullshit . . . he played me." Quiet, then an irritated, "I was so easy to manipulate . . . so full of ego." A sigh bled through the darkness. Calm came to his voice. "You see . . . I've had time to think about this."

"When did it stop? The grooming."

"Shortly after you hired me, that first summer."

"So . . . until then, they groomed you."

"They didn't call it grooming, but that's what it was, and you might not believe this." He paused. "I stopped . . . because of you. You were the very opposite of everything they said about you. All the lies they'd conditioned me to believe." He cleared his throat. "Remember how arrogant I was when we first met?"

"I don't remember it as arrogant . . . confident, standoffish maybe."

"That's your way, giving everyone the benefit of the doubt, like you're doing with that Mangum guy." Toby cleared his throat. "Did you know I tried being like that . . . giving people the benefit of the doubt . . . because of you? Did you know that?"

"Why did you come to work for me?"

"You don't remember?"

"Too much water under the bridge."

"Funny analogy." Toby forced a laugh. "Apropos. My hydrology professor. He introduced us. Thought it might lead to research projects, maybe one for a dissertation."

"The lies you talk about. After you started working for me . . . did you stay in that part of the game?"

"No. Might've been easier."

"Why?"

"I might still have friends. I backtracked, changed the things I said. By then, others were enlisted to keep the lies alive. My friends were conditioned to accept them as fact. If I'd just played along, people might not now see me as the enemy."

"Because you told them the truth?"

"Because I told them they were repeating lies."

"What's the difference?"

"People believe what they want to believe. You tell them their lies, you insult them, even though it might have been me who made them believe in the first place."

Jack drew in a breath. "Wow."

"When I say they shaped people, I mean it. You don't know what those people can do. . . . what they're willing to do. They're smart. They have tricks of the trade. How to manipulate."

"Example?"

"There's one that seemed so primal, I couldn't believe it'd really work. The guy had me try it. To watch how people responded to my words, to have me relish the power I had over others. He had me invent a lie . . . one tied to their worldview."

"Did it work?"

"Yeah, it worked. As if they had to believe it. They had to, to preserve their identity."

"Tell me."

"He called it the *those other people* method."

The words hit like a rock. "Hold it . . . say that again."

"The *those other people* method. Gives you great power. You mention outsiders. You come up with something that makes others look hypocritical. Maybe something funny. Then you tie it to someone with some imaginary influence . . . the more negative the better . . . something they fear. If it threatens their worldview . . . if it threatens their identity . . . then . . . they have to believe it. It *must* be true. They can't risk it not being true, because they need to preserve their identity or their life as they know it. Even when they know something isn't quite accurate, it's okay, because it's somehow tied to preserving a higher truth."

"Higher truth? Sounds wacko."

"It's not," Toby said, no longer offended. "Think about it."

"I'm listening."

"If you suggest *those other people* have influence over someone you want to screw with . . . ruin their reputation . . . then, you've planted the seeds of distrust. Not just distrust . . . division. Someone's gonna be toast. That someone was you. You were toast."

"You're saying . . . ?"

"That it was Doc's plan."

Jack bolted upright. "Did you say . . . ?"

"I said you were toast."

"No, did you say Doc?"

"Yes, . . . he was the one who painted you as an outsider. Someone controlled by notorious outside interests. To do that to you was easy. You're the government."

"I *was* an outsider," Jack muttered, "but, . . . who the hell is Doc?"

"I don't know . . . he changed the subject when I asked, but Doc was more an outsider than you were. You were invited . . . by people who wanted to preserve this place they loved. Make it a national park." Toby got to his feet. He began to pace, circling the camp, his dark form blocking the stars as he walked. "Doc wasn't invited. He showed up, acting like he belonged there. He painted a masterpiece . . . of you as the outsider, and in the end, of me, too."

Jack held his tongue.

"The same people who came to see you as an outsider . . . treated me as a traitor, blaming me in part for how their world changed . . . even though it was them who let it happen." Toby sat and pulled his knees close to his chest. He let out a whimper.

"Doc . . . *those other people*," Jack muttered to himself. Mexico. The faxes. Toby's sobs pushed the memory aside. "Okay, let's change the subject."

"For a bit, I tried acting like I was still part of the game, but everything about Doc's plan was right there in front of our eyes, and I couldn't keep quiet. I called Doc's rhetoric what it was. Lies. Doc called it rhetoric, said everyone used rhetoric. A sign of a good leader, the ability to convince, to make their case. But his were lies. Lies to blind us. I tried to explain that to my friends." Toby let out a long, painful sob. "Thing is, I saw behind the curtain. They refused to. Doc was making us forget what we valued . . . the things we thought important. The things we valued in each other. The things we wanted for ourselves and our community. I tried to reverse the damage . . . but everything went to hell. My friends were told to distrust me . . . and later, when their lives changed, they blamed me . . . and you. Doc won."

"I need to find out who Doc is. So, you really knew him?"

"Not at first. First, only the guy named Teague. Harper Teague, I think it was. The one who blew smoke up my ass. He introduced me to Doc and Doc took over."

"Took over? And where's he from?"

"Don't know. He wouldn't say . . . but he took over, with me at least, not everyone."

"He groomed you to not value the things you valued?"

"Hell no," Toby groused. "Not that. I don't think Doc cared about the outcome. He wasn't there for the *what*. He was the *how*. A technocrat. The end didn't seem to matter to him. Someone else's end justified his means. He never addressed *the ends*. Or who he worked for, or why. I know that sounds odd, but Doc made me think there was something out there to be conquered, something needing my leadership . . . an evil. Conquering that evil was the right thing to do . . . God's work. He could teach me how. The means."

"And what you saw today from Hide Mangum . . . what made you think about Doc? Why did it remind you of Montana?"

"Can't you see it? It's got Doc's fingerprints all over it. You're the evil, and Mangum is executing the plan. The *how*."

Jack fell quiet, thoughts coursing through his mind. *Mangum . . . did he send the guy with the lies to the public meeting? Aren't the feds at the motel his focus? Or is that a ruse?*

"In Montana, you were drawn to truth, ignoring the lies . . . until it was too late, when you went after those spreading the lies. If you'd gone after the lies you might've understood what was going on."

The lies.

"What have you pulled me into?" Toby said.

"Let's think about this." Jack rubbed his eyes, then a spot pounding on his head.

"Too late for that!" Toby shouted, irritated. "This is Doc's world. He controls the game."

"No!" Jack shouted back. "I refuse to let him win."

"So, now you believe me?"

"Guess I do . . . but this time he won't win . . . this Doc."

"Jack, you don't get it. Knowing doesn't help. What matters is how Doc wants to paint you. What matters is the plan. You don't know what the plan is." Toby got to his feet. "I'm going to bed." He slipped into the depths of the darkness.

Jack sat staring at the stars, tired, but he knew he wouldn't sleep.

Chapter 31

At the first light of day, after a restless night, Jack crawled from his sleeping bag and started a pot to boil. He packed up, made some coffee, and sat on a rock to drink his first cup, then his second. Johnny Reger came into camp first.

"You didn't need to worry about us," Jack said.

"I didn't," Johnny muttered, pouring himself a cup from the pot. "Not after midnight anyway. Kangaroo rats kept trying to keep me awake but . . . failed." He took a sip, a groggy stare barely clearing the rim of the cup. "You look like you got less sleep that I did."

Christy Manion sauntered in, her pack slung over a shoulder. "Did I hear coffee pouring?"

"You can have this cup when I'm finished," Reger said. "How late were you up?"

"Didn't last long, and I'll be fine, I'll use a water bottle." She dug one out and turned to the pot, giving herself an inch of brew. "I need water today. Might have to head to the river."

"You missed the big rumble," Johnny said, then noticed Toby staggering out from behind a boulder. "I'd offer a double shot cappuccino, but I think I just drank the last one."

Christy offered Toby her flask.

He waved it off. "Never touch the stuff."

"Can't trust someone who operates without caffeine," Johnny said.

Jack knelt over his backpack and dug out a handful of granola bars. "Anyone?"

Toby nodded.

Jack tossed him one. "Didn't give much thought to breakfast."

Johnny shook his head. "Got my own."

"Me, too," Christy said, digging into her pack.

"I was thinking," Johnny said, drawing all eyes. "Sitting there in the night . . . all by my lonesome . . . prepared for an attack, when the moon peeked over the ridge and at that moment, lucidity came over me." He awaited a response, eyeing the others. "Don't you want to know what lucidity came over me?" He waited another moment. "Guess you need more coffee. Anyway, in my moment of lucidity, I got to thinking. . . . since we cut into your food supply, we could help check those sites on your map, help knock a few off the list."

"We don't need help," Jack said.

"Seriously, boss, just give us assignments . . . places to check out. We can meet up later, let you know what we found. Maybe shorten your trip by a day."

"I'm not sure that makes much sense," Jack said, noticing Toby getting to his feet.

Toby went to his pack and pulled out his map. He unfolded it, laying it out on the ground.

Must need some distance. Still troubled about last night.

"We're here." Toby tapped at the map. Four distinct clusters. Two nearby. One in the slickrock, north of the trail. Another among the isolated outcroppings along downslope arroyos. "If we could get three done . . ." He pointed at the furthest west. "We can get this one tomorrow."

Johnny said it first. "Clusters. Which do you want us to take?"

"Know what you're looking for?" Jack asked.

"I think so . . . but tell us."

Jack glanced at Toby. "We're testing Toby's methods, seeing what we learn, seeing if there's ways to make the predictions more precise."

"We're quick studies. Christy is, anyway." Johnny flashed a crooked smile.

"How many radios do we have?"

"We've both got ours," Johnny said. He pulled his own from his pack.

"Three, then. Topos?"

Christy raised a hand. Then Johnny.

"Might work." Jack dug out his own topo, and a pencil. He held out the pencil.

Johnny—eyeing Toby's plot—started marking up his map.

"We can let you two take the ones down here in the sagebrush. The slickrock might involve some climbing." Jack gave a pat to the braided rope strapped to his pack.

"Don't baby us, Boss."

"Your hand . . ."

"My hand's fine, but I'm okay with the sagebrush." Johnny made circles on his map.

"Good." Jack gave a look at Johnny's map and ran a finger along the trail. "Let's meet up at 3 p.m. . . . about here. Near this little drainage." He waited for nods, then turned to Toby. "Wanna give a little more detail on what they're looking for?"

He sighed. "I can . . . but I've got another idea."

"Which is?"

"I'm tired. I have no desire to talk about that shit we talked about last night."

"I won't bring it up." Jack glanced at the others, then back.

"Instead of me explaining, let's split up. Me with Christy, you with Johnny."

Jack glanced at the others. No apparent concerns. "Which clusters do you want?"

"Doesn't matter. I'm no rock climber, if that's important."

Jack turned to Johnny. "Sure about your hand? The slickrock will require scrambles, maybe some ropework. Rappels, belays, that sort of thing. I could take Christy?"

"Don't baby me, Boss." He feigned indignation. "My hand can handle a rappel . . . and remember, I've got two of 'em."

—'—

Watching Toby and Christy on the trail, Johnny signaled Jack to wait. "Lover boy's not the most effusive or demonstrative, is he?" He turned to Jack. "Like those big words?"

"Yeah, but you're right. He's different than back then, or . . . what I thought I knew."

"He wasn't this oblivious about women?"

"I won't bore you with details." Jack started upslope. "Believe me, he's not oblivious."

Eyeing the slickrock rising in the distance, they weaved through sagebrush and four-winged salt bush, covering hundreds of yards before reaching the bottom layers of cross-bedded sandstone. From there the eroded rock rose in rolling swells and waves.

Jack glanced at his topo. "We're looking for perched deposits, maybe in draws . . . little valleys sitting in slickrock." He circled a spot on the map with his finger. "We may have to come in from above if the approach gets too vertical. Toby included this cluster as a test for locations in different strata . . . but, with similar factors. Might yield nothing. If so, no big deal."

Studying the lines on the map, he concluded one drainage might be too steep. The next one west looked less suspect. He ascended left, Johnny following, along a ridge the map suggested might take them directly to the first mark on the topo.

They trudged past scattered pockets of little-leaf mountain mahogany, their roots penetrating cracks in the rock, searching for water and nutrients. Determined little guys.

Johnny stopped, sucking in air. "You in a hurry?"

"You out of shape?"

"Light duty, remember. How far?"

Jack slowed to a stop. "The other side of this rise."

Johnny forced himself forward.

They topped the rise and dropped into the canyon below. A bowl, surrounded by swirls of rock. Level ground on its floor, windblown soils, rock of a different hue. Jack checked his map.

"You're thinking you're gonna find water here?" Johnny said, still sucking in air.

"Hoping to. This is the bottom of a different stratum than where we found water yesterday. This elevation marks the break between strata. Toby wanted to see what happens here. See if we find perched springs with the change in rock porosity, slope of the rock. That sort of thing." He spun around.

"Where?"

"I think we're looking at it." Jack glanced down, then around. No water. No springs at the line between layers. "Okay, we move on." He checked the map and started west.

—·—

After a quarter mile of gradual ascent, they reached a ridgeline and the beginnings of an equally gradual descent. At the bottom sat a bowl and a scattering of pinyon pine and cedar. Creeping, careful not to lose their footing, they started down. Reaching the bowl's grassy bottom, they found a small pool. And milkweed. Eggs and caterpillars, but no butterflies.

Jack scribbled details in his notebook, pulled out a GPS, and recorded the coordinates.

"You've got a GPS and you let yourself tramp around searching for this place?"

"Old habits." Jack chuckled to himself. "And what's a GPS tell me?"

"It tells you where you are."

"I know where I am. Call Christy, see how they're doing."

Reger pulled out his radio. "Manion, Reger."

A moment passed, then. "*Go ahead, Johnny.*"

"Checking on you guys."

"*We just left our last location in this cluster.*"

"Finding anything?"

"*At one spot. Water, milkweed, butterflies. Everything.*"

"That's better than us, but we're not striking out."

"*Copy. We're on to the next cluster.*"

"Copy." Johnny slipped the radio into his pack, staring over Jack's shoulder at the topo.

The next slope would not be easy. Not exactly vertical, but pretty damned close. "Maybe we should follow the drainage."

Johnny stared downslope. "Are you sure?"

"No. If it doesn't work, we'll have to go back the way we came, go up and around, see if we can get to our next target."

They followed the drainage down, ledging out above a thirty-foot drop. "No biggee," Johnny observed, "but enough to kill us."

"You have a talent for saying what I'm thinking."

"I know. I say the quiet parts out loud."

Jack eyed a mountain mahogany and gave it a tug. *Too small and too much wiggle. Can't trust that for an anchor.* He turned. Uphill, a cedar. Not a big one. Head high at most. He scrambled up and gave it a tug. *Solid.* "Trust this thing?"

Johnny stood staring. "I've had worse."

"Famous last words."

Jack slipped off his pack and unlashed the rope. Finding the midpoint, he draped it around the base of the juniper, walked it down to the lip and tossed the strands over the edge. With pieces of webbing, they made Swiss seats and prepared to go over. Having only one rappelling device, a figure-eight and carabiner, Jack offered it to Johnny. "Wanna go first?"

"You're the one trusting that puny-assed juniper."

He took a bite on the rope and slipped it through and over the figure-eight, then clipped it into his Swiss seat. He backed toward the edge. The rope grew tight. He loosened his grip, letting inches of rope slip through the device. Glancing at Johnny, then letting the rope slide through his fingers, he lowered his butt out over the edge. He looked down. A scattering of rocks and debris. Mostly clean. Mostly flat. Safe enough.

He gave Johnny a nod and began his descent, walking over the lip and into thin air, dropping, then settling onto rock. He stepped back and pulled enough rope through the rappelling device to allow himself to disconnect. "I'm off!" he shouted.

Johnny, out of view, pulled up the rope, the figure-eight attached.

In a moment, he tossed the rope over the edge and appeared, lowering himself over the lip. He descended.

"Hand okay?" Jack shouted.

"Gun hand, not a problem." He settled onto stone. "Funny I'm thinking of it that way."

He disconnected and they took hold of a strand of the rope and pulled, freeing it from the anchor above. Jack made a butterfly coil of the rope and strapped it to his pack.

They followed the drainage down and climbed out to the west, on to the next drainage.

This one had a longer, more gradual ascent, ending against a less vertical wall.

They approached, seeing a spit of soil at its base, and on that spit, milkweed, in a patch that spread over twenty linear feet. In the patch, three monarch butterflies.

Jack went about his business, tagging the two butterflies he could catch, while Johnny sat, and oddly, remained unusually quiet. Jack attempted to make light of the fact, but let it go, using the silence to concentrate on drawing a sketch and recording the coordinates.

"I'm done," Jack said, stuffing his notebook back in a pocket. "One more location and we can go down. Should make it before three." He picked up his topo and noticed a likely route for the next location. Turning, he caught Reger staring upslope, eyes wide. "What are you looking at?" Jack glanced uphill, expecting maybe some kind of critter. He saw none.

Reger remained speechless, as if he hadn't heard a word Jack said.

"You okay? What is it?"

Eyes still locked on something, Reger pointed. "Don't you see that?"

"What?" Jack scanned the hillside. Nothing obvious. Just slickrock. The high point, a round, layer cake of cross-bedded sandstone. A couple of trees. Big ones. Ponderosa. Not the most likely place for a tree of that species, but not that unusual. He squinted, making out the outline of something between them. At their base, in shadow. Dark, almost black.

"See it?" Johnny muttered, sucking in air, fighting excitement. "Right there! I think it's . . ." He held his tongue, gathering his composure. "Juan Rivera's cave!"

Chapter 32

"Can't be," Jack said, eyeing the cave, his heart pounding.

Johnny got to his feet. "Why?"

"Because . . . it can't be." He fell silent. Then words seemed to flow on their own. "It was just a bunch of guys on the internet . . . unsubstantiated."

"Unsubstantiated?" Johnny stepped closer. "I'm looking at it. And I saw the journals. This is just like it was in the journal."

Jack stared, piecing the memory together. A page, brown with age. Simple scrawling. A drawing, not really a map. A cave—la cueva—and two tall trees—pinos altos—on either side. *It can't be, can it? But there it is. A cave. Two tall ponderosas, framing the entrance. They could have been here—that big—two hundred years ago, right?*

"Everyone's searching in the park, because of the ponderosas," Johnny said. "They assume it's the high country. The plateau."

"Yes, they do."

"But . . ." Johnny turned and stared back at the route they'd followed to get here. In the distance, beyond the slickrock, open desert. Sagebrush. "This makes all the sense in the world," he muttered. "They give the slip to the Comanche, but they can't make good time because of the gold . . . the mules struggle with the weight of the plunder. Open desert, they make a run for it. That makes a hell of a lot more sense than getting caught on the plateau. There they'd be stuck . . . unless they knew the trails used for trade by the Ute, and the Comanche would know, too. So, the odds would go up that Rivera and his men would get caught."

Jack nodded. No argument. Makes sense.

"But here, . . ." Johnny looked back at the cave. "Not making good time, they duck into the slickrock. They come high, looking for cover. On rock, they can't be tracked. They plan on hiding or waiting till nightfall. But they see this cave. Now, they have a new option. Ditch the plunder, make a run for it, sneak back later with more men." Johnny nodded, growing sure of his assessment. "Only thing is, the Comanche still catch 'em. Rivera and most of his men don't make it. Those that do, can't find the cave, ever again."

"I can see that."

Johnny glanced over. "So now you're a believer?"

Jack cracked a smile, his heart pounding. "I don't know what I think."

"I do. I think we need to get up there and check it out. See if we're right."

"See if *you're* right."

Johnny gave him a glance. "We're a team, Boss. We'll split the . . ." He caught himself. ". . .the finder's fee. Let's go find us some treasure."

Jack let out a nervous chuckle.

Excited, Johnny hurried to the base of the slope and dropped his pack. Starting up, he plowed his way up several feet of gradual climb, then up stairsteps of cross-bedded sandstone. He steadied himself, finding a hold on a scrawny mountain mahogany.

Driven by adrenaline, he leaned into the rock and worked his way up a thirty-foot section on hands and feet, relying on friction.

Then he slowed.

Reger studied the last twenty feet, standing on an inches-wide perch. "Steeper than it looks," he shouted over his shoulder. "Not vertical but getting there."

Jack studied the route. Swells, breaks, and cracks all the way to the lip below the cave. At the lip it leveled out.

Johnny reached above his head and found a nubbin, lifted himself a few inches, reset one foot, and sought a higher step with the other. It wasn't there. He accepted the inches he could get, then felt higher on the wall for another handhold. His left hand reached a shallow crack and he lifted himself nearly a foot. "Don't wait on me, boss."

"I'm going to," Jack said, keeping an eye on him. "Sure Rivera's men could've made it?"

"Yeah. This climb would be easy for you."

"I'm not so sure."

"I am. Ordinarily, this would be a piece of cake, but . . ." Johnny reached with his right hand. No obvious handhold, so he returned it to its earlier placement and reached with his left. He pulled himself up another foot. Footing secure, he released his left hand and gave it a shake, flexing his fingers. "You go. Go ahead of me." Johnny shouted, over his shoulder.

"Problem?"

"I'm fine." He moved and his weight shifted. His left hand gave out, the right lost its grip. He slid down the face of the rock, slowing to a stop.

"You okay?" Jack shouted.

"Rock rash. Nose and hands mainly. Knees, too." He looked back over his shoulder. Red streaked his face.

"Want me to go? Top rope you from above?"

Johnny let out a loud grunt as he got to his feet. "I don't have the hand strength. Even if I was on a rope, I'd . . ." He shook his head, disappointed. "You go ahead. Go check it out."

"You need to go first. You saw it, not me." Jack studied the cave. Level ground either side. "Maybe we work our way up and around. Makes me wonder if Rivera's guys could've even gotten up there."

"They coulda," Johnny said. "It's not that bad a climb. I just can't make it . . . but they coulda. Get a few guys up there with ropes, and they coulda easily hauled the booty up to the cave." He sat back against the rock. "Really think there's a way in from above?"

"Hard to know. Let me see." Jack unfolded his topo and scanned the contours, first looking west, then east, near where they started. *The elevation difference from here to the cave, hardly more than the map's forty-foot contour interval. Still, the place where the gap between contours grew widest lay east, but the most likely route for getting to the cave lay west. If not from the front, maybe from the back side.* "I think so," Jack said, studying the route. "We could go back to where we started, go up and around, or . . . we go down a little, go west, we can see how high we can get."

"Which looks best?"

"Hard to tell. Probably west, and east looks farther."

"Too bad we can't plug the location into the GPS and ask it to tell us which way to go."

Jack laughed. "Haven't seen any roads today."

"I'm coming down." Johnny inched on his butt to a place where he could stand.

Jack dug out his first aid kit and waited as Johnny took easy steps the rest of the way. Jack tossed him the kit.

Reger cleaned himself up and waved off the Band-Aids, satisfying himself with pieces of gauze to dab at the wounds. Then, he plopped down with the map.

Jack tapped a spot to the east. "If we went east we'd miss our three o'clock rendezvous, but we could call, let 'em know."

"Show me west."

"Side drainage, then a gradual climb to this strata. We're supposed to go up the next drainage. Our next place to look for milkweed . . . but we could blow that off and . . ."

"Well, Jack Chastain," Johnny said, cutting him off. "Are you blowing off work?"

Jack fought off a smile. "I just thought, . . . it'd be hard for you go looking for milkweed until you knew what's up there."

"Ha, using me as an excuse." He leaned over the map. "But, hell, let's do it!"

"If we don't get to that last location, we don't get to it."

"That's a plan." Johnny grabbed his pack and started downslope.

Jack refolded his map and took off after Reger. Dropping down most of the way to the desert, they skirted west, then upslope, following less a drainage, more a gentle swell. Elevation gain, about 300 hundred feet before walls came together, the ascent now steep.

Johnny plugged on, sucking in air, not letting the climb slow him down.

At a wall, they clambered up through a break, then another gradual ascent toward a checkerboarded knoll.

"The cave should be on the back side," Jack said.

Johnny veered east but hit a slope as bad or worse than the one that stopped him before.

Hands on his hips, Johnny let out a long sigh of frustration. "Now what?"

Jack traced the contours on the topo in both directions. "Let's go around the other way."

"You lead," Johnny said, still sucking in air.

Similar topography. Boulders from old rock falls. Pinyon and juniper in pockets. Jack led them into what appeared on the map as circling the base of the knoll. "If I'm reading this right," he said, eyeing the map, "in a few hundred yards or so . . . we should come to the cave."

Johnny reached for his shoulder, stopping him, wanting to see.

A pop rang out, from both of their packs. Jumbled words.

The radios.

Jack checked his watch. Not yet three o'clock. He listened.

"*Chastain, this is Dispatch.*"

Jack unzipped a pocket and pulled out his radio. Now what? "Go ahead Molly."

"*What's your location*?"

"On the monument, South Desert."

"*Copy. Your former grad student still with you*?"

"Not exactly, but yes. Why?"

"*We've got a lost child report, maybe a runaway.*"

"Where?"

"*Near your location.*"

"Any urgency?"

"*The mother is frantic. Worried about his safety. We're still getting information on the kid's disposition, but the mother thinks he's in danger. She's talking to Barb now. I've tried calling Johnny Reger at his quarters, but no answer. If he's available, I'll send him up the trail to your location. If he's not, I need to find another body."*

"He's here, with me. So's Christy Manion . . . not with me, but in the area with Toby."

"*So, four of you?*"

"Yes. Three radios. Is this the same kid I saw out here before?"

"*Affirmative.*"

"Then I'm not sure we need to consider it urgent. He knows how to take care of himself." He glanced at Johnny. "And we're pretty busy."

"*I understand, but the mother seems to think he's in danger.*"

"Why?"

"*She's not absolutely clear on that. She's from the pueblo and her English is sometimes broken, but she's worried about something the boy said.*"

"Which was?"

"*Standby.*"

Reger fidgeted, eyes wide. He glanced east, anxious. "This can wait, can't it? I mean . . . we can check this out first, . . . right? We're almost there."

"Let's find out why the mom's worried."

A breeze whipped through. Jack raised the radio closer to his ear and turned away, to keep from being distracted by Johnny's nervous energy.

"*Chastain, this is Dispatch.*"

"Go ahead, Molly."

"*The boy is keeping some kind of secret. He wouldn't say, but the mom could tell he was scared . . . maybe for her . . . probably for himself.*"

"Then why the hell is he out here?"

"*She doesn't know.*" Molly let out a sigh. "*But he took his pack.*"

Chapter 33

Jack stared at the clear path before him, a sandstone shelf that circled the backside of the slickrock knoll. *This close. Why can't we just . . . ?* He forced his eyes from the distraction. He held the radio a moment, then keyed the mic. "Where's the boy supposed to be?"

"*His mother doesn't know for sure. Maybe South Desert.*" The repeater clicked off.

"She thinks? So, he could be anywhere?"

"*Yes, but she knows where you found him before. He told her. Says the boy has an attraction to the area.*"

"It's a pretty damned big desert . . . and . . . we're out here working. Maybe we could just keep an eye out for him."

"*Standby.*"

He turned to Johnny. "I'm sure that'll be good enough."

Fidgeting, Johnny gave a quick nod. "We could check the cave, then be ready to . . ."

The radio crackled. "*Chastain, Dispatch.*"

"Go ahead."

"*The Chief Ranger asks that you divert from what you're doing. There's something else going on, and the mom's not sure what, or won't say. On the call, she said the boy told her this morning that he's being followed. Barb is sending Luis Archuleta in from the main trailhead.*"

"Followed by who?"

"The mom doesn't think he knows. That, or he won't say. Barb asks you to check where you found him before and let us know if you see any sign that he's been there."

Jack unfolded the quad and checked the distance. "That's a few miles from here. How'd he get to the trail?"

"She doesn't know. He's a strong hiker . . . but he may've gotten a ride. Maybe someone from the pueblo."

"Yes, he is a strong hiker." He paused to talk to Johnny, then remembered. "Molly, do you know if the dog's with him?"

"No, I asked. The dog isn't with him."

"Okay. Not sure if that's good or bad. Any medical conditions we're not aware of?"

"Negative. This is priority because of the suspicion that the boy is at risk."

"Copy. What's the boy's name, by the way?"

"You don't know?"

"Nope, he wouldn't tell me."

"First name Miguel. Last name, the mother wouldn't say."

"Even with a missing child report?"

"That's one of the strange things about this. She wouldn't tell Barb. He made his mother promise not to tell anyone his or her last name. She honored that request, trusting there's a reason, but she panicked and turned to us for help. She's confused. She's scared."

"He's afraid someone will find him?"

"Yes, but he may be equally afraid someone will find her."

"Copy." Jack lowered the radio and shot a look at Johnny. "Change of plans, bro. At least for me. You go ahead. I'll go check where Kelly and I found him before. If he isn't there, I'll call, get you involved. It'll take me a while to get there. You should have more than enough time to get to the cave and check it out—if you can get there. Call and I'll let you know where I am."

"Nope."

"We're close. Go check it out."

"Nope. You coulda done so back there but didn't. Same thing applies here."

"I'm not sure I could've made it."

"Sure, you could."

"You're a better climber than me."

"Not today. I've got limitations." He gave his fingers a stretch. "And what if I encounter difficulties . . . beyond my limitations?"

"Then . . . don't take chances. I've gotta go. You check it out."

"I'm goin', too. If this is a bad guy, I'm prepared in ways you're not." Johnny reached back and gave a pat to the top of his pack.

His weapon. Jack sighed. "Okay . . . we'll come back."

"Deal."

"*Chastain, this is Manion.*"

Johnny leaned in. "Should we tell 'em about the cave?"

"I don't know. Up to you. You found it." Jack raised the radio. "Go ahead, Christy."

"*Where do you want us?*"

"Are you back on the trail?"

"*Not yet.*"

"In a place with a good view over the desert?"

"*We're in the rocks, but we can get to one.*"

"Do that. We'll head where I saw him last time. If you see him first, holler."

Jack started to slip the radio into his pack pocket but stopped. Someone's gonna call. Holding onto it, he backtracked along the shelf circling the knoll.

Once through the break in the wall, they hurried down the swell.

Reaching the bottom, Jack pulled out his map and set a course toward the sagebrush flats, hoping to intercept the line of travel he remembered the boy using before.

After crossing the trail, they adjusted their line, veering east, then south.

They encountered a deep arroyo and followed alongside it, staying out of the creek bed until finding a good place to traverse. After crossing the sandy creek bottom, they worked their way up to a high point with a view out over the plains.

The route where he'd seen the boy before lay before them.

Jack scanned the expanse of desert scrub, seeing no one—not

east, not south, not west. No one. *What if he doesn't want to be seen? What if he didn't come this way?* Jack ducked behind a taller specimen of four-winged saltbush and sat, signaling Johnny to do the same. "Let's just wait a moment. Might be too late, but . . . he might not want to be seen." He raised his radio. "Christy, go to channel 1."

"*Copy.*"

He twisted the channel knob from repeater channel to line of sight.

A moment's delay, then, "*I'm on.*"

"See anything?"

"*Nope.*"

Hot, afternoon breeze cut into his face. "Same. We're gonna sit here a few minutes and watch. We're keeping our heads down . . . he might be hiding."

"*Copy. We'll do the same.*"

"Copy." He lowered the radio and scanned the landscape, squinting, watching for details among the shadows, movement among the shimmering waves of heat rising off the desert floor, anything that might give the boy away.

Minutes passed.

Laying against his pack, Johnny drummed his chest with his fingers, eyeing the view to the west. He moved onto one elbow. "Should we tell 'em about the cave?"

"Your choice. You wanting to?"

"Kinda, but then it'd be embarrassing if it turned out to be nothing."

Jack turned his focus to the foreground. "Yep."

"What if the boy's already passed by here?"

"Real possibility." Jack checked his watch. Eight minutes. He picked up his radio and switched to the repeater. "Dispatch, Chastain."

"*Go ahead, Jack.*"

"No sign of him yet. Not where we first caught sight of him last time, but he's a hider so we're being careful, just in case he doesn't want to be seen."

"*Do we need to call in a helicopter? Maybe another team?*"

"Uh . . ." He glanced at the topo. "Hold off on that. He'd see that for sure. We haven't done an actual hasty search. We can divide up, hit a few likely places, then get back to you."

"Copy. I'll pass that onto Barb."

Jack turned to Johnny. "I'm in better shape than you . . . because you've been doggin' it lately." He flashed a tease of a smile. "Let's have you go to the trail. See if you pick up tracks that aren't ours. Check hard on any sections we haven't been on. I'll take a run across the flats, where we first saw him that day, see if I find any tracks."

"That's a lot of country."

"Not bad. About the same as one of my runs."

"What about Christy and lover boy?"

Jack glanced at the map and picked up his radio. "Manion, Chastain."

"This is Manion."

"Johnny's going back to the trail. I'm gonna take a run, check for track out on the flats. Post Toby on the trail checking for track coming from Johnny's direction. You could head to the breaks going to the river, see if that's his destination."

"Copy."

"Let's plan to talk in an hour if we haven't seen anything."

"Copy."

Jack dropped his pack, pulled out a water bottle, and stuffed his map into his shorts pocket. "I'm leaving that," he said, gesturing to the pack while studying the landscape he'd need to recognize to get back to it. He took off across the flat.

Setting his sights on the vicinity where they first saw the boy, Jack settled into a moderate pace, eye to the ground, hoping to cut across tracks.

Damned kid, why would you do this again? And why keep a secret from your mom?

After a several minutes, and seeing no track, he zigged to the south, just to check, covering a few hundred yards, then zagged back north. Still no track. Not even old track. Not even deer trail. He veered back to the east.

A stream of sweat rolled into his eyes. He wiped it away. *Even the wildlife is too smart to be out here. Why would he choose to be here now, in the heat of the day?*

Ahead, he could see the drainage they'd followed the boy into, the exposed rock he'd used to avoid being caught.

"*Chastain, this is Reger.*"

Jack slowed, taking a moment to regulate his breathing. "Go ahead, Johnny."

"*Boss, I've got tracks.*"

Jack stopped. "A kid's track?"

"*Yeah.*"

"Did we miss 'em when we crossed the trail?"

"*I don't think so. I got track on several kinds of substrate. Sand, dirt, gravel. These tracks look fresh. Nothing windblown about 'em.*"

"Serious? He just passed by?"

"*I think so, yes. One other thing.*" A sigh bled over the radio.

"Go ahead."

"*There are two sets of tracks. I think he's following someone.*"

Chapter 34

Jack took off in a jog. "Or is he being followed?"

"I don't think so. The bigger tracks seem relaxed, normal pace. The boy's . . . all over the map."

"Could they be together?"

"They're too close to be walking shoulder to shoulder. Too deliberately not on top of each other. It's as if he's following track, hanging back, not wanting to be seen."

"The other track an adult shoe?"

"Man's shoe, about my size, ten to twelve."

"Copy. Head toward Toby, see if he's met up with them."

"Copy."

"I'll get my pack and head your way." He picked up his pace. "Christy, hear all that?"

"Yes. I'll turn around." Breathing bled over the transmission. *"I'm almost to the river."*

"There's a chance these are different people. Just in case, go on to the break in the gorge, check for tracks. Eliminate it as a possibility. Then come back."

"Copy."

Covering ground for the second time, the return trip felt somehow longer. He darted past sagebrush, four-winged saltbush, winterfat, and the occasional desert marigold. Dust kicked up in the breeze. Reaching the crest where he'd left his pack, he took a moment to study the map.

Depending on where Johnny hit the trail, and how far west Toby had been working before being diverted, they could be a couple of miles apart, but more likely half a mile to a mile.

He took off, but his pack's weight and jarring wouldn't allow him to run. He slowed to a brisk walk and veered to intercept the trail close to where Johnny and Toby might meet.

Reaching it where it wound alongside a stand of weathered sandstone hoodoos, Jack raised his radio. "Johnny, I'm on the trail. Hooked up with Toby yet?"

"No. See two sets of tracks or three?" Reger asked, in quick, clipped words.

Jack looked down. Dirt and desert gravel. Not easy to read. Kneeling, he faced the sun. Breaks in the surface began to show. Compressed gravel. Fragmented shadows on the sunward edges of compressions. Shoe lugs, easy to miss in the dirt between pebbles. A man's shoe.

Now, where's the boy's track? He found it a little to the left, nearer the edge of the trail. Smaller. Swirls, an odd pattern. A kid's shoe.

He stood. That's two. Where's number three?

He stood a step along the opposite edge of the three-foot wide trail, looking for a third set of tracks. Those of the tracker, Johnny. There. The lug design of his lightweight hiking boot. Jack keyed his radio. "I'm behind you."

"*Copy. And I see LeBlanc, heading this way.*"

Jack took off.

"*Chastain, Manion.*"

"Go ahead, Christy."

"*Nothing here.*"

"Copy. Head back for the trail."

"*Copy.*"

"*Jack, this is Johnny.*"

"Go ahead."

"*We've got a problem.*"

"Go ahead."

"*I'm with Toby. He hasn't seen either party. And . . . I can't believe it . . . but . . . I took my eyes off the trail when I saw him and . . . I lost the tracks.*"

Damn. He's done it again. Jack shot a look at the map. "How? Isn't he following the other guy?"

"*They're both gone. They left the trail, somewhere near here.*"

"Copy." Jack counted the sets of track at his feet. One, two, three. "Come back my way. Find where they left the trail."

"*They were just here!*" Johnny said, exasperated.

"Go back and find 'em." Jack picked up his pace, eyes on the tracks left by the boy's shoes. *No fooling me this time.*

Rounding a bend, he saw Johnny and Toby, two hundred yards away, inching along the trail. Jack made a quick count of the sets of track. Three. He slowed, keeping an account of each.

Closing the distance, he crossed a flat strip of open rock. Beyond it, dirt. Only one set of track. Jack raised his radio. "I've found where they left the trail."

The two ran to join him.

To the south, beyond the trail, the rock ended at a pinch point between arroyos.

To the north, it continued unbroken, ending just short of a vertical spine, along which hoodoos shot from the ground. Beyond them, growing swells of slickrock.

Jack put his hands on his hips. Damn. *Did he go left or right? Downslope, finding him might be possible. Upslope? Never.* He turned to the south. Arroyos and sage brush. Then north. Slickrock. Patches of dirt and cryptogamic soil on the approach to the hoodoos. After that, continuous rock.

Johnny tapped at the rock with his boot. "I don't know, Boss. Looks impossible."

Jack turned to Toby and pointed into slickrock. "Keep an eye upslope. High ground. Watch for movement. We don't know how much of a lead they have. You might see 'em."

"Is that where you guys were?" Toby asked.

"We were working this way. Hadn't gotten here yet." Jack turned to Johnny. "If they went south, they'll hit dirt. Check for track." He turned to the approach to the hoodoos. "I'll check this way. I know his tricks. Just maybe he'll leave us a hint."

"What about the other guy? What about his tricks?" Johnny asked.

"Yeah, that's the question, isn't it?"

Head down, Reger scooted along the edge of the rock, starting from the last sets of track.

Jack followed the edge the other direction. Flat rock. Then, a break. Patches of sandy soil with scattered rock, then swells, scattered hoodoos, and slope rising to the highest slickrock. He made a quick pass along the edge. *If Miguel went this way, I'll spot his track here or never.*

No track.

He paced the edge of a sandy gap between the trail and the hoodoos. Scattered rocks. Last time, *Miguel had rock hopped. But if he's following someone . . . ?*

Jack checked a rock for movement. Then another. No sign of rocks shifting in sandy soil, but then he saw it. An adult-sized depression among desert gravel, then another beyond a boulder in line with the hoodoos, a gap too long for the boy to jump.

Would this guy he's following be doing the same thing? Rock hopping? Has he followed this guy before? Is this how Miguel learned to do this? Maybe they're traveling together. "Got track!" Jack shouted.

Johnny came running.

Eyes still on the slickrock above, Toby moved toward them.

Jack pointed at the adult-sized depression, then the boy's track.

Johnny gave a nod, then raised his eyes. "We'll never track 'em up there."

Jack eyed the slickrock. "Our only option is to figure out where they're headed. Let's see where this drainage goes." He pulled the topo from a pocket and took a moment to study. "I think we're here," he said, tapping the map. "The top of the drainage is there."

Toby looked over his shoulder.

"Is that near Rivera's cave?" Johnny asked, hopeful, then turning sheepish.

"No, it's a bit that way." Jack pointed east.

Toby cleared his throat. "That's near the approach to the Five Fingers of Tawa."

Stunned, Jack glanced up.

"Fingers of what?" Johnny huddled closer to the topo.

"It's not on the map." Jack turned to Toby. "You know about the Fingers of Tawa?"

He nodded.

"What are they?" Johnny asked, sounding left out.

"Fingers of Tawa, creator god. Potts told me about it, but not where," Jack said.

"Neither of you have been there?" Toby asked.

"Never been there, never heard of it," Johnny said.

"How do you know?" Jack asked.

Toby shrugged. "The GIS layer for cultural sites. I was looking at what's connected to various rock strata. Arch sites can tell you where to look for water. The fingers don't have the kinda places you're looking for . . . perched aquafers, that sort of thing . . . but the words caught my eye. Seemed interesting."

Jack looked down at the map. "Yeah, I only know about 'em because of Potts Monroe. Said he'd take me there sometime. Might be where he wants to work next. His next project."

"What is it?" Johnny asked.

"He described it as this strange place with five little canyons. Fingers, feeding into the same dry creek bed, which in turn dumps out on the desert west of here."

"Why haven't I seen these fingers?"

"Not easy to find, apparently, and Potts doesn't draw attention to them. Said they need protection." Jack laid the map on the ground. "Let's figure out what we're gonna do."

Toby gave five taps to the map. "The fingers."

Eyeballing the map, Jack slid his hand along the contours of the slickrock and beyond, to the base of an isolated mesa, sitting below the plateau. To the west of the mesa lay flat ground. The head of each canyon could be reached from there.

It appears easier to come in from below, if that's their destination. But the boy and whoever he's following chose to come this way. Then again, they could be going somewhere else. Maybe another route to Rivera's Cave. Maybe into the slickrock. Or maybe one of the fingers is easier to get into from above.

The creek the fingers fed into flowed south, dumping out onto rock before making its way to toward the river, northwest of where Christy intercepted it.

Jack took his eyes off the map and raised his radio. "Christy, this is Jack."

"*Go ahead.*"

"We need you to go west, then north, and take up a position where a little dry creek pops out of the canyon wall, a mile or so from your location." He read her the map coordinates. "I'm sending Toby your way since he doesn't have a radio. The boy and whoever he's following . . . if they stay ahead of us . . . you may see 'em first. We'll let you know if there's reason to believe that's not where they're heading." He slipped off his pack.

"*Copy.*"

Jack twisted a knob on the radio, changing channels. "Dispatch, Chastain." The repeater gave a pop.

"*Go ahead Jack.*"

"We've found track and that's about all we can say at this point. The boy is following someone . . . or they could be following him, but it looks like the former."

"*Copy. I'll share that with Barb.*"

"One other thing. It's gonna be hard to track him. They've gone into slickrock. Got an idea on where to pick up his trail, but if we can't find 'em, we'll need a helicopter."

"*Copy. I'll check on availability.*"

He slipped off his pack and pulled out food, divvying out granola bars, trail mix, cheese, tortillas, carrots, and peas to Toby and Johnny. "Eat." He bit into a carrot. "There goes tomorrow's breakfast, lunch and dinner." He switched back to channel one and keyed the radio. "Christy, got food?"

"*Not much.*"

"Copy. There's food coming your way." He grabbed a few items and handed them to Toby. "Take these to Christy." He turned back to his radio. "Got water?"

"*Plenty. I filled up at the river,*" Manion answered.

"Copy." He turned to Johnny. "Water?"

"Um . . . ." Sheepish, he said, "a little low."

Jack passed him one of his bottles. "Toby, you good for water?"

He nodded.

"Can Johnny have one of yours?"

He nodded and slipped off his pack, dug out a bottle, and handed it off.

Jack dumped his own pack and sorted through gear, keeping the rope, webbing, water, and extra radio battery, setting aside everything else—sleeping bag, pad, bivy sack, and stove kit. He stashed the discards in a cleft at the base of a hoodoo and threw on his pack. "Ready." He turned to Toby. "Be careful." Pointing Johnny upslope, he headed for slickrock.

They broke into a jog.

Chapter 35

Near the top of the slickrock, a vertical wall. They found a break and scrambled up and through, and there it was, the unnamed mesa, beyond it the plateau.

They veered toward the west side of the mesa. Swells gave way to a level bed of rock—the top of one formation, the base for the mesa. To the west lay five little canyons. Or so the map said. They counted off what they could see, three of the five. They didn't look so small from there. According to the map, the canyons lay over what was nearly half a mile, only three obvious from where they stood. Two others lay to the north.

Broken shale littered the ridges between canyons.

"So that's what they mean by fingers," Johnny said. "Ridges, reaching west."

"That or the canyons." Jack eyed the closest. "Let's look for track."

They spread out.

Twenty feet apart, heads down, they scanned the ground dropping into the head of the first canyon. Rock gave way to scattered slabs of shale. Shale gave way to soil and scrubby vegetation. Then came a steep, sandy bottomed creek bed.

No track.

They continued, toward the spine of the next ridge.

Nothing.

Ground dropped off to the north, into the shallow beginnings of the second canyon. Beyond it lay the next ridge.

No track, no people.

"We have no idea which canyon. No idea if they even came this way," Jack muttered, fighting uncertainty. He glanced at Reger, who shrugged. "Let's make a quick sweep across all five, see if we pick up anything."

"They could be here and we wouldn't know it, boss."

Jack let out a sigh. "I know."

They followed the ridge back to the level platform of rock at the base of the mesa.

"I'll anchor here on the edge of the rock," Jack said, "you take downslope. More soil. You're a better tracker."

They backtracked and began moving forward.

After covering over half the distance to the first ridge, Johnny, head down, shouted, "I think we should order the helicopter."

"Maybe." Jack stopped. A disturbance. In silt settled in a depression in the rock. A partial track. Not the boy's. The man's. "Johnny." Jack waived him over. "They're here."

Johnny stumbled upslope. He stared down at the track "Wow, Boss! If I were you, today I'd be buyin' a lottery ticket."

"So, we were right. This is where they're going. We need to figure out which canyon."

"Easy, peasy."

Ignoring him, Jack took a line of sight over the track. "Direction of travel . . . not the first canyon. Probably not the second."

"I'll confirm." Johnny swung left, toward the last half of the second. Nearing the ridge, he hollered, "So far, no track. You're probably right."

Trailing to his right, Jack saw a game trail heading back toward the second canyon. Glancing down, he noticed what looked to be brush marks. Like a broom. *You're kidding.* "You sure? No track?"

"What do you see?"

"Looks like they swept out their tracks." Jack pointed, twenty feet downslope. Tossed aside, lay snakeweed, pulled up by the roots.

"Serious?"

"Yeah. Check that for track."

Johnny approached the game trail. "Nothing."

"You're sure?"

Johnny followed it further. He stopped at a gap between boulders. A pinch point. He knelt and studied the ground. "Nothing here."

"Why would they go to that trouble? Do they know they're being followed?"

"Seems unlikely," Johnny muttered. "But . . ."

"Brushing them out suggests they do . . . and went that way.

"I'm not seeing it."

Jack studied the ground between them. Steep. Serviceberry and scrub oak. No sign of broken branches. "Go down a little more, keep checking. I'll check the next canyon. See if anything's there. Anything else that looks funny."

Heading north, he passed the beginnings of the ridgeline between canyons. Then the beginning of the third canyon. In the dirt, footprints. He keyed his mic. "Johnny, I've got track."

"*I'll be right there.*"

Jack headed into the draw. Track ended. *What's going on?* He looked around. Plenty of rocks, positioned nicely for a return to the slab. "I'm going to the next canyon," he said, into the radio. "The trail just ended. Something funny's going on."

"*Copy.*"

Keeping an eye over the edge, he moved toward the next ridge, watching for track and checking for broken branches. Still nothing.

Approaching the ridge, he turned to look for Johnny. He'd had gone high and past him, then stopped and knelt.

Jack moved his direction. "Got something?"

He stared over another thin layer of silt, barely present on the rock. "Boss, I think I was wrong about something."

Jack stopped beside him. "How so? Following the wrong people?"

"No, not that." Johnny pointed at an overlap of the tracks. "See it?"

"The tracks cross."

"They're on top of each other. The boy isn't following the man. The man's following the boy. The boy's funny moves below . . . must be jumpy . . . checking to see if he's being followed."

Jack leaned in for a closer look. The larger track covered most of a smaller one. "You're right! I wondered about that. At this point . . . will he still be on guard? If this guy's trailing at a distance . . . Miguel might be thinking he's safe."

"Maybe. With these few tracks, I can't tell if he's still being jumpy." Johnny gave a rub to his chin. "No sign of running. Whole foot compression, not just toes, so the boy's walking. But . . . why didn't the follower sweep out these tracks? Maybe he didn't think to watch for silt on the rock . . . because his eyes are on the boy."

"Maybe he thinks he's thrown us off the trail. That we've taken the bait, . . . gone down the wrong canyon. Or maybe he's in a hurry to catch up, afraid he'll lose the boy."

"Maybe to all those things . . . but if he's playing these games . . ." Johnny stared toward the next ridge. ". . . he must know we're here. Does he know we're on his trail?"

"How would he?"

"Maybe he has a radio."

"Or a scanner?"

"Maybe."

They broke into a jog, going to the next ridge. Track. Back to the third canyon.

Johnny headed down.

Jack stood staring. The man's track. No sign of the boy's. Words came to mind. Toby's words. About Montana and the games Doc played. The games Doc taught others to play.

'You were drawn to truth, ignoring the lies. If you'd followed the lies you would have understood what was going on.'

The lies.

Is this connected to all that? Could this be Mangum? Are the tracks another lie? A misdirection? Is this where he wants us to go? Where does he not want us to go? What truth does he not want us to follow?

Does he already know where the boy is going? Does he know the boy covers his tracks?

How would he know?

How much danger is the boy in?

Jack glanced north. "Johnny, I'm not coming with you," he shouted. "You check this canyon, but I have a gut feeling they didn't go this way."

Johnny turned his way. "Why?"

"Still got track?"

"No."

"Just a hunch. I'm gonna check the next canyon. I'll call, let you know what I find. I might be speaking in code."

"Gotcha," Johnny said.

Jack jogged past the canyon, past the next ridge, on to the head of the next canyon. Assessing the terrain, he noticed the ground falling away in a second direction. This was not the beginning of one canyon, it was the beginning of two. The ridge between them sat lower, less elevation. *That's why we couldn't see five.*

He pulled a water bottle from his pack and took a sip, studying the scene. Two canyons. The forefinger here, the thumb there, curving around the ridge.

Tracks?

He scanned. Nothing obvious. He walked downslope to the head of the last finger—the thumb. Brush marks. Sweeping away track.

Or, an attempt to look like he was sweeping away track.

Downslope, scattered boulders. Plenty to rock hop. Rock hopping downhill, not smart.

Which is the lie? The swept ground, or the ground with no track? Both could be lies. Which does he not want us to follow? Or is it both? Does he want us to think they came this far but didn't? Maybe they went back to where Reger is.

If he did, Reger will pick up his tracks.

Jack glared across the landscape. *The canyon to the left, or the canyon to the right?* His eye passed over the ridge in between, covered in broken shale.

What if the boy didn't go down either canyon? What if he took the ridge in between?

Did the follower toss in a misdirection to throw us off? Give himself time to set a trap.

He checked the map. The contour lines at the end of the ridge were so close they probably meant a near-vertical wall. The canyons looked severe, possibly requiring a rope.

Too little time to figure it out. Maybe too late already.

Jack keyed his radio. "Johnny, I'm going down."

"Which canyon? I've got nothin' here."

"You'll see when you get here." With a fist-sized stone, he scrawled the word *ridge* on the open rock. Then an arrow.

He headed down, eyes on the dirt between boulders, then between broken pieces of shale. On the ridge, no track. Thirty yards more, still no track, and a growing feeling of being outwitted. Then the ridge began to narrow. Then, there, track, veering right, into the thumb. Two sets, on dirt, dropping into the canyon, following a game trail, or one made by indigenous humans. Switchbacks wove through oak brush and serviceberry. Following, his feet slid on dirt. He slowed his descent, grabbing hold of brush. Reaching bottom, Jack stopped and looked out over the sandy creek bed. Two sets of craters in the sand. No longer did either make an effort to disguise their direction of travel. Downstream.

He glanced upstream. There sat the reason they'd come this way, and the reason for confidence in their earlier misdirections. A dry waterfall, a hundred feet high, possibly more. Too long a drop for the typical climbing rope, doubled over to be pulled down from the anchor.

Anyone coming downcanyon would be stopped.

Where the hell is Miguel going? And if this is Mangum, has he been here before?

Jack pulled out his radio. "Johnny, stay on my trail."

"*Copy. I'm following petroglyphs.*"

"Copy."

In a few hundred yards, willow and buffaloberry became

common. He came to a boulder holding back debris, below which sat what had been a pool in the not-too-distant past. Now dry and rung with detritus, it sat four feet below the rock, with two deep sets of evidence in the sand, of humans having jumped in from above.

He followed them down.

The canyon began to open. Around a bend, another dry pool, another jam of boulders, this one a six-foot drop. In the sand below, no prints.

Where'd they go?

They had to have worked their way around.

Too steep to have climbed out of the canyon.

He worked past the rock dam and back into the creek bed. Track. They'd done the same thing, but from the other side.

The canyon walls began to come together. Ahead he could see a ledge, and beyond it the ground falling away. He approached, slowing near the edge. A thirty-foot drop. Maybe forty. No jumping this one. *How'd they get down? Handholds?*

He leaned forward, bracing himself. In the sand below lay a rope. Pulled down by the last person over.

Jack glanced at the wall to his left. An anchor. A hanger, set with a star bolt. Threaded through the hanger, a short piece of knotted webbing.

If someone went to the trouble of bringing tools to set an anchor . . . what's down here?

More important, the follower knows I'm coming.

Jack dropped his pack and unlashed his rope. Taking hold of an end, he threaded it through the webbing, and started to pull, when his eyes were drawn downstream. Hundreds of yards away, on a long reach of the canyon, the boy ambled along the creek bottom.

Dark hair, red T-shirt, green backpack. No suggestion of concern.

In the willows behind him, movement. Deliberate, a few feet at a time. Short glimpses of someone closing the distance.

Is he trying to catch the boy or follow him?

Would Miguel be safer knowing . . . or not knowing? But if he's afraid . . . ?

Jack cupped his hands. "Miguel," he shouted. The name echoed down the canyon.

The boy spun around.

Jack caught the surprise on his face, even from a distance. "Miguel, you're being followed. Behind you."

Miguel's head jerked around, looking. He took off like a shot.

Through the willows Jack picked up glimpses of rapid movement.

He pulled his rope through the anchor and tossed it over the edge. Foregoing a Swiss seat, he went over, hand at his back, the other holding him vertical, rope sliding through his fingers. The drop came quick. He settled into sand, fingers burning.

He left the rope and darted after them, slinging his pack around, digging his radio from a pocket. He keyed the mike. "Johnny, I've seen the boy. He's in trouble. Hurry!"

Silence.

"Johnny."

Silence.

Damn. Radio dead spot. "Christy, this is Jack."

"*Go ahead, Jack.*"

"Come up the drainage. The last finger canyon. Have Toby explain. The boy's here and he's being followed. I'm behind 'em, but I might be too far away to help. Be careful."

"*Copy. We're on our way.*"

He ran up ahead, reaching the spot where Miguel had turned. Downstream, two sets of tracks, long strides.

They're running. On silt-covered rock, toe depressions. No heel at all.

The canyon constricted. Ahead, he could see the ground drop away at the end of a flat stretch of rock. Another dry waterfall.

He slowed.

An undulating cut in the sandstone, a slide that ended at a drop over the edge.

Downstream he saw the boy. No follower, yet. *Good.*

Approaching the edge, he eyed the drop and the rocks below.

How did they get down?

A blow, a sudden shove from behind. Jack's head and arms jerked back, rock flying at his face as he fell into the swirling undulations of sandstone.

He hit. A sandpaper-like bite. Then, tugging, sliding him toward the edge.

Then a sound. Like a gunshot, and an echo, then silence.

Chapter 36

His mind faded in and out. Jostling returned.

Pulling, sliding, his face scraping against stone.

He felt himself being flipped over, his back settling against rock. He opened his eyes, fighting the glare of the sun.

Johnny Reger stood over him, his face a palette of concern and confusion.

Jack felt throbs and stings, and blood and sweat rolling into his eyes. "Am I shot?"

"That was me," Johnny said.

"You shot me?"

"No, I shot at the guy trying to push you over the edge."

"What? . . . Why?"

"You don't remember what happened, do you?"

Jack sat up. "No . . . what happened?"

"I came around the corner . . . saw him hit you from behind. Looked like he was trying to throw you over the edge. I did the only thing I could think of. I fired my weapon."

"You had your gun out?"

"I took it out when you called on the radio . . . after I heard what you said to Christy."

"You could hear me?"

"I heard you. You couldn't hear me." Reger glanced down stream, antsy to go. "I need to get going, boss. If you're okay. The guy was packin'. Saw his holster as he ran off."

"He had a gun?" Jack gave his head a shake. "Who . . . was it?"

"He never looked my way. He just . . . disappeared."

"How'd you get here so fast?" Jack sat up, and Johnny helped him to his feet.

"I ran. You told me to hurry.

"But you couldn't hear me."

"I could hear you. Boss, I gotta get going, to protect the boy."

"The boy . . . ?" Jack looked downstream, then back at Johnny. "The guy's got a gun . . . ?"

"*Chastain, Manion.*"

"I'll get it, Boss." Johnny raised his radio. "They're coming your way. You have to be careful. Where are you now?"

"*Standby.*"

Woozy, Jack said, "You didn't tell her he has a gun."

—'—

Christy lowered the radio and turned to Toby LeBlanc. "Hear that?" she whispered.

"Yes."

Slipping behind a boulder downstream of the confluence, they listened.

Then they heard sobbing and hard breathing. Cobble knocking against cobble.

The boy appeared, running, looking back over his shoulder.

Toby grabbed him, picking him up off his feet, pulling him behind the boulder.

Christy cupped his mouth. She raised a finger. "Sh-h-h-h."

Wide eyed, he squealed, fighting to break free of the grasp.

"Sh-h-h-h," Christy said again. "We won't hurt you but you've got to be quiet."

The boy grew still.

Toby relaxed his grip.

Christy hunkered behind the boulder and keyed her mic. "We've got the kid. Now what?"

Johnny answered. "*Keep moving.*"

"We're hidden."

"*I'm not sure that's good enough. He's been tracking the boy. He'll find you.*"

"He's outnumbered. There's two of us."

"*He's got a gun.*"

Christy exchanged glances with Toby, then noticed the boy shivering. She studied the canyon. A straight shot with nowhere to hide. Sand, and slivers of light pouring in from above. A few willow. She keyed her mic. "Hurry."

—'—

Johnny broke into a run. "How far is it?"

Jack kicked into high gear. Still woozy, he couldn't keep up. "Your guess, good as mine."

One set of tracks in deep, dry sand. *Where's the other?*

Johnny plowed past a thicket of willow.

Jack cringed, seeing shadows in the brush, proving to be nothing. He turned his eye to the other side of the narrow canyon. High on the wall, cliff dwellings, what was left of them. Windowed structures. Granaries of mud and rock.

No time to be awestruck. He might be up there, ready to shoot. Jack broke into a sprint.

Ahead, the creek bed turned left, seemingly diverted by boulders and deposited debris, in reality bent by the sheer canyon walls.

The new path ran straight, gradual descent. No one in sight other than Johnny. Then, suddenly, there was.

—'—

Hearing sounds from up canyon, Christy sank behind the boulder, pulling Toby and the boy with her.

Clomping on cobble. Someone running.

Toby picked up a piece of driftwood.

She hunkered down. “Ready?” she whispered.

He nodded.

A light-haired man flew by, then stopped.

Toby stepped out from the boulder, raising his club.

“Johnny,” Christy Manion shouted, dashing past Toby.

“Where'd he go?” Johnny asked, breathing hard.

Jack rounded the bend, panic on his face, then relief. “Where is he?”

“I don't know,” Manion said.

“Where's the boy?”

Miguel stepped into the open.

“Good . . . but where's the other guy?”

Christy shook her head. “He hasn't come by here.”

“You mean?” Jack turned back. “He's still in the canyon?”

Johnny, nostrils flared, started back up.

“Whoa, Johnny. Let's think about this. I didn't see anyone.”

“Were you looking?”

“Kinda. I was afraid we'd be ambushed.”

“Okay, so now what?”

“Must've climbed out of the canyon, but where? How? If he wanted to get us, he would've had high ground, but I'm guessing he's running.” Jack raised his radio and changed channels. He keyed the mic. Nothing. “Can't hit the repeater. Not in the canyon.” He turned to Toby. “From the flats, how long did it take you to get here?”

“A few minutes. Ten if you take your time.”

“I won't be.” Jack broke into a run. “Meet you out on the flats. If the guy shows up, Johnny's here to protect you.” He stopped and turned back. “Miguel.” He eyed the boy. “Yes, I know your name is Miguel. So, tell me. Who is it? Who's following you?”

Miguel shook his head. “I don't know. I didn't know he was there . . . until you shouted.”

“Did you see him?”

“All I saw was a man in the bushes . . . in a brown shirt.”

Jack turned and ran.

Johnny shouted, “What are you gonna do?”

“Get the helicopter in the air. Get someone looking for him.”

“What do you want me to do?” Johnny shouted.

“Get ’em safely outta here.” Jack shouted back over his shoulder. “Learn what you can from Miguel.”

—·—

The dry creek bed spilled out of the canyon, onto cross-bedded sandstone. The sun hung to the west. Not many hours left in the day.

Jack pulled out his radio and keyed the mic. The repeater clicked on, then off. He keyed it again. “Dispatch, this is Chastain.”

“*Go ahead, Jack.*”

“Is the Chief Ranger still in the office?”

“*Yes. Standby.*”

After a momentary wait, “*Go ahead, Jack,*” Barb Sharp said. “*What do you need?*”

“A helicopter, and someone like Luiz on board. Or you. We’ve got the boy. He’s safe, but there was someone following him, and I think I know who it is. He ambushed me, took off, and is probably climbing out of the canyon. He has a gun.”

“*What canyon?*”

“All I can tell you is where he started from. I’ll give you coordinates. Start on the ridge.” He pulled the quad from his pocket.

“*Molly will get that from you. She has the helicopter on standby. I’ll grab my stuff. It’ll be me on board.*”

After calling BLM, Molly came back on. “*Jack, I’m ready to copy coordinates, and I’ll get back to you with an ETA.*”

—·—

Barb Sharp closed her office door, unlocked her gun safe, and retrieved her service belt and weapon. From her locker, she pulled the gray-green flight suit she kept for her own use.

After pulling it on over her uniform, she slung the belt and holstered 9mm Sig Sauer semi-automatic pistol over a shoulder, then headed to dispatch.

Waiting at the counter, she listened to the last of the exchange between Jack and Molly, including the route he took past the unnamed mesa, onto the ridge and into the fifth canyon.

When finished talking with Jack, Molly spun around to Barb.

"Call Luiz, get him on the trail, ask him to position himself where he can watch the trail and respond as needed. And I'm wondering if we shouldn't pick up Jack on the way," Barb said, thinking aloud.

Molly spun around to the base station and keyed the mic. "Jack, should the helicopter come pick you up? Barb wants to know."

"*Time's of the essence. He's got a head start, and there's not much left in the day.*"

Barb checked her watch. Six-forty. "Okay. Tell him to keep his ears on."

Molly passed on the message, then went to the supply closet and pulled out the Park's flight map binder. "One more thing," she said, turning back to the closet. She pulled out a clean quad map and marked the target ridge in black, then the larger search area, scribbling a few notes on the margin. She slid it across the counter to Chief Ranger Sharp.

Barb gave the quad a quick look. "Okay. I'll start at the ridge between the fourth and fifth fingers." She looked closer. "Interesting. Five little canyons."

—'—

On hearing the approach of the helicopter, Barb Sharp slipped on her helmet and took one last look at the topo map, then folded and slipped it into a pocket of her flight suit.

Rotor noise echoed off the sandstone walls. The Bell 407 circled and landed on the concrete pad.

A tall, wiry helitack foreman, in flight suit and helmet, climbed down from the passenger side and approached, signaling Barb to follow him back to the ship. He started for the rear door.

Barb tapped his arm and pointed to the open front seat.

The foreman flashed a thumb up, opened the door and waited as she climbed in, then secured the door and took his place in the back.

Barb connected her helmet to the intercom and keyed the button to transmit. "Did Molly tell you where we're going?"

"Affirmative," the pilot said, his microphone brushing against a red pencil-thin mustache. "Beginning coordinates. I'll get you there, you tell me where to go."

"Perfect."

The helicopter lifted off, and in a gradual ascent climbed out of the canyon and along the edge of the hamlet of Las Piedras. Skirting the South Desert, they veered west toward slickrock.

Off the right side of the ship sat the Enclave, a scattering of houses, barns and pastures. A few horses. Beyond it, a small, isolated valley. The mesa with no name came into view, the sun behind it. On approach, the pilot turned toward the broken shale ridgelines to the west.

The pilot keyed the intercom. "Your search area, as I understand it. Where to?"

"Hold this line. Let me get my bearings." Glancing from topo to the landscape below, Sharp counted off fingers, then pointed.

The pilot steered the helicopter north.

Sharp scanned the ridge, her eye sliding from the front to the side window. No sign of a man. No sign of anything on the ridge other than broken shale. She keyed the intercom. "Let's fly it again. Give me a view of the north facing slope."

"You got it."

The helitack foreman cut in. "I'll take the south facing slope."

"He's in a ruddy brown shirt."

After several passes, she pointed the pilot to the next finger, then to the open rock around the mesa. Staring out over the rock and vegetation-filled canyons, she knew she was out of options. *If this guy wants to wait us out, he can.*

Eyeing the position of the sun, she keyed her radio. "Chastain, Sharp."

"*Go ahead, Barb.*"

"At this point, let's focus on getting the boy as far away from this guy as we can."

"*Copy.*"

"I've got Luiz staked out on the trail, in case this guy leaves in the night."

"*I shoulda mentioned . . . there's a chance this guy has a radio.*"

Barb sighed and keyed the mic. "Now you tell me. We're coming your way to pick up the boy."

"*Copy.*"

—'—

The helicopter landed on a flat stretch of rock. The helitack foreman climbed out and opened the door for Sharp. She exited the ship, head down as she walked under the rotor.

Away from the ship, she approached Jack and the others, sitting near the break in the cliff where the side canyon poured onto the desert.

She pulled off her helmet and knelt before the boy. "Miguel, your mother called me. She's worried about you."

He lowered his eyes.

"We're gonna take you home. Okay?"

He nodded.

Sharp turned to Jack. "You look like you ran your face through a cheese grater."

He touched his nose. "This is the worst of it. I'm lucky he didn't get me over the edge."

"Need anything? Want us to ferry you home while we still have some sun?"

"Take Johnny and Christy. They don't have overnight gear. Maybe Toby, but not me. I've got gear scattered from here to breakfast, starting with a rope I left in that canyon. The rest of my gear's stashed at a hoodoo down in the slickrock."

She gave her chin a rub. "I don't think you should go get that rope, not tonight. Not with a bad guy still out here . . ." She lowered her sunglasses and glared over the rim. "Hear what I'm saying? You can get it in a day or two."

Jack hemmed and hawed.

She turned to the helitack foreman, ignoring the protestations. "Got any MREs?"

He nodded and went to the ship, opened a compartment at the back, and returned with five Meals Ready to Eat.

"Have we got room for everyone here?" she asked the foreman.

He did a quick count. "One, maybe two, too many."

"Got time to make two trips?"

He checked the sun. "Maybe, if we get moving." He took a look at the boy. "I won't have anything that fits him . . . not very well anyway." He left to get flight suits.

"Take everyone else. I'll stay," Jack said.

She pointed at Reger, Manion and LeBlanc, then waved them toward the foreman. "Get suited up."

Johnny got to his feet. "Maybe I should stay. Jack and I have . . ."

"Don't think it," Jack said, cutting him off. "Not tonight. I'm beat."

"I just . . . thought . . . we . . ." He stopped talking.

Jack sighed. "We'll come back."

"Jack," Sharp said. "The more I think about it, the thought of you being out here . . ."

"I'll be fine."

"Probably. But there's a bad guy running around with a gun. I don't want him getting another chance at you. Leave him to me and my people."

Jack rolled his eyes. "Why does everyone think they need to protect me?"

Chapter 37

Staring out the window, Toby LeBlanc's eyes darted up and down the sheer rock walls as the helicopter descended into the canyon, its second trip back to headquarters.

The pilot pushed the stick left, guiding the ship onto a new arc. Keying his mic, he reported his arrival to Molly in dispatch, and proceeded to set the aircraft down at the concrete helipad. Then, on a different channel, he reported into his home base at BLM.

The helitack foreman climbed out and opened the rear door.

Jack slipped out. He noticed Toby remaining seated. "You okay?"

"I'm supposed to wait here, right? Till that helitack guy says I can move?"

"Yeah, but . . ." Jack waved him out.

Toby released his seat belt and slid toward the door.

Jack led him out from under the rotors, stopping a safe distance from the ship. He unzipped his flight suit and slipped out of the sleeves. "What'd you think?"

Toby copied his actions. "Amazing. All that rock from above. Canyons deeper than anything I've ever seen in my life. In fact, everything about this day was amazing."

Jack stepped out of one leg of the flight suit. "You mean, hiking with Christy?"

"That woman is in shape. She hikes hard, looks hard."

"Being on fire staff does that."

"She looks pretty damned good . . . but it wasn't just her. It was the whole day." Toby pulled the flight suit off one leg.

"Finding the boy? Even after the man with the gun?"

"Yeah." He stepped out of the other leg. "Where are the others?"

"Inside, waiting. The gun didn't bother you?"

"Loved it. Is this what you do every day?"

Jack laughed. "Hardly."

The helitack foreman traded their packs for the flight suits, gave Jack a thumbs-up and returned to the ship. After stashing the suits in a rear compartment, he climbed into the helicopter. It took off toward the mouth of the canyon.

Jack signaled Toby to follow. "Let's go see what's happening."

As they started up the back steps, quiet settled over the canyon.

Inside, noise picked up again—Reger and Manion sharing their accounts of the day. Seated at the radio base station, Molly pivoted in her chair as they took turns with their stories.

Jack stopped at the door.

Molly's jaw dropped. "You okay?"

"Saying I need to clean up a little?"

"That or go to the emergency room."

Jack ran a hand over his nose and cheek, feeling the damage. Dried blood. Scraped skin. "A bit tender, that's all." He pointed at Johnny. "Not much worse than Johnny."

"The difference is, I'm presentable. I've got a Band-Aid®."

"Ha! Where'd you get that?"

Barb Sharp came in from the hall, squeezing past them. She pulled a soda from the back corner refrigerator and gathered a few things to eat. She threw something in the microwave, pushed a few buttons and started it humming. "For the boy," she said, as if someone had asked.

"How's he doing?" Jack asked.

"He's been a bit nervous since we got here. I'm not sure why. I set him up with the phone and told him to call his mom."

Jack nodded. “Did he?”

The microwave dinged.

“He’s talking to her now.” Barb removed her items from the microwave and departed.

Christy Manion leaned over the counter and reached for something out of sight. “Can I have the first aid kit?”

Molly pulled out a red bag and passed it her way.

Finding cotton balls and a bottle of alcohol, she turned to Jack, invading his space. “Do I need to tell you this is gonna sting?”

“Do I need to wash up first?”

Barb Sharp reappeared at the door. “Did Miguel come in here?”

Molly shook her head.

“He’s not in your office?” Jack asked.

“He was. Now he’s gone!”

Jack dashed out, Barb right behind him, running down the hall, checking rooms. At the end of the hall, at the main entrance to the offices, Jack looked outside. “He’s done it again!”

—·—

After mobilizing a quick search around the building, Barb called a young patrol ranger on the radio, directing him to drive the road between headquarters and the entrance station, looking for the boy. “He might be hitchhiking. He might be waiting for his mom.”

In a few minutes the patrol ranger called back. “He’s not on the road.”

She turned to Jack. “Should we worry about him?”

He shrugged. “Maybe he’s his mom’s worry now.”

“Feels like it, doesn’t it?” Barb muttered. She waved everyone inside. “Conference room. You’ve been on your feet all day . . . I know. But let’s debrief. A few minutes.”

They filed in. Sharp took the head of the table, and waited as others choose their seats.

Jack took a chair beside her. “Got his mom’s phone number?”

“No, she called from a gas station. She wouldn’t give me her number. Strangest thing. Tonight, Miguel wouldn't either. I gave him the phone, got an outside line, and let him dial."

"You're sure he talked to her?"

"He seemed to be. I tried the phone's redial. But . . . he must have played some funny game on the touchpad. Redial won't go through. We've done our job. I guess he's her concern."

"Until it happens again." Jack turned to Johnny. "When we were there in the canyon, I asked if he knew who was following him. He said he didn't. He said he didn't even know the guy was back there until I shouted. That sure seems unlikely. What did he tell you?"

"Same thing."

"Did he say why he was in that canyon?"

"Wouldn't say. At first, it was like we were his new best buds. I started asking questions and he clammed up. Wouldn't say a thing."

Sharp cleared her throat. "Do you believe he doesn't know who was following him?"

Johnny shrugged. "I don't know what to think. He seemed sincere but wouldn't talk. Hey, do you need a separate report from me for the discharge of my weapon?"

"Include it in the case incident report for the search." She turned to Jack. "Do you believe Miguel? Do you believe he doesn't know who was following him?"

"I don't know either. This is all so damned strange."

"Do you think he was in danger?"

"Yeah. The guy proved it." Jack ran a hand over the dried streaks of blood on his face. "He got me good. I might be lucky to be alive."

"You need some attention to those injuries."

Christy stood. "I've got it." She left the room.

Toby watched her go. "Is she an EMT or something?"

"Just suckin' up to the boss." Johnny flashed a teasing smile. "It's just first aid, but yeah, she's an EMT. Most of us are."

"Let's stay focused," Sharp said. "So, the guy's capable of aggression." She turned to Jack. "You really didn't see this guy? You can't give any description of him at all?"

"Correct. Didn't see him, other than from a few hundred yards away, moving through the willows. Didn't see him when he got me. It was Johnny who did."

She turned to Johnny. "What'd you see? Any idea who he was?"

"I saw a guy in a brown shirt and ball cap. I can't even tell you what kind of pants he was wearing, it happened so quick."

"You have no idea who this guy was?"

"None. Never saw his face."

"But you saw a pistol."

"Yeah. He was bending over Jack, and I saw a holster sticking out from under his shirt."

"Was he carrying a backpack?"

The question almost seemed to startle him. "I don't remember a pack. Just the holster."

Jack interrupted. "He was wearing a pack when I saw him."

"What color?" Sharp asked.

"Red or brown or dark orange? I'm not sure. He was in the shade."

She turned back to Reger. "So he ditched the pack before jumping Jack."

"Must've."

She sighed.

Christy returned, first aid kit in one hand, wet paper towels in the other. She pulled out the chair beside Jack. "Turn around." With a paper towel she made a gentle pass over his face, cleaning away streaks of blood, then swabbed his face with a cotton ball soaked in alcohol.

Jack cringed. "Where did the guy wear his holster?"

"Small of his back," Johnny said.

Jack fought another cringe as Christy moved to his cheek. "Then we know who it is."

"We do?" Sharp asked.

Jack turned to Johnny. "Hide Mangum."

Johnny held his tongue a moment, then scratched his cheek. "Yeah . . . probably. Didn't register because I never got a look at his face."

Sharp leaned toward him. "What do you mean, it didn't register?"

"Mangum's the reason Christy and I were there. He packs . . . Jack doesn't. The threats he made to Jack . . . we were there just in case he was serious."

"And you know what Mangum looks like?" Sharp asked.

"Hell, yeah. We encountered him yesterday . . . out on the trail. Chased him off."

Sharp turned to Jack. "Is there anything you know, or evidence you saw, that points to it being Hide Mangum?"

Before answering, he glanced around the table, knowing what he was about to say was unsubstantiated. He caught a wary, almost nervous look on Toby LeBlanc. "What's wrong?"

LeBlanc held his tongue.

Jack turned back to Barb. "He didn't want us on the trail. Maybe he didn't want Miguel out there either. Why he'd be following Miguel in town, I don't know. If Miguel told his mom he was worried . . . and thought he was being followed, he must know something."

"Evidence," she repeated. "Any evidence it was Mangum? If the boy is at risk, we need to take action, but not without evidence."

"I have none."

Sharp turned to Johnny.

"None."

"I'd bring him in for questioning, but everyone knows about this feud between you two, Jack. If we pick him up without evidence, how's it gonna look? With evidence, the FBI will take over . . . for attack on a federal officer." She paused. "I'll talk to the federal attorney, see what they think . . . but, in case Jack's right, keep doing what you're doing, Johnny. Stick to him."

Jack pulled away from Christy, a square of ointment-covered gauze stuck to his nose. "I don't need Johnny following me around. I can take care of myself."

Sharp ignored him. "Evidence, Johnny. When he goes for his equipment, go with him."

Johnny's eyes perked up. "Yeah, like maybe tomorrow."

She nodded, then turned toward Jack. "You may be right. It's probably Mangum, but here's the deal. Everything about today suggests you weren't the target. The boy was. Something strange is going on. The boy's mom thought he was in danger. Turns out he was. He wasn't hurt, you were, but still, today was about the boy. We need to find out why Miguel was in danger."

"And how he knew?" Jack added. "If he was afraid . . . why the hell did he go out there alone?"

"Exactly."

Jack stopped at the top of the stairs, looking down at the parking behind headquarters. "My Jeep's at the trailhead. We'll have to walk." He started down, lugging his pack.

Toby followed.

They reached the bottom and headed up the trail to Park housing.

The back door from headquarters crashed open.

"Hold up!" Johnny shouted, running down the steps.

They waited as he jogged toward them.

Jack flashed a quizzical look. "Aren't you a little spent at this point?"

"Yeah, exhausted."

"Then, why . . . ?" He shook his head. "Never mind."

"Going to Elena's?"

"No. Been a full day."

"Then let's make plans," Johnny said, making no attempt to hide his excitement.

"Let's talk about it tomorrow. Toby and I need to figure out what we're gonna do next."

Johnny gave a bug-eyed stare. "Boss, tomorrow, you know exactly what you need to do."

"What?"

"Remember?"

Excitement failed to ignite. "I'm sorry. I'm tired. Let's talk tomorrow."

Johnny kept his stare going. “We’ve got things we need to do. Your stuff. Your equipment. Evidence. All that.” He forced a wink. “Surely Toby has something he can do in the office, right? Maybe follow Christy around for a day?”

“Doing what?” Toby asked.

Johnny smiled and turned back to Jack, stepping closer. “It hit me . . . what the boy was doing,” he whispered. “I think he’s looking for Rivera’s treasure.”

“You didn’t mention that upstairs.”

“Well, you know . . .” He glanced back at headquarters. “I can’t prove it, so . . . anyway, that explains why he’s taking a risk, even if there’s something he’s afraid of . . . because of what’s at stake. He’s looking for treasure. The treasure’s a risk worth taking.”

“Johnny, he’s a boy. Why do you think he’d think like that?”

“The little guy’s clever. While everyone else is looking here in the Park, he’s figured it out. He knows where to look. Or at least he thinks he does, and he’s close.”

“That is, if *you’re* right about the location.” Jack dropped his pack, exhaustion washing over him. “If you’re right about Miguel, then someone else also knows he’s figured it out.” He crossed his arms. “Is that why you said you weren’t sure it was Mangum? Because you want to get there first?”

“No, Boss, honest. When I saw the guy, it didn’t register.”

“Okay.” He noticed Toby shifting on the balls of his feet. “Johnny, we only have so much time before Toby leaves, and I’m worn out.”

Johnny backed away. “Don’t jump to conclusions. We’ll talk tomorrow morning.”

“Why don’t you go? Investigate. Check out the cave.”

“I’m not going alone.” He glanced at Toby. “First, it might not be wise.” He raised a hand and wiggled his fingers. “Second, we found that cave together. I’m not going alone.”

“We’ll talk tomorrow.” Jack started up the trail.

With the cabin in view, Jack slowed. Without looking back, he said, “Not exactly what we’d planned, but tonight I get to sleep on a real bed. Want the sofa instead of the ground?”

Toby didn't answer.

Jack turned. "Wondering what Johnny was talking about? The cave?"

"Nope."

"I'll tell ya."

"Not necessary."

"Worried we won't get back to work?"

"It's not that. It's . . . when we got off the helicopter, I was thinking this was the best day I've had in a long time."

Jack laughed. "Even with a bad guy with a gun."

"Yeah, even that was exciting. Everything was exciting. The science. The search. Hiking with a hot lady. Rescuing the boy. The helicopter. All of it."

"What changed?"

"When you . . ."

Jack waited for the words. They didn't come. "When I what?"

"When you put your finger on it."

"Put my finger on what?"

"What you said . . . it explains everything. I see it, even if they don't."

"See what?"

"The Chief Ranger. Johnny. They don't know the connections."

Jack shook his head. "What are you talking about?"

"Mangum. Connections . . . they wouldn't know." He sighed. "But somehow, Doc is involved."

Jack sighed. "Doc . . . who is this guy?"

Chapter 38

Toby LeBlanc settled onto the sofa, his hair combed back, wet from a shower.

Jack tossed him a blanket and sheet. He pointed at a pillow at the opposite end of the sofa. "Will that work?"

"Yep."

"Tired?"

"Yep, but not sleepy. Not yet."

"Understood. Make yourself comfortable. I'm off to bed. If you're hungry, dive into the fridge."

"Jack, what I said earlier . . . about Doc. That was paranoia talking." His eyes broke contact, and slid across the wall, searching, not the wall but the dark corners of his mind. "Paranoia's done a lot of talking the last few years." He sighed. "He's not always right . . . he's not always wrong."

"Relax. Don't think about it." Jack plopped down on the chair next to the sofa. "I was thinking, too . . . while you were in the shower. Johnny's probably right. Now's the time to put Mangum away. We need evidence."

"Yeah, whatever that thing Reger's talking about, sounds like it needs attention."

"Maybe. Need to know what that's about?"

"None of my business."

"I don't mind telling you. In the meantime, if Christy's available, would you mind having help from her tomorrow?"

"She's sure as hell easier to look at than you are." He forced a grin.

"I'll see what I can do. When's your flight?"

"Day after tomorrow. Mid-afternoon. I'll need a ride. It'd be good to have a closeout."

"I'll drive you to the airport. If there's no other time, we'll talk on the drive." Jack stood. "I'm going to bed." After closing the bedroom door, he took a quick shower, and settled into bed. The phone rang. He saw the name on the screen as he reached for the nightstand. Kelly.

"What are you doing awake?" he asked as he answered.

"Can't sleep. I'm sorry to wake you."

"I'm not asleep, but I will be soon. Something wrong?"

"I'm torn. Between missing you and being mad."

"At me?"

"Of course. I talked to Father. Things aren't going well."

"What's wrong?"

"Everything. He needs you."

"For what?"

She snarled into the phone. "I don't know," she said, frustrated. "He needs you, and you haven't been easy to get ahold of. You need to put the butterflies on hold."

"We had a search today." He paused, refraining from mentioning Miguel or the hit from behind at the waterfall. "Kept me busy, and my phone was off."

"Sorry." She paused. "I jumped to conclusions."

"I'll call Kip." Changing the subject, he said, "I heard one of the attack ads on the radio."

"Don't tell me. I know what they say." Kelly sounded tired. "Makes me wonder if I shouldn't just go home, let someone else do this job."

"People don't believe those things."

"They sure as hell do. Ask Alex Trasker. He's worried . . . thinks I need to counter the ads. He's learned from an operative he knows . . . that the money for the ads comes from a non-profit 501(c)(4). Dark money. That bunch is funding a new super PAC set up in Virginia, registered to a mailbox in Alexandria."

"What's that mean?"

"It means, not only do they *not* have to report their donors, but the political action committee they're funding may not file quarterly reports until after the election, so there's a double layer of intrigue, and little we can learn. Alex is worried."

"And his worry has you losing sleep."

She sighed. "There's another thing. A bill . . . to eliminate the national monument, has been introduced in the house."

"Our national monument?"

She let out a cynical laugh.

"By whom and what about *your* bill?"

"Alex's old boss, Congressman Hoff. My bill might not even make it out of committee because of war drums he's beating."

"Don't worry, you'll figure it out."

"The governor should've found someone who knows what they're doing." She sighed. "I've got to go . . . I need some sleep."

"Sleep well." When her end went quiet, Jack muttered into the dead connection, "Tomorrow, Johnny Reger and I go into the backcountry to look for evidence to put away a guy who tried to kill me today, and there's another reason . . . Johnny found a cave. He thinks it holds Juan Rivera's gold."

—'—

In the office the next morning, Toby took over the computer. Jack settled back to watch after making arrangements with Christy Manion. Before he could even twiddle his thumbs, Johnny Reger appeared at the door.

"Ready?" Johnny asked, already anxious.

"Sure." Jack got to his feet. "I need to stop at the market, get food for the day."

Passing Dispatch, Molly hollered for them to wait. "Barb's looking for you, Johnny."

"What about?"

"I need half an hour of your time," Barb shouted from her office.

Johnny shrugged and headed up the hall.

"I'll go get groceries. That'll save a few minutes." Jack turned to the back door. "Hold it. I don't have a car. Mine's at the trailhead."

Johnny tossed him the keys to his patrol rig.

At the market, Jack grabbed a few veggies and fruits, granola bars and jerky, and a 'just add water' pasta dinner. He headed for the cash register.

The cashier, a young girl in a red apron, rang up the purchases for the man at the front of the line. He stood facing the window, turning only to pass her several bills. Buck Winslow, in jeans and a tan fishing shirt.

"Buck," Jack said, loud enough to be heard. "You were right."

Buck glanced over, uncertain or unsettled at the comment. "About what?" he asked. He held out his hand, anxious for his change.

"He jumped me."

Buck's eyes shot back. "Who? You mean . . . ?"

Jack nodded. "Yep. Him. You were right."

The cashier counted out several bills.

Buck nodded. "See ya." He took his bag and headed for the door.

"Hold up," Jack said, setting his groceries on the counter. "Got a moment?"

Buck paused at the door.

The young woman in front of Jack made her purchase and slipped past Winslow. Jack paid for his provisions and followed Buck out the door.

"You okay?" Jack asked.

Buck veered toward a pickup. "Some kinda bug. Taking the day off."

"I won't hold you . . . just thought you'd want to know . . . Mangum could've killed me."

Winslow, tired eyes, looked unconvinced. "What are you saying?"

"He got me. Good thing Johnny was there . . . but Mangum disappeared . . . thin air."

"What?"

"He got away."

Winslow turned, squaring his shoulders. "You're saying . . ."

"I'm saying I was stupid. Knew he was thereabouts . . . but, I just . . ." He shook his head.

Winslow rubbed his chin, his eyes becoming focused. "What are you gonna do?"

"Without evidence, not much . . . I actually didn't see him. We're about to head back out."

"On the desert? Why?"

"Look for evidence."

Winslow gave another rub to his chin. "What do you hope to find?"

"Not sure." Jack backed toward the patrol rig and sat his bag on the hood.

Winslow followed him. "Let's talk a moment, inside." He went to the passenger side.

Jack climbed in and unlocked the other door.

Keeping it open, one foot on the ground beside his groceries, Winslow sat and for a moment studied Jack's face. "I say this as a friend . . . and as a cop." He watched a patron cross the lot. "This may be unexpected . . . but I think you should play the odds. If you know the kind of evidence you're looking for, go for it. If you don't, your time might be better spent going after this guy. Put him in his place."

"That's not exactly taking advantage of the legal system."

His green eyes flared. "Damn it, Jack, are you blind? With his background, Mangum won't leave clues. He could be there all day and you'd never see him or any sign he was there. All he respects is conflict, so go the hell after him."

"What's his background? And we did find tracks."

"You did?" A cringe. "I heard military, special forces."

"Special forces? Really?" Jack let his eyes grow wide. "And yeah, not many. Tracks'll be gone by now . . . wind and down-canyon breezes."

Buck pointed a finger at his face. "I see where he got ya—and you listen to me. You need to hit this guy with everything you've got."

Jack sighed. "That's not what I'm about."

"Hell with what you're about." Buck said, his jaw clenched. "You said he could've killed you. You gonna let that happen? Take the fight to this guy. Make him cower. Put . . . him . . . in . . . his . . . place."

What's gotten into Buck? Jack frowned. "Why are you not telling me to let law enforcement do their job?"

Winslow gave his forehead a rub. "Sorry, man, maybe it's how crappy I feel." He pawed the floorboard. "There are different dimensions to things like this. If Ranger Reger finds evidence to pursue criminal charges, great. That's the best option. But what if he doesn't? And odds are he won't, so that means you have to put your emphasis on other dimensions of this conflict. You have to beat Mangum at the game he's playing."

"Why are you telling me this?"

Buck sighed. "Because . . . I'm worried about you. You're a good guy. You're someone I have a lot of respect for, and someone I need to have a good working relationship with. If I become sheriff, we'll need each other."

"I'm not in law enforcement." Jack laughed. "I'm just a simple country biologist."

Buck let out a chuckle. "That's why you need to work the other dimension . . . but I say that because you're important. Standing your ground might not be enough. Go on the offensive. To win. To beat such evil. Me? I need working relationships with more than cops. You connect with people . . . in ways your compadres don't. In ways that I need to." He tapped on his shirt pocket, searching for a toothpick. "I need you. You need me."

"That's logic. I guess I follow."

"Take my advice. Go after this guy. Don't let him destroy your reputation."

"What do you mean, *go after*?"

Winslow laughed. "I'm not saying, knock the guy off. I'm saying challenge him." He squirmed in the seat. "Gotta go. My shift's about to start. I'm suddenly feeling better." Winslow got out and sauntered over to his pickup.

Jack returned to the Park. Johnny stood waiting at the base of the stairs at headquarters.

He parked and climbed out. "I'll let you drive . . . but we need to talk."

Johnny turned serious. "Did I do something wrong?"

"Nope."

Johnny slipped behind the wheel. "You want me to drive fast, to make up for lost time?"

"Nope." Jack climbed in the passenger side and glanced at his watch. "A little after nine. I asked Christy to help Toby if he needs it."

"We don't need to talk about that. She's good with it. So am I." Johnny started the rig and headed for the entrance road. "Too bad Toby's not here for a while. Don't know what she sees in him, but whatever it is, she sees it."

"He's noticed her, too, and that's not what I wanted to talk about."

"Christy says he's got one hell of an ass."

"He said the same thing about her." Jack turned a curious eye. "She really said that?"

"Of course. We're buds. She tells me everything. I tell her everything. She even lets me complain about the boss."

"Talking about me?"

"Of course. Who else would I complain about?" He let out a laugh. "Is this what you wanted to talk about?"

"No, it's not. I saw Winslow at the market. Told him about getting jumped by Mangum."

"Does he know we need a little thing called evidence before we can say it was him?"

"Yeah, he knows, thinks trying to find it could be a waste of time."

"Yeah, kinda agree, but that's surprising coming from a lawman." Johnny made the turn onto the highway, accelerating toward the Park entrance. "Think he's protecting Mangum for some reason?"

"No, in fact, that's what I want to talk about. He thinks I should be going after Mangum."

"Going after . . . ?"

"It's not what you're thinking. He means, putting him in his place. Letting his followers know the game he's playing. Challenging him."

"Because of all the talk in town?"

"Yeah." Jack sighed. "Think this trip is a waste of time? Should I take his advice?"

"Well, I don't know about you, but I'm under orders from Barb to find evidence. But Boss, we don't have just *one r*eason for going, *we have two*."

Jack nodded. "Yeah, but what do you think about Buck's advice?"

"The trailhead first, or out where Potts left his pickup?"

"At the pickup."

"Agreed, and Boss, I see what Buck's saying. With all the talk, I'd be all over it, but that's me. You're not me."

Jack's phone rang. He glanced at the screen. Kip Culberson. He accepted the call and raised it to his ear. "Hi Kip. I was gonna call you. What's up?"

"Wondering if you have a little time to talk."

"Yep, got time now. I'm on the road . . . with about ten minutes before we lose signal."

"I didn't mean on the phone. I meant here, at the ranch, or someplace in town. We need to talk. It's important."

"Can it wait till tomorrow, or even better, the next day?"

"Needs to be now."

"What's this about?" He pointed at Johnny to pull onto the road shoulder.

Johnny braked and pulled over.

"It's about . . ." Kip pulled in a breath and exhaled. "It's about needs. It's about suspicions. It's about conspiracy theories."

"About me?"

"Let's just talk when I see you. Can we do this at my place? More privacy."

Chapter 39

"Detour." Jack pointed back the way they'd come. "That way. Culberson Ranch."

Johnny's eyes bugged out. "Boss, you can't get to South Desert from there. The day will be shot."

"I'll hurry."

Johnny whipped a U-turn and sped back toward town, turning at a fast clip onto the Terrace Road. Reaching the stone cairn at the edge of Culberson Ranch, he skidded into the turn, and followed the road around the hill, into the valley where Culberson's casita sat overlooking the plateau and the hamlet of Las Piedras.

"Looks like Karen Hatcher is here," Jack said, eyeing her tangerine Suburu, parked next to Kip's old Ford pickup.

Johnny parked in the shade of a cottonwood and killed the engine. "I'll wait here. They'll understand you're in a hurry, won't they?"

"That a hint?" Jack headed for the house and knocked on the door.

Kip answered, in old jeans and a tattered work shirt.

The sounds of another vehicle approaching blew in on the wind. Jack turned. A small grey pickup followed by a dark-colored sedan.

"You've got company," Jack said.

Kip stuck his head out the door. "Go on in, I'll wait for them."

Jack made his way to the sitting room. Karen Hatcher paced near the kiva fireplace, her hands clasped behind her back.

"Karen."

She turned. "Glad you made it."

"What's this about?"

"Rumors mostly, but not just that."

"Involving me?"

"Some of 'em. More importantly, we need you involved in something. It'll work a bit more smoothly."

Jack settled into a seat across from Kip's easy chair and the leather sofa.

Kip came in with the next two arrivals, the ranchers most involved in the effort, Ginger Perrette, in chore clothes, looking tired, maybe worried, and Daniel Romero, sporting a new beard to go with his dark mustache.

"Two more are coming, at least," Kip said.

Ginger and Daniel stood off to themselves, talking in a corner.

Thomas, the representative of the pueblo, appeared in the hall, his hair in a ponytail. "Hello, my friends," he said. Noticing Jack, he made his way over and shook hands.

"How's your niece?" Jack asked.

"Very good. I believe someday she will be chief."

"Hello!" came a call from the hall. Helen Waite, the county commissioner, gray-haired and in a business suit. "Am I late?"

"Right on time," Kip said.

Behind her another face appeared, the gaunt figure of environmentalist Dave Van Buren, the transplant from New England.

"Come in," Kip said, "Find a place to sit, all of you."

They settled into chairs and spots on the sofa.

Standing, Kip said, "Okay, we've got Jack Chastain, just as you wanted. Who wants to start this thing?"

"I can," Hatcher said. "You've been busy, Jack. We understand, but . . . we're heading down the home stretch and we need your involvement."

Jack took in the looks in the eyes across the room. Some

appeared to share the same sentiment, but not all. Some appeared circumspect. "I understand. Sorry . . . I've gotten pulled in a few different directions . . . looking for someone and starting a study of sorts. But . . . this is the priority. Something come up?" He forced a smile.

"Kinda . . . but might be nothing." Hatcher said.

Kip stood. "Who's next?"

Daniel Romero waved a hand. "We'll go." He turned to Ginger Perrette.

She shuffled in her seat. "Me or you?"

"Doesn't matter," Romero said. "You're better at this sort of thing."

She faced the others. "It's not that simple." She turned to Jack. "There are things you need to explain."

"Okay, what?"

"I'm told . . . you're making yourself scarce so . . . when things go to hell, everything is our fault." She scowled. "But . . . that's not the worst thing."

Jack held his tongue. *Let her finish.*

"Want me to say it?" she asked, glancing around the room and settling her eyes on Jack.

"Go ahead," Jack said.

"Why are you forcing us off our land? Why the big charade? Why tie us up in this made-up, make-believe work, taking two whole damned years? I've had other things I could've been doing. I didn't need to waste my time, if all you were going to do was take away our land."

He remembered Toby's words, about Doc's plans. "Ginger, where did you hear that?"

"Doesn't matter. Everyone knows about those damned land agents you brought in."

"Don't know 'em. Didn't bring 'em here," Jack said, as matter of fact as he could.

Ginger Perrette glared. "Prove it."

"How? I'm not allowed to even talk to those guys. You'll have to take my word on that."

"Hell no! Prove you don't know them."

"How can I? How do you prove a negative?"

"What do you mean . . . prove a negative?"

Jack got to his feet. "If I don't know them, what evidence would there be that I don't? If I did know them, there might be evidence. If I orchestrated something, you could look for evidence of what I did. Directing, coordinating, maybe even sharing information. But I can't share evidence that I didn't orchestrate . . . unless I find evidence of who did. I suppose you could ask 'em. . . . who sent you here?

"Hell no."

He sighed. "Courts of law require evidence. The burden of proof is on the person making an accusation, not the accused." He sighed. "I think you should look at this in the same way. Whoever told you I know those guys . . . that I'm orchestrating a way to force you off your land . . . well, put the burden of proof on them. Ask them to provide evidence, because there's no such thing as evidence that I don't know them. Make sense?"

Perrette glared. "Gobbledygook. Not buyin' it. If you expect me to believe you don't know those men, prove it."

"You realize this is how conspiracy theories get started . . . people hearing things, believing them without evidence, and Ginger, you know me. We've been at this for two years."

"That's why I'm so disappointed." She sat. "And why'd you shave you head? Some kind of disguise?"

Kip let out a laugh. "Shaving his head is his business."

Perrette turned a steady eye on Kip. "Doesn't doing something weird like that make you wonder if you know the real Jack Chastain? Especially with him hanging around your daughter."

"No." Kip scowled. "Maybe he did it because it's summer. Maybe he's always wondered if it'd help beat the heat." He shrugged. "Hell, I don't know . . . but doesn't bother me any."

"What's your daughter think?"

"I don't know, I haven't asked her," Kip said, his voice growing louder. "She's got more important things to worry about. Can we get back on track? Real questions."

"Why did you bring in those land agents?" Perrette asked.

"I didn't." Jack sighed. "Where did you hear that, by the way?"

"Hide Mangum."

Jack rose to his feet. "He's who you need to talk to. Ask him for evidence. If he can't give it, he's making things up. The question then would be, 'Why?'"

"He's not a bad guy," Perrette said. "I've known him for longer than I've known you. He's never steered me wrong."

"Have *I*?"

"Until now, I didn't think so." Perrette stood and took a step toward the door.

Romero started after her.

"Hold it," Kip growled. "We need to talk about this."

—'—

Jack stepped out into the sunlight.

Johnny sat staring over the steering wheel.

Jack glanced at his watch. Two and a half hours. Painful hours. He opened the vehicle door. "That didn't go as expected. Let's get out of here."

"What happened?"

"For a bit, I wondered if everything was falling apart." He sat. "Let's go. I need quiet."

Reger started the vehicle and put it in gear. "At this point, Boss, the trip we planned isn't gonna work. It'll have to be an overnight. To do that we need food and gear."

"Can't. Tomorrow I'm booked . . . taking Toby to the airport."

"Can Christy take him?"

"I'll ask . . . but he wanted time to debrief before heading home."

"Let's go grab a few things and you can ask him."

"My gear is still stuffed in the base of a hoodoo." Jack noticed others leaving. "Better get moving."

Johnny started across the meadow. "Sitting under that tree, I had a lot of time to think."

"Thinking is the last thing I want to do right now." He noticed Reger tapping on the dashboard. "Sorry, go ahead. What were you thinking?"

Reger cleared his throat. "I'll make it quick." He locked hands on the wheel. "One issue I can't get past. Why was Mangum following that boy? There's something we don't know."

"Right. Too damned bad he keeps running off before talking to us."

"Any evidence we find isn't likely to tell us anything about that, and yet it's got to be important."

Jack glanced out the side window. "I figured you'd be thinking about Rivera's cave."

"I was . . . but it made me anxious. Had to get my mind on something else."

"Well, you're right, that is important. We need to find the boy."

Reger turned onto the Terrace Road.

At the base of the hill, a deputy sheriff's vehicle sat off the road, lights flashing, deputy out of the vehicle. "That's Winslow," Johnny said, pulling in behind him. "Buckity," he shouted.

Winslow walked their way.

"Need any help?"

Winslow shook his head. "Nope. Just wrote up a speeder. He took off in a huff, and lucky for him, I'm not feeling good enough to give him another ticket."

"Nice of you. What happened to you?"

Buck rubbed a scratch that ran down his arm to the back of his right hand. "Run in with treasure hunters. A woman thought I was arresting her husband . . . took a swipe at me. Never been good dealing with women with long fingernails."

Jack cringed seeing the scratch. *Missed that this morning.*

Johnny laughed. "Arrest her?"

"No. Just a misunderstanding. She settled down. I let it pass." He leaned down to eye Jack. "Hope you're thinking about my advice."

"I am. Not sure what to do, but I'm thinking about it."

"You're gonna let him get away with it, aren't you? Damn it, Jack, go get the guy."

"Buck," Reger said, grabbing his attention. "Why would Mangum be going after that kid we've been looking for?"

"No idea. Is that what happened?"

Jack nodded.

"You didn't tell me that part."

"Spaced it, sorry."

Reger put the vehicle in gear. "Any new rumors about treasure?" He glanced at Jack.

Winslow scratched his chin. "Well . . . I guess I did hear something." He looked down at his feet. "Same guy whose wife cat-clawed me . . . something about information on getting to some arrows."

Johnny tapped the steering wheel. "You mean, quiver, don't you?"

"I suppose, but hell, I didn't interrogate the guy. I was protecting myself from his wife."

Johnny turned white. "Gotta go," he said, a sudden urgency. He shot a wave and accelerated onto the highway. "Boss, we need to go to the office."

"I thought we were."

"Well, I guess so, but . . . now . . . I need to go online, see if what Buckity heard, is something new in the rumor mill."

"About arrows? Or Quivira?"

His eyes narrowed. "It felt different somehow . . . but I don't want to get talking yet." He stared forward. "Let's talk after I dig into it." He remained silent, fidgety, his mind in two places. At headquarters, he dashed inside.

Jack plodded up the back steps, stopping at dispatch.

"What's with Reger?" Molly asked. "He blew by here like the Flash."

"In a hurry to look up something."

The Chief Ranger stuck her head in the door. "Find anything, Jack?"

"We haven't made it out there yet. My fault. Coalition business."

"Couldn't that wait?"

"Tried." He sighed. "We hope to get out there tonight . . . if I can rearrange some things."

She crossed her arms as he slipped past to go to his office. On his desk, he found a note.

Christy and I are in the high country.

Jack reached for his radio to call Christy.

Johnny rushed in. "Hold up, Boss. The latest . . ." He caught his breath. "It's not about the cave. It's what's in the cave. A map."

"A map? To where?"

"Quivira." Reger backed into the hallway. "I'm gonna grab my gear. I'll be right back."

"Hold up," Jack shouted. "A map to Quivira. How likely is that?" He pulled out his cell phone and dialed the international number for La Profesora. It rang twice.

"Buenos días," she answered.

"Hola, Angelica. This call might be a waste of your time, but . . . there's a new wrinkle." He toggled the phone's speaker.

"Okay, what?" she asked.

He waved Reger over.

Angelica spoke before Johnny could. "First . . . no one has yet found anything remotely resembling a treasure, correct?"

"Correct," Jack said. "Go ahead, Johnny. Give her the latest."

"I'm willing, Boss, . . . but I sense skepticism . . . which might bleed away some of my powers of wisdom and insight."

She laughed. "Skepticism? Not at all. I tingle in anticipation."

"Just tell her," Jack said.

"Okay." He composed himself. "Supposedly, Rivera, even with he and his men loaded down as they were, they had only a fraction of the riches. More trips to Quivira were planned."

"Stands to reason, if real. So, why is this significant?"

"Because Rivera left the map to Quivira in the cave with the booty."

"That seems unlikely," she said. "Why would he do such a thing?"

"Apparently, the threat of death wasn't only thing hounding Rivera. Trust was in short supply. Eroding fast. As they hid from the Comanche, some of his men wouldn't leave, fear they'd be cut out of the riches, that Rivera would return, take it all, and they'd see none of it."

"Why leave the map?"

"That was the offer he made—a token of faith, according to what's been deciphered from the journal. He alone had made the map, keeping it close to the vest. He offered to leave it, to calm those who were suspicious. They would return together, he promised. Each would get their due. Together, they'd return to Quivira."

"Did they supposedly know about this *supposed* plot for Rivera to take treasure to Spain . . . seeking favor from the crown?"

"Yes. If Rivera was successful, each stood to realize a place in society . . . in whatever Rivera created to the north."

"Who were these men?" Angelica asked.

"Hell with them," Johnny said, his body twitching. "At this point, does that matter?"

"It's a rather academic question, yes, but with names one could attempt to validate . . ."

He cut her off. "Hell, whoever finds the cave, finds Rivera's booty but also his map. With that map they can succeed where Coronado failed. They can find Quivira."

Whispered words bled over the phone. "Ay Dios mio."

Johnny turned to Jack. "What'd she say?"

"She said, *Oh my god.*"

—'—

"Let's go, Boss," Johnny said, after they ended the call.

The desk phone rang. A number scrolled across the readout, the direct line from Kelly's desk. Jack picked it up. "I better take this." He raised the receiver to his ear.

"Hi, handsome."

"I can't talk long . . . glad you're in a good mood."

"I'm not. Tomorrow, papers in Albuquerque and Santa Fe run stories about growing concerns . . . me not taking positions on important issues, and how that could mean I've sold out to Washington special interests."

"They don't buy that you're trying to understand all sides of the issues?"

"Reporters seem to want to believe that . . . but they're being barraged with information from a source that says otherwise. They talk to me, they think they understand, then someone gets to them . . . emphasizing a little factual matter they come back and ask me about."

"Factual matter?"

"Yeah, one I could never refute."

"Which is?"

"That I'm somehow connected to you."

Jack sighed. "What do I need to be prepared for?"

"I don't really know," Kelly said. "I guess . . . prepare to respond. Set things straight."

After they ended the call, Jack turned to Reger. "South Desert has to wait."

"But, Boss . . ."

"I need to see what's in the morning's papers . . . first thing."

"But we can't get Mangum without evidence . . . and what about Rivera's cave?"

"I'm sorry. Tomorrow . . . late, but no promises."

Johnny didn't fight it.

Chapter 40

Toby stayed late in the office to finish his project, Christy helping. Jack left for home.

He went to bed, but lay awake, staring out the window, tracking the moon.

What now? It all depends on what's said in the newspapers. But what can they say? Nothing wrong has been done.

Just wait and see. Patience.

But this is no time for patience. Barb Sharp wants evidence. And we've got to get to the cave before anyone else does.

He heard Toby come in, plop down on the couch, munch on an apple, then settle in for the night. Within minutes of the light under the door going dark, Toby was snoring.

Jack returned to his thoughts.

Whatever the newspaper says, Hide Mangum is probably behind it.

He remembered Buck Winslow's advice.

It's time to fight. It's time to go after Hide Mangum.

—·—

Jack left for the office early, with Toby still asleep on the sofa. First stop, Dispatch.

"Morning Molly," he whispered, as he entered, eyeing the *Gazette* on the counter.

"Mornin'." She took a sip of her coffee and made a quick check of her uniform.

"Anything in the paper?"

"About you? No."

"Good. How about the papers from Albuquerque and Santa Fe?"

"Don't know. I took 'em to the superintendent's office. Marge wants 'em first thing."

"Bad sign." Jack headed down the hall. Joe Morgan's office door stood closed, no light showing from underneath. Two newspapers lay on Marge's desk. He started with the Albuquerque paper. Sorting through pages, he found it, among the state and local news.

Group organizing to take on Senator Culberson.

She's accused of selling out.

The second paragraph got right to the point.

> . . . whereas Senator Culberson insists she takes positions on issues only after she understands the full range of interests and positions held by her constituents, others claim that is not her reason. And, while her seemingly naïve insistence on not fundraising may suggest integrity and objectivity, Max Cummings, a political strategist based in Virginia, insists it's a façade, that she has no need to fundraise because her campaign is funded by powerful, out-of-state interests. "There is ample evidence," Cummings asserts, but at present it seems cloudy at best. The senator does not refute an accompanying accusation that she is associated (in a relationship) with a man suspected of being connected to those same powerful interests. Though believed by many to be a government employee, others

suggest he's the actual architect of a grand plan to wrestle private lands from private citizens. Cummings claims the project will benefit the senator's financial supporters, but connections have not yet been confirmed. Limited evidence has not prevented the claims from going viral.

Senator Culberson insists all rumors are untrue, and that she has yet to decide whether she will run for her own term in office.

The page layout suggested a connection to an adjacent article.

Who is Jack Chastain and is he part of a secret government conspiracy?

The locals in and around Las Piedras have put their trust in a government insider and those locals are about to be swindled, this, according to a conspiracy theory making the rounds. The otherwise unassuming man is Jack Chastain. His title—Chief of Natural and Cultural Resource Management—seems fairly standard for a place such as Piedras Coloradas National Park. However, the conspiracy theory suggests nothing could be further from the truth. "Chastain is a charlatan, misleading the good people of Las Piedras. This is not the first place his skills have been put to such use," according to Suzanna Dove, Chastain's former colleague in Montana.

Before New Mexico, Chastain led an effort to study the suitability of certain mountain lands for a new national park. That effort fell apart, leading to a war between factions and a failure to preserve the lands in question. Afterwards, Chastain is said to have dropped out of sight, reappearing in his current position.

While in New Mexico, Chastain has played a principal role in several highly visible episodes that appeared to be victories in protecting Piedras Coloradas National Park and the adjoining National Monument. "It's all a sham," according to Dove. "As he did in Montana, Chastain first builds trust with dedicated citizens, and then forms a coalition, trapping them in an end-game that will lose them and their neighbors everything they own. The government plan is to turn those lands and the national monument over to an international syndicate of oil, gas and mining interests."

Those claims have not been confirmed, but Chastain has also failed to respond to interview requests. His supposed supervisor, the superintendent of Piedras Coloradas National Park, calls the rumors untrue but declines to provide information on an unusual set of activities being undertaken by federal agents.

The day approaches for a signing ceremony for the Piedras Coloradas National Monument Coalition's recommendations to Congress—on what legal authorities are needed to address the diverse interests of those who value the national monument. However, according to Dove, "The more important event will be in the days that follow, when all presumption of protection will be stripped away, and lands seized under legal authorities from World War II and the Cold War, used now only sparingly, without attention and without explanation."

"Chastain is not an actual employee of the agency managing the park," claims Dove. "He's left his fingerprints on similar but little understood actions across the nation. When finished with one project, he disappears until called to his next assignment, staying out of sight on his private island near Costa Rica." After Dove last visited the island—supposedly experiencing sordid events she is unwilling to discuss—she refused to ever work with Chastain again.

It has been confirmed that Montana was the location of Chastain's previous assignment, and that the effort to establish a national park failed. Afterwards, his whereabouts were unknown for months. He reappeared in New Mexico. Also confirmed: Chastain recently flew to Mexico City. While rumors suggest he was there to attend meetings

> regarding his next assignment, those details have not been confirmed. It should be noted that with the coalition's signing ceremony on Saturday, his current project will come to an end.

Jack slammed the paper down. "You've got to be kidding! How'd they learn about Mexico? Costa Rica? Yeah, right. An island? I wish. Whereabouts not known for months? Hell, I was here, not hiding. And who is this Dove person?" He pounded his fist on the desk.

"May I help you . . . before you destroy my office?" Marge slipped past him, purse in hand.

"Sorry, I shouldn't be reading things on your desk." Jack sighed. "Is Joe in today?"

"No, he's not, but he wants a report first thing on what's in those papers."

"Can I finish reading first?"

"Go ahead, and if you'd rather make that call, you're welcome to do so."

"Where is Joe?"

"Denver. Regional Office. That's between you and me, and if I were you, I would not want to make that call."

He glanced at the other paper, seeing similar coverage. "Will he be back today?"

"No idea. The trip was rather sudden." She opened the paper. "What page?"

"State and local section. Did Joe know to expect this?"

"He did, yes. Called last night. He knew something was happening. Told the papers he couldn't say more, except they had their story wrong." She scanned, then looked up. "They admit they're reporting on a rumor?" She chuckled to herself. "No one will believe this."

Shaking his head, Jack left for his office.

—·—

He expected a call from Kelly, but no call came. He jotted down a few phrases, to use in responding to reporters, but their calls never came.

At a little after 9 a.m., Toby appeared. “Can I use the computer?”

Jack moved out of the way.

“Taking one last look at something.” He pulled up a map layer. “I think I’m done.”

“Good, thank you for coming.”

“I hear you might want Christy to take me to the airport.”

“Yeah, but . . . I think I’d rather take you myself. I need to get out of here.” He turned to the door, then stopped. “Disappointed?”

“You mean, Christy not taking me? No. I hoped we could talk. About the map.”

“Good. Got your stuff?”

Toby grabbed his bag. Walking down the hall, they paused at Dispatch.

“Molly, I’m taking Toby to the airport,” Jack said. “Tell Johnny I’ll try to be back in time. He’ll know what I mean.”

She gave a thumbs up.

They left in an agency pickup. Turning toward the Park exit, Jack pulled out his phone. No signal. *Call Kelly down the road.* “So, what do I need to know?”

“Need to know? You know everything . . . except maybe this. If you really want to find butterflies and milkweed, we haven’t looked in the best place.”

“Best place?” Jack glanced his way. “Where?”

“Outside the monument. North.”

“The Enclave?”

“No. Public land, but close.”

“I might avoid that for now.”

“You’ll find it on the map . . . latest version. What I really wanted to say is . . . thank you for asking me to help, for letting me see myself in the way I once did. The way I want to see myself . . . as someone who has something to contribute.”

Jack managed a smile. “Kid, you’ve always . . . Sorry, didn’t mean to say that.”

“It’s okay.”

“Toby, that’s why I called. You’re smart. You know things and how to get things done.”

“I appreciate that. If you ever need help again . . . ever . . . I’ll come back. In fact, I’d love to move down to this part of the world, get a fresh start.”

“I’ve got ideas.” He laughed. “Christy might have a few, too.”

A smile formed.

Jack glanced at his phone. Three bars. “Excuse me a moment.” He tapped the number for Kelly and waited for the call to go through.

It got a prompt pickup. “Jack?” A man’s voice.

“Alex?”

“Yes. Kelly asked me to watch for your call. She’ll ring you back when she can. She’s getting barraged by reporters and constituents. Don’t worry, she’ll call.”

“She okay?”

“She’s worried about you.”

“Tell her I’m fine. Bye.” He set down the phone. “Well, . . . everything’s going to hell.”

“What happened?” Toby asked.

“Conspiracy theories. Today’s paper. Me. Kelly. Believe me, you don’t want to know.”

Toby stared out the windshield at something in the distance. “I know . . . even if I don’t.”

Jack took his eyes off the road. “What’s that mean?”

“It means I know what’s in that paper, even if I don’t know the specifics.” He turned to the side window. “There’s a little bit of truth. Just enough to make anyone who knows that truth wonder about the rest of it.” He rubbed his chin. “There’s a suggestion of pattern. We humans always look for patterns. The conspiracy theory will give them one. It’ll tap into the kinds of common bias you find here, making people open to new information, whether there's evidence attached or not." He turned to Jack. "And . . . it's threatening . . . overwhelming . . . value laden . . . geared to create a great deal of uncertainty. What it doesn't do . . . not yet . . . is suggest a path for people to regain control . . . to feel secure." He gave a slow, stern nod. "But . . . that'll come."

"How do you know all this?"

"I'm an expert."

Jack slowed the vehicle. "Doc taught you that?"

"Not on purpose. Most of what he taught me on conspiracy theory comes from the school of hard knocks. I too was a target, remember? With you." He sighed. "And I was there after you left, trying to figure out why people who knew me, friends who trusted me . . . so willingly came after me, came to hate me. Why would they let themselves believe what they did? I studied conspiracy theory. I know more about that subject than I've ever known about hydrology."

"You're kidding me, right?"

"Why would I kid you?" He grimaced.

"Well . . . you don't look mad . . . like you did a few days ago."

"Being here's been good, . . . but, let me tell you what I know. There are people who study conspiracy theories and why they're so common. They do research, trying to understand. But people like Doc, they know things . . . innately. He's built on what he's always known with his own kinds of research."

"How do I stop him?"

"You can't." Toby let out a sad little laugh. "It's his world, remember. You're just living in it. The people who believe his lies twist themselves into logical knots to keep believing. Those beliefs become core. Important. They won't let go."

"Be serious. How do I counter him?"

"I am serious. The only thing I've seen in research . . . the only way you can hope to beat it is to act early, inoculate people with a weakened dose of the conspiracy, show them why it's a lie before they start accepting it as truth. Build up their cognitive antibodies before they hear repetitions of the whole lie. If they hear it a lot—and they want to believe it—it's too late."

Jack tried to laugh. "Cognitive antibodies. Now, you're kidding, right?"

"I promise, I'm not. That came from a report. The only research I saw that really suggested a solution. Attack the lies early. Lies are contagious. Conspiracy theories are deadly."

"I have no idea how long this rumor's been bouncing around. Just learned about it this morning, but the story says it's been making the rounds. That a reporter tried calling me and I didn't respond . . . but no one called me. I've had no message."

"Yep," Toby said. "They got you with that one in Montana, too."

"What do you mean by that?"

"You don't remember? Reporters saying you weren't responding to inquiries. My guess is . . . someone gave a reporter a phony number, saying it was yours, counting on the fact that they would trust it was. Maybe the call kept ringing, or maybe someone left a phony message . . . as you . . . saying . . . leave me a message . . . that sort of thing. Then, they never hear from you. Who looks bad? You do. In Montana, that happened after the conspiracy theory broke that you were in cahoots with the mine company that eventually bought most of the land—after the congressional hearing in Missoula. Before people started fighting among themselves."

"How do I find Doc?"

"Might be hard." Toby turned to the window, appearing to search his memories. "He's a guy you see, and yet you don't. Wants it that way. Blends in. He's got a strange bend on his nose, otherwise, nothing would catch your eye. Where is he? No idea." Toby faced him. "What are you gonna do?"

"Fight back. If I can't find Doc, I'm going after Hide Mangum."

"I'd tell you it won't work . . . but . . . I won't."

—'—

With a handshake and a promise to return, Toby LeBlanc slipped out onto the curb at Albuquerque International Airport. In a few quick steps he was inside the sliding glass door.

Jack sped into traffic and looped around toward I-25. He took the on-ramp and drove through the city heading north. Near Taos, it began to rain. Dark clouds hung over the horizon.

Evidence could be washed away. That would be bad, but then again, there were more important things to do.

Chapter 41

Eyeing the rising cliffs before him, Jack made a call to Dispatch. "Molly, Johnny isn't answering his phone."

"He's on patrol. I can call him in, but . . . there's something I want to show you. Something I missed. In the *Gazette*."

"About me?"

"Doesn't start that way. We'll talk when you get here."

Jack sped along the edge of Las Piedras and into the Park. He bounded up the back steps of headquarters, stopping at Dispatch. "Whatcha got?"

Molly passed him the folded copy of the *Gazette*. "Letters to the editor."

He laid it out on the counter and flipped through the pages. Among the letters, one from a name he didn't recognize. The subject of the letter, Mangum.

> I'm troubled by rumors I'm hearing about Hide Mangum and his followers. This stand they plan to make, with over a dozen people, all armed, pledging to rip the national monument out of the hands of the government, to use it for whatever they think is more important. It scares the hell out of me. He certainly doesn't represent me. He's crazy.

> So what, that the constitution makes no specific mention of national monuments or national parks or the laws he claims the feds use to control us. The constitution was written over two centuries ago, as a framework, not a lawbook. Those laws work as far as I'm concerned.
>
> Mangum's scaring the hell out of people. Nobody will come here. Our economy will tank. We won't be able to pay our bills. We'll lose everything.
>
> Jim Espinoza

Jack looked up from the letter. "About time someone paid attention to Mangum, gave him a little pushback."

Molly turned in her chair. "Yeah, but you need to see this." She brought up the browser on her computer.

Jack came around the counter and stood over her shoulder. "What are you looking at?"

"Responses to that letter . . . online edition of the *Gazette* . . . coming in all day."

Jack leaned closer, bringing the words into focus. Words from anonymous writers.

> "Hell no, I'm not worried. Get the feds out of here and we'll make real money."

> "Sign me up. While we're at it, let's run the outsiders out of here. I'm tired of their antics. Damn haters are ruining everything."

"I've seen enough." Jack turned to leave.

"No, you haven't." Molly scrolled down.

He settled in behind her.

> "Jimbo, obviously today you haven't read the Albuquerque and Santa Fe newspapers. Read those before you jump to conclusions. Read and you'll understand

> Mangum. Jack Chastain is planted here to execute a grand plan that'll help no one but a bunch of foreigners. They want our land, and he plans to give it to 'em, lock, stock and barrel. Land agents are in town, ready to rob us of our land. If anyone profits from the land here, it should be us. Hell with the Endangered Species Act. Hell with the national monument."

Jack sighed. "And therein is the lie." He settled against the counter.

"Whatcha gonna do?"

"Go after Mangum. Put an end to the conspiracy theories."

A shadow cut across the light gleaming in from the hallway. Reger came in the room, in a Stetson and class A uniform. "Give me a minute and I'll be ready to go."

"No. I've got something else I've got to do."

"Now what?"

"Hide Mangum. It's time to confront him."

"Boss, the way to get Mangum is evidence. The evidence is in the backcountry."

"Maybe." Jack drummed his fingers on the counter. "But what if there isn't any? Then, it's wasted time. The longer people hear this crap, the harder it'll be to get it out of their minds." He paced the length of the counter. "I've got to confront Mangum, on the Enclave. Let the people there see that he's lying."

"Calm down, Boss. You're rattled . . . like I've never seen before."

Jack returned to drumming his fingers. "I've done everything I can, always . . . to earn people's trust. To not choose sides. To get people to talk. To realize they're in this together." He slammed his fist on the counter. "Now this. Going after my reputation. What do I have if I don't have my reputation? It's everything." He let out a growl. "Everything, and he's trying to take it away, along with the work people have done . . . like in Montana."

Johnny took a step forward. "Boss, what needs to happen?"

"What do you mean?"

"If this wasn't happening, what should be happening?"

"The signing ceremony."

"It's still scheduled, right?" Johnny said, his voice in a whisper. "Focus on evidence. We can take care of the other thing, too. The thing that's driving me crazy . . . and I can't believe it's not doing the same to you." He glanced at Molly. "I'll tell you about it, but not now."

She turned to her desk.

"I think I need to go at the newspaper," Jack said.

"I'll be here when you get back. We'll leave then, right?"

Jack followed him down the steps to the vehicles. Johnny left for the ranger dorm and Jack headed into town.

On the square, at the offices of the *Las Piedras Gazette*, Jack parked. Inside the mid-twentieth century building, in the newsroom, he saw a pair of people working, heads down.

After a moment, a young dark-haired woman, hardly out of college, ambled toward him.

"I need to talk to a reporter. I'm mentioned in letters to the editor. Need to give my side."

"I know who you are," she said, sounding uncertain about what to do.

A voice boomed from across the room. "I'm afraid the reporters are busy . . . finishing stories." The thin, balding editor left his glassed-in office along the back wall, and advanced to the front of the room. "I'll take it Kitty. Hello Jack, what's on your mind?"

"Henry, sorry. Thought I needed to respond to everything."

"You are the news, so . . . what'd'ya got?"

"I don't have that much to say . . . just that it's all unsubstantiated crap . . . most of it erroneous. I want to say lies, but I guess I'll say erroneous. But, first, I live here, not on some bogus island off Costa Rica. I don't know anyone named Dove. If reporters want to talk they can call me. Use *my real number*. I'm not connected to any international corporations. And last, people should have faith in the coalition. Let them finish their work. They've worked hard and listened to everyone. We're about to sign their recommendations and there are no surprises. It'll present ways to protect what people value. It's not a fight, it's a recommendation."

"Well said," the editor muttered, scribbling a few last words on a pad. "I'll carve out a space on the front page . . . but I want to follow up with you later . . . cover this thoroughly"

Jack mouthed his thanks and turned to leave. Outside, he let out a sigh. He checked his watch. A little before five.

Mangum. How do I take on Hide Mangum? Who names their kid Hide, anyway? No one. Must be a nickname. Sounds ominous. Why go by a name that telegraphs that sort of message? But, what do I really know about him? Not much. Just where he lives. But that's a start.

He sped toward the county office building, climbing the stairs to the second floor, rushing in before they could close.

A gray-haired clerk looked up from her work.

"Jack Chastain, Park Service."

"I know who you are" she said, getting to her feet.

"Just wanted to check some land records. Are the parcels on the Enclave kept together?"

"Same book, yes."

"Plat maps?"

"Most, yes, why?"

"I just want to see if we have an issue along one of the public land boundaries." *And learn as much as I can about one owner in particular.*

"The papers say you're up to something other than that, but these are public records, so I'm not sure how I would deny you access."

"Thanks, and don't worry. The real story will come out."

She led him to a back room and pulled a book from a shelf. "We close in five minutes."

"Thank you. I'll hurry." He thumbed through the books. There were more houses on the Enclave than he realized, but he found Mangum's. His full name, Malcom Henry Mangum. Jack wrote down the property address. References to county tax records suggested a birthdate in 1971 and a wife named Jean. No other information of interest, other than he'd owned the property since 1996. *Malcom, I'm gonna learn what you're up to, and what the lies are about.*

Jack thumbed through one more time, then left, giving a wave to the clerk.

As he exited the building, he called Johnny Reger.

"I'm waiting in your office, Boss."

"I'm headed that way. Question for you. If I give you a full name, can you check and see if someone has a criminal record?"

"What name?"

"Malcom Henry Mangum." He opened the vehicle door and climbed in.

"I could, Boss, but . . . the day after the search for the kid, Barb and I went through everything there is about Mangum. Found nothing, not even a speeding ticket."

He started for the Park. "Are you serious?"

"Yes."

"Why haven't I ever seen this guy until recently? Sure he really lives here? Could he split his time between here and someplace else, where he has a record? Maybe he's here to lay low."

"Possible, I suppose, but we'd still see his real record, and we've found nothing to suggest that's the case. It's actually rather spooky. Rabble-rousers don't appear out of thin air."

"What if he's not the real Hide Mangum? Maybe just some guy sent in to cause trouble. Acting like he's Mangum. Spreading lies."

"What do you want me to do, bring him in, fingerprint him, interrogate him?"

"I don't know what I want, Johnny." Deflated, he said, "I'll be there in a minute." As soon as he hung up, his phone rang again. "Hello."

"I've been wanting to talk to you all day." Kelly sounded exhausted. "You okay?"

He pulled over. "Of course," he said, after a moment.

"You're not fooling me. You sound strung tight as a fiddle . . . and I've talked to Father. The latest is making it difficult for the coalition."

"I'll call him. Do what I can to help. How about you?"

"Constituents calling. Demanding I distance myself from you. Or, to demand my position on foreign syndicates trying to take our lands for their gain and profit."

"What'd you say?"

"Staff did most of the talking, but Alex and I crafted a statement." She paused. "I said he's a sweetheart and I love him dearly . . . that I will protect our treasured lands and I will not let private lands be taken, till the end of my dying days. If it kills me, so be it."

"No, seriously, what'd you say?"

"Something pretty damned close to that. I wish I'd been able to talk to more constituents, not just reporters." She sighed. "What are you doing now?"

"About to go in the backcountry, but first . . . I'm driving to the Enclave and banging on Hide Mangum's door . . . finding out who he really is and why he's spreading lies. If I can get a few of his neighbors to hear what I have to say, all the better."

"Are you sure that's a good idea?"

"It's the only option I've got."

"You're not thinking clearly. He's dangerous. Take someone with you. Like Johnny."

"He's going, but I can take care of myself."

"You should wait till tomorrow. Think about what you want to say. You're more stressed than I've ever heard you." She waited for his response. Getting none, she said, "Promise me."

—·—

Jack walked into his office and found Reger, anxious and ready to go.

"I've made a promise to Kelly not to do anything tonight."

"We're just going into the backcountry."

"Well, I told her I was making a quick stop at Mangum's."

"Boss!"

"Let's go first thing in the morning. There's got to be something there that tells us what he's after and why he's targeting me, maybe even why he's after Miguel."

"We need evidence," Johnny said, sounding frustrated. "If we don't try to prove it's Mangum, those answers hardly matter." He moved to the door. His shoulders slumped. "Okay, get your head on straight. You need a drink, and I'm starving. Let's go to Elena's."

At Elena's, Jack looked in the restaurant, and seeing people he knew, pointed Johnny to the bar. "Do you mind?"

Johnny led the way to his usual table.

The bar began to fill. Treasure hunters giving up after a long day, many looking frustrated, some quite testy.

"We're looking in the wrong damned place," a voice bellowed from a nearby table. "We should be looking south."

Johnny turned to find the source of the voice.

"Hell no," a man said, in a lowered voice. "It's gotta be where we're looking. We just . . ."

"We looked," shouted a blond, wiry man, cutting the other off. "I'm going south. Satellite images suggest better places to look down there."

"Not good," Johnny muttered between locked lips.

"Finders keepers, you ass. If I find it and you're not there, hell with you, it's all mine."

A fight broke out.

Franco, the sturdy part-time bartender, part-time river guide, rushed over and tried to get them to behave. That worked for only a moment. He made a call for a deputy.

In minutes Buck Winslow entered the bar and sauntered over, relieving Franco. The two men, both bruisers compared to Winslow, calmed enough for him to escort them to the door. Then he made his rounds through the room, making his presence known.

"Buckity!" Reger yelled.

Winslow stopped at their table.

Reger pushed a chair toward him. "You handled that beautifully."

"Getting hard. The latest on Rivera is a couple of day's old now. People are getting feisty. Best guesses haven't made 'em rich and they're worried someone else's gonna figure it out." Winslow turned to Jack. "You're awfully quiet."

"Yep."

"Nice article in the papers. Didn't realize you had such a colorful past."

"Yep. Colorful."

"You gotta take me to that private island of yours. Sounds inviting."

Johnny sat down his beer. "If I'd thought that would get any laughs I woulda tried it."

Winslow pulled a toothpick from his pocket. "Are you gonna take my advice?"

"Yes. Was thinking about doing something tonight, but . . ." Jack sighed.

"Damn it, Jack, you're gonna let him get away with it, aren't you?"

"How long have you been here in Las Piedras, Buck?"

The question seemed to catch him by surprise. "Why do you ask?"

Jack took a sip of his beer. "Just wondering. How well do you know Hide Mangum? Me, I'd never encountered him till recently."

Buck glanced at Johnny. "I don't know him well. Only been here a few years myself. Not till I started talking to kids at school did people even try to remember my name. Mangum still doesn't. Treats me like I'm a nuisance." He flashed a grin.

Jack sat up. "Johnny could find no criminal record . . . of any kind."

"Doesn't mean anything. What the man's doing now isn't a crime, but it isn't right. He's smart, but you can't trust him. Papers say he's building an army." Buck stepped closer. "I'm worried about you, Jack. You're thinking too hard. Does it matter *why*?"

"Well . . . yeah."

"If you say so. I think finding a way to stop *what* he's doing is a bit more important."

Chapter 42

Winslow made one more pass through the bar, then slipped out the door.

Johnny leaned toward Jack. "Those guys Buck ran off." He pointed at the empty table. "You heard 'em, right? One's heading south. We don't want him getting to the cave before us."

"I want to get to that cave as much as you do . . . but I've got things to do first."

"Got a plan?"

"Not really."

—'—

Jack lay in bed, watching the clock, wishing he'd ignored Kelly and done something.

Can't let what happened in Montana happen here. Can't let these people down. But what does it take to challenge Mangum?

What if Mangum's right about the guys at the hotel? Damn them.

At a little after two in the morning, with moonlight sifting in through the curtains, he decided his plan would be to confront Mangum about the lies and following Miguel. To make it hard for Mangum's followers to believe in him. How could they continue to follow Mangum, knowing he'd been after the boy? Maybe to hurt him. No one can follow a man who is a threat to a boy, no matter how slick Doc's lies are.

And who is Doc, and what's he trying to accomplish?

—·—

At 7:00 a.m., Molly met Jack as he entered the back door to headquarters. She held the *Gazette*, a finger on an article at the top of the page. *Local Ranger Denies Accusations.*

Jack scanned the article. A one sentence introduction, the rest being Jack's words. "Good."

She turned to her computer and opened the browser. On it, the same article. She scrolled down to the comments. "There's two more since I was on last, six altogether."

"Already?" He came around the counter and read them, one by one.

> Bob3289. "What a crook. Chastain played us for fools. His land agents will slip a notice under our doors any day now, and we'll have no choice but to sell. Nothing will protect us. This is my home. I don't want to be anywhere else but here, but I can't fight the government."

> Anonymous321. "I heard someone is building a war chest to challenge Senator Culberson. If anyone knows how to contribute to electing someone new, please share."

> GoodGrief. "Mangum's going to ruin us. Who'll come here to enjoy the beauty if he gets his way?"

> Cowfrank. "I have respect for some of the good folks on the coalition, so I'm curious what final recommendations will look like, but I'd sure as hell feel better if the damned enviros were kicked off, as well as the feds.

The coalition needs to work for us, not a bunch of San Francisco enviros and a government that wants to kick us off our land.

Getajob. "How can we trust the coalition to come up with anything good? Government is involved. Nothing good ever comes from the government."

Anonymous14. "Could it be Mangum that actually wants to put our lands into the hands of international mining interests? If Mangum wants to get rid of the National Monument, maybe even the National Park, doesn't it seem more likely that he's the one with that kind of plan?"

"War's coming." Jack slipped to the other side of the counter. "I'm driving to the Enclave, then to the backcountry."

"What's happening on the Enclave?"

"You don't want to know." He sighed. "Tell Johnny I'll meet him at the trailhead."

"I think you can tell him yourself." Molly pointed out the window. Reger's rig made the turn into headquarters. "He came in early to gas up."

Jack met him in the back lot.

Lowering his window, Reger said, "Morning, Boss. I was laying there last night, thinking. If we don't get a move on, someone's gonna find our cave. Do what you've got to do, then let's focus on evidence, then on making a run to the cave . . . and yes, I mean run."

"Johnny, just go. You don't need me. What I need to do, I should do alone."

"The Enclave?"

Jack nodded.

"Then I'm going."

"Nope, I don't need you."

"You're not going alone. Kelly made you promise."

"Only because she thinks Mangum's dangerous."

"And you don't? He packs a gun and he's got no apprehension about wrestling in the dirt." Johnny pointed Jack to the passenger door.

"That was me. He was bluffing."

Johnny shook his head. "I don't think so. Load up. You're not going alone."

Jack sighed, walked around the vehicle, and climbed in.

At the edge of town, Jack pointed to the main road. At the motel, on impulse, Jack gestured for him to turn. Johnny parked alongside the big white SUV with General Services Administration plates. Mud filled the wheel wells and dust covered anything not muddied.

"Are you sure about this, boss?"

Ignoring him, Jack mumbled, "Why would realty specialists need a rig like this?" He climbed out and approached the room. "And with four-wheel drive?" He banged on the door.

No answer.

He knocked again, then heard sounds of movement from inside, then of the chain being removed from the door.

It swung open. The tall, African American man, sleepy eyed, peeked out, first at Jack, then at all directions behind him. "What do you want?"

"Letting you know, I'm blowing your cover. Whoever's plan this is, it's making people fight. People deserve to know what you're doing. I'm telling the newspaper you're here."

The man stared back with tired, bloodshot eyes. Exasperated, he closed the door.

Jack went back to the rig and climbed in. "The Enclave."

Johnny flashed a smile as he backed up. "Feel better?"

Jack didn't answer.

No sooner had they turned in at the Enclave, than a pack of ATVs appeared on the road, coming fast. The ATVs surrounded them, one in front, blocking the rig from going any farther. The others circled, engines revving, tires throwing gravel at the white ranger rig.

Hide Mangum, on the lead ATV, in desert camo, pistol

strapped to his side, sat in command. He cut his engine and crossed his arms. Others surrounded the patrol rig.

Exhaust fumes came in the window as Jack rolled it down.

"You've been avoiding me," Mangum shouted.

"Not exactly. I saw no reason to play your games, but now I do. I'm here."

"The games aren't mine. They're yours and you're going to stop playing them."

"You're saying I want to take your land, and that's a lie."

"You won't get our land."

Jack glanced around, checking the attentive eyes of the others. "Mangum, why were you following the boy?"

"What boy?" Mangum scowled. "You mean that wise-ass kid at the trailhead?"

"Yes. Why were you following him?"

Mangum laughed. "I wasn't following him. I was going for you."

"I'm not talking about the first time. I'm talking about three days ago, and you know it. On the trail. You followed the boy. He ran before you could hurt him, then you jumped me."

"Jumped you?" Mangum looked amused. "Did I do any damage?"

Jack ran a finger over his nose. "Hardly."

"Too bad."

Jack turned to the nearest ATV rider, a woman, blonde, dust-covered scarf over her face. "How can you follow someone who would hurt a boy?"

"You're lying," Mangum shouted. "Three days ago, I was here. All of us were."

"That's right, he was," a steely-eyed man said, from behind the vehicle.

"Making excuses for him?" Jack said, challenging his word.

"No," the man said, his voice not wavering. "I was here. He was here."

Jack scanned the eyes of the other riders, not sure what to say. "What do we do, Johnny?"

"Don't ask me."

Jack turned back to Mangum. "Did you invent the conspiracy theory about me, or are you just the messenger?"

"Those are questions you need to answer, government man. Why are you doing what you're doing?"

Jack gave him a cold hard stare, not sure what to say next.

"Leave." Mangum rested his hand on the butt of his pistol.

"Boss, we better go," Reger said, sounding antsy.

This wasn't working. Jack shook his head. "Yeah, I guess so."

Johnny put the engine in reverse and waited for one of the ATVs to move, then backed toward the county highway.

"And if I catch you on the Enclave looking for gold," Mangum shouted. "I'll kill ya!"

Jack flashed a look at Reger. "Is this a new lie he's feeding his followers?" Jack sighed. "That didn't do any good."

"No, Boss, it didn't, but a little evidence might."

"Okay, you're right. Let's go to the trailhead." Jack's phone rang. He pulled it out of his pocket. "Hello."

"Call Father. Get back to me." Kelly ended the call.

Jack pulled up Kip's number.

Kip answered quickly. "Can you meet?"

"We're about to go into the backcountry. How about tomorrow?"

"Tomorrow's too late."

Jack cupped his hand over the phone. "New plans." He dropped his hand. "Sure, Kip."

"My place."

Frustrated, Johnny slumped over the wheel, then sat up and started for Culberson Ranch.

Kip met him at the side door of his casita and walked him back to the dining room. The regular members of the coalition sat around the table or against the wall. Karen Hatcher and Dave Van Buren, representing the environmental community; Ginger Perrette and Daniel Montoya representing ranchers; Mack Latham, manager of the Inn of the Canyons, representing business interests; Thomas, representing the pueblo; Helen Waite, county commissioner; and Paul Yazzie, Bureau of Land Management.

Kip made eye contact with each attendee. "Jack . . . we have a new wrinkle as of today. A rumor that the President is being lobbied to issue a new proclamation, one that does away with the national monument." He pointed Jack to the chair at the head of the table.

"I don't think it works that way." Jack took his seat.

"We're not sure either, but it sure takes the wind out of our sails. Paul?"

Yazzie took a moment to speak. "Likely scenario . . . if the monument is gone, it reverts back to simply being public land. But there's another rumor, different source. That lands would be withdrawn from all uses except mineral exploration and mining . . . maybe oil and gas."

Jack leaned over his hands. "Folks, I think that makes it all the more important that you issue your recommendations, make it known that people here want to protect what they value."

Kip sighed. "There's another issue . . . making things complicated."

"Support for the monument is fading," said Ginger Perrette, sitting to Jack's left at the table. She pointed at Dave Van Buren. "Because of the games being played."

"What games?" Jack asked.

"Enviros want it easy to get what they want . . . hard for everyone else. That's not gonna work." She glanced around the table.

"That's not true, and you know it," Van Buren said.

"It is." Perrette looked not at Van Buren, but Jack. "Plus . . . there's what you're doing."

Thomas squirmed in his seat.

Jack caught the movement. "Something you want to say, Thomas?"

He scooted up to the table. "We refuse to sit by and lose the things important to our culture. The national monument is important. Our being at the table is important, part of decisions being made."

"You can do that without the national monument," Perrette said.

"That has always proven difficult. This rumor of mining . . . it gravely concerns the elders. So, too, do the letters in the *Gazette*."

"Hell, mines bring jobs," Daniel Montoya said from across the table.

"And years of ruin!" shouted Van Buren. "What are you, a sell out?"

"Folks, let's not attack each other," Jack said.

"We don't need that from you now." Montoya eyed Jack. "You expect us to believe you were behind us the whole time? Hell, we know what you were doing. It's all over the papers."

"I wasn't doing what the rumors say. I was here, with you, trying to do the right thing."

"Yeah, right."

"Seriously. I want this finished as much as you do."

"That's not what we're hearing," said Ginger Perrette. "Your land agents are about to swoop in and take our land."

"They're not mine." Jack sighed. "Sign the recommendations and show people the conspiracy theories are fake."

"How will they know that?" Montoya asked.

Jack swallowed, fighting the lump in his throat. "The purpose of the conspiracy theory is to make you afraid. To make you feel helpless. They want you to have doubts. I want you to succeed, to preserve the things you value. Even though you value things a little differently, and for many different reasons, together, you'll defend each other's reasons, and your own."

"When are you going back to Costa Rica?" Perrette asked.

Jack scowled. "I've never been to Costa Rica. That's a lie . . . to stoke anger."

"Prove it," she said.

Jack turned to Kip. "My being here isn't helping." He glanced around the room. "Saturday . . . at the signing . . . I'll be proud of you." He stood.

Karen Hatcher, close to tears, looked away. Faces showed a range of emotions, some only glared.

Jack walked out of the room and let himself out. He slipped inside the vehicle and Johnny started the engine. They crossed the meadow and climbed the hill at a fast clip.

At the bottom of the Terrace Road, Johnny turned toward Las Piedras.

Jack's phone rang. He glanced at the name on the screen, then answered. "Hi Kip, did I forget something?"

"Nope, I need to tell you what was unsaid when you were here. That we were in a tenuous place. I was hoping your being here would change that. It didn't. You deserve to know. There will be no signing ceremony tomorrow."

"Rescheduled?"

"Cancelled. It won't happen. Ever."

"But we're so close."

"No, we're not. We're miles apart. Today sealed the fate. The coalition is no more. It's over. We've parted ways."

"I'm turning around. I'll be right there."

"No, Jack, it's too late. The moment you left war broke out. That fast. We all knew it was coming. Half the people in the room were ready to fight. The other half left after you did."

"Karen Hatcher?"

"She tried holding it in, but . . . she shared a few choice words I don't care to repeat."

"But . . ."

"Gotta go, Jack. I need to call the newspaper, let 'em know there will be no signing ceremony." Kip ended the call.

Jack ran his hands over his face. "Pull over, Johnny."

He pulled onto the shoulder.

Jack climbed out of the car and trudged across the desert, his head full of thoughts. About people he'd been proud of, the hope and promise he'd felt, the people who had vested so much in preserving a place they valued. A place they loved.

They would now let those feelings fade and find it more important to hate their neighbor.

It's happening again.

Chapter 43

Jack climbed back into the patrol rig. "Johnny, let's go to the *Gazette*. The least I can do is speak in defense of the people on the coalition. Make sure no one thinks it's their fault." He sighed. "And while I'm at it, I can *out* those guys at the motel."

"Bad news, huh?"

"Yeah, sorry. You can listen in while I talk to Kelly." He pulled out his phone and called her cell. It rang twice.

"Hello, Jack," she said, sounding occupied.

"Bad news."

"I've heard," she said, sounding tired, distant, and unwilling to show emotion. "I talked to Father . . . so I know. No signing ceremony. No coalition. He doesn't blame you."

"And you?"

"I'm in New Mexico, on my way there. Gotta go, I've got a call coming in." The phone went dead.

Jack dropped his head.

—·—

At the *Gazette*, Jack slipped into the newsroom, finding two reporters pounding away on stories. The editor came from the back room and crossed the newsroom floor.

"We're a little busy, and we've already heard what you're here to tell us. No signing ceremony, right? Coalition disbanding?"

"No, I'm here to say, please don't let anyone attribute blame to the people who served on the coalition. If anyone failed, it's me."

"Jack . . . I'm not taking that as an admission. I'm referring to the conspiracy theories."

"Correct, but what good is that?"

"Understood. I'll be fair."

"Thank you." He turned to go but made an abrupt stop. "One other thing. There's a rumor that there's a secret team of feds working out of a motel here in town. Supposedly land agents. It's true, they're here. It's true, they have some sort of secret assignment, but no one will tell me what it is, and I really know nothing more than that. They could be land agents for all I know."

"That's interesting, but . . . maybe not as important as . . ."

"Henry," a reporter shouted, cutting him off. She jumped up from her desk. "Threats."

His brow furrowed. "What?"

Scurrying across the floor, she waved a page full of scribbles. "I just got off the phone. Threats to Senator Culberson."

"What kind of threats?" Henry glanced at Jack.

"Multiple kinds." The young button-nosed reporter tried to calm herself. "He plans to unseat her, challenge her for her senate seat, and if he can't do that, he'll do whatever it takes to keep her from ever setting foot in Washington again. Sounded like a physical threat."

"Sounds like a rambling fool. Who was it?"

"He wouldn't say, and no, he was no rambling fool. He was very calm. Very deliberate."

"So, what'd he want?"

"He wants people to be at the Senator's town hall. That's where he'll make his play. He wants a showdown." She frowned. "Weird. Probably nothing."

"I agree . . . but could be something big. He surely wouldn't hurt her in front of that many people." Henry turned to Jack. "Know anything about this?"

Jack shook his head, fighting to stay calm. "No, nothing."

The editor turned back to the reporter. "Go ahead, cover it. Emphasize the town hall, not the threat . . . but call the sheriff. For the town hall, take your camera."

"There's one other thing," she said. "I had a call I was about to tell you about, but the second call came in. The first was a Virginia phone number. I wrote down the guy's name. He's building a war chest to defeat Senator Culberson. They plan to use it to let people know she's selling out to Washington interests. He claimed a challenger will be stepping forward. He said . . ." She paused to read from her notes. ". . . the challenger is someone who will keep the tribe safe from the monsters that threaten those who cannot defend themselves. A gunslinger, willing to do what it takes to solve a problem. Someone willing to kick some ass."

Henry shrugged. "Typical election-time rhetoric."

Jack felt his heart pound. *That's typical?* He rushed the door and dashed down the sidewalk. Slipping into the patrol rig, he pulled out his phone. The call went to voicemail. "Kelly, there's a threat against you. Call me."

Johnny started the engine. "What kind of threat?"

"A physical threat. And a challenger."

"Mangum?"

"Sounds like it . . . let's go back to the Enclave."

Johnny sped out of the square, onto the road leaving town. Reaching into the back seat, he dug into his pack and pulled out his service weapon.

"You won't need that."

"Hope you're right, Boss, but I'm keeping it handy."

Jack pulled in a breath. "Everything's gone to hell."

As they turned into the Enclave, another vehicle—a gray sedan—pulled onto the highway toward town, the female driver watching them closely.

Johnny slowed on approach to the first set of homes. Wooden fences, houses set on acreages, some with horses. Ahead, a group of people stood assembled at a wide spot in the road. An unmanned table and two chairs sat off to the side.

Johnny slowed to a crawl.

Several in the group started walking toward them. Hide Mangum stepped past the others and made an abrupt stop. He crossed his arms and glared.

Johnny brought the vehicle to a stop, keeping it in gear, his foot on the brake.

Jack jerked the door open and stepped out of the car.

"The guest of honor," Mangum shouted. "Interesting. How'd you know we were assembled in your honor?"

"No time for small talk, Mangum. I'm here to tell you one thing. I will not let you hurt Kelly Culberson."

Mangum unfolded his arms.

"Got that?" Jack waited for an answer.

Mangum smiled. A spark lit in his eye. "I don't know what you're talking about."

Jack took two steps forward, stopping as Mangum moved his gun hand. "You try to hurt her, I'll get in your way."

Mangum laughed.

Jack tromped back to the patrol rig.

"So, government man," Mangum muttered, "Don't leave so soon. Don't you want to know why we're gathered?"

Jack turned. "No, why?"

"Because we figured out why you want our land. It's that treasure, isn't it?"

"The Rivera treasure?" Jack glanced back at Johnny. He cocked his head. "No one's said the treasure is on your land."

"Then why are you wanting it?"

"You're crazy. I don't want your land."

"Nice try. What I haven't figured out is, whether you really think it's here, or you made up the whole damned crock just to get our land." Mangum turned to the others and nodded.

Is he checking his audience? Is this an act? A misdirection?

"That's the only thing that matters," Mangum continued, "keeping you off our land."

"I'm leaving . . . stay away from Kelly Culberson." Jack turned to leave, but stopped. “Why did you say I’m the reason you’re assembled?”

“Because you are.” Mangum’s eyes flared. “We just signed a poison pill to keep you away.”

“Poison pill? What’s that?”

Mangum glanced back, eyeing several bystanders.

An elderly man, gray, stooped, looked uncomfortable, uncertain.

“Don’t worry.” Mangum raised his hands, tamping down emotions. “As I said before . . . it’ll never come to that.”

“Come to what?” Jack shouted.

“You just missed ’em—we signed over mineral rights to people with deep pockets and lawyers who can kick your ass . . . beat you at your own game. With them on our side, them with a stake in the game, you’ll take us seriously. You’ll never get us off our lands.”

Jack’s jaw dropped. “You convinced these people to risk everything they own?”

“It’ll never come to that.”

What had Mangum done? “Then why guys with lawyers?”

Mangum’s smile radiated through his mustache. “To take on the feds. That’s their purpose in life . . . and mine.”

A gray-haired woman pushed her way to the front of the crowd. She threw up a fist.

Johnny stepped forward.

Jack waved him back, then noticed a familiar bearded face. Rancher Daniel Montoya.

Montoya looked away, then caught himself.

It’s done. Kip was right. It’s fallen apart. It’s over.

A woman shouted, “Why do you feds keep doing this? You shoulda learned years ago.”

Not a taunt. A question.

“Learn what? What should we have learned?” Jack asked.

“You people tried this before. It didn’t work then. It’s not gonna work now.”

“What are you talking about?” Jack studied her eyes. Sincerity.

"Stop playing dumb," she said, her voice growing angry.

"I'm not." Jack waited. No explanation. He pointed Reger to the vehicle.

Jack settled into the passenger seat. *You feds keep doing this.* He shook it off.

Reger made a U-turn.

How can Mangum do that to those poor people? They can lose everything. They're his neighbors. Why? "Stop," Jack said.

Dust wafted past as the vehicle slid to a stop.

Jack let the words sift through his mind once more. *Why do you feds keep doing this?* "Johnny, never mind, but I need to check something."

"Boss, we need to go to the cave." He sighed. "Okay. Where?"

"Headquarters."

Johnny stepped on the gas.

At headquarters, Jack left Johnny and followed the hall to the stairs descending into the basement to central files. There, he passed rows of file cabinets, stopping at the locked door at the back of the room. Archives. Retired files. He pulled out his master key and unlocked the door.

More file cabinets lined the wall.

He pulled open the file drawer that held the Park's only original copy of the presidential proclamation establishing the national moment. He knew what the signed version said and ignored it. Instead, he flipped through earlier drafts, along with memos and directives and all manner of instruction on carrying out the intent of the final proclamation. He found the earliest draft. It said nothing about lands other than those in the final proclamation. Nothing suggested intent to include the Enclave, and nothing suggested a different boundary, or more or less land.

Nothing gave support to what the woman said.

He closed the folder and returned it to the file cabinet. As he did, he noticed other files, five or six in all, bound together with a rubber band. *Never looked through those.*

He pulled out the stack and slid it onto the table in the center of the room. Taking a seat, he pulled off the rubber band and sorted through the files. They appeared to be working papers, documentation of legwork done locally, copies of originals sent to a solicitor in Washington, D.C., the person tasked with the job of consolidating the recommendation to the President.

One file held pictures of lands now part of the national monument. Another, phone records documenting conversations with elected officials, none mentioning anything about the lands within the Enclave. He set aside a file labeled *Discussions*, then decided to give it a look. Flipping through, he scanned page after page of support and opposition to the concept of a national monument, a few with notes from working meetings with various individuals and organizations. Most with familiar names. Kip Culberson. Karen Hatcher. County supervisors. Business interests. He came to a set of papers clipped together, a yellow note attached to the front, written with heavy black marker, the words *Misinformation Campaign*. He peeled away the note. The top page spoke to a rumor that landowners would be forced to sell. The source of the rumor was unknown, but it appeared to be aimed at countering a suggestion by an elder from the pueblo, a man who had since died. The suggestion had died with him. The stack included a copy of the elder's obituary. Jack continued through the pages. Nothing suggested the elder advocated for anything other than that a piece of public land be included that abutted private land. The elder had partially prevailed, getting planners to include—and keep secret—an extensive area of cultural heritage—habitation sites, etc.—but the elder had also wanted to include lands west of the private parcels, to protect current traditional uses. Here he had failed, possibly because of his passing, but—from what Jack could see—more likely because of a misinformation campaign. The adjacent private lands? The Enclave.

The purpose of the misinformation? It appeared to be solely for the purpose of scaring the inhabitants of the Enclave. They were made to feel certain they would be forced to sell.

Lies.

Jack tapped on the table. Told they'd be forced to sell. Told old stories from other places, where that sort of thing had been done decades before. Told stories from bygone days that still haunted the agency, even though as a practice it was seldom considered or approved for use today. But stories were used to raise suspicion and resistance—just as had happened in Montana.

He thumbed back through the pages, finding information on the tribal elder, and a detail he'd missed on the first pass through. On a record-of-call documenting not just a conversation with the elder, but also the name of the person who prepared the record. Third line from the top, a name scrawled just legibly enough that it could be deciphered. Charles Monroe. Jack squinted, taking it letter at a time, confirming the name. Charles Monroe. Not Potts, but Charles. *Potts was brought in as a subject matter expert? He never said anything. Never even mentioned it.*

Why didn't he?

Jack studied the language for clues. Nothing suggested how well Potts knew the elder, or if he had a personal interest in what the elder had to say. All very professional.

So, what happened to the elder?

Jack thumbed back to the obituary, published in the *Las Piedras Gazette* three years before. Cause of death not mentioned. If suspicious, it wasn't noted. He read to the end. Survivors, two. A daughter and a grandson. The daughter, different last name. Sanchez—rather than her father's name, Tsadiasi. Rebecca Sanchez, of Las Piedras, and a grandson, Miguel.

Miguel. What are the odds?

Could this be our evasive little guy?

He glanced around the room and spotted the collection of old phone books.

He pulled one down from five years back, thumbed through and found an address for Rebecca Sanchez. He wrote it down, then turned back to the files.

So, why did Tsadiasi want the area behind the Enclave to be part of the monument? Jack flipped through the pages. Nothing concrete. Indication of Tsadiasi being secretive.

What's there?

Could it be because of Juan Rivera's treasure? Quivira gold?

Jack slipped into the larger room, to a topo map tacked to the wall. The road through the Enclave ended where terrain became difficult. Considering only contour lines, the land appeared nondescript. A drainage. Variable elevation. Open areas between sections of near-vertical cliff.

But the flow of the terrain came from the direction of Johnny's cave.

Is that what this is about? Was Tsadiasi a protector of Quivira gold? Was he trying to assure the hiding place remained wild, that road access would be limited? If so, did Potts know?

And equally important—those behind the misinformation, what did they want? Maybe Gilbert Tsadiasi knew. Maybe that was why he wanted that land in the monument.

Jack flipped through the pages. No answer. Potts had delved into the question of what was behind the misinformation, but nothing in his notes suggested a clear answer. It appeared that with the death of the elder, and without a champion, the proposal was dropped. The unseen antagonists remained a mystery.

Jack slipped the rubber band over the stack of files and returned it to the cabinet.

Leaving the building, he took only the address he'd written down from the phone book.

He drove along the edge of Las Piedras and turned onto the street where Rebecca Sanchez lived, stopping at a simple adobe home with a small garden surrounded by a low wall.

He parked, approached the door and knocked. Inside, a dog began to bark. A moment later, the door swung open. A woman, tired eyes, gray streaks in black hair, stepped from the shadows into the light. A suspicious look came over her.

"Rebecca Sanchez?"

"Yes," she muttered.

"Jack Chastain, National Park Service."

"I know who you are. I'll see if Miguel wishes to talk."

"Wait . . . that answers a question, but . . . I'm not here for him. I'm here to talk to you."

"About Miguel?"

"No."

Her dark eyes narrowed to a slit. "Why would you want to talk to me?"

"It's about your father, Gilbert Tsadiasi."

"We no longer use his name." She dropped her eyes. "That is our way."

"I understand, I'm sorry . . . but there are things I think I need to know."

"Ask your question."

"He wanted the national monument to include lands it doesn't now include. Know why?"

"Yes."

"What can you tell me?"

"It was painful."

"I'm not here to drag you through pain. I wonder if it's something I need to know."

"Does it matter? It's done. It's not included . . ." The words hung like a sentence unfinished.

"His death, was it foul play?"

"You mean murder? No. Foul play? Yes. It was as it always is. Our people marginalized, ignored. That's what happened to him. Lies. Things said that people wanted to believe."

Jack remembered Miguel's words to Mangum. *Is that what you want to believe?* He looked into her eyes. "Can you tell me what your father wanted?"

"To preserve our ways, our traditions. He should have seen himself as successful. A vast area of cultural heritage—homes of our ancestors—protected, with little attention, but he believed the unincluded area was just as important, maybe more. It must have been important to others . . . but he didn't know their reason. Whatever that reason, he was marginalized for it."

"What's there? Why's the site important?"

Her eyes narrowed. "You don't know?"

"There's nothing about it in the files. In fact . . . it seemed like he was being secretive."

"He may have come across that way." She sighed. "A gathering area . . . abundance even in dry years. Important for the silks used in thread and rope, even fabric woven for the clothing of dancers."

"You said, silks?"

"Yes. From the seed pods of milkweed."

Chapter
44

The heavy wooden door closed, a quiet click into place.

Milkweed. Jack staggered back to the rig, lost in uncertainty.

It was important to Tsadiasi. Had meaning to him, but there's nothing you can do. Leave it be. Tsadiasi . . . another soul for whom hope was lost. A mess that wasn't his fault.

But this mess of mine . . . why didn't I see it coming? Why am I so damned naïve? Why weren't my eyes open, aware of what could happen, what others could do, that bad things could happen? Now, a signing ceremony canceled. The coalition, no more. Next, war. With each other. People, neighbors, similar lives, different details. They'll battle over details. And you? You were naïve and didn't keep it from happening.

He started the truck and headed for the park.

The story of your life. Just like in Montana. Next time, if there ever is one, don't be so damned naïve.

Kelly will arrive tonight but with no legislation to discuss, no feel-good ceremony to plan. No recommendations from the coalition. She'll likely have a challenger. And a threat to hurt her. My failure, her ball and chain. Guilt by association.

And now, impetus for eliminating the monument, maybe the park. For whom? And why?

And how? Guess that's obvious. The machinations of a ghost named Doc. Conspiracies planted in the minds of those who do his dirty work.

But . . . those poor people of the Enclave. They could lose everything. They bought into it. Deep pockets they think will protect them, now can take it all. Their own doing, against their own best interests. They won't blame Mangum. Or themselves. They'll blame me.

He dug out his cell phone and called Reger.

"Go ahead, boss."

"Johnny, in case you're waiting, thinking we might still go to the cave . . . I'm not going."

"I kinda figured that, Boss."

"I need to be here when Kelly arrives. She knows the signing ceremony is off, but she doesn't know about the threats."

"I understand. You're gonna need a drink . . . so will Kelly. I'm buying."

Jack ended the call, slowing on approach to the park entrance station. He waited as the line metered past, weekend arrivals, some likely treasure hunters. When his turn, he pulled forward, expecting to be waved through. The entrance station ranger signaled him to roll down his window. She straightened her Stetson. "Hello, Senator Culberson's beau."

"Hi, Just Jen." He made no attempt to smile.

"Meeting the senator?"

"Later tonight."

"Nope, she's in your office . . . came through a few minutes ago, asked if you were in."

Accelerating out of the gate, he headed for headquarters, parked in the back, and dashed up the steps. Inside, he went straight to his office. As he stepped in, he became aware of two visitors, not one. Vera Martinez sat with Kelly against the back wall, both in dark suits.

Kelly looked up, her eyes tired.

"I'm so sorry," he said. "I should've done something . . . sooner."

"I'm still processing what it means. Right now, I'm worried about you."

"You've got more important things to think about. You've got threats."

"What kind of threats?"

"Threats of a challenger. Physical threats against you." He sat, facing her.

"A challenger? Well, that's pretty obvious from the newspapers."

"But a physical threat. That's serious."

She turned to Vera. "May I have a moment alone with Jack?"

Vera nodded and stood.

"The conference room is likely empty," Jack said. "Across the hall, two doors down."

Vera slipped out, closing the door behind her.

"Who made the threat?" Kelly leaned over her knees.

"Heard it from a reporter. She didn't have a name. Probably Mangum. He's said some things. You need to cancel the town hall."

"I can't do that. People are waiting. They want my answer . . . am I running or not? They deserve to know. With the signing ceremony cancelled, there's no point bringing up legislation to implement the recommendations. So . . . Vera and I have work to do. I need to anticipate the issues constituents want to talk about. I need to be ready to listen and respond."

"What about Mangum?"

She shrugged. "What's he gonna do? Shoot me? Not likely. Not there."

"You have no idea what some of his followers might do. They're hopped up on lies and they're angry and scared."

"Why would they be scared?"

"Afraid they'll be forced off their land. Scared enough that they did something foolish, and whether they know it or not, what they did should scare them." He sighed. "Instead, they're afraid of me and what they think I'll do . . . and they think you're letting it happen."

"What'd they do?"

"They think it's a sly move . . . to counter what they think the land agents might do . . . but . . . it could cause 'em to lose everything."

"What . . . did . . . they . . . do?" Kelly asked, her words staccato.

"Signed over mineral rights to someone with deep pockets.

Someone they think will be on their side . . . fighting the feds, keeping them from being forced off their land."

Kelly gasped. "Oh, my God!" She stood and paced the floor. After a minute, she turned. "Gotta go. Gotta prepare for tomorrow. I'm sorry this happened. You've worked so hard."

Jack dropped his eyes. "I'm worried I may've caused this. I went there first thing this morning, and again this afternoon after hearing the threats against you."

She spun on her heels, her eyes turning cold. "Damn it Jack, sometimes you can be so damned naïve. Can't you be more astute? Can't you think before reacting?"

"I know." He sighed. "And now . . . not only that . . . it's over. Everything."

"How will you fix it?"

"Too late. The coalition is gone. The recommendations won't happen. The monument might soon be gone. The only thing to worry about is you. I won't let Hide Mangum hurt you."

"Look, Jack Chastain . . ." She raised a hand and pointed into his eye. "I will take care of myself. He will not do anything there. Not in the open."

"He might. Even if it's only to say he's running against you."

"Let him. It's a free country."

"But what if that's just a ruse? An act that triggers a follower to do something desperate. Something worse than shouting."

"It won't."

"What if it does?"

"Jack, you're paranoid. Promise me, you will NOT try to protect me. I have to stand on my own two feet. In front of all those people, I have to show I can take care of myself."

"Does that mean you're declaring your candidacy?"

"I don't know. I'll decide during the meeting. If I'm convinced people think I can represent them and be helpful, I'll announce that I'll run. If I'm not convinced, I won't."

"Are you sure that'll work?"

"No, but I've been all over this state, and it's left me with more questions than answers . . . about myself. I want to serve. I want to do the best I can . . . but they deserve someone who can do the work well. I'm too new to this. It takes confidence but also humility."

"You've got plenty of both."

She shook her head. "I don't know. But I know this. This is home. People know me and I know them. If I'm lucky I'll learn something tomorrow. I'll make my decision then." She leaned over, kissing him on the forehead. "Sorry this happened. I won't see you until the meeting tomorrow. I'm locking myself in at the ranch . . . with Vera and Alex. He's flying in tonight."

"I can help."

"It'd be a distraction. Understand this, whatever happens, do NOT protect me. Promise?"

After a moment he gave a reluctant nod. "Promise."

She slipped out the door.

—'—

Evening came. Tired of the walls of his cabin, Jack drove to town. He parked, crossed the graveled lot, and approached the steps to Elena's Cantina.

The sounds of a bustling crowd drifted onto the porch. He slipped inside. Tightly wound treasure hunters vented frustrations. A few locals endured the horde, giving Jack plenty to avoid. Lowering his head, he stepped past the ring of patrons, locating Johnny against the back wall.

"You must have gotten here early."

"Not early enough. Almost got in a fight getting in line for a beer. Where's Kelly?"

"Preparing for tomorrow." Jack slipped into a seat, his back to the crowd.

"I'm buying. It'll be faster if I go to the bar." Johnny hopped up and made his way through the throng.

Jack studied the crowd through the corner of his eye. Tension, anticipation, and desperation. Optimism and disappointment. Not the typical Friday crowd.

"You're not drinking?" a voice asked from behind him.

Jack turned.

Deputy Winslow stuck a fresh toothpick between his teeth. "Heard the big ceremony's off. You must be disappointed. Also heard folks on the Enclave have someone willing to go after the monument. Get rid of it, give it back to the people. I told you to go after him."

"I did . . . and that's not what they'd be doing."

"Well, that's what they're saying anyway. Whatcha gonna do next?"

"I'm done. Everything's fallen apart."

Winslow sat and turned to face him. "I'm worried about you, Jack."

"There's no point in that."

Johnny returned with the beers. He handed one to Jack. "Deputy Buckity, you're here early. No fights yet. Need me to start one?"

Winslow laughed. "Quiet, like controlled explosions." He pulled off his hat and wiped sweat from his brow. "Ranger Reger, you need to convince your buddy here that ol' Mangum ain't easing off the pedal. He can't either." He glanced at Jack. "Mangum's planning something."

"I know. He told me."

"When was this?"

"Today."

"You were at the Enclave?"

"Twice. He now thinks I'm going after his land because Rivera's gold is on the Enclave."

"Hold it." Winslow pulled the toothpick from his mouth. "He said what?"

"You heard me."

Winslow turned serious. "Isn't the gold supposed to be in the high country?"

"Tell *him* that."

"Odd." Buck reinserted the toothpick. "What else did he say?"

"I'm not in the mood to talk about it."

"Fine." The deputy nodded. "Take my advice, bro. Do whatever it takes." He flashed a wave and started for the door. "Don't let him win."

"Too late," Jack muttered to himself, watching Buck thread his way through the tables.

"Drink your beer." Johnny took a sip of his own. "Something just came to me, Boss."

Jack stared at the beer. "Shoot."

"Mangum's telling people that you believe Rivera's gold is on the Enclave. He's telling 'em you want their land. You told them neither's the case, but they don't believe you. Those stories are triggering everything, right?" He took a sip of his beer and flashed a smile. "You know what you need to do? Or rather, what we need to do?"

"No clue."

"Go to the cave. Tonight. Prove you don't need their land."

Jack eyed him.

"You know I'm right." Reger chugged his beer and slammed the mug on the table. "Drink up."

—·—

They avoided the trailhead, choosing to take the old two-track road across BLM land. Jack's Jeep sat beside Potts' abandoned-looking pickup. New layers of dust lay over both, dull reflections of the moonlight on their metallic paint.

Striking out for the monument boundary, they left head lamps off in case Mangum indeed had a secret vantage point among the buttes on the northern horizon. That decision felt paranoid for this hour, but the lights were unneeded. The moon gave the desert an almost daytime feeling. Shadows felt deeper, a little darker, but otherwise the moon cast a glow over the desert.

They reached the fence in short order, then the trail. They headed for their first stop, Jack's stash of gear. Everything was as he left it.

The hour grew late, the moon low, the shadows deeper. They headed up the slickrock draw they'd ascended before, Johnny in the lead. A rolling swell caught him by surprise, throwing him off balance, causing a near fall. He stopped, overlooking a precipitous drop. Dead in his tracks, eyes on the chasm, he drew in several quick breaths.

"Let's think about this," Jack said, taking hold of his shoulder from behind. "We're almost there. We're tired. Let's not get ourselves killed. Let's find a flat spot, make camp, and get there in the morning."

Johnny nodded.

They made a quick camp and slept until first light, making lukewarm cups of coffee to get started, and striking out before sunrise.

The higher they climbed, the more anxious Reger became. Walking behind him, Jack felt it himself. "Remember, we can't keep it," he said, at one of Johnny's moments of effervescence.

"But isn't the hunt the best part?" Johnny glanced back. "Just think, . . . the map to Quivira. With that, we can do what Coronado couldn't. Imagine the stories we can tell."

Jack shook his head. Interesting. Most people would be thinking about getting rich. Johnny's thinking about telling stories. "I just want to shut down Hide Mangum."

"You're thinking too small, boss."

They reached the wall at the top of the drainage and found the break they'd climbed through before. Remembering having gone right, only to have to backtrack, they headed left, following the ledge of eroded sandstone that circled the dome. Passing the spot where they'd gotten the radio call to go search for Miguel, Jack checked his map. The cave must be close. They continued around. Off to the north, a view opened through a saddle between buttes.

Grasslands divided by an arroyo, cottonwoods lining the bottom. The plateau in the distance. Jack stopped to catch his breath. Must be the place Tsadiasi wanted to protect, poor guy. "For sure, we didn't get this far last time. We're right on the monument boundary."

Reger took off, picking up his pace. Jack fought to keep up as they circled the base of the dome. After several hundred yards, Reger made a sudden stop and stared into the head of a drainage that fell away to the left. He appeared to tick off familiar features.

Undulations of slickrock. "That's where we were." He pointed. "That's where I tried climbing." His head slowly turned, eyes zeroing in on a bend up ahead.

Beyond it would be the cave.

Johnny took off. Determined, steady steps, Jack behind him.

A ponderosa pine came into view, rising alongside the base of the dome.

"There it is," Johnny said. "The first pine." He started to jog.

Jack felt his own heart pound.

The second ponderosa came into view. Big yellow bellies, both of them.

Johnny broke into a run.

Jack tried to keep up, taking a straighter line, cutting through grass. Broken stems caught his eye. A spot where deer might have bedded down.

Johnny slowed, then stopped, and stared at the opening to the cave. Rock overhung the entry, keeping sunlight from reaching the floor. Beyond, darkness, almost foreboding. Hands shaking, he wriggled out of his pack and dug into a pocket for a head lamp. Nervous fingers fumbled to turn it on. "Ready, Boss?"

Jack nodded.

Reger took a deep breath and directed the beam into the cave. A small circle of light registered against the back wall. "Here we go." He stepped inside, keeping the beam steady. Ten feet in, he stopped and directed the beam along the base of a wall, then another. He stood motionless. "Maybe it's . . ." He ran the light again along the back. "Maybe there's a passage."

"Don't see one." Jack looked down. Dry, lifeless dirt. Enough reflection off the walls to see footprints. Hundreds of them. Relieving Johnny of the flashlight, he directed the beam at the floor. Boot tracks. To and from the walls, exiting the cave below the highest point of the ceiling. *The boot impression, one he'd seen before. The same boot that had followed the boy.*

Jack raised the beam enough to check Johnny's reaction.

Mouth gaping open, eyes wide, he appeared in shock.

Jack stepped into the light, returning to where he'd noticed broken stems in cured grass. Looking closer, he saw tracks. Tire tracks, reworked with windblown sand.

Jack returned to the cave and guided Johnny out. Without words he pointed at the stems, then the tracks among the long shadows cast by the morning sun. "Sorry, Johnny. This is my fault. You wanted to come. I was distracted."

"I can't believe it," Johnny muttered to himself, kneeling over tracks.

"I am so sorry," Jack repeated.

Reger dusted away the sand. He studied it a moment. "Might not have mattered."

"Why?"

"When was the last rain? A month ago? The tracks in loamy soil are distinct. Filled with windblown sand but distinct. Balloon tires. ATV."

Jack stared over his shoulder. The pocks of stubby tread. A month? He gasped. *Before Paris and little gold men.*

"Not much of a story." Johnny sighed. "Doesn't help you one bit. Not with Mangum."

Jack looked east. Out beyond buttes lay the Enclave. *Rough country, traveled by someone who knew how to get here, and knew what was in the cave.*

Johnny sighed. "Hell of a consolation."

"What do you mean?"

Johnny pointed. "Monarch butterfly."

It settled on the bright red petals of an Indian paintbrush.

Jack noticed a line on its hind wings. "Nope. That's a viceroy. A mimic."

Johnny frowned. "Damn imposter."

—'—

The hike back to the vehicles took them well past noon, the sun heating up fast.

Jack took his own vehicle and turned onto the road into town.

Reger, following in his patrol rig, called on the radio. "Where are you going?"

"Sheriff's office."

"You're gonna report that? That someone got to the cave before we did?"

"No. There's something else I need to do. See you at the town hall."

Sheriff Mendoza was in his office. The receptionist sent Jack back. Partially packed boxes sat against the wall. Mendoza, at his desk, studied a carved glass memento.

Jack waited for the introspection to pass, then knocked on the door.

"Come on in." Mendoza stood. "I'm just packing a few things. Any day now, Deputy Winslow is gonna slip in here and want to measure for curtains. What can I help you with?"

"I'm worried about tonight. You know . . . the meeting." Jack stayed at the door. "Mangum. What he might do. Maybe nothing. Maybe embarrass Kelly, but what if it's more serious than that?"

"We've been discussing that. Deputy Winslow thinks he knows how to handle it." Mendoza set down his memento. "Don't worry. Buck's way ahead of you."

Chapter 45

Jack drove to the Inn of the Canyons, alone. Wearing a hooded sweatshirt, he bowed his head as he joined the throng of people under the porte cochere, unable to escape the human current flowing into the hotel. It continued through the lobby, into the hall to the meeting rooms. Somehow, he managed to remain unrecognized. Just inside the door of the largest room, an eddy formed, and he broke away, working his way to a back row seat along the side wall.

The hotel staff had set up a slightly elevated stage in the middle of the room, rings of chairs encircling it. Many rings. Jack watched as people worked their way to preferred seats. The phone call made to the *Gazette* had worked. This crowd would be huge, with some here simply to see the blood. Some wanted to see it up close, while others sought a safer distance from the splatter. Some tried to sit off to themselves but were quickly surrounded by the others packing into the room. Tonight would be a full house.

Nothing to do but watch. With the promise made to Kelly, and being irrelevant on all other fronts, he sat back and watched. Helpless. Useless.

A woman sat on the front row, opposite the stage from Jack. A jacket lay across the empty seat beside her. He'd seen the woman before. Several times. Yesterday, at the Enclave. The first time, at the trailhead. Usually on an ATV. Now, probably saving a seat for Mangum.

Vera Martinez and another of Kelly's aides, a young, slightly built male—dark hair, dark complexion, ill-fitting suit, probably from the office in Santa Fe—scurried about making last minute preparations. Alex Trasker—gray suit, red tie, beard neatly trimmed—made a quick appearance, studied the room, then ducked into a door at the back.

Sheriff Mendoza took a position against the opposite side wall, watching the crowd. *Who else is here, on guard?* Glancing around the room, Jack noticed a female deputy, in uniform, along the wall behind him. Deputy Chavez, he recalled. Johnny Reger and Luis Archuleta, in plain clothes and probably fooling no one, took positions a few rows from the front on opposite sides of the room. Even with the promise to Kelly, Jack wouldn't intervene if those two felt they needed to take action.

He kept scanning. *Deputy Winslow. Where's he?* Third row, near an aisle. Not in uniform. Jeans and a dark sport coat. No toothpick. Close to the stage, ready to move. *Hope he knows what he's doing.*

At the main door, a blonde woman appeared. Tall, willowy, tight skirt, blazer, hair up. *Erika Jones? Why is she here?*

She searched the room. If attempting a subtle entrance, she failed. But when did Erika ever try being subtle? Her eyes stopped on his. She made a beeline toward him. "Unabomber look? Again?"

"You working?" he asked, still eyeing the crowd.

"No . . . well, mostly. Nice haircut."

"Why are you here?"

"Can't a girl come see an old friend announce her campaign for the Senate?" Scanning the room, she let out a chuckle. "You musta never found your clothes that day at Caveras Creek . . . if you had, you wouldn't be here in a second-hand store hoody. Did you hike back to the road in your birthday suit? Fun, wasn't it? Let's do that again, someday."

"Have you been in Las Piedras all this time?"

"Hell no. Denver. The regional director had things she needed me to do, speaking of which, I'm here . . . on her orders . . . because of you. You screwed things up."

"Me?"

"You couldn't stay out of things, could you? You had to bring attention to the team. Because of that, you can expect to be disciplined. Expect a downpour."

"Talking about the realty specialists?"

"They weren't realty specialists . . . you idiot."

He shook his head. "Now you tell me."

"Now, I *can* tell you, not that it matters." She scowled. "They're criminal investigators, looking for pot hunters. Trying to break up an international ring looting archeological artifacts. Because of you, the trail's gone cold. They missed an exchange with the fence, and nothing's happened since."

"Why couldn't you just tell me that? I would've left 'em alone."

"You know the answer to that. If people ask questions, you have to answer."

"Bull. All you or the regional director had to do was tell me. Would'a had less impact."

"Would you have kept it secret? Hell, no. You would've blabbed to the first person who asked, thinking you had to be transparent, trusting they wouldn't tell anyone." She poked his shoulder. "Only two people here were allowed to know. You weren't one of 'em. Neither were the rangers. The investigators wanted it that way. Secrecy was paramount. The bad guys somehow had fingers on the pulse of every attempt to break up the ring. It's an inside job. I don't know how you did it, but even with precautions you managed to screw things up."

"Why do you think it was me?"

"You so much as told them yesterday, at their motel." She turned, watching someone cross the floor. "I'll be back. Save my seat." She headed for a group gathering near the entrance.

Jack returned to studying the people in the room.

Hide Mangum had entered. He stood inside the door, his beard neat, hair combed, his usual cargo pants and T-shirt replaced with tan slacks and a brown sweater. He seemed to be casing the room. Abruptly, he walked to the front row and sat as the woman picked up her jacket.

Mangum all cleaned up. That must confirm he's throwing his hat in the ring.

Johnny Reger left his seat and slipped around the room, squeezing past others to take an open chair two rows behind Mangum.

Jack detected more movement and turned. Behind him, the boy—Miguel— stood at the wall, fidgeting, his eyes searching.

"Miguel," Jack said, in a loud whisper. "Who are you looking for?"

He jumped at the sound. He offered no answer.

Jack waved him over. "Sit here. Hey, I met your mom."

"I know." Miguel came around to the aisle and slipped into the open seat.

The room neared full capacity. Hopeful attendees worked their way to remaining seats.

Jack caught sight of Sheriff Mendoza approaching Mangum. He said a few words. Mangum stared without responding, then turned and—through glances—connected with others from the Enclave. Mendoza stepped back to the wall, keeping his eyes on Mangum.

Kelly appeared, slipping in from a side door, wearing a navy business suit and white blouse, her hair down. She exchanged a few words with her father, following in his usual garb, boots and a western-cut sport coat. As Kelly continued to the dais, led by Alex Trasker, Kip took a seat against the wall with Vera. Stopping at the dais, Alex scanned the crowd, then departed as Kelly stepped onto the platform. She took a deep breath, and suddenly ceased to be Kelly Culberson, hometown girl, becoming instead, Senator Culberson.

"Thank you for coming," she said, her posture stiff. "As I like to say in town halls, this is your meeting. And, as I promised, at the end I'll announce whether I'm running for this seat in the next election. You will have an influence on what I decide."

"Are you playing games with us?" came a voice somewhere near the back of the room.

"No," she said, looking for the speaker. "But let's not make this about me."

Another voice shouted. "Tell us what you stand for."

Mangum edged forward in his seat, a sly smile on his face, his eyes locked.

Kelly turned to the second voice. "I represent *you.* Isn't it more important that I hear what *your* needs are? Why does it matter about me?"

"Because we need to know what you'll do in Washington."

"I'll take what I hear, carry that into deliberations. Fight for your needs."

"Really?," a man shouted, sounding skeptical.

"Yes, really." Kelly smiled. "So, let's talk . . . what issues concern you?"

Mangum stood. "Government trying to force us off our land . . . to control our lives."

Kelly looked him in the eye, then glanced around the room before settling back on Mangum. "I've looked into this with every federal agency that could have any kind of jurisdiction over such an action. No agency has plans to force people off their land. I would fight it if that was the case. . . . but I can't find an actual example of government wanting your lands or trying to control your life. Conflicts? Yes, and they appear to be of your making, Mr. Mangum."

"You believe that?" Mangum spat.

"I do."

"You're either bought off or naïve as hell. Or lying." Mangum made a move to the dais.

Officers around the room came alive. Johnny, locked and loaded, appeared ready to pounce. Luiz as well. The female deputy behind Jack moved to the head of the aisle. Buck Winslow stood, shooting a cold stare at Mangum.

Mendoza stepped away from the wall. "Let's go," he said, signaling Mangum to the door.

Kelly raised a hand. "No, he's okay. Please let him stay."

Mangum eased into his chair.

Sheriff Mendoza returned to the wall. Winslow sat.

"If you're not gonna keep the government out of our lives," Mangum growled, "then I'll take you on. I'll bring you down. I'll replace you or fight you. Either way, Senator, take a stand."

"I have," Kelly said, her eyes growing cold. "I've found no evidence of what you're claiming, Mr. Mangum, but that doesn't mean I'm not serving your interests."

Mangum clenched his fists, scooted forward, then eased off the front of the chair.

Jack's muscles tightened, even as he fought to keep from leaving his seat. The promise.

Mangum inched toward the dais, eyeing Mendoza.

Winslow stood and ran one index finger down the length of the other. Naughty, naughty.

Mangum stopped.

Winslow stepped into the aisle. "Interesting situation we've got here," he said, as the eyes in the room shifted to him. "Senator Culberson . . . trying to conduct a meeting, with the possibility . . . and I would speculate, likelihood . . . she'll announce a run for her own term in office. And . . . I heard a rumor that Mr. Mangum here is gonna challenge her for office. That or try to ring her bell." Winslow laughed. "I'm not gonna let the latter happen . . . standing here, with the best view in the house."

Kelly, her eyes locked on Mangum, sighed. "Thank you, Deputy. I'll be fine."

"I'm sure you will."

Mangum growled and scooted back, stewing in his own juices.

Jack caught the movement of Deputy Sanchez backing, returning to the wall. Glancing her way, he noticed Miguel, eyes wide, shaking. Scared. The same fear he had seeing Jack the first time, that day in the side canyon. "You okay?" Jack whispered.

"Will he hurt her?"

"No, too many people." Jack turned back to watch.

"But he . . . could . . . like he did . . ." Miguel let the last word hang.

"What did you say?"

Miguel held his tongue.

"Interesting quandary," Winslow shouted, filling the silence. "For all of us."

Kelly and Mangum kept eyes locked on each other.

Kelly started to speak, her mouth moving, but no words coming. Thrown off her game, she cleared her throat. She seemed to be trying to collect her thoughts.

"Hide, I guess you have every right to challenge the senator." Winslow gave a rub to his chin. ". . . if the rumor I heard was correct. But do we want someone like Hide representing us in Washington? Maybe we do, maybe we don't. He's a bit of an outlaw, but not really. Mostly antisocial. There are people who like that sort of thing. Me, I guess I'd have to think about it."

Kelly seemed unsure how to proceed.

Mangum took a step toward her.

Winslow pointed. "Take your seat."

Mangum sat.

Kelly stared at the floor.

"Maybe Hide's got valid points," Winslow said, rubbing his chin. "About choosing sides. . . . choosing between right and wrong. Good and bad."

"Yes, absolutely," came a voice from the audience.

"But I'm sure the senator has a good response to that, right Senator?"

Kelly looked up. "I'll try."

"Good," Winslow said. "I'm sure you've got a plan for giving those folks in Washington a damned good kick, don't you?" A smile grew on his face. "We'd love to hear that part."

Jack took his eyes off Mangum. Buck was getting a little carried away. Mangum was tamed for the moment. Buck should sit down and shut up.

Winslow continued. "I think we're all looking for someone willing to make a sacrifice. Willing to fix what needs fixing. A gunslinger. Someone who'll keep the tribe safe. Protect those who can't defend themselves. You know . . . from those other people

. . . who threaten our way of life, want to take everything we have. Could you speak to that, Senator?"

Mangum, brow furrowed, scooted forward in his seat.

Winslow raised a hand, looking at Mangum. "Senator Culberson, go ahead. People want to hear from ya. I'll keep Mangum on a leash."

"I believe," Kelly said, then paused. She glanced around the room. "I believe in representing all of you as best I can. I try not to pick winners and losers. I try to find ways to bring people together, find solutions for all their needs . . . if I can. And, *what I* believe, myself, matters least of all." She eyed Mangum, clearly distracted. "In a democracy, what is leadership . . . for those who serve?"

Winslow took a step toward her. "Look Senator, I'm trying to give you a hand here."

Mangum stood. "My turn."

Jack shifted his weight to his feet. "Poor Kelly," Jack muttered, then realized he had said the words out loud. He glanced at Miguel.

Miguel hadn't heard him. Shaking even more violently, he stared, eyes wide.

Jack turned back to the room. Mangum, angry, seemed ready to launch.

Chatter rose across the room.

Kelly, confused, turned toward Winslow.

A man on a middle row jumped to his feet. "Maybe we should send Deputy Buck to Washington. Send someone who's willing to kick some ass."

Winslow smiled and raised a hand. "Don't get me wrong, that would be an honor but . . . sheriff is a better fit for me."

What is Buck doing? Kicking off his campaign for sheriff?

Mangum, angry, took two steps forward.

Kelly stepped back.

They stared at each other, tensions mounting, the room growing quiet.

Jack wrung his hands, fighting a need to do something. *Hold it. Those words.*

Kelly backed to the edge of the dais, wilting.

Jack stared. *Why didn't I see it? There in plain sight.* He rose to his feet, events and words racing through his mind. *A mimic.* Stepping past Miguel, he turned down the aisle toward the dais.

Kelly saw the movement. She shook her head. "No, Jack," she mouthed.

He did not stop.

Winslow waved off the shouts from throughout the room, fighting a smile.

Jack kept walking.

Kelly's face turned cold, glaring, watching Jack approach. "I'm gonna withdraw," she said to him. "Do not do this. Please do not try to defend me."

"I won't. I promised you that," Jack said. "There's something I need to do." He stopped in front of Mangum, and whispered, "Let's talk. In the hall."

"Anything you have to say to me, you can say right here!" Mangum shouted.

"Not a good idea."

"I'm not leaving this meeting."

Winslow pointed. "No fighting you two. Got that?"

Mangum clenched his fists.

"I'll make this quick." Jack looked deep into Mangum's eyes, past the anger, past the confusion. "That story . . . about government coming to take your land . . . about land agents . . . did you tell Deputy Winslow, or did he tell you?"

Mangum scowled. "Go to hell."

"No, Hide, please, just answer the question. Did you tell him, or did he tell you?"

"I'm not playing your game, government man."

Jack sat on the edge of the dais, feet away from Mangum. "No game, Hide," he whispered. "Please. Who told who?"

Mangum drew in a breath and let the question settle. He sighed. "He told me."

"Whose idea was it to sign away mineral rights? Who told you that was a good idea?"

Mangum's eyes sank deep into their sockets. He drew in a deep, hot breath, and looked up, eyeing Winslow. Mangum bit his lip. "He introduced me to a guy who did . . . then . . . I told everyone else." His voice went soft. "What are you saying?"

The room fell silent.

"I'm not sure yet." Jack studied the faces behind Mangum. Mangum's neighbors. Most of their faces wore shock. "I'm trying to figure this out."

"Figure what out?" Mangum asked.

"What Winslow is doing and why."

Winslow laughed. "I'm doing what you won't, Chastain. Cleaning up a mess."

Jack ignored him, eyes still on Mangum. "You didn't destroy the milkweed, did you?"

"No."

Jack rubbed his chin, studying the expression on Mangum's face. "I'm wondering if we've both been set up. Strange to say . . . but I'm wondering if we're both victims . . . targets."

"I ain't no god-damned victim," Mangum growled, rage contorting his face. It melted into confusion. "What did he do?" Mangum whispered to himself. "What did *I* do?"

"What *did* you do?" Jack asked.

"I signed the papers. I convinced everyone to sign those damned papers. Because . . ."

Jack stood and took a step toward Winslow. "What's your game, Buck? Are you the big purveyor of lies and conspiracy theories?" Over Winslow's shoulder, on the back row, Jack saw the face of Miguel, shaking uncontrollably. Jack took another step. Miguel cringed. Jack stopped. He turned back to Mangum, stepping toward him, keeping an eye on Miguel. The boy's shaking subsided. Jack turned and approached Winslow. Violent shaking. Cringe on his face.

That first encounter, at the trailhead, Miguel wasn't afraid of Mangum. He was afraid of me. And now Winslow. "Miguel, when we met that day on the desert," Jack shouted, "you were afraid of me. Was it because of the uniform? The badge?"

Miguel nodded.

"Have you seen Deputy Winslow in uniform?"

He nodded.

"Does he scare you?"

He nodded again.

Jack paused, soaking it in, remembering. "That day, talking to Kelly, you said something. What was that?" He looked down, summoning recall. "Something about . . . faces . . . no, spirits. Was that about Winslow?"

Miguel shook his head, no, then stopped, and nodded.

"So somehow it was? What'd you mean by spirits?"

Miguel cowered, giving half a shrug. "Spirits," he repeated.

"Spirits? Faces?" Jack dropped his eyes and ran a hand over the stubble topping his head. "Do you mean masks?"

Miguel nodded.

Masks, like in Paris. Damn, exactly like Paris. Not little gold men from an anonymous collector, but masks. That's why Teague was there. The masks, not the little gold men. "Does Deputy Winslow know about the masks?"

He nodded.

"So, artifacts . . . you're a pot hunter," Jack said, directed at Winslow, then turned back to Miguel. "There's more to this, isn't there? That's why you're afraid."

He nodded.

"Did Deputy Winslow hurt someone?" He waited for the nod. "Who?"

Miguel's mouth opened. Words did not come.

Not a good sign. Jack tapped the floor with his toe, gathering his thoughts. "I think I understand. Your people don't use names of the dead. So let me. Did he hurt Potts Monroe?"

He nodded. A tear streamed down his cheek.

Jack turned to Winslow, who now stood wide eyed, his expression blank. "Miguel, can you show us where Potts is?"

Nodding, Miguel began to cry.

Kelly walked up the aisle to the boy, taking him into her arms.

Winslow, still as a statue, glared, eyes wide.

Realization hit. Jack dropped his head, recalling details. Marks in the dirt on the floor of the cave. "It wasn't gold in the cave, was it? It was the masks. Artifacts."

"I don't know what you're talking about," Winslow said.

Jack closed his eyes and raised a hand to his forehead. "I'm missing something. A detail." *Something obvious. What was it?* He eyed Winslow. "Everything I ever heard about Mangum I heard from you. Same with the rumors of Juan Rivera's gold. First, I heard it from you. Always. Did you make that up, too?"

Winslow wouldn't answer.

"Why?" Jack dropped his eyes to the floor. *Why would he do that?* "Hold it. Investigators were coming. Looking for pot hunters. You knew that, didn't you? Even though I didn't. I learned that just tonight but . . . you were one of the two in the loop, weren't you? You knew everything. Things the rest of us didn't. They were on your trail, but you wanted more time. So, you invented a fake story about a real man, Juan Rivera, a man few of us knew anything about, but real. Why?" He ran a hand across his forehead. "Yeah, that's it. To flood the park with treasure hunters. Make it hard for investigators to do their work."

Winslow's eyes turned cold.

"And you wanted me out of the way, too . . . didn't you? Told me to avoid the monument. You wanted me nowhere near." Jack turned to the wall. "Sheriff, am I making your job harder?"

"You're doing fine, son," Mendoza said, stepping away from the wall, pulling out a pair of handcuffs. "I can take it from here if you'd like." He took Winslow's arm and placed a handcuff on one wrist, then the other. "Never thought I'd be doing this."

"One last question," Jack said.

Mendoza turned Winslow to face him.

Jack approached, studying his eyes. "Who's Doc?"

Winslow's eyes twitched, pulled left.

Jack caught the movement. He turned. In the midst of people he recognized sat one he didn't. A balding man with a crooked nose. A man he'd seen somewhere before, but whose common appearance made him almost invisible.

The man froze as others watched him. Eyes shifting, he looked for an escape.

"Is this connected to anything?" Mendoza asked. "Like, what happened to Dr. Monroe?"

Jack rubbed his chin. "I . . . uh . . . I don't know."

"Go ahead," Mendoza said. "Let's see where this goes."

"Doc, who are you?" Jack walked up an aisle and stopped. "Why are you here?"

The man held his words.

"Our paths have crossed, haven't they?" Jack stepped closer.

Doc said nothing.

"Well, maybe not you, but I've crossed paths with your handiwork, your lies. Maybe you, but I'm not sure." Jack glared. "Were you involved in what happened to Potts Monroe?"

The man shook his head, eyes wide.

"You weren't?"

The man clammed up.

"Okay. You may or may not have been," Jack said. "But I know this. You killed a lepidopterist . . . a butterfly biologist in Mexico. You didn't pull the trigger, but your lies killed him. An unintended consequence. But those things happen, right? The end justifies the means."

Doc squirmed.

Jack turned to a solitary television cameraman, set up at the back of the room. "Be sure to get this guy's face. He's an important guy. A brain trust, the puppet master behind conflict you've covered and assumed happened on its own. But no, it was his handiwork. He's good. Give him all the credit he deserves."

Doc froze as the camera trained on him.

"And . . . if the end justifies the means, what end are you seeking? Why are you here?"

Doc glared.

"Not gonna tell us?" Jack took another step toward him. "You've committed crimes against all of us here. Maybe nothing illegal, but crimes none the less." He sighed. "Lies. Propaganda. Conspiracy theories. Fabrications to cause division, . . . distrust.

Made us do things not in our own best interest. Even me. I thought I was above all that . . . I guess I'm not. I believed what was said about Mangum. Even let myself believe things I wanted to believe . . . with no evidence . . . hook, line and sinker.

Jack continued. "Tonight was . . . I suppose . . . intended to put Buck Winslow on the path to becoming a U.S. Senator. You employed your best tactic, the *us and them.* When there is no *them*, you create one. The . . . *those other people* method."

Doc's jaw dropped.

"Yes, I know your games. Some of 'em. That one you used in Mexico, on a good man named Professor Morales. He died. The wrong people heard your lies and took action. Cartels, maintaining control." Jack looked around, catching the wide-eyed stares of people throughout the room. He turned back to Doc. "Here's a coincidence. The butterfly biologist was here a few months ago, with his wife. Someone learned he was coming, didn't they?" Jack locked onto Doc's eyes. "Had him followed, to find out why he was here. Maybe they were afraid he knew about a piece of land on the back side of the Enclave, land someone wanted to get their hands on, maybe your boss. Land they probably feared the professor wanted to protect. Is that right?"

Doc shook his head.

"I'm piecing this together as I go, so correct me if I'm wrong." Jack paused, remembering details. "FYI, you . . . or someone . . . didn't understand the connection. Morales wasn't here on *his* business. He was here on his *wife's* business." Jack stopped. "Hold it." He stewed a moment. "That's how Buck came to know about artifacts, isn't it? Buck was hired to follow Morales, wasn't he?" Jack glanced at Winslow, then back at Doc.

Stone-faced, Doc avoided eye contact.

"Doc!" Jack shouted. "Pay attention."

Shuffling. Restlessness. People sharing glances and uncertain looks.

Jack turned to the opposite side of the room, then pointed. "Doc here knows us better than we know ourselves. He knows what to say to make each of us do what he wants."

"I do not know what you're talking about," Doc muttered.

"He speaks." Jack clapped his hands, slowly, three times, then let silence fall over the room. "What happened here is your specialty. Making us quit thinking for ourselves. That's what you wanted."

Doc forced a smile. "I provide services. To clients. Specialized services. That's all. Nothing more. What they do with those services is their business."

"But lies are your product. If truth would work, you'd give it a try, but people are triggered more by lies, so that's what you use. The end justifies the means."

"I didn't say that. I give them messaging . . . rhetoric."

Jack turned to face the crowd. "Your neighbor is not your enemy. This guy is your enemy. His lies are your enemy. The things he does to divide us, they are the enemy. They make us do things *not* in our best interest." He turned to Doc.

No response. Doc stood and made his way to the aisle, then turned toward the door.

Deputy Chavez took his arm, stopping him in his tracks.

Surprised, Doc attempted to pull his arm away. "What are you doing? I had nothing to do with killing that archeologist. That, he did on his own."

The deputy held firm. "We need to talk . . . tie up a few loose ends."

Sheriff Mendoza guided Winslow past the two of them. "Deputy Chavez," he said, not looking back. "Ever think about running for sheriff?" He pushed Winslow into the hall.

Chavez motioned for Doc to follow, her hand still locked on his arm.

Jack walked to the side wall, where Kelly stood embracing Miguel, the boy still sobbing. He took the boy and pulled him close. "You're safe," he whispered. "And you've been a big help." He watched Kelly approach the dais.

She looked tired. Resigned. Stepping onto the stage, she said, "I'm sorry folks, let's call it a night. I'll put out an announcement tomorrow that I'm not going to run."

"No," a woman shouted from the front row, stopping Kelly

from talking. The woman next to Hide Mangum. "You're willing to listen, and that's what we want. We want you."

A man stood near the back. "I have no idea why you don't have more ego than you've got, but . . . hell, that's fine by me. I want to be able to vote for you."

"I . . . I need to think about what's happened tonight," Kelly said.

Throughout the room, people stood, but not to leave. Her father stepped away from the wall. Then Alex Trasker. The room remained quiet, expectant eyes upon her. No one moved.

She dropped her head a moment, then looked up. A tear formed, then a smile. "I'd like to announce my candidacy for the office of Senator."

Respectful applause filled the room.

She ended the meeting, but stayed, listening to anyone who wanted to be heard.

Chapter 46

Sitting in her car, Kelly watched the seconds tick down. At eight o'clock on Monday, she stepped out and headed into the county courthouse, her bag over her shoulder. She climbed the stairs to the second floor, stopping at the words *County Clerk* stenciled on a glass-paned door, knocked, then entered.

The county clerk, a graying woman with thick rimmed glasses—sipping coffee as she worked with an assistant—glanced up as the door swung open. "Well, you weren't the person I expected to see first thing this morning. How can I help you, Senator?"

"Morning, Cas. Thought you could help me. How do I file for office?"

"Interesting. I've got an appointment in an hour to talk about that same subject with Sheriff Mendoza and one of his deputies. I can answer her questions, but . . . the answers for you would be different." She pointed Kelly toward her office, her brown sleepy eyes unchanging.

Kelly followed her in and sat in the chair across from her desk.

"You would file your papers with me *if* you were running for county office. But you're not. For federal office, you file with New Mexico's Secretary of State. Plus, you'll need signatures from two percent of voters, statewide. That shouldn't be a problem for you." She let out a little chuckle. "I'm surprised you didn't know that."

"There's a lot I don't know. I'll reach out to the secretary, but I wanted to start with you, since this is home."

"I understand. Sorry I can't be much help."

"No, this is very helpful, and it's always good to see you. Did you hear about the folks on the Enclave?

"You mean, the thing about mineral rights?"

"Yes, and rights of way."

"Sad, isn't it."

"They're suffering a little remorse." Kelly sighed. "A lot actually. They're scared."

The county clerk's eyes grew wide, signaling a realization. She turned to the wire basket inbox on the corner of her desk.

Kelly followed her eyes.

File folders, envelopes, papers—all likely waiting to be sorted. On the very top, a deed clipped to a stack of other pages, likely other deeds, all clipped to a larger envelope.

Kelly eyed the stack. Originals, the top page signed and notarized, a yellow sticky note attached. *They haven't been recorded?* She leaned forward and read the words on the note, upside down from her angle. *Goes to State Land Office, not us. Call filing party.* She sat back. "I uh, . . ." She turned to the clerk, catching her still staring. "I talked to several after the meeting Saturday. They're not sure what to do."

"Is that so?" The county clerk sat a moment, in thought, then stood. "How about a cup of coffee? It'll take a few minutes to brew a fresh pot, but while I'm doing that, I'll find the forms you need to start getting signatures."

Kelly smiled. "That would be great. The coffee and the forms."

The clerk slipped out, closing the office door behind her.

Kelly stared a moment. *Would it be wrong?* She reached for the package. Thumbing through the deeds, she confirmed what she already knew. She slipped them into her bag.

—·—

Jack climbed out of his Jeep as Kelly reached into the back seat for her bag. She followed him toward the steps into Elena's Cantina. The morning sun, now above the canyon walls, shot a beam past the shadows of the bar, into the hallway, toward sounds of conversation and dishes clinking. The smell of coffee pulled at them. The hostess grabbed four menus and led them along whitewashed walls, under vigas and latillas, to the table Kelly had called to reserve, the one nearest the kiva fireplace.

"You're the first to arrive," the hostess said. "Can I get you some coffee?"

"Please," Kelly said, checking the hallway.

The hostess dashed to the waitress's station, picked up a coffee pot, and returned to pour them two cups. "Your waitress will be right with you."

Jack glanced around the dining room. Tourists mostly. Quieter than a few days ago. The word had gotten around. No gold to be found.

Hide Mangum appeared in the hall, his wife Jean by his side.

Kelly raised a hand.

Hide said a few words to the hostess and started across the dining room.

Kelly and Jack stood.

"Thanks for coming." Kelly gestured them toward open seats.

"Yeah, we, uh . . . or at least I . . . ," Jack said, stumbling over his words. ". . . wanted to try getting off on a better foot. I'm sorry. I've been a jerk."

"It's gone both ways. I'm sorry, too," Mangum said, eyes dropping to the table. "I'm okay talking about anything else." He sighed. "Did they find the archeologist?"

Jack nodded. "Yeah."

"Just as you suspected?"

"Yeah. Pretty much. Shot . . . body hidden. The sheriff went out with Miguel and his mom, and one of the ARPA investigators —the guys Winslow described as land agents."

"ARPA?"

"Archeological Resource Protection Act."

"Must've been traumatic for the little guy."

"It was, but he was brave. His mom had him point at where to look for the body, then put him on a helicopter. Got him out of there fast. The helicopter came back for the body."

A waitress delivered two more cups of coffee and refilled the others. "Need some time?"

"A little," Jean said, poring over the menu.

Mangum tugged at his mustache. "Had the little guy seen everything?"

"Apparently." Jack took a sip of coffee. "After Winslow shot Potts—late that night—Miguel hid . . . scared, not sure what to do. The next morning, he saw enough of Winslow to realize he knew the man. He'd seen him at school, in uniform, for one of his dog and pony shows. He didn't tell his mom, knowing who the shooter was, fearing for her safety."

"Why was he out there?"

"He and Potts Monroe were friends. Potts knew the boy's grandfather, formed some kind of connection to Miguel. Took him to one of his research sites. They camped on a ridge overlooking the desert, watching the stars. Saw pulses of light from a flashlight—Doc hiking across the desert—and decided to check it out. They dropped off the ridge and there they saw a campfire. Winslow was there. Potts stashed Miguel and went to see what he was doing. It's an area he knew well . . . an important archeological site. Not the smartest thing Potts ever did."

"What about that Doc guy?" Jean asked.

"For some odd reason, he'd chosen that location to enlist Winslow for his games. Admitted to seeing the shooting. After Winslow buried the body, Doc finished sharing his plans, then left."

"Weird," Mangum said. "Do we know his real name? Doc sounds like an alias."

Jack laughed. "Does, doesn't it? His real name is Herman Durfey. Consultant to corporations and politicians, doing what he did here . . . and in Montana. His mission . . . to divide us . . . and he did. In Montana, I accused a partner of spreading lies that he knew not to be true. He turned against us. I figured I'd been too slow in responding to the lies—Doc's lies. I realize now, it played out just as Doc wanted."

"So, there was no Juan Rivera?" Jean asked, ready to change the subject.

"Juan Rivera was real," Jack said with a nod. "But Winslow's story was not. Rivera was a man largely forgotten by history. The first person of European descent to go north into what is now western Colorado. Passed through this part of the world, going as far north as current day Delta, Colorado, near the confluence of the Gunnison and Uncompahgre Rivers."

"So, it's true." Mangum said, sounding uncertain. "Never heard of him before this." He opened the menu and glanced down the page.

"Rivera's journals were found a few years ago . . . in Spain. There's a recent book," Jack said. "Academic piece, done by an anthropologist in Colorado. Winslow may have seen that book but more likely—and this is the interesting part—he may have first heard the name at the same time I did." Jack let the thought sink in. "Someone—probably a man named Harper Teague—paid Winslow—a bad cop, probably off duty and who happens to be a good tracker—to follow the butterfly biologist, thinking the good professor was here to give trouble to whoever Teague and Doc work for. Doc won't say who that is but confirmed Winslow was recommended by Teague. The professor may not have known either one, but *they* knew of *him* somehow . . . but the trip here had nothing to do with the biologist or butterflies, and everything to do with his wife. She's an archeologist, an old friend of Potts, here to help on a project . . . and to reconnect. One night, while Winslow was lurking in the trees, listening, Potts and his friend joked about Juan Rivera and reasons why he disappeared from history. Winslow remembered the joke . . . and used it . . . to throw off the ARPA investigators, to keep 'em busy dealing with treasure hunters.

"Rivera was real," Jack reiterated. "Established trade with the Utes and looked to see if there was gold or silver to be had. Made two expeditions, found a little silver, but not enough to stir much interest. Essentially, he was forgotten. Nobody knows anything about him after that."

The waitress refilled their coffees and stopped at the fireplace to toss in a stick of wood.

"So those stories of treasure maps, and caves, and loot from Quivira . . . ?" Jean asked.

"Fabricated," Jack said, "all of it, but Winslow had help . . . from people good at faking old documents . . . and stories."

"Documents?"

"Yeah, the pictures online . . . of a journal. Made things look legit. The map made for a plausible story. They let the journal pages trickle out a few at a time, increasing the excitement, and making the ARPA investigations more difficult. The important stuff was fenced, then sold . . . masks and other rare artifacts. They were sent to Paris to be auctioned. But there was more to be found and Winslow was greedy." Jack leaned over the table. "He told me to stay away from that part of the monument, saying it was provoking you."

Mangum let out chuckle. "He told me you were sneaking around, making plans."

Jack shared in the laugh.

The waitress stopped at the table. "Ready to order?"

Mangum glanced at his wife and said, "Yep. We know what we want."

"Us, too," Kelly said.

The waitress took the orders and scurried away to the kitchen.

"One more thing," Jack said, "and this part answers a lot of questions."

Mangum leaned in.

"The investigators . . . the guys he called land agents."

"Yes?"

"Anytime you and I had a run in, I'd always run back to the Park, angry someone was undermining the work of the coalition. I tried getting information. No one would talk. Told me it was none of my business, even though the rumors were tearing the community apart."

"I'm sorry for my part in that," Mangum said.

"Not your fault." Jack sighed. "The reason Winslow knew as much as he did . . . he was one of only two people here who knew what the investigators were doing. The other was the Park superintendent, who was sworn to absolute secrecy. The sheriff, knowing he was retiring and thinking the investigation could go on for a while, named Winslow to be their point of contact. The investigators talked to only two people. Winslow knew everything."

Mangum's brow furrowed. "And it was Buck who told me they were land agents."

"Me, too. I was so damned disappointed in my agency. How could they be working against us like that? But I couldn't get anyone to confirm anything. I felt caught in the middle."

"I saw those guys on occasion, working. Made me so damned mad, thinking they were eyeing our property." Mangum tugged at his mustache. "To think it was Winslow playing us all."

"Know anything about butterflies?" Jack asked. "Monarchs and viceroys?"

"Yeah, there's lots of monarchs up the creek from our place. Because of the milkweed. Don't know a thing about viceroys." He glanced at his wife, catching a shrug. "Why?"

"The viceroy butterfly is a mimic. Looks very much like a monarch, which is toxic . . . from feeding on milkweed. Having a similar look, it deters predators. Winslow was a mimic. Maybe to all of us. He looked like so many things. None of us suspected he was doing what he did."

Jean shook her head. "And he might have become our sheriff."

Jack glanced at Kelly. "Or our senator. Doc was grooming him to run against Kelly. And who knows for what purpose? During interrogation, Doc folded like a house of cards, but he didn't know Winslow's future purpose."

The waitress arrived with their meals, three plates on one arm, the fourth in her hand. She circled the table, setting them down.

"Sorry I've talked so much," Jack said, eyeing his plate. "Enough about that. All that's left now is fixing the damage."

Mangum sighed. "I'm just waiting for the next shoe to drop. Someone's gonna show up, throw their weight around, and take everything we've got. That's when I'll feel the full wrath of our neighbors, people I care about, people I somehow misled."

"What's up above your place, by the way?"

"A nice little valley."

"Mineral claims? Oil and gas?"

"Mineral claims, so we hear. But with the monument there, the only way in is through the Enclave. I don't know why I let myself forget that."

"That's the strength of Doc's lies and conspiracy theories. They blind us."

Mangum unfolded his napkin and picked up his fork. "Remember that day at the trailhead? We were all there. So was the boy. He said something that day that pissed me off. He said, '*Is that what you want to believe?*' All I could think was, '*damned smart-ass kid.*' "

Jack laughed. "He's some kid, isn't he?"

"Yeah, he is. But he was right. There are things we all want to believe. Things I wanted to believe, and I convinced others to believe, too. Believe one thing . . . it gets easy to believe the next. You even want it to happen, so you can get pissed off about it." He slipped back inside himself, dropping his eyes to his plate. "I watched my old man . . . a Viet Nam vet. Dedicated to the cause . . . until they released the Pentagon Papers. Ate him up inside. The friends he lost in Nam. His disappointment became the filter through which I saw all things government. So much so that I never entered the military, despite family tradition."

"You weren't in the military?"

"Nope."

Jack shook his head without commenting.

"I've never trusted people like you," Mangum said, no tinge of animosity. "I just haven't, because . . ." He didn't finish the thought.

"No need to explain."

Mangum nodded. "But the division . . . is something, I suppose, that will always be there."

"Why?" Jack asked.

"For me . . . because I want to be left alone." He looked at his wife. "We both do. We want our freedom."

Jack sighed. "I'm not after your freedom, or to intrude on your life. I admit, I know there are people who say that I am. I accept that they say that. But I hope you realize that sometimes there's a motive behind their saying it."

"I do. Now." He took a bite and turned to his wife. "Remind me of something on occasion?"

"What?"

"All you need so say is, '*Is that what you want to believe*?' "

Jean nodded.

Mangum looked at Kelly. "You've been quiet, Senator. Can *you* forgive me?"

"Don't have to," she said. "You owe me no apology, but . . . I have something to give you." She picked up her bag and pulled out a stack of papers, bound with a metal clip. She dropped them on the table.

Mangum's eyes grew wide. "Where the hell did you get that?"

She laughed. "I shouldn't say. They were sent to the wrong office. Honest mistake. I made it, too, but there they were. Borrowed 'em . . . kinda. Thought you might want to check your work before sending them to the right office."

Mangum sighed. His shoulders dropped. Relief poured over him. A tear came to his eye.

"I'll take those," Jean said, picking up the papers and slipping them into her own bag. "I know right where they need to go."

Chapter 47

The dust lay a little heavier on the pickup than when Jack last saw it.

Johnny pulled to a stop beside it. "I'll wait to see if it starts."

"It will. Go ahead, I know you're busy."

"I'll wait."

Jack climbed out and fished a set of keys from his pocket. Keys given him by Sheriff Mendoza. Keys found on the body of Potts Monroe. He opened the pickup door and inserted the key into the ignition switch. He started the engine, then gave Johnny a nod and thumbs up.

Johnny put his patrol rig into a quick three-point turn.

Jack watched the vehicle round a bend, leaving a cloud of dust. *Should have said something. Through it all, with everything going to hell, with conflict from everyone, Johnny was there. Always insisting on protecting me. Maybe he'll get some good stories out of it.*

I need to let him know he's appreciated.

Jack turned off the engine and let the quiet return. Staring into the distance, he sat as an image of Potts appeared, climbing the ridge and fading into the expanse.

"Oh, Potts, how could I have kept this from happening to you? What could I have done?" He settled into the driver's seat and stared through the hazy windshield a moment more, then took a glance around the cab. Nothing here. No trash. No stray pens or pencils. Not even lip balm or sunscreen. Nothing.

He pulled on the latch to the glove box. The lid dropped open.

An accumulation of vehicle service records—and an envelope, stamped and addressed to La Profesora Angelica Vargas.

The call to her two days before had been hard . . . now this. Jack sat staring at the envelope and decided not to wait. He pulled out his phone. "Hola. This is Jack," he said once she answered. "Just found a letter, addressed to you. I'll stick it in the mail but . . . I wanted to save you from the shock of getting something from Potts . . . something you weren't expecting."

"Would you read it to me?"

"What if it's personal?"

"Please read it."

Jack tore open the envelope and pulled out a single page, revealing words more deliberately written than anything he'd ever seen from Potts Monroe. He began to read aloud.

> *My dear Angelica,*
>
> *I hope this letter finds you well. I've thought about you often in the last couple of weeks and not for reasons you might expect.*
>
> *I'm not sure exactly what to say, or even how to begin, but I owe it to you to be the one who hears it first. I know you'll laugh when you finish this letter. Enjoy it. I wish I could hear your beautiful laugh.*
>
> *Your journey over a decade ago . . . I didn't understand. I'm sorry I didn't even try.*
>
> *I suppose I should say that I know you better now. At least I think I do, because of a new friend. A young fellow. He's not quite as young as he looks, but he's still young. Lives in town but he's really from the pueblo. He's the grandson of an old friend.*
>
> *We ran into each other one day in the backcountry. I was amazed he was there all alone, him and his dog. He thought I was a pot hunter. Lectured me up one side and*

down the other. When I finally convinced him I wasn't, and I learned who he was, I let him know I was a friend of his grandfather's. He let down his guard and I attempted to teach him a thing or two. But—it turns out—he's taught me more. So much so, I'm seeing things a little differently.

His connection to places never ceases to amaze me. Before long I was following him. He took me to places I never knew about, but he would only show me if I promised to do nothing more than protect them. These are places of cultural significance. To him they are places of connection.

His knowledge of the living world, and of the culture and traditions of his people, seems to grow with each passing day, building on things he learned from his grandfather. It came to settle over me another thing he has in common with his grandfather—a constant, persistent gratitude for the gifts of the earth and the creator.

You, my dear profesora, described it all as traditional knowledge, and I remember encouraging you not to give it the same credence as the scientific method, but to partition it off as something else. You struggled and I remember telling you to "consider it knowledge on its own merits—whatever that means—but not to call it science." I could see that uncertainty haunted you and I didn't make it easy. I understand how that uncertainty led you to seek new directions. I know I said silly things. Undoubtedly insulting. Maybe hurtful. So, let me say it here. I apologize.

And let me continue. My indigenous friends have long told me that the past is connected not only to the present but also to the future, an unbroken continuum, and I always thought I knew what that meant. I now have more questions than answers, and that's okay. The one thing I do know . . . my young friend is a caretaker. Same as his grandfather. A caretaker of the present. A caretaker of an ancestral past. A caretaker of connections to the future.

I knew his grandfather, considered him a friend, but realize now that I didn't fully understand all he tried to teach me. At least I tried to listen. Others wouldn't. Still, it is now me who is haunted.

As all of that settled into my little brain of late, I began to think of your choices.

You felt you were intruding on something you might not understand. You thought it best to pull back. I thought you were being silly. It affected the depth of our friendship. Forgive me.

I will say, I'm not pulling back, I still have a purpose here, but my methods and reasons seem to be changing as this caretaker educates me.

I look forward to talking about all this with you, sharing experiences like we did so many years ago. Thank you for coming here this past year. Both you and your husband."

Glancing at the letter's final paragraph, he stopped, seeing words he wasn't comfortable saying. Words she needed to read to herself.

"He signed it, simply, Potts," Jack said, feigning conclusion. He listened to her sobs.

"Gracias, Jack."

"I'll stick it in the mail."

"No, keep it for now. Could you arrange for me to meet this young man?"

"I can try. His name is Miguel. He's a big fan of Kelly's."

"And, when I'm there, I'd love to see the places you've found la mariposa monarca."

"Well, I could show you sites we've found, but . . . apparently . . . Miguel's better at it than I am. Despite all our science, he knows right where they're at. When would you like to do it?"

"In a few days. I'll make plans and let you know."

—·—

Angelica hiked up the draw with Miguel and his mother, sharing a private conversation. Jack and Kelly held back, choosing not to intrude. The destination would be the place Miguel's grandfather had hoped to protect.

Hide Mangum had given his blessings for crossing his land, joking not to make it a habit, but then stating a desire to give Miguel a proper right of way.

In the distance, the rock rim stood over the valley. Topping a rise, the canyon bottom came into view. Cottonwood trees along the creek bed. Upslope, scattered single-leaf ash.

In the distance, high and to the west, would be the cave Winslow used to stash his booty. To the south, Jack could make out the trail he had used to cart his treasures out by ATV.

Plopping down in the shade of a cottonwood, Jack and Kelly waited. Miguel, his mother, and Angelica continued to talk.

"Had a message from the superintendent," Jack said, breaking the silence. "It was short. It said, now you understand, sorry, and well done." He chuckled to himself. "That's Joe."

At the sound of a ping, Kelly glanced at her phone. "Whoa," she said after reading the first few lines. "One of my aides shared something on the grapevine." She scrolled down, scanning the content. "A television station in Albuquerque had an ad buy. Big one. One that would start the day after the town hall, cancelled a few hours afterwards. The news side of the shop wouldn't have even known about it, except someone from the revenue side came down the hall asking questions, wondering if reporters knew why they lost the buy."

"What was the ad?"

"Attack ad—I was the target—intended to open doors for an unnamed opponent. Danced around what can and can't be said but hinted at support for someone like Winslow. Paid for by the Super PAC recently registered in Virginia. A reporter found a contact for the PAC . . . called, acted like they wanted to confirm the ad buy had been cancelled, but the operative wasn't too bright, didn't understand it was someone from the station, thought he was talking to the man paying for his services. Answered all sorts of questions, confirming that the bank account he'd created had received a wire transfer, that the exchange rate from France had been about as expected, maybe a little less but not a problem." She looked up from the phone. "When he realized he wasn't talking to the client, he hung up."

Jack gave her a slow nod. "Paris? Wow! Can we find out who's paying?"

"Super PACs don't report dark money donors. Not sure what more can be learned."

Jack watched Miguel, kneeling in the midst of milkweed, pulling strands of silk from a seed pod, then demonstrating something to Angelica. "Let's think about that later."

When finished, they hiked back to their cars. Miguel and his mother left in an old green Ford pickup, Angelica waving goodbye. She stood a few moments, deep in her thoughts.

Jack and Kelly waited, giving her time to process what was on her mind.

When finally she turned, she had an overcome look about her.

"You okay?" Kelly asked.

"I'll be fine."

"Maybe this wasn't a good idea," Jack muttered. "Too soon."

"No, it's fine." Angelica dropped her eyes and stepped toward them. "I've offered to help prepare something to restart a discussion begun by Miguel's grandfather. I told them I knew you would want to listen." She turned to Kelly. "And you, too."

"Yes," Kelly said. "Send it my way."

She nodded and turned back to Jack. "You need only listen. You don't have to understand their traditions or their culture . . . just respect the importance it has for them." She paused. "Miguel remembered Potts telling him he wanted to show this place to someone—but only when Miguel was comfortable doing so. Miguel now believes that person was you."

"Why does he think that?"

"Because Potts referred to this person as a good man."

Jack toed the ground.

"This is a special place for them," she said, looking upslope. "It would be special for me, too, for other reasons. A place to continue work of two special men. Mí amor and my friend."

"Sure you're ready?" Jack asked. "The connection . . . to both . . . could make it difficult."

"Yes, difficult . . . but, as my love often said, think of the monarch. For them, death is a phase of life. One they do not fear. Generations pass before they return to Mexico, and life goes on. I must now find a way to see the lesson in that. The same is probably true for a young woman—a graduate student—who must now find a way to quit fearing life."

"You'll try to interest her in helping?" Jack asked.

She nodded, looking up canyon. "Miguel's mother worries about drawing attention. The attacks it could bring. Someone . . . wants this land. Why, is a mystery."

"Yes, it is," Jack concurred. "I've heard rumors of impending filings from my contacts in the Bureau of Land Management . . . mineral claims . . . but that hasn't happened. As if they, too, don't want to draw attention. Maybe, waiting until everything is in order. Rights of way across the Enclave may have been part of that." Jack sighed. "Is Miguel afraid?"

"Miguel, less so, because of what's happened in the last few days. But his mother, yes. What happened to her father was painful. Lies intended to marginalize. The division those lies caused . . . the healing that couldn't occur."

"We'll protect them," Jack said. "We won't let ourselves be afraid of a few little lies."

"My dear, Jack," Angelica said, stepping closer. "Lies have shaped history more than anything I can think of. Look no further than Coronado, a man you've given much thought to of late." She watched his eyes. "The Coronado Expedition was all about lies . . . and look at the consequences. Beginning, middle and end. First, lies from a man trying to impress the Viceroy. Lies that fell on the ears of Franciso Vazquez de Coronado, triggering greed . . . for more wealth and power. Coronado risked his wife's family money, seeking more, and he bankrupted himself, and in desperation, left a trail of destruction. He tortured the indigenous people of New

Mexico, stole their food to provide for his men, and took their shelter. He left them to starve. Those indigenous people, in their quest to survive—seeing the greed, desperation and entitlement in Coronado and his men—created their own lie, Quivira. And lies —or falsehoods—continue to this day, as if he was a great explorer. He was not. He was a conquistador, and he followed a lie, even after learning it was a lie . . . his ego not letting go. Who knows why he would do that?"

"Maybe it became a core belief. His worldview. That it had to be true. He was entitled."

She considered it. "Maybe. Interesting choice of words."

"Not mine. A friend's. One who's thought about these things. But . . . my dear Angelica." He shared a teasing, sympathetic smile. "I do understand. There will be more attempts to do the things that have happened here. We'll try to be smarter. We'll be circumspect. We'll seek to understand. What other choice do we have?"

Angelica turned away. "I'll do what I can to help . . . even with the risks."

Seeing her pain, Jack looked upslope, hoping to change the subject. "See up there." He pointed. "There's the cave with Juan Rivera's stash from Quivira." He laughed.

Angelica sighted in on the distant ridge, looking confused. "You found something?"

"No. It's empty." He gave her a wink. "So, professor, who was Juan Rivera, really?"

"My dear Jack, we may never have answers to your questions. They are lost to history."

"Not the answers to my questions," Jack said. "For me, they're not lost."

"What do you mean by that?"

Jack glanced at Kelly, then back at Angelica. "I look at Juan Rivera this way. He was a man who did what he was asked to do. He finished the job. He charted a route into what is now Colorado, doing what the governor asked. His journals gave Escalante and Dominguez a beginning for their historic journey, and he established trade with the Utes, making friends, not enemies.

He looked . . . and found a little silver. He did what he was asked to do."

"Is that enough?" Angelica asked, sounding analytical.

"What more do you want? He didn't slaughter the Utes or use torture to get answers. He didn't steal their food or leave them to starve. He did his work, without drama, and maybe without ego. He did not leave a trail of destruction, like Coronado or other egos like Magellan."

She let out a sad little laugh. "Sometimes big egos accomplish great things. Coronado and Magellan are remembered. Rivera is not."

"But you said it yourself, Coronado was after riches. He wasn't successful. He failed. Rivera accomplished most of what he set out to do. In scale, there were differences in their missions, but why should that matter? Just because he didn't stumble onto something like a Quivira doesn't mean his accomplishments were inconsequential. He did what he set out to do." Jack gave a rub to his chin. "Know what else? I suspect he was fair."

"Fair," La Profesora said, echoing the word, then turning to face him. "I struggle with fair. What does it mean in a world that has a way of justifying anything it wants?" She paused. "I'm not the optimist I once was."

"I'm sorry . . . but . . . fairness is on my mind. After lies, fabrications, and conspiracy theories, I've been thinking a lot about fair. How important it is. Not winning at all costs. Not letting the end justify the means. Hearing what others have to say, accepting who they are, and what their needs are. Fair is being willing to be vulnerable, to accept having to build trust. Coronado was none of those things, but . . . I want to believe Rivera was."

Angelica dropped her eyes. "Without evidence, you don't know that . . . but evidence supports that as a possibility . . . just as evidence confirms Coronado to be an entitled bastard." She laughed. "I will say, my dear Jack, . . . maybe what you look for in Juan Rivera, is not so hard to find in someone else. Fair, trustworthy, hardworking, respectful of others. What you see in Juan Rivera, I see in you." She smiled. "And you seek to finish the job.

I will tell Miguel, despite all that you don't understand . . . their culture, their traditions, the things they value . . . you will seek to understand what his grandfather sought to do."

"Fair enough."

Chapter 48

Looking out over the water, Kelly approached the boulder's edge. "I told you not to protect me."

"Didn't think I was," Jack said, appreciating her perfect backside. "What are you gonna do?"

"Punish you." She jumped, pulling her legs into a cannon ball, hitting the surface with a splat. The eruption of water covered him. She came to the surface near the travertine edge of the pool and blew water from her lips. "Feeling punished? Or must I continue?"

Cool water on warm skin, shocking, but refreshing. "Uh, . . . I'm wet, . . . but punished? Afraid not."

Hefting herself onto the boulder, a mischievous sparkle formed in her eyes. Water streamed from her dark wet hair, over her neck and breasts, and down the length of her body. She sprang, landing on top of him, wet and slippery. Sitting up, she put her weight on his belly and held down his arms.

"You're a wrestler now?"

She giggled. "Afraid?"

Shifting his mass, he flipped her onto her back and rolled on top of her. "Very. You never know what a guy might do when he's this afraid."

She draped her arms around his neck and pulled him to her.

After a moment, Jack came up for a breath. "Senator, what if someone comes down that trail? Remember the lecture you gave me . . . about how you must worry about your reputation?"

"I said that?"

"Yes."

"And you listened?

"Yes."

"I also told you not to protect me, yet . . . you did." She giggled. "So, I trust you know when to ignore what I have to say." She pulled him closer.

Appetites and passions took hold under an early summer sun.

Afterwards they lay on the boulder, watching Caveras Creek pour over a ledge of sandstone, cascading over the boulders below.

She put her head on his shoulder.

"I really did intend to keep that promise," Jack said. "In fact, I thought I had."

"I know." She kissed him on the cheek. "You were good for your word, but . . . you protected me nonetheless . . . and lots of other people."

"Probably myself more than anyone. I'm just lucky I heard what Winslow said."

"I guess we're all lucky."

"Feeling good about making your own run for office?"

"Yes." She snuggled closer. "If elected, good. If not, that's okay. Part of me misses being here every day. With you . . . but that day will come. Until then, I've got a job to do." She sighed. "I've been pretty uptight . . . just getting to know this gig. Sorry I was so hard on you."

"Not as hard as I was on myself. The last few days I've been thinking about lessons I need to take from what happened here. I now know the game Doc played, the ways he divided us, and the ways he made people to do his bidding." He let out a sad little laugh. "But . . ."

"What?" She looked into his eyes.

"I've always known, what I've had to say wasn't important."

"You're the only one who thinks that."

"Hear me out." He put a finger to her lips. "What mattered was, I kept the important people listening to each other. That was my role. Same in Montana. But the lies . . . even though I was slow in Montana to take 'em seriously, I reacted . . . and that's what Doc wanted. He wanted to keep me from doing my job, so he could divide the public. Same thing happened here.

"That's what you learned?"

He stared at the slice through the sandstone where water poured over the edge. "Also . . . feels like I learned that . . . truth can deceive, lies can reveal."

"That's confusing."

"It is. And . . . it disappoints me that I can't automatically believe what I hear from people I want to trust. On the other hand, it troubles me that I might do something to cause someone else to question whether *they* can believe *me*." He touched her cheek. "Most of us think lies are a problem, but not that we're part of that problem. We think it's our neighbor, or our uncle who blathers on at Thanksgiving, not us. We can't be the problem, we're smarter than that. We think we see the difference between truth and lie, fact and fiction." He sighed. "But that's what afflicts society now . . . all of us are the problem. Somehow, we've got to be smarter about what we accept as fact, and what we don't."

"Truth can deceive, lies can reveal," she said, contemplating his words.

"Strange, huh?" He rubbed the corner of an eye. "As children we're taught to tell the truth. As we get older, the rules seem to change. It's okay to lie if it hurts only the people who think differently than we do." He clenched his fist. "There are those who lie, afraid they'll get caught, but the dangerous ones lie, feeling entitled to be believed." He turned back to the waterfall. "Sorry. After the last few days, I'm not as pessimistic as I sound."

"Tell me, what do you see as the future?"

He looked into her eyes. "For us?"

"No, for you." She looked away. "A few weeks ago . . . a monarch landed on your arm."

"I remember."

"I commented that some believe it means a season of transformation . . . determined by what's going on in your life when it happens. You took that comment to mean transition . . . back to something you love doing. But transformation doesn't mean that. What happened here could trigger the beginning of a major change. A transformation."

"Whatever happens, happens."

"I know, but . . ."

"What?"

"I really don't want you to change. I love you just the way you are."

"But what about that lecture you gave me about being naïve . . . about not being astute?"

"Forget I said that."

"I can't. You weren't wrong. Those are my weaknesses."

"I don't really see it that way. You couldn't lie if your life depended on it, but your naïvety makes people trust you. You're hard-wired to deal with things. Most people aren't."

"Kelly, I made the same mistakes here that I made in Montana. I can't stay in those old grooves . . . the same old patterns. If I do, I'll keep making the same mistakes."

"Jack, we're all just one decision away from a totally different life."

"Like you, my dear? You say that like it's a bad thing, but there are people who think you'll do great things in Washington."

"But this is the place I love. It's my home. It's your home, too."

"I'm not going anywhere, but I'm open to transformation . . . if it means being a bit smarter . . . less naïve . . . more astute. Might be scary. I'll make mistakes, but different ones."

"Promise you won't let us grow apart."

"You're worried about that? I'm the one who should worry, Senator. You're a big shot."

"I am not."

He laughed. "There's a ranger here who doesn't seem to know my name. She calls me Senator Culberson's beau."

A smile started to form. "And what do you say?"

"What can I say? She's right. That's a badge of honor."
She poked him in the ribs. "Good to know you're still naïve."
He smiled. "So much for transformation."

Author's Notes

All along I've figured this would be the most important part of the Jack Chastain story. Its subject strikes close to home for most of us—misleading rhetoric and conspiracy theories that divide our communities and, in some cases, our families.

Conspiracy theories, small and large, play prominent roles in this story, as they do at present in our society. I have had my own personal experiences with conspiracy theories, although I didn't want any of those to be the basis for the ones in this novel. I will, however, share one story. One night—I won't say which national park I was working in at the time—while catching up on work, an email directed my attention to a letter to the editor of a local newspaper. The letter was from someone who claimed to know my motive on a project, supposedly because of a conversation that person had with me. However, I'd never had such a conversation, and I didn't have such a motive. In fact, I didn't know the person and had never heard their name. I thought, *how could they do this?* I remember thinking, "*How very, very interesting. Someday—if I write a novel—I'll use that.*"

I've also borrowed from a matter I was slow to accept—that there are people who seek to divide us, using any means that works. That the end justifies the means. Although I came to accept that those people exist, I continue to believe most of us don't think that way. That the end does not justify the means. I've also seen—as occurs in this novel—that means have unintended consequences, that weren't the primary objective, but occurred just the same. 'Oh well,' the creator of the lie may have thought, and they may have even shrugged it off. But we, as a society, don't shrug it off, we live with those means, ends, and unintended consequences, often feeling bitter about things we have no business taking seriously.

A few other things:

Yes, Juan Rivera was real. He was the first person of European descent to explore territory that is now western Colorado, and yes, he was largely lost to history. There were parts of his assignment that he failed to achieve, e.g., getting to the Colorado River, and investigating native accounts of bearded men who looked like Europeans. I admit I was more taken by his travels in Colorado, than in his failure to make it to present day eastern Utah. I've likely traveled some of the same ground Rivera explored on the Uncompahgre Plateau, and in what is now Colorado's Montrose and Delta Counties.

Could Rivera have found gold, maybe even the mysterious Quivira? No. His journals document having found silver, but it was not enough to stir much interest. Historians take him at his word. If you want to know more about Rivera's explorations, I recommend *Juan Rivera's Colorado, 1765: The First Spaniards Among the Ute and Paiute Indians on the Trail to Teguayo*, by Steven G. Baker. It's an interesting read, and the source for many of the descriptions I use in this novel. However, everything beyond Baker's analysis of Rivera's (real) journal is a work of fiction . . . my own imaginings, portrayed as the game played by Deputy Buck Winslow. Some information dug up by la profesora, Angelica Vargas, can be found in the history books but had nothing to do with Juan Rivera. It was used as a plausible foundation for the fictionized parts of the Juan Rivera story, much like what was portrayed in the fake provenance used at the auction in Paris.

There's a scene where Joe Morgan said, "If anyone gets hurt, I want it to be me." Those words came from a real-life experience at about the mid-point of my career. I had been trusted by my park superintendent to handle whatever came our way on a highly contentious issue, meaning work with members of Congress, special interest groups, adversaries, news media, and others. But then political forces got involved, and my boss called and said, "Until you hear otherwise, refer all calls on this issue to me. If anyone gets hurt, I want it to be me." That moment stuck with me. The situation was very different than what Jack Chastain dealt with, but I used it to illustrate integrity and the complexities of trusting and protecting your staff when orders and involvement from others make things difficult. I experienced that from one of the best bosses I ever had, and Joe Morgan—when ordered to keep Jack in the dark—deserved to be characterized as handling the situation in a similar way.

And finally, I want to thank Mary Bisbee-Beek, publicist and sage; Lynn Steger, editor; Ann Weinstock, cover designer; Kris Weber, book designer; and Sue Carter, proofreader. It was a great pleasure working again with each of you.

I want to thank Geraint Smith for the use of his evocative photographs on the book cover and encourage your support of his favorite charity, riversandbirds.org.

I also thank those who gave me feedback on early versions of the manuscript: Michael Madigan, Virginia White, Julie Mulford, Jan Balsom, Greer Chesher, Karen Merritt, Denny Dressman, and Cassy, my wife. Thanks folks, your comments and perspectives were helpful and greatly appreciated.

And now, an epilogue.

Epilogue

Harper Teague pulled the phone from his pocket and switched it on. Messages scrolled across the screen. It began to ring. He raised it to his ear. "Teague, here."

"You're not answering your phone," said a gruff, entitled voice. "Where are you?"

Teague eyed the crowded corridor. "Albuquerque. Airport. Just got off a flight."

"What weird-assed task did you give Doc?"

"Nothing. I helped with the task *you* gave him . . . going after Senator Culberson."

"What did you do, Teague?"

"Suggested the guy he groomed to run against her." Teague forced a chuckle. "How'd that go last night? Wish I coulda been there to watch."

"You do, do you? So you're the one who suggested the clown that got Doc arrested?"

"Arrested?" Teague took a step, then stopped. "What do you mean?"

"Arrested, idiot. Both of them. What'd you have Doc do?"

"Nothing. He followed *your* instructions . . . from the back of that photo you sent . . . of the Senator."

"You saw this photo?"

"No, why?"

"I didn't send any damned photo. The job I gave Doc was to turn those bleeding hearts against each other . . . and against Chastain . . . like in Montana."

Teague swallowed hard. "Doc thought you wanted 'em both targeted. Two birds with one stone. Thought this would be his masterpiece."

"Masterpiece? Hell." A growl, then, "Get him bailed out. Don't show your face. Let the bail bondsman do it . . . and find out if Doc has been talking."

The line went dead.

—'—

Watching through binoculars from behind a low earthen wall, an observer noticed movement and cracked a smile. "There you are, Doc. I've been waiting."

The balding man with a crooked nose stopped outside the door of the criminal justice building, wearing a crumpled white shirt and slacks, having spent the night in a holding cell.

Another man met him on the sidewalk, his beefy arms covered in tattoos. They signed and exchanged papers, and the tattooed man departed in a gray sedan. Doc glanced around, then plodded to the road, appearing uncertain about where he was going.

"So, Doc . . . or rather, Herman, . . . still think you're the smartest guy in the room?" The watcher lowered the binoculars, reflecting on the moment. "Probably . . . but you're not. You were tricked into overplaying your hand. People now know your name and your game. As for what happened in Montana, you . . . are one more down. That makes three. One more to go."

A mud-covered pickup appeared on the road. It slowed on approach, then stopped.

Doc climbed in the passenger side.

Is this the boss? The watcher raised the field glasses and focused on the driver. Serious eyes. *Harper Teague.* "You're not the boss, Teague. You're not that smart." A sigh. "Still . . . you've given me no clues, and that's what I need. So . . . who the hell do you work for?"

Discussion Questions

1. Is there anything Ranger Jack Chastain could have done when he first met Hide Mangum that might have contributed to a different outcome?

2. On page 124, Angelica Vargas, comments that finding no evidence that Juan Rivera wasn't a military man, ". . . is hardly evidence at all. In fact, it isn't." In Chapter 39, Jack tells Ginger Perrette he doesn't know the "land agents," but there would be no such thing as evidence that he doesn't. Do those arguments make sense to you, or do you feel, as Ginger does, that the burden is on Jack to prove he doesn't know them?

3. While in camp, Toby LeBlanc tells Jack of a method he was taught that was effective in marginalizing others. Do you think you would be affected by hearing someone use the "those other people" method?

4. Have you ever found yourself *wanting* to believe something, even without evidence? If so, why do you think you felt that way? Have you felt you *needed* to believe something, even without evidence? If so, why?

5. When Jack drives Toby to the airport he mentions breaking news—conspiracy theories about Kelly and Jack—Toby tells him he knows what they say, even if he doesn't know the actual details. Is that possible?

6. In the story, Jack works with people who have different reasons for loving the same lands. Do you think it's easier to keep people working together or to drive them apart?

7. Can you trust people who value something for reasons different than your own?

8. At the end, Jack believes he needs to be less naïve, and claims he's not afraid of transformation, because—without it—he's likely to keep making the same mistakes. Do you think Jack can change?

About the Author

J.M. Mitchell grew up in Texas, now lives in Colorado, and spent the years in between on some of America's most cherished landscapes—Yosemite, Grand Canyon and Zion National Parks. He had a long career with the National Park Service, retiring as Chief of the agency's Biological Resource Management Division, where he worked on the technical and sometimes politically charged issues facing the National Park System. He is the author of three other novels: *Public Trust*, *The Height of Secrecy*, and *Killing Godiva's Horse*. His writing has appeared in scientific and conservation journals, travel magazines and newspapers. He and his wife split their time between Littleton and their ranch on Colorado's western slope.